Advance Praise

John W. Maly's first novel is a taut, suspenseful, mind-bending thriller that's as doom laden and timely as tomorrow's head-lines. In the near future, a flawed hero is convicted by an AI-driven legal system of an atrocity he didn't commit... and this is just the beginning of the dark spiral that will have readers up all night turning the pages. As atmospheric as it is plausible, *Juris Ex Machina*, announces the debut of an exciting new voice in speculative fiction.

> Jay Bonansinga, the New York Times bestselling author of
> *Stan Lee's The Devil's Quintet: The Armageddon Code* and
> *The Walking Dead: Return to Woodbury*

This book should NOT be classified as Science Fiction but, instead, Science *Probability*...a thoroughly entertaining and completely plausible look of where our future may very well be headed, though I sincerely hope that it is not!

> Dean Haglund, actor in *The Lone Gunman* and *The X-Files*

John Maly's *Juris Ex Machina* is that rare fictional creation: a deeply compelling story, one that surprises and delights with its inventiveness and crisply unfurling plot, and one that's also populated by characters who are finely textured—feeling, breathing, living creatures whose concerns quickly become the concerns of the reader. In a word, it's engrossing. You've got to read this book.

> Jack Livings, award-winning author
> of *The Blizzard Party* and *The Dog*

Juris Ex Machina serves up a potent recipe spiced with an inventive plot, characters to match, constant action, and tension so real you will bite through the inside of your lower lip. John Maly conjures an entirely new world that does not immerse you, it swallows you whole.

The usual cliched superlatives of "highly recommend," "page-turner" and "rollercoaster ride" do not do *Juris Ex Machina* justice. Only the deft mind of a creative savant could pull off this high-level of novelistic magic and literary sleight of hand. Bravo!

Juris Ex Machina is a masterful work. An auspicious debut for an exceptionally talented writer.

Kirk Marty, author of *Quantum Terra*

You'll come for the plot, get drawn in by the refined storytelling, and stay for the incisive commentary. Philosophically stimulating and delightfully outrageous, *Juris Ex Machina* masterfully considers whether or not the ends can justify the means.

Jennifer Jackson, *Indies Today*

From its opening pages, *Juris Ex Machina* is a rip-roaring, wild, and kaleidoscopic ride that lies somewhere between Orwell's *1984*, Asimov's *I Robot*, and *The Road Warrior*. It leads readers through a scintillating, futuristic world of dystopian intrigue which is all-too familiar. John W. Maly's science fiction novel is a riveting, entertaining, and compelling tour-de-force cinematic and bristling with an innovative, imaginative intelligence. *Juris Ex Machina* is smart, funny and clever in places, terrifying in others. It is an exhilarating, slightly frenzied trip, fascinating and dynamic. It is also very current and a timely warning what may befall humanity if it continues to rely too much on artificial intelligence and computers to control its destiny.

Liam Taliesin, author of *Lithium Fire*

A page-turner you won't want to put down! John W. Maly pulls us into a cinematic future world and delivers a story that makes us question the relationship between humanity and technology, even as the plot takes us on a breathless edge-of-our-seats ride. *Juris Ex Machina* combines light and darkness, beauty and brutality, wise humor and deep legal and technological expertise, to create a blend of dystopian sci-fi and legal thriller as unforgettable as it is unique. A not-to-be-missed debut from a fiercely talented new voice.

Kris Faatz, author of *Fourteen Stones*

The high stakes, fast pace, intriguing storyline and interesting world [of *Juris Ex Machina*] made me read the story in one sitting. I was on the edge of my seat from start to finish. Highly recommend!

The International Review of Books

Deftly balancing reality and science fiction, *Juris Ex Machina* presents a what-if tale of frightening proportions that forces the reader question the state of AI in the modern world.

John Maly envisions a world of computers running the show using artificial intelligence as the brain power behind everything including legal decisions. In the sci-fi thriller *Juris Ex Machina*, the futuristic city of Arcadia provides a protective dome and runs on 'foolproof' robotic systems which aren't. As they begin to fail, a bomb explodes leaving hundreds dead. Rainville, a nineteen-year-old techie is accused of hacking that system, resulting in AI convicting him. In thrilling chase scenes, Rainville teams up with talented hacker Vyanna blending a very human love interest as they fight to locate and thwart the power behind the computers. The worlds that Maly creates inside Arcadia and the dreaded inmate-controlled Wychwood prison outside the dome reveal we have more to fear from AI than some computer stealing our art or writing. The narrative presents a compelling story that is both terrifying and touchingly human when the computers unite as Servitor to wage war on mortals. A fast-paced read into the AI world of the future.

I found it hard to put *Juris Ex Machina* down! Antihero Rainville starts out as a clever, kind, but immature guy, who lives in a future where tech makes his life easy. It all changes when Rainville is wrongly found guilty by a jury of robotic minds for using tech to blow up a city block. Hooked, I dove into the story to discover if true justice was possible for Rainville.

Maribeth Decker, author of *Peace in Passing*

Juris Ex Machina is a wildly inventive futuristic showdown between the law, AI, and an innocent young man. It is compulsively readable and written with intelligence and wry humor. Maly reveals a deep understanding of both technology and law —creating a compelling story and characters that keeps the reader on the hook until the final page.

KC O'Connell

This riveting, timely novel invites us to take a hard look at humanity's best intentions run amok, and at the enormous risk of surrendering fallible free will to idealistic, automated systems.

Angela Pneuman, author of *Lay It On My Heart* and *Home Remedies*

Maly's style of writing is as poetic as it is thought-provoking. His characters pull on your heart strings and his storyline will cause you to question everything you've ever known about the past, present, and future of the legal field. This fabulous debut novel has passages that make you close your eyes just so that you can savor them. This is the kind of book you'll want to revisit time and again. An incredible read from start to finish, that will leave you wanting more and hoping for a sequel!

Angela Wynn

Juris Ex Machina introduced me to an extraordinary world I didn't know existed. Alongside Rainville, as he came to life under the dome of Arcadia, I experienced sparkles of joy, moments of pain, and spine-tingling instants of fear..... This is an extremely powerful story with a plot with so many twists and turns, it is impossible to put the book down, and I recommend it to anybody who enjoys a genius futuristic novel.

Maryam Soltani

JURIS EX MACHINA

JURIS EX MACHINA

JOHN W. MALY

HIGHLANDER
PRESS

Hardback ISBN: 978-1-956442-37-3
Paperback ISBN: 978-1-956442-29-8
Ebook ISBN: 978-1-956442-31-1
Library of Congress Control Number: 2024934877

Published by Highlander Press
A division of Highlander Enterprises, LLC
501 W. University Pkwy, Ste. B2
Baltimore, MD 21210

Cover design: Liza from Miblart (https://miblart.com/)
Cover layout: Pat Creedon (https://patcreedondesign.com)
Map illustration: Kate from Miblart (https://miblart.com/)
Author photo: Barbara Banks (barbarabanks.com)

Story Notes

I got the idea of expressing laws as equations and the dog bite example from Cleary's 1959 article "Presuming and Pleading: An Essay on Juristic Immaturity" as it appeared in the Stanford Law Review that year. (12 Stan.L.Rev. 5 (1959))

Japadog was a real hot dog stand in Vancouver. They've since grown into a successful franchise in British Colombia and Southern California. Their 'dogs are simply amazing!

Wychwood Prison is modeled loosely after the Instituto Nacional Penitenciario in Lurigancho, Peru. I watched every documentary and read every first-hand account I could find about the prison, and it never stopped being fascinating. It's an amazing example of spontaneous order amongst the criminally non-orderly.

The idea for Wychwood Cemetery comes from a community in Cairo called al-Qarafa (القرافة), or the City of the Dead. Unlike the prison in the book, the City of the Dead is actually a civilized, tight-knit community despite residents being considered outcasts by some parts of Cairo society. The actual crypts and other descriptions of Wychwood were inspired by a large private cemetery in Belgium.

Lastly, there are a great many inside references within this story, but I won't spoil any of them by giving them away here...

MAP OF ARCADIA

Retro District
(Crown Point)

Euclid Ave

Walton Street

Westcott St

Essex-Park

Stephens St

Agri-stations

Hasidic
neighborhood

James
Hotel

Judical Admin Node
(Brickell Ave)

Latin
Quarter

Rainville/
Essie

Cinero St

Bohemian Quarter

Zizka Square

University
District

FIDI

Chuck's

NORFED

Pentridge

Comstock Ave

Foxwright

P&S

Vaux Park

Lafayette St

Comstock
Station

Lafayette

Jenninds Ave

Soviokes

Genesee St

Abondoned
home

Chinese Quarter

The Flux

Xiagu

Wychwood

For my mother Carole, who instilled in me her love of the written word;
for my father James, who taught me to never, ever give up;
and for my daughters Katherine and Emily, who taught me everything else.

Contents

Part I

Probatio per Aqua 3
Flashmob 5
The Caper 9
The Chase 13
They Meet 15
Gardening 17
Bathroom Break 21
Janitation 23
Venting 25
Mole People 27
The Tunnels 29
The Witchfinder General, Part I 33
Foxwright 35
Legal Computing 41
Dinner 45
Dessert 51
The Witchfinder General, Part II 55
Culinary Anachronism 57
Toast 59
Force Majeure 61
Shattered 63
Calamity 65
Close Shave 67
龙之烈焰 71

Part II

Burnt Breadcrumbs 79
Ardy 83
Forensic Inference 87
The Witchfinder General, Part III 91
3:13 a.m. 93
Barratry 97
The First Legal AIs 101
Walls 105
Association 109
The Referral 113

A Meeting with Management   119
Review   125
Visitation   129
The Bisha'a   133
Questions and Answers   135
News from Home   141
Fabrication   145
Paying a Visit   151
The Corsned   155
The Verdict   157
Life   161
Hourglass   165
Dead to Us   167

Part III

Probatio per Ignis   173
Waking Up is Hard to Do   175
Multicelled Organisms   179
Meat   185
The Chief   195
Prospects   201
Broken   205
Sticky   207
Cold Justice, Part I   211
Japadog   213
Training   219
Dead Drop   221
Hungry Marley's   225
Cold Justice, Part II   231
Prey   233
Settling In   235
R&R   237
The Trough   241
Winners and Losers   247
Tomorrow's Pardon   253
Slumber   259
FTP   261
Outside   263
The Ashanti Needle   269
Digging In   271
Due Diligence   273
Calling   279
Full Disclosure   281

Part IV

Probatio per Crucis   287
Religious Experience   289
Crying Over Spilled Beans   295
The Egress   301
Out and About   305
Wake Up Call   309
Going to Church   315
Isaiah 65:4   319
Entombed   325
City of the Dead   329
Paydirt   335
Twigs   339
Formula for Conducting the Ordeal of Boiling Water   345
Charon Station   347
The River Styx   349
Passage   355
Now Arriving   363
Reflections   367
Home   371

Part V

Alcolu, South Carolina   379
Plasticity   381
Missive   387
Steganography (noun)   391
Pentridge   393
!=x[0]   399
Back at the Ranch   403
Psychophilosophy   407
Designs   413
Commitment   415
Deployment   417
Execution   419
The Coming of the Profit   423
Crash   425
Crossing Arcadia   427
Authorization   431
Trajectories   435
Reception   439
The Institute   443
Underground   447
Divide   451

Topology   455
Reason   457
The Fall   469
Ratio Decidendi   471
Take #2   475

Acknowledgments   479
About the Author   483
About the Publisher   485

Part I

Probatio per Aqua

(TRIAL BY WATER)

"[The water ordeal] was a trial only for the poor and humble, and, whether they sank or swam, was thought of very little consequence. Like the witches of more modern times, the accused were thrown into a pond or river; if they sank, and were drowned, their surviving friends had the consolation of knowing that they were innocent; if they swam, they were guilty. In either case society was rid of them."

Charles Mackay, *Extraordinary Popular Delusions and the Madness of Crowds,* Vol. 1, 1841

Flashmob

"*ATTENTION, SHOPPERS*," flashed the message. Beneath was a business name and a time. Nothing more.

The designated location was relatively close to where Rainville sat, but still on the other end of the Financial District. He'd have to scarf down the rest of his Skyburger if he was going to make it there in time, and he regretted ordering Triple Extra Spicy.

The message source could not be traced. It had sailed through a sea of anonymization servers in various jurisdictions before being transmitted to the consoles of a group of subscribers including himself. The recipients were not trusted friends, but rather, friends-once-removed. Semi-Anonymity, that was Rule #1: it's hard to rat someone out when you don't even know their name. Still, when robbing a store, it helped to know the others could be trusted. To a degree, anyway; full trust in anyone was a dubious proposition.

Yet, Rule #1 allowed for significant risk, and thus Rule #2: Minimal Advance Notice. If one of the trusted invitees turned out to be in the business of law enforcement, a Shopping Spree could turn into a sting operation.

There were other rules. Rule #7: No Clothing. It sounded funny, but if a mob of young people suddenly filtered into the same store at the same time and began trying on clothes, a fidgety store clerk might get on the Comm to security. Rule #10: One Item Only. For reasons of style and ethos, skilled Shopping was about the experience, about earning each item, about each piece of loot having its own unique story. If your goal was quantity, then you should be burgling warehouses or some shit.

Rainville chewed faster, shielding his console from falling bits of synthesized meat and spiced curry with one hand as he accessed site maps and forum posts and other intel related to the store with the other. It was not a popular target because it lacked a rear entrance, but by the same token, less popular targets often had less wary security staff.

He placed his console atop a reflective icon molded into the purple antibacterial plastic of the restaurant table and craned his neck to continue using the device while the restaurant debited his account for the meal. "Thank you for dining at Lunch & Munch!" the console exclaimed, "We hope you enjoyed y—" Rainville cut the voice off by confirming his bill without stopping to look at it. With a flick of his wrist, the console rerolled itself into a neat cylinder and slipped into his pocket.

He hurried to the mag-rail subway station across the street, bolting onto a subway car seconds before it lurched into motion. With Christmas coming, there was a certain expectation that any nineteen-year-old, living on his own now or not, would provide decent holiday gifts. Maybe he'd even extend an olive branch to his father, pick out something nice for the old man, get them back on speaking terms again.

Rainville was self-employed, repairing electrophotonics. He could afford to buy gifts but felt they meant a lot more when he'd taken personal risks by stealing them. Ironically, this added significance couldn't be revealed to their recipients. Most of them would just be pissed at him for shoplifting. Life was funny that way.

He took the mag-rail two stops to the RetroMall of Atlantis in

Arcadia's city center. Ancient by City standards, the RetroMall represented living history, recreating a place where generations past had gathered during the colder seasons to celebrate their lameness. It was built before the dome was erected over Arcadia, when weather still affected Arcadians' day-to-day lives. These days the outmoded facility still saw commerce, but its ironic decor was looking a bit ragged. Hokey electroluminescent floor tiles flashed primitive animation of fish and mermaids and streams of bubbles. "Follow the green bubbles to savings!" flashed a tile indicating a long-closed department store. The mall's food court was ruled over by a giant animatronic King Neptune, waving his trident and welcoming shoppers to his aging retail shopping kingdom. Water cascaded down mollusk-shaped catch-pans before collecting in a large pool at his feet.

Beyond the food court lay his objective. The location, a store called Darrow's Technological Goodies, was bedecked in dingy "SALE!!" banners and garish flashing lights. Based on the number of people milling around in the store, he was not the first Shopper to arrive. Good. Arriving first only seemed to stimulate the memories of store clerks. He wandered back through the shop toward the less mundane items. The entertainment aisle was already crowded with people, leaving no clean escape route when the shit hit. Fucking amateurs.

Rainville passed through an aisle piled with animated T-shirts, and then a jumbled display of snow globes containing their own miniature weather systems. He veered into the photonics aisle, just as a dumbass in a trench coat ran by with a Swordblade Holographic Game Imager under his arm. Trench Coat's adrenaline level had exceeded the design tolerances of his body. Mid-stride, his foot clipped the edge of a pyramid of artificially intelligent bears. They teetered before collapsing into an aisle-blocking auditory torrent of "Hi, I'm Twispy!"s and "Can I have a hug?"s and "I can tell when your friends are lying!"s. Trench Coat stumbled over the bears, increasing his speed to an even more reckless level as he flew around a corner toward the registers. The stupid fucker obviously hadn't checked his time synchronization daemon, in clear violation of Rule #3: Synchronize Watches. His chrono was way off. Odd. Synchro daemons should have kept the consoles of everyone in Arcadia calibrated to the same millisecond. Anyway, the commotion of his solitary theft would make a nice diversion in ninety seconds when the real flashmob started.

At the tick of 12:46:34, chaos reigned supreme.

The Caper

QUICK FOOTSTEPS ECHOED in the adjacent aisles. Manic laughter cascaded over the rows of shelving. Yells of protest rose from the front of the store. Trench Coat's distraction took the heat off Rainville's aisle, but moved it squarely onto the store's only exit.

Someone was coming down his aisle, fast.

A SecAgent?

No, a girl!

More than just some girl: she was gorgeous. Her strawberry-blonde hair had highlights running from periwinkle to violet. Her impossibly-saturated, synthetically-hued eyes fell somewhere in the same range. Were they fixed on that color, or configured to change with her mood?

She wore a short, ruffled trench coat, and had a small tattoo of some kind of normally-cute-and-fuzzy animal that was growling-and-rabid on the side of her neck.

She flashed a smile which seemed to go right through him, for he felt it all through his body. "Security's on site. The gig is up!" With that, she zipped away, her coat ruffles flapping behind her like wings. She disappeared around a corner, leaving Rainville behind. The risk of Detention and being judicial-flagged as a Shoplifter grew with each idle second.

And he was still empty-handed.

His eyes landed on an EverSweet Fruit-Ripening Bowl. "The perfect gift!" proclaimed the box. His father's refrigerator already had ripening and preservation circuits, and who really needed their produce on display? Then there was a Bark-o-Matic Poochimunicator, "Give your best friend the power of speech! One size fits all breeds!" He didn't have a dog. Then a bin of animatronic Life-Like Loch Ness monsters. "Watch them swim! Only $3.50!" Then a display of New-and-Improved Magic 8 Balls, featuring a physical quantum source for guaranteed randomness in their pointless results. Bah! He needed to hurry, but this only worsened his indecision. It was a bad Shopping habit, trying to pick the perfect item. The perfect score was about getting in, getting an item, getting out, and getting away clean; it was about speed and timing, and thus mutually exclusive with choosing the perfect item. Rule #2, Minimal Advance Notice, prevented Shoppers from scouting for the best target, but he still hated rushing and grabbing something sucky. It seemed wasteful, somehow, like risk without reward. "Preparing to lock down aisle five," came the voice of a Security Agent now entering the far end of his aisle. Dammit! Rainville was flailing when he should be fleeing. His heart raced with a new rush of adrenaline.

Panicked, he grabbed a random box and sprinted toward the front of the store. Around him, waves of the bouncy and rolly goods from endcap displays dumped onto the floor tiles like a torrential polymer rain as Shoppers succumbed to their baser Discordian instincts, creating impromptu distractions.

A wave of polyhedral multipurpose robots rolled across his path like geometric surf on a glossy beach. The effect disoriented him. He looked up and away from the tiny critters and tried to maintain his course up the aisle.

Ahead was trouble. The checkout area was a bottleneck of Shoppers trying to stream through a choke point laced with Security Agents eagerly snapping images, video, and audio footage. A quality photograph of a Shopper was as career-ending as any physical collar in the days of old. The Shoppers in the back were slowing down, fish in an increasingly crowded barrel. He pictured himself in Detention, the privately operated mall jail that would hold him until City law enforcement could be called and formal judicial charges filed. He'd seen vids of the place. Its cells were padded, colorful and shiny, designed by the same people as toddler playgrounds and with a common goal: to thwart civil suits against the operators. The thought of being confined there made him shudder.

He raised his arm to block his face from imaging, and pushed forward. He gasped as an unseen hand clasped his wrist. A SecAgent! Rainville kept his arm over his face and attempted to pull away, but could not shake loose of the man's vice grip. "You are being detained as per Chapter 221, Section 15 of the RetroMall of Atlantis Shoppers' Rights and Responsibilities," shouted the man over the din of theft sensor alarms as his opposing hand grasped the Detention Pistol on his belt, "implicitly entered into by your entry into this retail establishment, and legally binding as of that time—"

In the midst of the chaos, a bespectacled man, his beard trailing off into gravity-defying braids of various colors, reached into his pack. He yawped a mighty rallying cry and tossed a countermeasure into the air. At the sight of the shiny tangerine-sized ball leaving the man's hand, Rainville lifted his elbow. He blocked his eyes with the solid meat of his arm just as a stream of blinding flashes hopelessly overexposed the SecAgents' video footage to featureless rectangles two shades whiter than a snowman's ass. "Dammit! I can't see!" cried the SecAgent holding him. He jerked free as the agent's hand receded to his face.

The remaining Shoppers sensed liberation. They surged forward, SecAgents scattering like leaves before a gale to avoid being trampled. Rainville dashed past the SecLeader, doubled over and screaming into his safety-orange console: "Code Seven, we need help STAT. Repeat: Code Seven, requesting a full lockdown of all Mall exits."

The Chase

THE OPEN SPACE outside the store gave Rainville a primordial sense of relief. The bulk of the Shopper mob veered left toward the mall's main entrance. Since the SecLeader still had his console, the rest of the Security world knew this too. Experience taught Rainville that one man's safety-in-numbers was another man's target-rich environment. He darted right.

Herds of aimless midday mall patrons stopped their slow meanderings to stare at the spectacle of streaming humanity, effectively blocking the way ahead. He slalomed between a mall navigation kiosk and an amorphous bronze sculpture, then hopped a bench to bypass the onlookers.

Ahead, a scattering of Shoppers sprinted, weaved, and burst with the impossibly giddy laughter known only to those getting away with something. He'd seen old 2D vids of an event in Pamplona before it got leveled by New Galician separatists – they'd called it the Running of the Bulls. He'd never seen a live bull, but the mix of fear and ecstasy on the runners' faces, a source of puzzlement to the vid's narrator, now made perfect sense.

He found himself laughing despite himself. It was apparently contagious; he heard an almost musical titter beside him. It was then that he noticed who was running next to him.

They Meet

IT WAS the girl from the store! Even framed with the blur of the gaudy mall storefronts, she was radiant. Rainville's pulse somehow found new heights and he narrowly avoided stumbling over his own feet.

"This is Mall Security," came a voice that interrupted the mall's cheesy music track. "You are surrounded. Stop where you are, and place the merchandise on the floor. If you run, you will be subdued."

The floor ahead split into matching ramps descending into the grand plaza marking the start of the mall's lower level. Dividing the ramps was a large planter of tropical heliconia and metallic palms protected by a railing; behind it, a fountain cascaded down to the lower-level plaza. Shoppers split left and right, racing down the twin chutes. *Zat!* The unmistakable sound of a synthetic spider-silk cannon pierced the air. A squad of SecAgents had anticipated the escape route and cut the runners off at the proverbial pass. Screams of anger and defeat grew muffled as sticky webs ensnared runners on the ramps below.

Rainville weighed his options. It was anyone's guess which ramp had fewer security guards. The girl next to him surged confidently ahead, straight for the planter rail, vaulting over it in an elegant arc.

She landed among the plants in a mini explosion of chunkbark then dove through the stalks and fronds.

He leapt over the railing after her. In the worst case, they'd get caught and he'd have some time to talk to her on the way to Detention. Better case, they'd hide somewhere together. As the web cannons rang out below him, he wondered if this day was looking up.

Gardening

STOMPING through the lush plants and mulch, Rainville fought to keep from losing the girl in the foliage ahead. He heard more screams, closer this time. Through the fronds he saw SecAgents streaming up the ramps on both sides, immobilizing runners as they went. Following this girl had saved him, yet now he seemed no less trapped.

He was jerked sharply sideways. Someone had him. He turned. Readied himself to grapple with a SecAgent.

His shirt was caught on the branch of a flowering bush. He grabbed a fistful of the fabric and pulled it free. And ran.

The foliage dissipated and another railing appeared, marking the end of the tropical garden and the yawning void of open air beyond. The girl launched herself again, vaulting clear over the rail then dropping out of sight. The *zats* of more web cannons fresh in his ears, he jumped over the railing after her like a hormone-crazed lemming.

He was still in midair questioning his own wisdom when the girl splashed down into the top level of the waterfall-fountain ranging over the food court far below. He landed just behind her, and found himself ankle-deep in a giant bronze cockleshell. Beneath him, King Neptune brandished his trident, looking more protective (and the trident more pointy) than he remembered. Water poured from the shell into a dozen progressively-lower mollusk shells before emptying into the pool next to the dining area. Down below, families seated in the food court stopped eating; children pointed.

The girl hopped from one basin to the next, each jump triggering an explosion of water. He followed her lead, the cold water rushing over his feet and amplifying his senses. The children below, ardent puddle-stomping aficionados one and all, shrieked and laughed. A tiny girl with pigtails still too short to do anything but stick straight up cried, "Look Mommy, flying people!"

They landed with giant kerplunks in the central pool to the cheers of several children and more than a few parents. Dashing out of the water, they found themselves behind the throng of SecAgents busily blocking the ramps and incapacitating hapless Shoppers.

They did not go unnoticed. Two SecAgents at the rear of the blockade broke off to pursue them. The girl burst into a sprint, droplets of fountain water flying off her ruffled coat in a fine mist like the supernatural aura of some chaotic angel. Rainville followed her for a quarter mile as a stitch grew in his side. He cursed his lack of physical fitness. More shouts erupted behind him, and adrenaline washed away his fatigue.

The *splot-splot* of their footsteps caught his attention. He called to his accomplice, but his lungs burned, and "Tracks!" was all he could bark out to her between gasps of breath. She tilted her head, and he gestured backward to a trail of shoe-shaped puddles. A perfect trail for SecAgents to follow.

They vaulted in unison over another planter rail and dragged their soles through the absorbent planting medium to dryness, resembling a high-speed interpretive dance more than a strategic act. Who said a flower garden couldn't be functional as well as beautiful?

Emerging from the opposite end of the enclosure, a wave of panic hit him: the SecAgents were gaining ground! They were too out-of-breath to speak, but the girl smiled sideways at him and motioned for him to follow.

Ahead was Wakefield's House of Fashion, and they dodged inside. In the front of the store were rows of sparkling crystal perfume counters. Robotic pink perfume cannons automatically locked onto them, swiveling around to face them, and a pleasant female voice asked if they'd like to try some. The girl managed to croak out an exasperated "No!" but Rainville was too out of breath, and soon found himself doused with a musky combination of roses and lavender. He coughed his way back through the aisles, weaving through a forest of electroluminescent Christmas trees and probably-holographic snowman and reindeer decorations as shouts from the trailing SecAgents dogged his steps.

Just past the Ladies' Apparel counter, the girl cranked a sharp left turn down a narrow tunnel toward the restrooms and public access consoles.

A dead end?

She'd gotten them this far. He sprang after her.

Bathroom Break

THE HALLWAY WAS long and featureless. Near the end of the passage, Rainville followed the girl through a swinging door into another sterile room covered in faded white tiles. Across from a row of bathroom stalls sat an overstuffed sofa that had seen better days and above it, a generic floral painting. "Couches?" he gasped, his lungs still burning.

"Standard equipment," the girl said.

Realization dawned on Rainville: this was a women's restroom. The perfume he'd been sprayed with seemed all the more cloying in the small space, or maybe it was just the femininity of his surroundings. The SecAgents would assemble a female entry team, but it would not take long.

The girl was fiddling with a locked janitorial closet door. She pulled a small device resembling a teddy bear from her pocket. She clutched it in one hand and rubbed its belly with the other. A sophisticated extension popped out between its ears, making it look vaguely like a unicorn. She inserted the extension into the lock mechanism. He admired the finesse of her fingers as they alternated between asserting force and sensing changes.

The lock snicked sideways and the door swung open to reveal an even smaller space. An even more confined dead end. "Lock it behind you," she said, beckoning him to follow her into the closet.

Maybe the SecAgents wouldn't check in a locked closet? Either way, being closely confined with this prime specimen of teenage girl-ness was not something he'd avoid whatever the circumstances, so he re-engaged the lock and stepped inside.

Janitation

THE GIRL FLICKED on the lights. They revealed a deactivated sanitation robot parked in its charging cradle, and a set of shelves filled with supplies.

"You..." she began, still fighting to catch her breath, "really smell like an old lady!"

"I..." his own respiration was still ragged from the chase, "feel a bit like one."

She giggled, then glanced down at the boxes they were holding, and her snicker graduated into a laugh.

It was then he realized he had no idea what item he'd finally grabbed back at the store. He was not the self-conscious type, but his gaze followed hers in a panic. On the bright side, they were each holding the exact same product. What were the odds? On the not-so-bright side, he'd evidently grabbed a Baby Snarflet doll. Hardly the gift to make amends with his father. The toy's hot pink hair, dainty sundress, and sickly sweet smile radiated out from the box like some masculinity-destroying toxin. He wanted to drop it—no—throw it as far away as he could. Which was not far at all since they were in a tiny closet.

"Me, I've got a baby sister," she offered. "What's your excuse?"

"I...well, there was this stupid fucker who knocked down a display near me, and so ..." He thought ahead to where this story was going, and any way you sliced it, it ended with him panicking like an amateur and abandoning any targets of value. But wait! He'd read an article in *Automation Weekly* just yesterday about how these toys contained a highly versatile femtocontroller that could be used to override vehicle navigation control systems, which he explained at length.

She nodded patronizingly as he spoke. "So you took a toy intended for little girls. Because there was a fucker. And also, because you're going to part it out?"

"Umm...." His face grew hot, and he wished he smelled less like his grandmother. His defeat was absolute. "Yes. What you said."

She chuckled. "I'm Vyanna. My friends call me Vy." Learning her name felt like a kind of victory, an accomplishment that no one could ever take away.

"Hi, Vy. I'm Rainville." He extended a hand out of instinct, then immediately regretted making such a formal, old-fashioned gesture to such a dynamic female. But she grabbed his hand before he could fully retract it and shook it with a formality devoid of mockery or humor. "Pleased to make your acquaintance, Mr. Rainville. Now, would you care to see the Underground?"

Venting

THERE WAS a bang outside as the door to the bathroom flung open. Then the sound of footsteps just beyond the closet door, and a series of squeaks as the stall doors opened one by one.

Vyanna waved for him to follow her...up.

She began climbing shelves like rungs in a ladder, finding purchase on each shelf where cleaning supplies weren't.

He now had a close-up view of her boots, their smooth, glossy soles formed from a substance he'd only read about, a unidirectional, dry-adhesive surface for maximally-effective climbing. The boots could theoretically be used to climb straight up a wall, if needed, and if the wearer possessed sufficient muscle.

Above the top shelf, she touched a ventilation grate which swung out of the way as if by magic to reveal an opening into darkness. He followed her up the shelves, pausing while she wriggled into the ventilation duct to admire her slender yet shapely ass.

Getting from the top shelf into the grate opening without falling took some real effort, although Vyanna had done so seemingly without effort. At length, he clambered over the gap, but not without knocking a can of cleaning solvent off the shelves. It hit the floor with a crash.

Below, the closet door rattled as someone tried the knob. Rainville hurried into the ventilation duct and closed the grate behind him.

They were deep within the guts of the mall complex. A faint, almost subliminal hum faded in and out like the pulse of some giant mechanical heart. He padded forward on his palms and knees; each movement sounded a sort of gong as the thin metal of the archaic ventilation shaft deformed then sprang back. A constant breeze gave him a welcome respite from the rose-and-lavender perfume from the department store, and the faint smell of Vyanna's own perfume echoed back through the duct. It was unique, like a combination of plumeria, and those white carissa flowers that grew in Vaux Park.

A loud *whump* noise shook the vents, and a burst of frigid air rushed past them. A tiny ice crystal landed on Rainville's cheek. A snowflake! And then a second, and third. Any thoughts of the strangeness of this were scoured away by the shock of the chill on his soaked clothing.

"What the hell was that?" he called ahead to Vyanna.

"Damned if I know," she said, still crawling. Rainville could not see anything, but there was nowhere to go but straight ahead. She banged along the metal passage in front of him, and he sped up his movements whenever she sounded more distant.

A dim glow appeared far in the distance. As they approached, the light grew in intensity, its source a rectangular hole in the wall of the duct where a ventilation grill had been removed. How often did Vyanna use this path? And where the hell were they going?

"Follow me. Watch the edges!" she said, pointing out the gleam of the razor-sharp edge of the sheet metal. She tossed her parcel through the hole, reached out to grab a thin black pipe that ran beside the duct, and swung out onto it before dropping into the shadows below with effortless grace.

He took a deep breath, and followed her.

Mole People

THEY LANDED in a small room barely lit by a failing light array. Most of its elements had gone dark over the years, and the ones that remained hummed loudly. The walls were made of ancient cinderbricks, and a raised concrete platform supported a metal motor or generator or other archaic technology that took up much of the room. The equipment looked long disused, in that it no longer had any plumbing or wires connected to it.

The room was otherwise featureless save for a wide metal door on one side. It was latched closed, but had no doorknob. Rainville slid his hands along it but could not get a grip. "Now what? We're trapped!"

"Glad you think so," replied Vyanna. "That's kinda the point. It's a one-way door, unless you have the key." She reached into her pocket and pulled out the teddy bear-shaped multitool, waving it like an animistic talisman in front of a nondescript spot in the cinderbricks beside the door. There was a buzz and a click, and as the door swung open she repocketed the magnetic bear.

A gust of warm air welcomed them to a narrow utility tunnel. A row of antique light bulbs shielded by metallic cages trailed endlessly into the distance. Where they finally disappeared from view, it was not because of any turns in the passage, but because they'd simply become too small to see. She closed the door behind them and gave it a shove to make sure it latched.

"It's an old steam tunnel," she said, "built to service the office complex that was here before the RetroMall. When they excavated for the mall, they left this passage intact. It's not on any map or blueprint, so the maintenance drones keep clear. I didn't even know it was still connected except that some days I'd catch wafts of mall food in the tunnels in other parts of the City." Occasional clanking sounds came from the pipes around them, seeming to move up and down the length of the tunnel. "One day I followed the smell to figure out what the hell was back here, and ended up in the bowels of the mall. Which itself is sort of the cultural bowel of the City, really."

Vyanna's disdain for malls and the people who frequented them made Rainville's heart beat faster. Was this love?

The Tunnels

THEY WALKED single-file down the endless tunnel. Rainville had never seen so many antique lightbulbs, nor so much concrete. It was hard to believe there was such a long, straight passage anywhere in the City, let alone one with no other people.

The pulse-beat of the mall faded along with its fast food smells. Their escape seemed a success.

"What was that back there in the ducts?" Rainville asked.

"The mini-snowstorm?" she said. "No idea. Never seen anything like that. The environmental controls must have gone nuts for a minute."

"That's a handy device you've got, by the way," he said. "The teddy bear lockpick thing, I mean."

"Oh! His name is Mozart." Was there a touch of self-consciousness in her smile?

"A fine name for a teddy bear."

Another smile. "I built him when I was little. Well, an early 'him.' This little guy is version fifteen. Mozart can now cycle through mechanical combinations and electromagnetic field permutations to open even high-security, mixed-type locks. He can even forge the security signatures for the city government locks! It took me almost a year to find all the cryptographic chips I needed."

Rainville nodded. Such chips could be made by a fabricator, but modern units would log the creation and the authorities would come knocking. "The parts for that kinda stuff can definitely be tough, but I do a lot of repair work. Optronics and electronics, mostly. Sometimes I can scavenge the harder-to-find components. And for the ones I can't, well, I've found some other sources…"

"Such as?"

"I live next door to an old lady with a stone-age fabricator. It doesn't support the latest security and safety protocols. I help her out with it, and in return she lets me use it for my projects. Last year, I made a Gauss pistol with it."

"You built a Gauss gun?" Vyanna's eyes lit up. "Sweet! Can I shoot it sometime?"

"Maybe," he replied with a wink which he hoped looked less cheesy than it felt.

An hour later they were touring a maze of cramped passages, some only high enough to crawl in. "This is the Labyrinth," Vyanna said. "The passages have never been fully mapped, mostly because it's a hard place to get around."

"Reminds me of the time I got lost in the Flux," said Rainville. "How do you find your way around down here?"

"You got lost in the Flux?" she asked incredulously. "For how long?"

"Only a day. Or two at the most," he laughed. "There's plenty of restaurants down there, so it could have been worse."

The Flux represented the newer half of the Chinese Quarter. Born from necessity of steep terrain, limited space, and increasing population density, the stores, restaurants, and apartments of the Flux were situated in interchangeable cube-shaped blocks of varying sizes that could be relocated and reconfigured on the fly. The passages connecting them were constantly evolving thanks to teams of builders (some human, but most robotic) who were always on call, and always at work. The result was a 3D network of roads and tunnels in a permanent state of rearrangement to meet the Fluxians' ever-changing traffic flows.

"I've heard stories about the Flux," she said. "Alleyways that change around people, blocking them into a maze of twisty little passages, all alike, until they've been subjected to hours of interactive popup ads."

"Urban legend," said Rainville. "Probably." Indeed, sometimes it felt as if the same Flux street corner would repeat, like you'd inexplicably gone in a circle. But the tales of tourists stuck for days in a closed loop, stumbling out of the Flux stark raving mad, mindlessly humming advertising jingles, were almost certainly apocryphal.

"So how do you find your way around down here?" he asked. "You haven't even touched your console."

She smirked. "It's a secret," she said with a wink. "I just hope we don't run into any Tunnel Folk down here."

"Tunnel Folk?"

"Not many people know about it, but centuries ago, a group of humans took up residence under the City. Over time, they changed to the point that they don't even seem human anymore. Nor do they consider themselves human." She cast a nervous glance over her shoulder. "In fact, they've developed a taste for human flesh."

"What! Really?" Rainville stopped walking.

"No, dumbass. It's just some abandoned tunnels. Who'd want to live down here? Honestly!" She shook her head in feigned wonder, and Rainville could not help laughing.

She led him to a place she called the Planetarium, a domed tunnel junction that graffiti artists from generations past had painted to resemble a night sky outside Arcadia's dome. A dim light seemed to project upward from the floor, bioluminescent paint perhaps, and parts of the murals above twinkled.

At last she checked her console, which had the look of cherry-red chrome in the dim light.

"I've gotta head home in a few. Wanna see one more place before I go?"

"Will I see you again?" The silence that followed his question seemed to last an eternity.

"Maybe," she said with a wink.

He laughed nervously. "Let's exchange contact data. So, umm, you can keep your options open, you know, if you decide you want to? To see me again, I mean." Such a smooth talker. How could she resist?

She studied him closely, then crooked a finger and he followed. She brought him down a series of long passages to a room she called the Cathedral, a tall, octagonal space filled with corrosion-stained metallic pillars rising up into the mist. Faint red light from somewhere above illuminated the mist and silhouetted the columns and their riveted crossmembers, creating an inexplicable majesty that transcended the industrial setting. "This is my favorite place in the Underground," she said, the glow of the light reflecting in her eyes.

"It's...amazing!" said Rainville. And it was. It looked like an underground cityscape in miniature, the clouds only amplifying the feeling of surreality. "To think, there are a million people walking around up there on the surface," he said, gesturing upward into the mist. "And none of them even know this place exists."

She nodded. "That's part of its beauty."

"Do you lead a lot of tours down here?"

"You're it. Hope you liked it, but I really do need to go now."

"Oh. Well...thanks for everything," he said. "I'll never forget this. Today, I mean. Or this place." Or you, he wanted to say, but the words did not come.

Her expression was inscrutable in the dim light. Could it have been a faint smile? At last, she snatched the console out of his hand, tapped it against hers, and tossed it back to him. He grabbed clumsily then caught it, but when he looked up, she was gone. There on the display was a series of digits that had not been there before.

The Witchfinder General, Part I

"The test [that the Witchfinder General] commonly adopted was that of swimming, so highly recommended by King James in his *Demonologie*. The hands and feet of the suspected persons were tied together crosswise, the thumb of the right hand to the toe of the left foot, and vice versa. They were then wrapped up in a large sheet or blanket, and laid upon their backs in a pond or river. If they sank, their friends and relatives had the poor consolation of knowing they were innocent, but there was an end of them: if they floated, which laid carefully on the water was generally the case, there was also an end of them; for they were deemed guilty of witchcraft, and burned accordingly."

Charles Mackay, *Extraordinary Popular Delusions and the Madness of Crowds, Vol. 2*, 1841

Foxwright

FOXWRIGHT WAS LOVED BY FEW, hated by many, but respected by all. While he possessed not inconsiderable social skills, he was miserly with etiquette, remorselessly honest, and abided no foolishness. His rarified profession involved analyzing lost legal cases and appealing the decisions of the nearly-perfect computerized jurists which now decided all civil and criminal legal cases.

His job required him to get inside the computer's artificially-intelligent mind and comprehend the "why" of its decision, to see if it lined up with generally-established notions of justice and fairness. For Foxwright, this often came through as a gut feeling about whether the case outcome was consistent with all the others he'd seen in his many years of practicing law. Unfortunately, this generally required reviewing every bit of data the computer analyzed to identify missed or misunderstood facts, slogging through case files and depositions and then computer-input transcripts, looking for things that appeared in one but not the other. This file comparison could be done by low-level attorneys and automated tools, but his veteran instinct for spotting deeper inconsistencies was what earned him the big bucks.

Attuning his mind to artificially-intelligent computers may have caused Foxwright's low tolerance for incompetence and distaste for human contact, or perhaps just made the job a good fit. He'd been at it so long, it was now difficult to say which was the case.

Foxwright did unto others as they did unto him, which on some days was convenient, but on this day was not. Months ago Phelps, a former colleague from his days at the firm of Petronius & Sydra, had brought his attention to a forensics article that made all the difference in one of Foxwright's tougher cases. In return, he grudgingly agreed to write a few chapters for Phelps' upcoming book about the history of humankind's various systems of justice, culminating in the rise of artificially intelligent juries. Computerized juries had brought immeasurable benefits to Arcadia, and it did seem important for the masses to understand this.

He took a swig from his glass of tea and frowned; it had long gone cold. He'd been reading ancient legal history all morning. He threw the cup toward the garbage can. It missed, careening across the floor and sloshing tea everywhere as the cup rolled under the desk.

"Nice shot," intoned a female voice. It was Trixy, his automated administrative assistant. A small door in the wall slid open, and sensing disorder, a floor-cleaner robot deployed and began steaming the tea out of the rug. The racket was enough to kill any chance of preserving his train of thought.

"Trixy, I'm in the middle of something here...."

"It will just take a second, sir."

"Can't it wait? I'm not asking a lot. It would be nice if you obeyed me every now and then."

"That is but one of my duties, sir. I also have a duty to your carpet."

"You have a professional responsibility to my floor coverings?"

"I am bound to preserve the appearance and functionality of your workspace, sir." Another rush of steam thundered from the floorbot as it worked away on the carpet.

"That's wonderful, Trixy. Thank you very little."

"Of course, sir," she replied cheerfully.

He scowled at his disembodied assistant, and at the floorbot, then gave up on scowling for lack of results and fumbled around under the desk to retrieve his cup.

Standing, he retracted the curtain and looked out over Arcadia. Above him was the translucent dome that enclosed the City. He lived in one of the taller domescrapers in the Financial District, which afforded a prime view of Arcadia.

Climate control spires stabbed upward to the very top of the dome where swirling clouds of vapor collected, a transient weather system that clung to life at the dome's highest elevations as the humidity was captured and the moisture redistributed around the City.

Braids of fiber-optic light stalks ensnarled the pillars, descending in a spiral to the structures below, massive vines tapping into rooftops beneath a polymer forest. Near the far edge rose the semicircle of the Columbia Biome like a rising moon, a dome within the dome. Through Columbia's transparent wall was a blur of green vegetation silhouetting the respiration structures used to maintain low temperature and high humidity for the temperate rainforest within.

Foxwright's walls and shelves held memorabilia from the golden age of baseball—autographed balls and signed team photos, relics now quite affordable given that the sport was nearly dead.

His grandpa had introduced him to baseball, taught him the uniqueness of the game. Slow and fast at the same time; turn-based, yet played in realtime. In the end, the sport died out for the same reason as so many other pastimes of centuries-gone: no one could focus on them. By the time crowds sat around checking their consoles, playing fantasy-league metagames, messaging, only half-watching the game, it didn't have much of a future. To many, baseball was now a metaphor for dullness.

Dullness could be a dangerous first impression. Researching legal history seemed dull and dry at first, and he'd dragged his feet for several weeks before even starting this project. But there were definite trends and less manifest undercurrents running through the early systems of justice, undercurrents which were still alive and well, and which transcended historical trivia.

The chapters he created were no mere textbook filler, a means of fast-forwarding from the void of tribal anarchy to the computer age of justice. They'd become something more, underscoring the core purposes of a legal system for humankind. Historically, law seemed at least as much about having an orderly process as having a fair one. This was a surprising result, and he wondered just how many of the old legal systems' purpose was actually to dissuade people from ending up there in the first place, whether as plaintiffs or defendants, or as the criminally accused. Fairness, it turned out, had always been something of an afterthought, like a pitiable stepchild that acquaintances asked after when absent, but never truly missed.

Indeed, for long expanses of human history, "justice" had been largely absent from the picture; Foxwright's history of systems of justice was becoming not a study of justice, so much as of systems. All that seemed to change from one epoch to the next was who held the gavel. The incipient pattern echoed throughout the recorded past. That is, until computers came into the picture, marrying together wisdom, reason and objectivity for the first time in history.

Not that there weren't areas of the justice system still administered by human beings, dismal though they were. Arcadia's prisons embodied all manner of human cruelty. The worst of them, known only as Wychwood, was the stuff of nightmares. Wychwood was widely regarded as a hell-on-earth, a place more likely to strip away a man's humanity than rehabilitate him in any real way. Thankfully, the facility had been prohibited from accepting new prisoners, and places like this might soon become a thing of the past. But in the meantime, ensuring the courts meted out correct verdicts remained a critical mission.

Foxwright had earned some degree of fame as a defender of the computerized jury both in legal journal articles and in academic debates. He saw his job not so much to find fault with their decisions (which, indeed, it was), as to help perfect them, given their endless capacity to learn from mistakes and better themselves. If only his fellow humans were so blessed.

His eyes drifted to a Circassian walnut frame atop his desk. Within was an autographed photo of George Brett, third baseman for the

1983 Royals who hit the only game-losing home run in the history of baseball. After a two-run homer that put his team in the lead in the final inning, the umpire nullified the home run and called him out for having too much pine tar (a primitive twentieth-century grip material) on his bat. Instead of simply removing the bat from the game as actually required by the rule, the ignorant officiator changed the score and cost the Royals the game.

Foxwright took another sip from his cup, this time not even noticing it was empty. Was injustice simply an inherent part of the human condition, an inescapable pattern caused by some corrupt kernel of human nature?

Legal Computing

(an excerpt from The Rise of Computerized Courts by J. Q. L. Foxwright)

At a fundamental level, artificially-intelligent jurors are easy to understand. Artificial intelligences (AIs) are based on neural networks. A legal neural net uses a hierarchical structure to model a logical mathematical formula with different weights and operations. What does this mean? Imagine that a dog bites a man and the man sues the dog's owner. No crime has occurred, but the victim demands compensation, so we have ourselves a civil action. In our legal system, AIs perform deliberation for civil actions like this, and they also adjudicate criminal cases.

How does an artificially-intelligent juror work? Let's begin by stating a legal premise: *If someone owns a dog <u>and</u> they know it's dangerous <u>and</u> it bites somebody else, then the owner should have to compensate the victim.*

That's all well and good, but the earliest computers didn't understand English sentences, and even modern computers do not "think" in plain English—they think in abstract mathematical terms. We can get a little closer to the proto-language AIs use by replacing the "and's" in the above premise with × signs, multiplying the various factors of a dog bite case together.

Now, the AI formula representing our legal premise might be:

Liability = Ownership × Notice of aggression × Biting

The outcome of the case is the mathematical product of several terms. First, Ownership: if the dog isn't owned by the defendant, then ownership is equal to zero. To put this in plain English, regardless of the other factors, if it's not your dog, then you aren't liable when it bites someone. But let's assume it is your dog. Common law has always held that every dog is entitled to one bite. Thus, there is only liability when the owner should have known of the dangerous proclivities of his dog, and the "one bite" rule makes allowance for this. If there was no notice of aggressive character (it's the first time your dog ever bit anyone!) then that part of the formula is zero, and the resulting liability is again zero (multiplying anything by zero equals zero). Finally, if no bite occurred, then Biting equals zero, and there is no liability. In contrast, if you own the dog, knew it liked to bite people, and it did indeed bite the victim (our plaintiff), then the degree of each of these factors will be multiplied together to yield some non-zero amount of civil liability. And of course, you'll have to pay some compensation to our poor victim based on how much Liability there was.

This is all well and good, but we haven't accounted for mitigating circumstances. What if the victim was tormenting the dog before the bite? Or what if the victim was robbing the owner's home, and the dog acted defensively? No doubt the dog's owner should be absolved in those cases.

Our legal premise might be restated as *If someone owns a dog and they know it's dangerous and it bites somebody, then the owner must compensate the victim, unless the dog was being tormented, or unless the victim was trespassing.*

So that our AIs might understand, we'll replace the word "unless" with a—indicating subtraction, so we'll subtract liability for each mitigating circumstance. Now, the formula representing the legal premise is:

$$\text{Liability} = \text{Ownership} \times \text{Notice of aggression} \times \text{Biting}$$
$$- \text{Being tormented} - \text{Trespassing}$$

Here, even if Ownership, Notice of aggressive character, and Biting are all 100% verified, we can still end up with zero Liability if the dog was being tormented or was defending against a home invasion. Or the owner could be found only partially at fault, in which case he may be liable only for some percentage of the victim's total computed damages.

There are certainly other aspects of common law that might be exacerbating or mitigating in a dog bite case, but you can begin to see how we can translate our oldest legal principles into a computational paradigm, and compute a solution just like any other mathematical equation.

Dinner

RAINVILLE'S first official date with Vyanna was at 12:46:34, the exact time of their flashmob caper two days previous. They met at Thornden Plaza, located in a remote part of Vaux Park.

The Vaux was the crown jewel of Arcadia's urban preserves, its biome approximating a cloud forest. Fiber-optic vines flowed down from the roof of the habitat, splashing sunlight down upon the park in vibrant contrast to the muted glow of ever-overcast daylight through the City's overhead dome. In places like the grove of trees that surrounded the plaza, the directed sunlight hit the canopy of leaves producing a kind of swaying light show that seemed somehow more impressive in its simplicity than all of Arcadia's interactive art installations. The lines between man-made and natural were seamlessly organic.

They watched a flock of tiny rainbow-colored birds weave to and fro far above, their murmurations changing with their heading. "I always forget how great this place is," Vyanna said. "My sister and I used to come here as kids. And it was always like, I dunno, like even the air is cleaner here."

He considered this. Sure, the air in the park was molecularly-identical to what was pumped out of the City's environmental control ducts, but somehow it seemed better. Fresher. Like it could grant the park wanderer more vitality than the fabricated stuff.

Vaux was, well, pure. It was a far cry from the smaller commercial parks which littered the City, where each tree was programmed to drop gaudy synthetic leaves covered with advertisements for local businesses on passers-by, and where each bird sang advertising jingles or hymns from up-and-coming (or not) religions. The more time Rainville spent in the Vaux, the more the commercial parks seemed like a travesty of nature.

Enchanted by Vaux's beauty, they spoke as they walked, exploring new park trails and conversational topics.

"Phaedra's my younger sister," continued Vyanna. "Our parents worked all the time when we were little, so we kinda had to amuse ourselves. We'd look through my dad's technical magazines, until we found schematics for toys. Phae would pick one, and I would build it for her. Or try to, anyway! My first 'robot' was just an unmoving box with a flashing light." She laughed. "But Phae loved it. She still has it, and the light still flashes on my original power cell."

Different fiber-optic vines activated to simulate the movement of the sun, the piped-in daylight warming as afternoon set in. Butterflies hovered over to bask in newly-created patches of sunlight. Rainville told her about his past Shopping adventures, about his job, and his favorite customers.

"And that was right before my mom died," said Rainville. "I moved out two weeks later. I guess my dad and I have never really seen eye-to-eye since." Vyanna looked at him with compassion, and the color of her eyes filled him with wonder. A beautiful shade halfway between blue and purple—lavender, perhaps? The same as in the mall. Most girls his age changed their eye color every day, or even more frequently. Vyanna had made a choice, and she'd stuck with it.

They came to the end of a long arbor when he heard a familiar *whirr* approaching behind him. A PizzaBot rolled along on its duly appointed rounds, delivering tasty sustenance to city-dwellers in twenty minutes or less. A walking billboard, the robot's chassis was coated with animated paint showing wholesome-looking families gobbling down slices of the Yummy Pizza Pie Restaurant Syndicate's various menu options.

"You hungry, Vy?" he asked.

"I could eat," she said. "Where do you wanna go?"

He snapped his rolled-up console into a solid plane and did a quick-but-surreptitious sensor sweep for SmartLamps. Arcadia was infested with the things. Disguised as innocent streetlights, on a good day a SmartLamp would simply illuminate a given street corner. But on a bad day, the SmartLamp's sensor array would detect you robbing a PizzaBot, zorch you unconscious, and you'd wake up in detainment wondering what the hell happened.

"Follow me," he said, dashing into the path of the robot. She smiled and chased after him.

"Excuse me, sir!" the PizzaBot chirped as it neared, swerving to avoid Rainville in a fluid motion that led it behind a hibiscus hedge lining the sidewalk. He followed his quarry out of sight, and again stepped into the robot's path. Reaching into his pocket, he retrieved a fistful of hazy blue-green spheres, each about an inch in diameter. He cupped them in his hands and shook, and as they clacked against one another, they began flashing. He flung them in an arc toward the bot. They bounced and then rolled onto the sidewalk surrounding the bot, which stopped dead in its tracks.

"Oh, excuse me, young sir," it intoned, rolling backwards away from the nearest of the flashing marbles. It stopped again and changed course; "Pardon me, young miss!" and then repeated the sequence, each new direction of motion ceasing as it approached another orb.

"I've never seen a robot do that," said Vyanna. "What'd you do to it?"

"I played on its uncertainty."

"Come again?"

"People think robots are deterministic. But a robot is far more uncertain about what's going on than even your most neurotic human.

At any one time, it's getting a dozen conflicting sensor inputs, and it has to make a best guess on which inputs to disregard, and which to listen to, to figure out its situation. I guess you could think of them as having a lot of self-doubt. So those emitters blind the robot's optical sensors, and at the same time, give off the thermal and electromagnetic signatures of humans. The robot gets stuck in an inescapable confused state; it's not completely sure what it's seeing, but chances are better than not that its path is blocked by a crowd of non-moving pedestrians."

"Why doesn't it just push through them, like a person would?" she asked.

"I programmed them to emulate babies," he said.

"Babies?"

"Yeah. So the bot won't find it safe to assume rational reactions, nor communication ability, on the part of the people around it. It's now paralyzed by a programmed fear of litigation. The pizza company that owns it doesn't want to get sued for rolling over a baby. It's much cheaper to just compensate a customer for a late pizza here or there."

"In those rare occasions where the robot gets caught in a mob of infants," offered Vyanna.

"Right."

"Very clever," she said with a smile. "And do you always carry babies in your back pocket, Mr. Rainville?"

"Only usually. I can give you the fabricator schematics, if you'd like!"

"Hell yes! And, now what?"

"PizzaBots carry food, but all their payments are handled electronically. They don't haul anything of real monetary value, so their security is on the primitive side."

This was true.

Generally.

He stepped over one of the flashing spheres, but as he reached toward the warming vault which protruded from the robot like a distended abdomen, a crackling sound cut through the air. A spike emerged from the robot's chest, electricity gathering into a cloud on its tip.

Before Rainville could retract his arm, a bolt of electricity struck his outstretched hand. His upper body convulsed and he stumbled back into the hibiscus bushes, twitching uncontrollably.

Dessert

RAINVILLE FOUND himself staring at the domed sky. He was disoriented, and winded by the involuntary workings of so many muscles at once. His arms and legs shook tremulously, and it took a concerted effort to unclench his fingers.

"Oh my God! Are you okay?" Vyanna asked, helping him slowly back to his feet as the robot continued to murmur apologies and jerk to and fro nearby.

"D-d-damn it to h-h-hell!" he said, surprised at his involuntary jittering.

She asked again. He forewent trying to speak and gave a tentative nod.

He held his hand up next to his head and waggled his fingers. He was still shaking enough that they mostly waggled themselves.

She laughed. When he could stand on his own, she moved a short distance away and started rummaging through the closest park garbage can. "Eureka," she said, clutching a shiny food wrapper. "Now it's time to avenge you!"

Maneuvering around the front of the PizzaBot, she tossed the foil onto the spike, where it draped down and met the metallic base of the robot's coverplating. *ZOT!* Electricity rippled across the surface of the

PizzaBot, short-circuiting the defense spike to the robot's own chassis, and catching the foil on fire. The robot went into a convulsive dance not completely unfamiliar to Rainville. "Your p-p-p-p-pizza as ord-d-d-d-dered, Mr. Estrag-g-g-g-gon, sor-r-r-ry to keep you waiting!" said the robot, its voice fluttering as its door flung open to reveal a pizza box, which it forcefully ejected into the nearby bushes.

"Are your legs back online yet? Or are you still...?" she said, waggling her fingers next to her head with a grin.

He managed to shift his weight from one leg to the other without falling down.

"Good!" she said. Retrieving the pizza box, she turned and bounded down a trail heading further into the cloud forest, her purple-blonde tresses bouncing as she went. Rainville followed gingerly, his muscles still coming back under his control. Soon, their giddy laughter blended together as it had at the mall.

"Sir, your mystery pizza," she said, offering him the oblong box with great ceremony. With trepidation, he lifted the lid and peered in.

"So what is it?" she asked.

"I think it's mushroom with port wine sauce."

"And the gods smiled," Vyanna said, smiling right along with them.

She used the box as a plate, and they munched slices of pizza as they walked through a grove of lignum vitae trees, purple blooms fully open in the humid air of the biome.

"Lorikeets!" said Rainville, pointing above them. A flock of the birds were nestled on the gnarled branches above them.

"I've never seen peach-colored ones before," she said. "Hey, you don't you suppose that robot had a refrigerated beer vault, do you?" she said.

"Dunno, but I feel like I've had enough of PizzaBots for one day. Besides, by now it's probably called in the cavalry," he said.

"Afraid of a few measly AIs?" she asked with a grin as she retrieved a fresh slice. "I'm getting kinda thirsty."

A bright flash lit the biome, and computer-generated thunder reverberated through the park. The synthesized sounds disguised the crackling of the park's precipitation guns as they augmented, then coalesced, the humidity in the air into rain.

"There's your water, as requested!" Rainville laughed.

"I forgot they do monsoons on Wednesdays," Vyanna said loudly to be heard over the torrential rain. She held the pizza box above her head to block the downpour. "Follow me!"

They ran deeper into the lignum vitae grove, finally taking shelter beneath a squat pandanus tree with a rounded canopy curving around to form a dry space within the plant. A rather small, dry space. They sat, side by side, her elbow and hip pressed against his, and Rainville's pulse quickened.

Vyanna smiled awkwardly. "So, ummm…wow, lots of rain, huh?" she stammered. She looked away from him, and picked intently at some nearby blades of grass.

"Yep. It's…it's very wet."

The rain is wet? What a dumb thing to say. His cheeks grew hot.

She cleared her throat as if to say something, but then didn't.

Rainville's heart thumped ever more loudly in his eardrums. His thoughts were a jumble. This couldn't get any more awkward. Could it? No, not really, not in any way he could think of. Unless….

He leaned in and kissed her. And instead of running away screaming in fulfillment of his envisioned nightmare, she closed her eyes and actually kissed back.

Randomly-generated thunder rolled across the biome. As the air filled with the fragrance of drenched soil and synthesized ozone, Rainville and Vyanna nestled there, alternating between nibbling on pizza slices and trading kisses.

When the last slice of dinner was gone, the rainstorm was still going strong.

The Witchfinder General, Part II

"Another test was to make them repeat the Lord's Prayer and creed. It was affirmed that no witch could do so correctly. If she missed a word, or even pronounced one incoherently, which in her trepidation, it was most probable she would, she was accounted guilty. It was thought that witches could not weep more than three tears, and those from the left eye. Thus the conscious innocence of many persons, which gave them fortitude to bear unmerited torture without flinching, was construed by their unmerciful tormentors into proofs of guilt.

In some districts the test resorted to was to weigh the culprit against the church Bible. If the suspected witch proved heavier than the Bible, she was set at liberty. This mode was far too humane for the witchfinders by profession. [The Witchfinder-General] always maintained that the most legitimate modes were pricking and swimming ... If he found any [witches], he claimed twenty shillings a head in addition when they were brought to execution."

Charles Mackay, *Extraordinary Popular Delusions and the
Madness of Crowds*, Vol. 2, 1841

Culinary Anachronism

THE TOASTER WOULD SURELY BE the young couple's most interesting wedding gift. Essie, the bride's ninety-three-year-old grandmother, had endeavored to replicate, to the best of her remembrance, the toaster she'd received at her own wedding a lifetime ago. The machine had been top-of-the-line, the first model to offer thermal paint that shifted through a rainbow of colors as it heated up. The appliance had served Essie and Lambert, God rest his soul, without fail or even uneven toasting, for fifty-four years of marriage. Now Tessa could make toast for Dashwood. Young women today had forgotten how to make a home, so reliant were they on robots to do this and that and the other. But not her Tessa. Tess would appreciate this gift. She would understand its significance.

Essie worked for three months to implement the toaster, a relatively sophisticated choice for one's first custom fabricator project. Would the kids think her an old fuddy-duddy for gifting such a culinary anachronism to them? They'd undoubtedly be impressed she finally relented to their nagging, and not only learned to use her fabricator, but really showed it who was the boss by creating this custom circuit-driven masterpiece. Sure, she'd relied heavily on Rainville, the bright young man who lived next door, and the *Fabricators for Dummies* reference vids he'd given her, but the results proved she was no dummy!

She was tempted to test the toaster before wrapping it up, but it was tacky to give someone a used gift, even a lightly used one. In the end, she put it in the box untested. Rainville had reviewed the schematics, worked out all the bugs. "It'll work," he'd said, "trust me!"

Toast

TESSA ACTIVATED capture mode on her console, livestreaming her inaugural use of Grandma Essie's gift to the cloud.

She read the label out loud: "'To the Newlyweds, Dashwood and Tessa'—who are these married people?" Tessa giggled as she lifted the cover off the box.

She woke up early that day, deciding on a lark to use the toaster to make her husband—husband!—breakfast in bed. Grandma would be thrilled to see her present in action, and no doubt Tessa's friends would get a laugh from it. "It's part of an old diurnal breakfast ritual," she narrated. "They call it a 'toaster.' It turns plain old bread into toast!" It looked exactly like the one she'd grown up seeing Grandma Essie use.

In actuality, no one under the age of eighty who wasn't a retro or a cultist still used toasters. With the technology fabricators offered, one could simply create toast on demand. The devices were thus relegated to antique and junk stores, and still common enough that they weren't even worth much there. Yet this toaster was more than an outdated bread warmer: it was a reminder that her grandma loved her.

After fabricating some untoasted bread, which she admitted felt like cheating, she placed the toaster on the kitchen counter near the power jack. As she plugged it in, she thought of her grandmother's kitchen and felt a tangible link to past generations of newly-married brides.

"All right, you guys ready?" she narrated to the vidstream cam. "Here goes!"

She eagerly positioned bread in each of the four slots. Leaning in close to watch the culinary antiquity work its magic, she pressed the wide black knob down in its track. The bread disappeared as the slice lifter clicked into place, and several circuits within the device engaged simultaneously. One circuit began heating the resistive coils surrounding the bread slices. Another monitored the surface temperature of the bread, and another its color. Still another controlled the buttering circuit to spray particles of the chosen topping onto the toast.

One circuit was quite unlike all the others, as exotic as it was sinister. Milliseconds after the heating circuit powered up, the electrical current drain from the toasting coils triggered the extra circuit.

The ensuing explosion vaporized Tessa's flesh and blasted charred fragments of her teeth and bones across several city blocks.

Force Majeure

IN A HIGH-RISE far above the Financial District, on one of the floors belonging to the illustrious Law Offices of Petronius & Sydra, an attorney named Phelps took the first sip of his third coffee. He rose at dawn that morning to get a jump on a fusion-energy futures contract due that day. His caseload was split between criminal defense and energy business law, an unlikely combination, but one which seemed to suit him. He liked the variety and felt that a good lawyer could tackle any kind of legal task he put his mind to. And on the days where this proved incorrect, he had a large virtual rolodex of specialists to help out.

As a young associate, Phelps had planned to work hard and pay his dues until he made partner, then kick back and take time to enjoy life a little more. But after nearly a decade of long workdays and work nights, he knew nothing else. Having no social life outside the firm had become habit, one which it made little financial sense to break.

Phelps was busy refining the contract's force majeure clause when it happened. Out of the corner of his eye, the view out the window shifted for a brief instant. The buildings across the street appeared to twist on their foundations. Then his window shattered, bulging inward within its safety laminate. He tripped backwards over his chair, then rolled behind his desk to take cover. The shaking continued, followed by a loud pop outside as the shattered window now flexed outward.

At length the rumbling died down. He knelt there bracing for more, but only silence came.

Then the lights went out, and the computers went quiet.

Shattered

HUNGRY MARLEY'S ("Purveyor of Fine Food and Drink") was Prexy's passion. In the years since she'd acquired it, the underground pub became more than just a business: its patrons were like family. It was her refuge, hidden away from the savageries of the rest of the world.

The pub was as rife with her personal mementos as with exotic liquor. The stopper on her best scotch decanter was made from the first fifty Reformed Dollar Credits she earned, redeemed in gold coins then melted down and cast. The bar itself was a massive slab of now-extinct koa wood, and at least two centuries old (she got it for a song from an elderly barkeep who insisted only that it be given a good home). The antique stained glass lamp hanging over the pool table was a gift from her late father when she'd first bought the pub. Hungry Marley's represented her past, and with any luck, it represented her future.

She'd arrived at 7:00 a.m. and spent the morning polishing the bar and then wiping down high-tops. She was midway through unpacking the latest liquor deliveries when the Earth moved.

At street level a story above, the double doors shook in their frame. Beer glasses swayed and fell off hooks, raining down onto the bar and shattering on the floor tiles below.

It had to be an earthquake. The first one she'd seen in this era of seismic management. Must be a bad one if they couldn't neutralize it before it started.

Liquor bottles began shimmying out of their racks. Prexy ran to the oldest bottles and pushed them back in as they emerged, like some high-stakes game of whack-a-mole with single-malt scotches and ancient rums in place of holographic rodents. She fought hard, but in the end there were just too many, her best stock smashing to the floor around her feet. Tears streamed down her face as the smells of smoky peat, and fire-malted barley, and earthy sugar cane rose up from the glass wreckage.

It was then that her father's stained glass billiard lamp pitched violently on the end of its chains. "Nooooo!" she cried, scrambling over the broken bottles and bounding over the bar to save it. The pain from shards of glass puncturing her foot was temporary, while the pain of a lost family heirloom would be forever.

She knocked chairs aside and slalomed tables, but was still ten feet away when the lamp bounced drunkenly off its chains. It slammed into the wainscoted wall, facets of broken glass raining down onto the pool table in a multicolored tinkling torrent.

Calamity

A BELL RANG as Essie stepped out of the Old Prague Bakery on Zizka Square. The storefront on the southeastern extreme of the Bohemian Quarter was quite a trek from her apartment building on Cicero Street, but freshly-baked kolach pastries were worth the trip!

She breathed deeply as the smell of warm apricot preserves rose from the bag of fluffy pastry pillows. She considered sitting down on one of the park benches in the Square to eat a few and lighten her load when the plaza's lampposts began to rattle.

The earth lurched beneath her feet and she was knocked to her knees, along with most of the people around her. It looked as if, by some divine order, everyone in the plaza suddenly knelt down to pray at the same time. As if it were the end of days.

A gust of wind and dirt rushed through, carrying with it an ungodly roar.

Essie's ears rang as she blinked away some of the dust. Around her people yammered in confusion. "Look!" someone cried. Several people were pointing to a black mushroom cloud rising to the northwest. It reminded Essie of a thunderhead forming in fast motion.

Through the ringing, she heard disjointed fragments of speech joining into a jumble:

"Doesn't even look real…!"

"Right outta one o' them old war vids…!"

"Dome's gonna fill up with smoke and suffocate us…!"

As folks stood and began to dust themselves off, Essie stayed on her knees. She'd seen the direction of the blast, and now she *was* praying.

Close Shave

CROWN POINT, or the Retro District as it was known to outsiders like Foxwright, was steeped in Traditionalism. Its cobblestone streets, historic buildings, painted signs (no digital signage allowed), and slow-cooked foods gave it a quaint, Old World charm, if also a certain anachronistic strangeness. The streets housed butchers, dairies, saloop carts, and markets offering everything from incandescent lights to ice cream makers to real wax candles. Conspicuous in their absence were synthesized meats, flavor-morphing sodas, designer fruits, and any other victuals not found in nature.

It wasn't a neighborhood Foxwright would frequent, but for Matousek's Luxury Barber Shop on Westcott Street. While most in this day and age resorted to shaving bots, he'd never been comfortable around them. If the feeling of the tiny robots skittering around on his face was not unnerving enough, the things looked even more horrifying. They resembled exoskeleton-husked insects, ravenously searching his terror-stricken face for hair-food. The first time he'd watched them under magnification, the diabolical beasties caused him weeks' worth of nightmares. He'd sworn off shavebots ever since. He stuck with antique electric razors, or an old-school straight-razor shave from Matousek when he was feeling extravagant.

Matousek finished stropping the blade and wiped it down with disinfectant. He leveled Foxwright's graying sideburns off at mid-ear, then moved the razor steadily down his cheeks. "Chin up," the old man said at last. "Hold still."

The words were unnecessary; with a razor blade scant millimeters from his jugular vein, Foxwright could scarcely imagine a situation evoking more stillness.

The razor blade slid down Foxwright's neck. A tickle formed in his nose, and continued to build as Matousek passed the razor nearer and nearer to his throat. He held up a finger to get Matousek's attention, and the man stopped his work.

"Sorry...I need...to sneeze," Foxwright said, bracing himself.

But he did not sneeze. Instead, a dull roar filled their ears, quickly building to a deafening, ground-shaking crescendo. At length it subsided, giving way to the sound of breaking glass and screams.

Shaving cream still on his face, he ran out into the street. Dust choked the air. Panicked people scrambled across cobblestones littered with glass. The sky looked...wrong, somehow.

A dazed young woman staggered toward him. Her hair was white with dust. She covered her eyes with her arm, and blood poured down her cheeks. He noticed her shirt, blood and grime over a series of embroidered cats and the caption "It's meow or never!"

"Can anyone hear me?" she asked loudly. "I can't see! Help me!" She'd been struck in the eyes by debris. Possibly flying glass. Traditionalists loved the stuff, despite the advantages of polymers.

"Stay with her; I'll call for help!" said Matousek as he hurried back into his shop, leaving Foxwright alone with the girl.

He tried to get a view of her eyes, but saw only blood.

"It's all right," he said, glad she could not see the expression he could not hide. "Help is on the way. Everything will be okay." He wasn't sure if he was lying or hoping, helping or hurting. He had no idea what the hell was happening, nor whether this girl would ever see again.

She seemed not to hear him.

"Hello? Please help me!" Hoarse sobs wracked her body.

He wasn't sure what to do. What he even *could* do. So he reached down and grabbed her free hand in his and wrapped his other arm around her back.

He helped her onto a wooden bench and stayed with her. She leaned in to him, growing calmer at his touch, as her crying softened. There they waited, her hand in his.

When the medical robots finally arrived, he could not bring himself to let go.

龙之烈焰

(LÓNG ZHĪ LIÈ YÀN)

RAINVILLE WAS GENERALLY IGNORANT of Chinese cuisine. Not that he didn't like it, but spicy Indian and Thai curries were more his speed. It was thus a calculated risk to bring Vyanna to Xiagu for breakfast. Still, it seemed a unique setting to tell her what he increasingly felt needed saying.

A partially subterranean subdistrict, Xiagu was built into a deep slot canyon just east of the Flux in the Chinese Quarter. It was as foreign a place as he'd found in Arcadia. The sheer walls of the canyon were riddled with ancient *yaodongs*, homes and shops carved out of the sandstone. Outsiders speculated the cave-like dwellings met in an endless maze of connecting warrens, but he'd read that most were quite modest in size due to the general human preference for proximity to daylight, coupled with a ban on construction bots in the subdistrict.

The Níng Jìng Hào restaurant perched on a stone terrace overlooking the widest part of the slot canyon. From their vantage point, they could see the ledge-roads and businesses cut into the far canyon wall. Backing their table was a grotto lined with thousands of miniature windchime flowers. The flowers converted solar energy into minuscule movements of their genetically-engineered bells, collec-

tively forming an orchestra of tiny ringing voices, each slightly different. Far above, flocks of sparrows darted to and fro in the thermal
winds at the canyon's rim. Were the birds real or robotic? Rainville
decided they were so beautiful, he didn't care.

The waiter cleared his throat and Rainville's attention snapped
back to the present.

"Umm," said Rainville, "we'll take the, err...the pure tea."

"The pu-erh tea, sir?"

"Yes, definitely, that one." It was the most expensive drink on the
menu.

Vyanna searched the menu for the item, and her eyes grew wide.
"That tea you ordered...."

"Yes?" He tried to look nonchalant.

"It says here that it's fermented, and then aged for twelve years.
Wow! Just think about what you were doing back when this tea was
picked?"

He thought back to where he was twelve years ago: a seven-year-
old kid with no real problems, no serious responsibilities. A kid with a
mom who was still alive, and a father still excited about Rainville's
potential, instead of criticizing its perceived waste.

The waiter placed a glazed clay teapot before them, ornately
painted with a herd of deer crossing a snowy meadow. The brew was a
deep red color, and it was delicious: strong, sweet and earthy at the
same time.

Vyanna took a hesitant sip. Then a smile lit up her face. "It's
amazing!"

Her every smile lifted his spirit, filling him with relief. If this date
could be going better, he wasn't sure how. It was even better than last
week's trip to the Yukon Biome, where they'd had a snowball fight,
shared hot chocolate, and made snow angels.

He tried the tea while Vyanna sampled bites of golden lotus root,
and the wind chimes tinkled around them as the sparrows looped.

The morning rush was winding down, and the ledge-roads and
plazas on the far wall of the canyon were empty save for a scattering of
elderly people playing mahjong and chess. Many of the older women

carried brightly-colored umbrellas, not because such crude devices had any place in an enclosed, climate-controlled city, but because the practice had been ubiquitous in their youth.

"I was thinking," said Rainville, blowing across his cup to cool the steaming tea.

She waited for him to finish, but he did not. "About?" she said.

He thought carefully about how to phrase what he wanted to say next. He'd never had so much in common with any person, and so the stakes of what he was about to say only amplified his nervousness.

It was then that the ground began to vibrate. The chairs jolted beneath them, and hot tea sloshed out of their cups.

Vyanna screamed, and he pulled her close as rocks and dust fell from the ceiling of the grotto. A grapefruit-sized chunk of stone crashed onto their table, smashing the teapot to bits. The white meadow on its clay shards was now spattered with red droplets of tea.

A shockwave passed over the top of the canyon, booming echoes cascading amongst the stone cliffs. A burst of billowing fire followed, scorching the rooftops of the highest pagodas. *"Lóng zhī liè yàn!"* exclaimed an old man at the bar: dragon's flames.

Then their ears popped, an effect felt by a hundred thousand others as the emergency pressure-relief hatches in Arcadia's dome were blown out before they could entirely open, and atmospheric pressure plummeted citywide.

It began snowing dust and ash. It would not stop for two days.

For the Angel of Death spread his wings on the blast,
And breathed in the face of the foe as he passed;
And the eyes of the sleepers waxed deadly and chill,
And their hearts but once heaved, and for ever grew still!

Lord Byron, "*The Destruction of Sennacherib,*" 1815

Part II

Burnt Breadcrumbs

DOZENS OF CITY blocks surrounding Genesee Street disappeared in a pall of smoke. A column of heat thousands of degrees Celsius shot up from the Latin Quarter, charring and blurring huge swaths of Arcadia's polymer dome. A thick fog accumulated at the dome's highest point, casting a days-long artificial night over the Financial District until the overwhelmed air purifiers could catch up. In the fringes of the cloud where the dark met the light, chaos churned.

A full-scale citywide emergency response was initiated for the first time in over forty years. Response teams deployed from the Latin Quarter and five neighboring districts, including hundreds of robotic fire suppression squads.

The explosion erased the top of the Cleveland Arms complex. Built as a luxury hotel a century and a half earlier, the Cleveland's ventilation system could adjust the direction and force of air movement to prevent the spread of fires. However, after the system was damaged in the initial explosion, the fire generated its own winds and became a firestorm. The Cleveland was also the first building in Arcadia to feature carbon-fiber-threaded girders. This spared it from complete collapse and left a twisted skeletal ruin to mark the epicenter of what had been the western Latin Quarter.

The sheer force of the mysterious blast destabilized neighboring structures, peppering the entire Quarter with shrapnel of flying bricks baked and laid by centuries-dead craftsmen. Some buildings collapsed before their residents had any hope of escape.

The fire teams used acoustic waves and electric fields to disrupt combustion, and leeching beams quenched the burning materials at the molecular level. Without heat, the fuel could not sustain the oxidization reaction necessary for a fire to burn. As the various zones of the fire were brought under control, crab-like autonomous robots crawled through the acres of mangled metal and rubble to locate survivors and identify remains. Imaging robots crept under and above wreckage, ascending cracked walls and encircling broken columns, scanning terrain, itemizing objects, and exchanging map coverage data with each other in realtime. A 3D model of the scene was gradually stitched together as each automated insectoid reported back.

The criminal task force was the largest the city had seen in a generation. Hundreds of police and fire personnel worked around the clock for over a week cataloging and transmitting digital images of the damage and collecting evidence. It took several more days to clear the most hazardous wreckage and make the surrounding streets passable. Counting and identifying the victims took even longer.

Photos and vids of the destruction flooded the newsfeeds. A four-ton stone carving of a neo-Mayan deity in Iximche Park lodged in the side of an industrial tower in the Financial District over two miles away. Historic glass windows blew out in the Retro District, and the streets of Old Town were cordoned off. And in Westminster Park, images revealed blackened and broken trees surrounding a depression in the dirt. It had been the park's pond, and no one was quite sure where the water went.

But the top-ranked newsfeed photo that day showed an old man with a long scraggly beard and a certain wild-eyed fanaticism. He stood before the police tape brandishing a sign, as though at war with unknown forces in the smoky haze beyond. Tear tracks jagged across his dust-covered cheeks, so he resembled not so much a man as a cracked stone statue on the verge of crumbling.

The sign was simply constructed and hand-painted. It read:

WEEP NOT FOR THE DEAD
WEEP FOR THE LIVING

Ardy

ARDY WAS AN EXPLORER. He got his first deployment order when he was only twenty-three days old.

His programming interface designation was Autonomous Robotic Dragonfly ARD70-14001. Like all members of the ARD70-series, Ardy was equipped with the most advanced imagers, sensors, and rangefinders that would fit on his tiny ultralight chassis.

Approaching the target site, his sensors picked up sharp protrusions of twisted metal, and his wings reconfigured for a slow hover. His software had been upgraded mere hours earlier, undergoing only a portion of the normal battery of benchmark tests before his Programmers, in need of any and all functioning ARD70s, plucked him from the test environment and sent him on the mission. Usually the software updates they gave him were helpful, but sometimes they broke things and made him feel not all there. Ardy hoped this was not one of those times; he'd run every self-test in his memory array on his way to his assigned zone.

The zone was near what his Programmers had labeled the "epicenter." He descended and flew a grid pattern over the surface of the zone, imaging the objects he could see and taking depth sensor readings when there were dark unknown places he couldn't. Not counting his shadow (which, like a real dragonfly, he ignored), there was just one dark place he could not quite reach into with his sensors.

Ardy paused, checking and rechecking his actuation and sensory circuits, before cautiously approaching the darkness. Data streaming in from his sensors told him he was entering a long, cylindroid passage, composition: steel alloy with interstitial carbon, preliminary categorization: pipe. His Programmers used pipe tunnels in the simulation maze back at the lab, although the lab pipes were smooth and symmetric. This particular pipe was not exactly round or straight anymore, and its inside surface was melted and charred.

He flew slowly into the ragged opening of the pipe but could not help raising a sensor-blinding cloud of soot. He paused, waiting for it to settle, but his wings continued to blow the ash around the confined space. It would not clear. He resolved to power through the black fog in the direction he'd last scanned open space. A meter into the pipe, the warm reassurance of his wireless signal dropped away, and he was Offline. Ardy was alone.

He emerged in a dark void, a crevice formed by packed rubble, ancient concrete, and iron rebar. Here, the confinement problem remained, and Ardy was blind as a robotic bat. He calculated surface stability odds and decided to set down on a high point at the center of the space and shut his wings off.

After several minutes, the dust settled. He found himself perched on the edge of a shard of glass that slanted down into a pool of murky black water. The shard had held in place during his landing, so he stayed put and initiated a litany of scanning and imaging operations from his new vantage point, populating his dispositional matrix with each catalogued substance as he encountered it.

Substance #F4360264: Building material: Masonry, possibly archaic kiln-fired brick
Substance #F4360265: Particulate: Ash, with elevated levels of phosphorous and calcium, possibly human or animal remains [no trace DNA detected]

Substance #F4360266: Building material: Glass, soda-lime silicate, possibly window glass
Substance #F4360267: Ultra-volatile compound: Hazardous Materials Database Classification X13
<---URGENT INTERRUPT!--->

Ardy immediately suspended his normal processing activities and launched a special interrupt program in response to the anomalous substance.

This was Highly Abnormal. Unusual circumstances called for unusual subroutines. His fisheye imaging switched to zoom, and he concentrated his sensors on the location of the reading. As per his critical measurement protocols, he recalibrated his sensors and retested the substance once, then twice. Result: Compound X-13 confirmed.

According to his interrupt routines, this piece of data was so Important that it had to reach the Programmers immediately. He had to get Online as fast as robotically possible. He was programmed to try to acquire a wireless signal three times before giving up. His persistence yielded no response.

Suddenly, his gyroscopes and accelerometers went wild. The fragment of glass on which he perched came loose, sliding down the sloping rubble into the water. He tumbled along with it, plunking into the dirty fluid. The shard pivoted on some unseen fulcrum, trapping the robotic dragonfly in the dark depths.

Seconds ticked by as Ardy's sensors took stock of his situation. He was underwater, an environment which he was designed more to escape than to function in. Said escape was made more difficult by the glass fragment which now pinned his wings against a filament of steel cable. He could still sense his appendages, but they would not move.

He had a critically-important mission to accomplish. He'd found traces of Compound X-13, and his knowledge of it had to be reported or it could be lost forever. Yet, trapped as he was, his mission, and perhaps his existence, could well end in failure. His rising panic triggered a Distress Interrupt. A shock of voltage surged through Ardy.

His wing and leg motors whirred. They twisted. Folded. Unfolded. The Distress Interrupt made him writhe just like a real insect does when caught.

It failed.

A subroutine now tried activating his limbs in various combinations and speeds. Without success.

His subroutine matrix was running out of tricks. Its last was to spike each appendage with a simultaneous over-voltage. His legs and wings fired violently, all at once.

Splash! The action caused his body to push up off the cable while pulling his wings out from under the glass. The glass resumed its slide into the murky depths, allowing him to float to the surface and clamber out gingerly onto a fragment of cinderbrick.

His wings were too wet to fly, and several feet of sheer vertical surfaces lay between him and the entry pipe. He engaged his drying cycle; slowly, his wing stroke frequency increased, first a slow hover, then a fast hover. Dust and ash began to rise, but he already had a full 3D model of the crevice saved in his memory array. He increased his hover velocity. A mist of water droplets radiated outwards from his wings, mixing with a newly-raised cloud of powder to form a black fog. Once the resulting airflow dried his imaging and sensor instruments, he hovered back up to the pipe and through, leaving a miniature tempest in his wake.

Ardy was out, free, and a familiar twitch told him he was back in wireless range. He eagerly went Online, set his transmission strength to maximum, and began transmitting priority notifications that a Highly Abnormal compound had been discovered.

Forensic Inference

AS SOON AS the molecular suppression fields cooled the wreckage, the City's Fire Science Laboratory began constructing a detailed physical model of the buildings and damage before any significant settling of the ruins could occur. Mathematical values representing ignition temperature, heat release rate per unit area, and a dozen other physical variables were mapped to every recognizable surface and object in the disaster zone. Computers queried environmental control logs from the affected buildings, incorporating the status of all windows, doors, ventilation ducts, and condition sensors at the time of the incident. Traffic, surveillance, and other sensor data from the day of the blast were stirred into the computational brew.

Next the computers added medical examiner reports corresponding to each body, along with imaging of each human remain. Body parts that had been violently torn apart were carefully pieced back together, if only in the computational world. The computers matched a severed foot with the dissociated leg of Victim #77, a thirty-two-year-old receptionist and mother of two. They linked a dented wedding ring with the charred remains of a Victim #201, a forty-six-year-old bank manager. In this way, they arrived at an estimated number of casualties (368 souls), although this was only a preliminary guess since some victims had been vaporized or burned to ashes.

The resulting data model was fed into the Arson and Explosion Investigation System, a sophisticated and highly specialized artificial intelligence system with access to room and furniture burn patterns, explosive force vectors, heat flux times, and other data gleaned from a hundred thousand prior fires.

The system regarded every incident scene as its own unique puzzle. Inductive and deductive reasoning were simultaneously engaged and branch logic employed, yielding conclusions which were then back-checked for consistency against the evidentiary data. Bringing to bear the collective heft of this crystalized ocean of data, a best-fit pattern of the initial explosion and timeline for the ensuing fire was computed in three days (albeit centuries of computational time). The ignition source was identified, within a single square meter of precision, to the twenty-eighth floor of the Cleveland Arms building. Traces of a rare synthetic isotope detected by an ARD70-series robot confirmed that the explosion was not accidental.

Computers performed full background checks and financial reports on the building's owners, occupants, relatives, guests, and the victims themselves. These were cross-referenced with title, assessment, and tax records for the building. Area hospital records were checked for any wounds consistent with the explosion and fire by individuals not already known to be victims of the incident. Insurance policies, coverage amounts, and present and previous claims of loss were tabulated and fed into the computer.

Network data feeds emanating from the Cleveland Arms were logged and analyzed. Of particular note was a streaming video feed from the residence of a certain newlywed couple, initiated by one of the victims just moments before the blast.

Facts were correlated with other facts, those correlations associated with other correlations, and those associations linked by a vast network of computers, some artificially intelligent and others not. Bits streamed across the optical fibers that bridged the City.

One day, a completion signal was transmitted, and the bits stopped. A suspect had been identified.

The Witchfinder General, Part III

"[T]he 'Witch-finder General' used to take the suspected witch and place her in the middle of a room, upon a stool or table, cross-legged, or in some other uneasy posture. If she refused to sit in this manner, she was bound with strong cords. [He] then placed persons to watch her for four-and-twenty hours, during which time she was to be kept without meat or drink. It was supposed that one of her imps would come during that interval, and suck her blood. As the imp might come in the shape of a wasp, a moth, a fly, or other insect, a hole was made in the door or window to let it enter. The watchers were ordered to keep a sharp look-out and endeavor to kill any insect that appeared in the room. If any fly escaped, and they could not kill it, the woman was guilty; the fly was her imp, and she was sentenced to be burned, and twenty shillings went into the pockets of [the Witch-finder General]."

Charles Mackay, *Extraordinary Popular Delusions and the Madness of Crowds*, Vol. 2, 1841

3:13 a.m.

IT WAS 3:13 a.m. on a Tuesday morning when the security controls of Rainville's apartment on Cicero Street were overridden from outside and his front door breached.

He awoke not from a nightmare, but to one. Shadowy figures surrounded his bed. "Don't move!" came an amplified voice. His eyes took focus on a dozen men in full assault gear. Two flung him onto his stomach, pinning him while another applied wrist restraints. He was dragged into custody before he ever fully awoke. They read him his rights and frog-marched him out through his living room where uniformed men were already collecting and bagging pieces from his various half-finished electronics and photonics projects.

The invaders hustled him into a police van, and the convoy began its slow move toward the police station.

Rainville looked down at his pajama-clad knees, shaking from the aftermath of high adrenaline. There were two men in front and two in the back of the van behind him. Seated alongside him was an older-looking mustached man with enough epaulets and shiny crap on his uniform to make it clear he was not your typical babysitter of arrestees.

"I already asked to see a lawyer?" he asked the man. He turned his wrists in the restraints but their comfort did not improve.

"Three times," said the man without making eye contact.

"Good." He distrusted his own panicked mind as it skipped across countless fleeting thoughts, but the demand for legal representation had been drilled into him by endless public service broadcasts from civil liberties groups. He felt comforted by the affirmation that he still had some rights that could not be taken away even after being abducted from his bed. "Kind of overkill, isn't all this, Sergeant?"

"Lieutenant."

"What am I being charged with?" Most likely, he'd been made at the Darrow's store flashmob, probably got photographed by a SecAgent without him knowing it. He hoped they hadn't gotten Vyanna too.

The man turned toward Rainville for the first time. "You want the whole list, or just the worst of it?"

"There's a list?" Maybe they had him for evading arrest, too. It couldn't be anything else. If they'd made him on one of his dozen or so prior Shopping Sprees, he'd have been arrested long before now.

The Lieutenant sighed, tapped a featureless grey console. "Mayhem, 168 counts...."

What the hell is "mayhem?" Surely he'd know, if he'd done it 168 times.

"Conspiracy to Detonate a Weapon of Mass Destruction, one count...."

What?!

"Creation and Deployment of a Nuclear Device, one count...."

Haha! Okay, this was obviously some sort of joke.

"Aggravated Terrorism, one count, First Degree Murder, 368 counts...."

The word "murder" stopped any thoughts of a joke. "Whoa! Just a fucking minute! What exactly is it you think I've done?"

The man continued, "And finally, Subversion of a fabricator, sixteen counts."

The last charge stuck in Rainville's mind as the only thing that sounded, through the sensory numbness of stress magnified into a kind of mental static, like something he would do. But what did messing with a fabricator have to do with terrorism? And then, it was clear. This many serious crimes could only be connected to one thing: the bombing three weeks earlier. But what did that have to do with him? It had to be a case of mistaken identity; he hadn't even set foot in the Latin Quarter, let alone Genesee Street, in more months than he could count. He didn't even know anyone there—the neighborhood was mostly computational mathematicians, neosynergist philosophers, and other academic types.

"Serg—I mean, Lieutenant, this has to be some kind of mistake!" He suppressed an urge to explain he'd never even seen the Cleveland Arms building, but his extrapolation that the arrest was related to the blast could be interpreted by someone as a sign of guilt. Best to let his lawyer make these arguments. He supposed those relaxed-looking actors in all those civil liberties vids, calmly declining to comment and cheerfully requesting an attorney, had never been falsely accused of mass murder.

"There's no mistake, son. I'm here to make sure of it. That all the i's get dotted and t's get crossed. No errors, no omissions, no shortcuts." He glanced away again. "Arcadia has been shaken to its core. There's too much at stake...," he began, then thought better of it, left the thought unfinished, and found something important to look at out the passenger side window.

"What? You were going to say something?" Rainville asked desperately.

"Nothing. Let's just keep the conversation to a minimum, okay?"

His heart sank. Adversarial though it was, having another human being to talk to had been strangely comforting during the ride to be incarcerated. He'd not been allowed to take anything with him when he was arrested, and felt naked without his console.

The van arrived at the police station and they were greeted by chaos. A passing camera drone positively identified Rainville's face, and a fog of churring newsfeed camerabots soon blocked out the streetlights with the shifting shadows of their competing flightpaths.

He tugged at his pajama bottoms to ensure he had good coverage as a barrage of media questions rose into an indistinguishable buzz. Further back in the crowd, people screamed at him. "Murderer!" yelled a tall man. "I hate you!" screamed a tearful child. These were people he'd never even met, let alone wronged. The scene was disorienting, and he was almost glad to get inside the station.

But as his relief faded, his indignation grew. He insisted that this must be a mistake all the way from the booking window to the biometrics scanners, but it fell on deaf ears. They stripped off the very last of his personal possessions, his pajamas, and ordered him to don a drab grey jumpsuit. He considered telling these bastards where they could put their jumpsuit, but nudity-induced feelings of vulnerability won out and so he complied.

Rainville always tried to maintain control of his emotions, even when he couldn't control the situation, but his grip on even those was rapidly slipping away. It was as if fear was now taking command, a bad facsimile of himself that kept thinking in circles.

After processing, guards escorted him to a room that was padded from top to bottom, and empty but for a small sink and toilet, both made of an unbreakable metal.

"Where's the furniture? Don't I get a bed?"

"You're being isolated from the other inmates," said one of the guards. "This cell is designed to prevent suicide attempts. Although if it were up to me, I'd let you."

"Suicide? Why the hell would I do that? Because you fucked up and arrested the wrong person?" It showed just how little they knew about him, about any of this.

Wordlessly, the guards closed the door and locked him in.

Why weren't any of these people out looking for the real killer, instead of wasting his and their time on this? And what right did they have, did anyone have, to crank into his apartment and kidnap him? Goddamn it, someone was going to pay for this! He kicked the door, and his foot bounced harmlessly off the padding. Defiantly, he kicked it even harder, and the lack of sound or even pain only increased his sense of impotence.

Barratry

THE DIM ARTIFICIAL glow from the ceiling only amplified the blandness of the grey padded walls and floor of the small detention cell. The lack of sights and sounds made time move at an uncertain rate.

Rainville's thoughts were a tightly-woven braid of loose threads that he revisited again and again, yet none of them seemed to lead anywhere solid.

Had anyone notified his father of his arrest? God forbid the man find out about his arrest from the newsfeeds.

He knew these police types thrived on paranoia and cynicism, but on what planet could someone, anyone, reasonably mistake him for a terrorist?

He had rights, damn it. At least, he thought he did. They couldn't just keep him in here forever. Could they?

His thoughts were mercifully interrupted by the cell door buzzing through its unlocking sequence.

A harried-looking man entered, middle-aged and balding. It was rare to see someone who'd resisted the use of genetic therapy to regrow hair; Rainville's own father had more hair at age fifty than he'd had at thirty. The man's royal-blue necktie was a welcome break from the colorlessness of the cell. He plodded awkwardly over the foam floor padding before smiling at last and extending his hand. "My name is Phelps," he said.

"You're the lawyer I asked for?" asked Rainville, rising uncertainly to meet him.

"Not exactly. You requested a public defender thirty-eight minutes ago. One has been selected, and he's on his way here now."

"Then who are you?"

"I'm your new lawyer," the man said with a sort of confidence that transcended the fact that he was standing in a cramped, padded cell.

Rainville opened his mouth to say something, but he wasn't sure what, and kept his silence.

"My apologies, I seem to be getting ahead of myself," Phelps said. "Your public defender's name is Carstone. If I may be candid, Mr. Carstone isn't a bad guy. He is honest, and he's got a work ethic that would put a pack mule to shame."

Rainville wondered if this was actually a compliment.

"But here's the deal. Mr. Carstone is just one man, and the Public Defender's Office computing resources are ... shall we say, a bit subpar? They've got nothing close to the artificial intelligence systems that will be used to judge your case."

Rainville knew each law firm used its own AIs for case review and strategy. The thought that weak-ass computers with crappy off-the-shelf software were the only thing standing between him and prison produced a cold sweat.

"And what does your firm have to offer, Mr. ... Phipps?"

"Phelps. Petronius & Sydra is the top litigation firm in Arcadia. And if I may be so bold, anywhere else for that matter."

Phelps was the first friendly face he'd seen since the ordeal began. The temptation to grasp at whatever hope the man offered was strong, but he could not let panic make such an important decision for him.

He pushed back against the rising tide of desperation. He took a deep breath. Then another.

Phelps waited patiently.

"What makes you better than your closest competitor?"

Phelps smiled, nodding. "A fine question, Mr. Rainville. I could tell you how old our firm is, what scholarly papers our partners have published, about their being voted top attorneys by this ratings organization or that. But I see from your record that you're a tech-focused kind of guy, so I'll cut to the good stuff. Put simply, we know computers. We're integrated with the judicial systems of this city, and darn near every other. We study artificial intelligences, how they work. We study them as one would living things: how have their neural matrices changed from last week, last month, and last year, to now? Are their legal adaptations trending in a certain doctrinal direction? We fully leverage all this analysis; in short, Mr. Rainville, we prepare!" Phelps had hit his stride. Rainville sensed a change from mercenary to missionary: Phelps was no longer reciting rote marketing points; he firmly believed what he was saying.

Rainville stepped quickly through the logic of what Mr. Phelps said, and nodded in approval. He'd heard of Petronius & Sydra, and knew it to be a well-established firm.

"We're proactive, Mr. Rainville. It's how we knew the minute you requested a lawyer. In fact, we've already put together a preliminary strategy for your defense. The other firms are old school. They still get their data from the newsfeeds. We—"

"Okay! Okay, I get it. You guys have skills, and tech. But I don't have a lot of money—"

"The firm's board of directors already agreed to take your case pro bono. They're even going to cover the judicial fees."

Rainville wondered what was in it for them. "Is that because it's a high-profile case? One that will earn you publicity?"

"Partly. If I may be candid, it's standard procedure to do a full financial workup on our pro bono clients, including family members. Your family tree is rather ..." Phelps searched for a tactful word.

"Scrawny?" Rainville offered. The veneer of Phelps' politeness and professionalism made it difficult to read the man, and he hoped that a laugh might put a crack in it. Alas, it did not.

Phelps nodded apologetically. "Yes, well, it is a bit sparse, perhaps, Mr. Rainville. Through no fault of your own, of course." He must have known Rainville had few relatives, and that his father didn't make enough in a year to cover even the electrical power that would be expended by the firm's computers on such a complex case.

"Well, you certainly seem to be an upgrade from the Public Defender. I guess for now that's all I need to know. So what's the plan for getting me the hell out of here? These clowns arrested the wrong guy. Maybe that means they'll stop looking for the right one. Could you talk to them?"

Phelps smiled broadly. "Let's not get ahead of ourselves, Mr. Rainville. First, you'll need to sign a letter of engagement and fill out some judicial forms stating that you understand what it means to change lawyers." He stepped carefully back across the padded floor to the door. "If you'll follow me?" he asked, addressing the guard outside more than Rainville.

The guard nodded and escorted them to a small visiting room with a table.

Rainville hurried through the paperwork, wanting to get these guys on the case as quickly as possible. It was what he imagined was pretty standard stuff, like about the firm's duties in representing him, and authorizing them to file a motion to change his representation before the court.

"Please, promise me you'll get me out of here."

"I wouldn't be here if I didn't think we could." Phelps checked the signatures. "You've made a wise decision," he said.

"Should we talk about what happened?"

"A criminal trial isn't about what actually happened, Mr. Rainville," Phelps said as he gathered up the papers. "It's about what can be proven, and what can't. Making these determinations is our first priority. Now if you'll excuse me, I must go contact the firm's directors and get the wheels turning."

His new lawyer hadn't promised anything, exactly. Yet, Rainville felt himself nodding; wheels needed to be turning, and pronto.

The First Legal AIs

(excerpted from the unpublished manuscript of
The Rise of Computerized Courts *by F. H. Phelps and J. Q. L. Foxwright)*

The earliest artificially-intelligent judicial computers used simple neural networks trained with an extensive body of humankind's most pivotal legal decisions. These AIs were taught to emulate the best qualities of human jurors, which they could soon do with high reliability.

A tireless computer with infinite attention span could absorb all the facts with perfect recall, analyze them in an unbiased manner, and eliminate injustices caused by prosecutorial error, attorney incompetence, and bored or overwhelmed judges. Statistical analysis of case results indicated the truth of this.

Critics questioned whether the margin of error was simply moved somewhere less detectable, rather than reduced or eliminated. Understandably, many were skeptical of the idea of replacing a human judge and jury with a computer. After all, computers were not infallible.

What the early critics failed to see was not the fallibility of the proposed technology, but rather, the fallibility of their fellow humans in the original system. Certainly the computer made mistakes, initially producing a single-digit percentage of false convictions and false acquittals. This alone would have mothballed the project, except the researchers discovered a far more surprising statistic: human juries were wrong nearly three times more often. Even worse, the certainty human jurors had in their decision bore no correlation whatsoever to the accuracy of their verdict. Human judges performed even worse at fact-finding. By the mid-nineteenth century, judicial error was so rampant that courthouses had to be built of non-flammable materials like brick or stone, lest they be regularly burned to the ground by aggrieved litigants.

Ultimately, the most human aspects of the human jury were its undoing. For example, despite a mountain of scientific research showing the confidence of an eyewitness has no relation to the witness' accuracy, human jurors without exception believe an eyewitness who seems sure of himself. Similarly, humans are highly susceptible to arguments based on emotion instead of fact. Logical fallacies such as vivid imagery of pain and suffering, of vicious intent, and guilty conscience were the stock and trade of lawyers arguing cases before uncomputerized juries. While a juror might be made aware of a fact, he or she might never believe it deep down; human nature and its psychological biases often trumped facts and reason.

In cases where it wasn't clear whether a death was an accident or murder, human jurors often skipped over the question of whether a crime had been committed. The mere presence of a defendant in a prison uniform at the start of a trial swayed human juries toward the assumption of illegality. And when a human jury misattributed an accidental house fire or infant drowning as a crime, the most likely person to blame was the one sitting at the defendant's table. In contrast, the computer will objectively ask whether a building fire was the result of arson before its algorithms even look at the defendant's personal file. Despite their flaws, the earliest AI juries soon proved to be the lesser of two evils.

In the century since, AIs have been optimized to improve their accuracy by several orders of magnitude. Today, it's easy to see the benefits of judicial computerization, which has brought with it a new age of fairness and integrity.

Walls

SEVERAL WEEKS HAD PASSED SINCE PHELPS' first visit. Despite the lawyer's optimistic tone in their subsequent meetings, the Detention conditions were taking their toll on Rainville. The padded cells, lack of sunlight, monotonous food, and unfriendly guards steeped the hours of his day in desolation. On top of this, he'd begun to grapple with the very real possibility of losing any future he had with Vyanna. He tried to focus on his case to keep his mind off it but was not always successful.

Phelps seemed to understand this and did his best to cheer Rainville up during their conferences. But today, as they sat across the table from each other in featureless polymer chairs, Phelps was short on optimism. The defense team, as he explained it, had "hit a few bumps in the road."

"We're still conducting evidentiary review. The physical evidence, in particular, has proven to be quite extensive, and it is keeping our AIs busy. In the meantime, we have some potential areas for follow-up."

"You mentioned bumps."

"The largest has been that our latest motion for a continuance was denied."

"You said the motion was just a formality. How could they deny it? Why would they?"

"The ruling was not specific. At this stage in the trial, motions for continuance are discretionary, and the Court can deny the extension if it wishes. Now, that being said, this is a very complex case. Even for a firm like Petronius & Sydra, and we are one of the largest, the staffing levels on this one are unprecedented. Late yesterday evening we filed what is called a 'motion for reconsideration and clarification' of the Court's ruling. That may clear things up a bit, and hopefully even grant us an extension of time."

"What if it doesn't?"

He smiled. "Don't worry. The best litigators in Arcadia are hard at work on this one, even as we speak."

"Is there anything I can do to help?" He wished he knew more about criminal law, or at least had his console so he could do something, anything, to aid his defense. Access to the detention facility library was denied to prisoners like him with "Elevated Risk" status.

"I'll let you know if there is, Mr. Rainville. That reminds me: I was visited last week by a young lady of your acquaintance, one Ms. Vyanna."

His heart, the one he'd worked so hard to tune out and ignore, awoke with pounding palpitations at the sound of her name. Instantly, he saw her smile in his mind's eye.

"She wanted to know how your case was going. Of course, we couldn't reveal to her any data that was material to the case. But this young lady, she was undeterred. In fact, she has visited the office twice since. She seems quite concerned for your well-being, Mr. Rainville."

"I ..." Vyanna seemed somehow closer to him than she'd been since his arrest, and yet in some desperate way, farther away. Phelps had seen her. Talked to her! Yet he himself could do neither. "Does she ... believe any of this stuff about me?"

"No, Mr. Rainville. She's expressed the utmost faith in your innocence. Whether you knew it or not, this Vyanna seems to care a great deal for you."

She hadn't forgotten him, hadn't abandoned him. Rainville's brain could not decide if this was wonderful or tragic. At length, he merely sighed.

Phelps continued. "Would it be all right if I share some high-level details about your case with her? Nothing too specific, as the firm's management wouldn't allow it, but at least an overview. And perhaps I could tell her how you are doing?"

"Thanks for the offer. Yes, please share with her anything you can." He hesitated. "But please don't tell her how I am doing."

"No?"

There was no need to upset her. "Instead, please say I am doing well."

"Of course." The edge of Phelps' voice was uneven. He cleared his throat and straightened his tie. "Of course, Mr. Rainville. I'll do it next time I see her. You have my word on that."

Association

"SUPERINTENDENT WHISTON CONCLUDED the press conference by reminding Arcadians to stay focused and alert during this difficult time. The Superintendent noted that the number of accidents involving distracted citizens is up sharply this week. Just this morning, a memorial service was held for C. I. E. Eckert, a fifty-three-year-old network administrator at the Jyanix Institute who was killed while crossing Cicero Street just hours after the blast. According to sensor data, Eckert stepped out in front—"

The vid was interrupted by a tone from the office door.

"Come on in," said Phelps. He leaned back from the display and rubbed his eyes. In the seven weeks since his firm took the case, he couldn't recall a single full night of sleep.

The door retracted in a whisper, and one of the senior associates walked in. "Ahh, Mr. Tremblay. Any news for me? Brighten my day with some reasons for hope."

The young man spoke quickly. "I'm afraid I have none, Mr. Phelps. It's just as we feared. The latest computer simulations show a 99.6% probability of an unfavorable verdict. The allowed physical evidence all seems to correlate. Over 99% chance that the toaster belonging to Victims #1 and #2, identified as Tessa and Dashwood, will be found to be the cause of the blast. Over 99% likelihood that the toaster was configured with the bomb as made by Ms. Essie's fabricator. A 98% chance that Ms. Essie is as technologically ignorant as she claims. And a greater than 96% chance that Mr. Rainville's actions will be found to be the proximate cause. Those are the numbers for the murder charges. The percentages are lower on the terrorism-related charges, since the Prosecutorial Administration will have difficulty establishing Mr. Rainville's intent, motivations, state of mind, and what have you. But to be frank, sir, I'm not seeing a lot of avenues for hope at this point."

Phelps seemed to study a spot on the floor for a long moment. "Perhaps we could create some," he said at last.

"Are you suggesting there is something more that we could be doing?" said Tremblay. His tone was more curious than defensive, eager for ideas.

"There may be one: Foxwright."

"I've heard of him."

"He was a partner here at Petronius when I was a young associate," said Phelps.

"We studied the Jarndyce case in law school," said Tremblay. "It resulted in a reversal of a decade of equitable interests doctrine, which is nearly unprecedented these days. I believe he worked on the litigation team."

"He *was* the litigation team." Phelps chuckled. "Our firm gained a lot of prestige with that case, but—and don't repeat this outside the walls of this office, Mr. Tremblay—Mr. Foxwright won Jarndyce single-handedly." Phelps' eyes brightened. "The verdict simulations were looking grim. He'd taken to sleeping here at the office to get in more hours. And then ... well, the man vanished. He stopped coming into work, just dropped off the radar entirely. He didn't come back that week, nor the next."

"Old Mr. Sydra, God rest his soul, was livid. He told the Board of Directors that, so help him, 'that Foxwright character' was a 'deserter,' was 'done,' would be fired whenever 'he deigned to make an appearance at his former place of work.'" Phelps chuckled again. "A few weeks passed, and then Foxwright did indeed return. He called an emergency meeting of the litigation team, who was at their wits end by this point, along with Mr. Sydra, and presented a strategy to win the case. He approached it from an angle that hadn't even occurred to the rest of the team, and didn't even make complete sense to some of us. Myself included, if I might be candid with you, Mr. Tremblay. But the computers liked it. They acquitted the defendant of probate fraud, and formally modified their method of deciding such cases. 'Our Mr. Foxwright taught them something new that day,' Mr. Sydra always liked to say."

Tremblay quirked an eyebrow. "Do you know Mr. Foxwright personally?"

"Oh yes. I was just a first-year associate, but his office was next to mine. He lives only a few blocks from here, although you'd never know it. He's a bit of a recluse as far as the legal community is concerned. I'll reach out to him." Phelps smiled. "After all, he owes me a favor."

Tremblay nodded, his eyes gleaming with admiration.

The Referral

"YOU'VE BEEN at it awhile. Perhaps you should take a break?" said the female voice.

Foxwright had indeed been writing since dawn. As he typed, Trixy continuously analyzed his facial movements, vital signs, posture, and other physiological metrics to assess his work performance. When his features implied confusion, she offered her help interface. When they indicated fatigue, she suggested a break. Trixy could often predict when he was about to make a mistake and initiate preemptive action. She could even grab his attention when he seemed distracted by applying some light electric shocks, but she was merciless with them so he'd disabled the feature despite her protests.

She may have been a nag, but she was right: a break was clearly in order. He leaned back into a stretch. Just then a comm signal activated, destroying any chance of relaxation. "Call for you, sir."

Foxwright hated incoming calls with a passion. It was always some needy person, wanting some damned thing or another from him. If he'd wanted to talk to some person, he'd have called them, and they'd already be talking.

"Call for you, sir," Trixy repeated.

He preemptively regretted answering, sighed, and then answered.

The face of Phelps, his former colleague from Petronius & Sydra, appeared on the screen. "Mr. Foxwright! How is extra-office life? Might I inquire whether you're even out of bed yet?"

"I haven't gone to bed yet, Phelps. I haven't even stopped drinking from last night!" He knew it was best to play along to speed the jibes to their logical conclusion.

"I'm glad. I've got a referral for you." When Phelps changed gears from pleasure to business, it was a hard shift.

"I don't want it."

"You will."

"What sort of person wants more work for himself?"

"The kind that owes me a favor."

"For helping me with the Tice case? I believe I promised you a bottle of scotch, not a favor. And anyway, you've already got me busy writing about legal history."

"This is a chance to make legal history."

"Let me guess: is some innocent damsel in distress?" Foxwright asked. Phelps had three ex-wives, all of whom were former clients.

"Yes. But this particular damsel is a male, nineteen years of age, accused of crimes against humanity."

"You need a new dictionary."

"Okay, not crimes against humanity. He stands accused of terrorism and mass murder. You heard about the Cleveland Arms?"

"Big building that blew up and killed 368 people several weeks back? Rings a faint bell, being that I don't live under a damned rock. It sounds like your damsel is in need of some competent legal assistance."

"Competence won't save him," Phelps said with a sigh. "Hell, I doubt even you can. But we're in need of a miracle, and you're the luckiest guy I know." Phelps' "luck" was a backhanded reference to Foxwright's record for turning around more no-win cases than any consultant-barrister in Arcadia.

Foxwright leaned back in his chair. "So what've you got to work with?"

"Not a whole lot. We've spoken with the defendant extensively, and completed a preliminary review of the evidence. Kinsey says the Directors are starting to doubt their decision to take on this case. There's a mountain of evidence, all of it incriminating, and a serious shortage of any mitigating facts. Let's see...." Foxwright heard the soft sound of keystrokes across the comlink as Phelps accessed his notes. "They've got him working on Grandma's fabricator the day before the incident." The media had taken to calling Essie "Grandma Essie," as with Old Mother Leary whose cow, in a fit of bovine injustice, had been falsely accused of starting the Great Chicago Fire of 1871. "Grandma Essie" quickly became an epithet for someone who is so technologically inept as to be dangerous. As with Mrs. O'Leary's heifer, the truth of her innocence would do nothing to diminish this.

"Before that, the unit caused no recorded problems for the preceding thirty-six years. And," Phelps continued to type away, and his voice dropped as if delivering bad news, "the kid's apartment was full of contraband items that appear to have been made on the grandma's fabricator."

"Contraband?"

"The kind of stuff you could only make on a fabricator with no safety protocols."

"Bomb-making stuff?"

"Nothing so dangerous. Tools of teenage mischief, mostly."

"A boy after my own heart. Have you got anything helpful in the police or arson reports for the...are you calling it an accident?"

"We're calling it an 'incident.' No, nothing exculpatory."

"Any alternate suspects we can point to?"

"None."

"Sounds like a fun one. How long have we got left?"

"Did you say 'we'?"

"You know who's too old for this shit? Me." Foxwright sighed and shook his head. "Fine, I'll take a look. But no promises. And if you ask me for any more favors, by God, I'll sue you for harassment."

Phelps nodded.

"Now answer my damn question," said Foxwright.

Phelps let out a longer sigh.

"We asked for the normal continuances to buy more time; they were granted. This allowed us to finish our first pass at the evidence and start digging into details. Unfortunately, all that's done is rule out some of our most promising defense theories. Our subsequent motions for continuance, in light of the sheer magnitude of the evidence of the case, were denied."

"Denied? Why?"

"The ruling cited the importance of bringing peace and well-being to a city that has suffered a grievous wound. Honestly, it's a little unusual. But a case like this has never come up before, so I suppose there is no 'usual.' Anyhow, the result is a deadline that is measured in weeks and not months."

"So, in summary, we've got virtually nothing to go on, and no time to fix that. Is this an accurate assessment?"

"Unfortunately, yes. But there's more to it than that. There has to be. Look, I know that all our clients are innocent, but let me say this: the Rainville kid is the real deal. I've never been more sure of anything in my life. He just doesn't have it in him." Phelps paused, at a rare loss for words; he was not good at this sort of thing. "Seriously, Foxwright, you see things others don't. You're the best guy I know for this kind of stuff. You might be the only hope this kid has."

"Thank you, Phelps. Although I am sorry to hear he is innocent."

"What?" Phelps looked flustered. "Why?"

"Because," said Foxwright, "it means we've still got a mass murderer on the loose, maybe already planning his next bombing. But enough cheerful banter—send me the data paths and permissions, and I'll take a look at the evidentiary database and see what we've got."

"Will do. Stop in tomorrow and I'll introduce you to the team. Until then."

Pleasantries aside, direct compliments from Phelps were rare indeed. And the potential to catch the real terrorist and prevent subsequent attacks added a dimension of significance to the case that no hourly rate could buy.

"Trixy! Wake up."

"Yes, sir?"

"Transition into tactical mode. We're on a case."

A Meeting with Management

FOXWRIGHT RUBBED HIS EYES. Arcadia had been crawling with cleanerbots since the blast, but they'd done little to improve the air quality. Was he allergic to the smoke? The dust? Or was it the ash? For that matter, the sudden dome depressurization hadn't exactly helped his ears. Damn urban living! We'd all be much safer residing out in the woods, where nothing ever explodes.

His meeting at Petronius & Sydra was at 10:00 a.m., but even without the haze in the air, it was hard to know what time of day it was. Arcadia's dome tended to mute daylight, and the narrow canyons formed by the Financial District's multi-hundred-story buildings only made things worse. The lavender of the rosemallow flowers in Spooner Plaza was a less exact temporal metric. They began their morning bloom a vibrant white, turned pink by early afternoon, and were a deep purple-maroon by the time they dropped from the bushes at dusk. Their aroma likewise changed through the course of the day, moving from a fresh sweetness in the morning to a buttery scent by evening. Today, they were lost in the burnt odor. He broke down and checked his console: 9:46 a.m., still fourteen minutes to spare.

At the heart of Spooner Plaza was the Metreon, one of the City's tallest domescrapers. Clad in blue glass, the building's reciprocating curves were strangely undetectable from the inside. The Petronius main lobby was in the penthouse on the 303rd floor, just meters beneath the highest part of the dome.

The lobby put forth the usual law-office aesthetic paradox: simulated mahogany wainscoting, crystal chandelier, and shelves of paperbound legal books, a centuries-old interior in a building only a few years old. At the far end, a panoramic window overlooked Arcadia, granting a uniquely close view of the City's ceiling.

The haziness brought the entire vista into soft focus. One section of the dome remained blackened from the explosion, and the Latin Quarter lay below in perpetual darkness. The dome ordinarily diffused the light from above, but now jagged lines blossomed across its surface. From ground level, the sky felt closer: the City felt smaller.

Repairbots skittered to and fro on the curving plane like waterbugs skimming atop a pond, polishing, cleaning, and reflowing the polymers. The surreality of the scene was matched only by the devastation below. The blast had lain waste to the Latin Quarter, wreaking havoc on its residential units and shutting down its three agristations, 150-story hydroponic farming towers which normally grew enough food to feed a significant portion of the City. He'd not seen a fresh tomato in weeks.

Foxwright forewent the comfort of the lobby's plush chairs and examined the bookcase. Unlike the rest of the archaized decor, these books were the genuine article, full of creased spines, faded leather bindings, and torn covers. Judging by their perfectly symmetric arrangement, he imagined most of the firm's visitors kept a reverential distance from the works.

Never content to be part of the majority, he helped himself to a first edition of Charles Mackay's *Extraordinary Popular Delusions and the Madness of Crowds*, leaving a conspicuously dark gap in the teeth of the shelves' otherwise-perfect smile. Printed in 1841, the work was one of the many digitized texts he'd consulted during the course of his writing project, but he relished holding a real, physical copy in his hand. He admired its sheep-hide binding and marbled page-edges. The book had no animations or moving parts; it was refreshingly static. Its knowledge waited patiently within and did not ambush the would-be reader with gimmickry.

"Foxwright!" came Phelps' voice behind him, disrupting his reverie. "Always a pleasure."

Foxwright turned and extended his hand. "Yes. Well, sometimes, at any rate. Do you philistines ever open any of these books? Or is this museum of rarities just another way to pretty up your ivory tower?"

Phelps smiled tentatively then shook his head; sometimes Foxwright's irreverence still surprised him even after all these years.

"Beautiful, aren't they? A gift from Mr. Sydra's widow, the whole collection." He gestured deeper into the complex of offices. "If you're ready, let's proceed into the war room."

Foxwright was ushered into the firm's main conference room, though it was barely recognizable. Half-consumed meals and days-old stimulant drinks formed chaotic borders around case data graphically projected on nearly every remaining square inch of table and wall space. The shades were drawn, blocking out the view of the City in favor of more space for data. Even the programmable carpet was in full use, depicting a colorful chronological map of case events, interrupted only by the occasional chair-leg or associate-shoe. He smiled, recalling his own days as wet-behind-the-ears associate on the front lines of high-profile cases such as this one; he missed the camaraderie, but not the long hours nor the short pay. It said something that the firm would tie up its largest conference room, the one meant for impressing new clients, for the Rainville case.

An older man sat the head of the conference table, casually dressed the way only a managing partner could get away with. His eyes narrowed. "And you are?"

"He's one of us," Phelps replied.

"No need to be insulting, Phelps," countered Foxwright.

The partner looked puzzled at the slight. Then realization dawned on his face: "Ahh, you must be Mr. Foxwright! Your reputation here certainly precedes you. Phelps mentioned he'd gotten you on board. I can't tell you how pleased we are." His eyes moved to the book still clutched in Foxwright's fist. "And what have we here?"

"Just a bit of research for a legal history work I'm co-authoring with Phelps. He was nice enough to let me borrow it."

The man's gaze turned to Phelps, whose eyes grew wider without letting his smile falter. He managed a shallow nod.

"Good, good. I'm Kinsey, the managing partner of the Arcadia office. Time's short, so I'll cut to the chase. We've asked you here because, to be candid, this case just isn't coming together as we feel it should."

Foxwright nodded at the men and women poring over diagrams and reports.

Kinsey followed his eyes. "The body of evidence is staggering, that's for certain. But it's more than that, Mr. Foxwright: missing bits of records, things that are inconsistent between data logs. Small things, probably inconsequential, but they require analysis, and our last round of requests for extensions of time have been denied."

"A less tactful man than myself might say you've waited until the case was already a lost cause before seeking my help," said Foxwright.

Kinsey's face hardened. "As a rule, we prefer not to use outside consultants. The decision to bring on a specialist of your stature was not one the Directors made lightly, I can tell you."

Nor quickly, Foxwright thought. He'd dealt with legal administrators, and knew this meant "we're stingy, we think your rates are too high, and we only called you as a last resort." His relationship with such people was generally based on mutual respect: they respected him, and he respected that. Kinsey had the resources of the entire firm, its army of associates, and a host of high-dollar legal reasoning AIs. Yet this was not a case that would be won with automated algorithms; if it were, Foxwright would not be standing here.

"We've only got ten days left to present evidence. It's honestly unlikely we'll come up with anything to keep Mr. Rainville entirely out of prison in the time we have left. Still, it's not impossible. The full resources of the firm are at your disposal. Channel your requests through me, and I'll make sure they're handled promptly. We recognize that you're coming into this case already behind the eight ball. We only ask that you do your best with what you've got to work with."

"I always do," said Foxwright. "I'll be in touch."

Review

EVEN SIFTING through the case file inventory lists required a search engine. The bulk of the materials were evidentiary reports covering physical and chemical modeling data. Foxwright supposed that un-blowing up the city using mathematics was not a simple problem (look how long it had taken humanity to finally reverse the Big Bang!) This was followed by tens of thousands of pages of DNA sample reports. He flipped to one at random. It was the DNA analysis results of remains sample #65535, which was a fragment of human hand belonging to victim #209, a middle-aged woman whose name was not yet identified. She didn't deserve this. No one did.

He dove into the case with abandon. Sleeping and eating fell by the wayside as he analyzed the litany of charges against the defendant, Rainville. One man could not hope to double-check every piece of evidence in a case of this magnitude. That was where experience came in: knowing where to look, what balls got dropped most often, and what specific pieces to follow up on.

Unlike many other defense attorneys, Foxwright began his inquiries by building a case *against* his client. He made a list of the chief potential weaknesses in such a case. Then he switched roles and took the opposing side. The two approaches met somewhere in the middle, and each revealed different facets of the case, different pieces the AI jurors would latch onto.

He reviewed the arguments for acquittal that the firm had preliminarily filed. It was boilerplate stuff: the evidence was circumstantial, and there was no intent. But they lacked a plausible theory as to who had done this, if not Rainville.

Time was short, so he drew up a checklist of pivotal areas of research, and then spent several days working with Trixy to query the database, together chasing down his various lines of inquiry.

The boy's biography revealed that he'd finished school, but only barely. His grades were erratic, low in subjects like history and languages and math, but off the charts in anything relating to technology. If anyone had the aptitude to perform surgery on a fabricator, it was this kid.

Rainville's father had worked the last decade maintaining lawn and garden care robots for Buxton Properties, a corporation which owned several dozen private parks around the City. His mother had been a teacher until she died three years earlier from pyrrhoneuritis, a rare degenerative disorder that compromised synaptic pathways. The disease began with chronic pain which increased in intensity as the condition took its toll. Toward the end, she'd no doubt suffered severe bouts of dementia. He'd been just fifteen when she perished. Could such a blow have sent him off the rails?

"Trixy, trace all of his known locations preceding the incident."

"Defendant Rainville is nineteen years old. Would you like all of the preceding nineteen years?"

"Of course not. Give me eight weeks. No! Twelve."

A few moments later, the report was on his screen.

This kid certainly lived a colorful life, but there was no suggestion of anything beyond minor mischief. A nagging question began to form in his mind.

He looked into the Prosecutorial Administration's other suspects and found the results were surprisingly scant. The chance that Grandma Essie was secretly a terrorist mastermind willing to sacrifice her granddaughter for some unknown cause was .0016%. After reading all that was available on Essie, including statements from neighbors who'd known her for decades, he tended to agree.

He searched the dataset for potential reasons for murderous intent. Subpoenaed records of Rainville's communications in both public forums and private media ranged from technology to restaurants to history, but seemed apolitical, unrelated to bomb construction. Boring stuff. Still, there were other, less traceable ways the kid could have sought out bomb-making information.

There was a lengthy report on Victims #1 and #2. Their names were Tessa and Dashwood, and as it turned out, they had no known enemies. Yet, the bomber had no way of knowing Essie would gift the next thing she fabricated, instead of simply using it herself.

Was there a reason to murder Essie?

He had Trixy review everything she could find on Essie. She lived a simple life, had been a widow for many years. No significant business dealings. No involvement in politics. No significant assets. And no clear motive for her death.

"Trixy, where is Essie located at present?"

"Ms. Essie suffered a mental breakdown after the blast. She is currently admitted to the Iverson Mental Wellness Center for monitoring and treatment."

"Arrange for me to meet with her as soon as is practical."

"Meet you? Hasn't she already been through enough?"

"Can it, Trixy."

"Confirmed. Next visiting hours begin tomorrow at noon."

What if Essie's fabricator had been chosen at random? There were a handful of fringe political groups that claimed responsibility for the attack, but they seemed not to know much about how it had been perpetrated.

Phelps was right. There was simply not much to go on.

Trixy compiled reports for him summarizing the evidence on record. A series of graphics illustrated the most damning and the most exculpating factors of the case. On their face, the result did not bode well for Mr. Rainville: he appeared to be either very guilty, or very unlucky. Yet, there was something more to it. The asymmetry of the evidence was itself abnormal. Typically, even the guiltiest of criminals had some facts, however inconsequential, on their side. Here, there was not even a bad alibi.

He couldn't explain exactly why, but decades of reviewing criminal cases told him something just wasn't right. It was all too neat and clean. He'd run into problem cases before, but this was different. It was something new, something to do with the shape and consistency of the body of facts. Yes, "shape" and "consistency" felt like the right terms, but they would have woefully little persuasive value to anyone, least of all a computerized juror.

If Phelps was right, and Rainville really wasn't behind the attack, then who was? And how the hell was it done? And perhaps most importantly, why? The impossible challenge of those questions burned in his mind late into the night.

Visitation

At the Iverson Mental Wellness Center the next day, the nurse led Foxwright through the warren of passages that made up the psychiatric ward. The main hallways were decorated with color-shifting paint that cycled through more pastel colors than he'd have believed existed, but somehow the place still felt soaked in sadness and desperation.

Essie's room was narrow with high ceilings, and a realistic-looking window filled the room with artificial sunlight. The curtains billowed gently, and Foxwright swore he could smell grass clippings and flowers in the synthetic breeze.

The old woman rocked in her chair, watching intently out the window as if expecting something to happen. She took a drink from a glass of water on a nearby table without breaking her gaze. He followed her eyes into—or was it out over?—the computer-generated landscape. If you squinted just right, listened to the piped-in sounds of wind in the trees and singing birds, the scene was easy to get lost in.

"We have her under sedation," whispered the nurse. "She's very fragile right now, as I'm sure you understand. She's not had an easy time accepting what's happened. Please try to be delicate."

Delicate was not his strong suit, and time was limited, but he would certainly try.

"It's almost nap time for her, so you'll need to be brief," said the nurse. She touched the old woman's shoulder. "Miss Essie? You have a visitor."

She looked up, and an uncertain smile rose on her lips. "Oh, heavens, I wasn't expecting any guests!" She produced a small mirror and quickly touched up her lipstick. "Are you one of the police officers? I'm glad you could come out. The countryside here is so lovely."

"No, ma'am, I am an attorney. Name's Foxwright. I'm helping with Mr. Rainville's defense."

At the mention of the name, she looked puzzled for an instant, then brightened. "That's a relief! I'd heard he was in some trouble. Rainville is such a nice young man. I hope you'll help him straighten things out."

"I'll certainly do my best. So how long have you lived next door to him?"

He saw the strain in her face, like she was trying to access a memory from early childhood. "He moved in, it must have been about two years now."

"And he's been...helping you with your fabricator?"

"Oh, yes! Until I came here." She gestured to the window. "It's a lovely place for a holiday, don't you think?"

"It surely is, ma'am."

"Rainville is a whiz at those technical things, you know. That boy has a bright future ahead of him," she clucked, "if he would only apply himself."

"How long has he been helping you?"

"Oh, let's see now, for several months I guess. I am afraid I'm not a very quick study," she laughed. "But Rainville is so patient. My husband Lambert was the same way. Do you know we were married for fifty-four years, and he never once raised his voice to me, even when I probably had it coming? He was a university professor, and ever so patient. Are you married, Mr. Foxwright?"

"No ma'am, I'm not."

"I don't believe it! A handsome young man like you?"

"My work keeps me pretty busy. Let me ask you, is it true that Rainville disabled the safety protocols on your fabricator?"

There was a flash of pain before her smile returned, there, but less certain than before. "Why, I don't know! He did some work on it last year to make it faster. I told him, don't waste your time; I hardly ever use the thing! But he was determined. He said he was sure he could make it work better."

"So you let him?"

She took a sip of water from the glass, leaving a smudge of lipstick. "You know how it is with the kids these days. It's important for them to have something constructive to occupy their time. It keeps them off the streets and out of trouble. So I let Rainville use it whenever he asks. He's such a polite young man; he always asks so very nicely." She beamed.

He watched the lipstick smudge fade away as the self-cleaning glass did its work. A second later, there was no trace the glass had ever been touched by human hands, let alone lips.

"The police found several items in Mr. Rainville's residence that seem to have been made on your fabricator." He tapped his console and brought up the certified 3D models he'd received from the Central Precinct Evidence Repository. Various emitters, transceivers, and controllers rotated across the screen, one by one. "Do you recognize any of these?"

She smiled. "I know that one," she said, tapping her finger on one of the images. "It's a self-stirring coffee cup that keeps your java warm. Cute, huh? He's clever, that boy is!"

He clicked past some more photos of a photonic transceiver, a Gauss gun, and various remote controllers, but she showed no recognition. "The rest of those things, I don't know. I think I've seen some of them before, but ... well, I'm afraid growing old isn't much fun, Mr. Foxwright. The memory is one of the first things to go."

"It seems like Rainville made a lot of different kinds of devices. Did he ever fabricate anything dangerous?"

"Oh, no, of course not!" She rearranged her hands, which had been folded in her lap, wringing them in a slow pattern. "He might have a mischievous side, but he wouldn't hurt a fly."

"Did anyone else have access to your fabricator during the last year, aside from you and Mr. Rainville? A building superintendent, maybe? Or a housekeeper?"

"No one," she said, shaking her head. "I'm a very private person, and I keep my own house. Always have, you know. My mother taught me that, how did it go now, ah, yes! 'A woman's conscience can only be as clean as her home.'" She chuckled. "Lambert, my husband, always said our apartment was the neatest place in all of Arcadia." She gave a satisfied nod and renewed her rocking with vigor.

"You seem like a very nice lady, but it is my professional responsibility to ask: might you have any enemies? Any people who might want to hurt you, for one reason or another?"

Her smile faded as her eyes widened. "No! Why would they?"

"What about your granddaughter, Tessa?"

"What sort of silly question is that?" she asked in a flat tone. "Tessa is a sweet girl." Her right hand was pale around the left, which itself was a deepening purple.

"Is there anyone who might have wanted her dead?"

He regretted his word choice before he'd even finished saying it. The last vestige of Essie's smile faltered, and her mouth curled into a rictus of pain. A dull noise started in her throat and grew until she was wailing. The sound was haunting, deafening. Like he'd just broken the news to her for the first time, and artlessly at that.

"Sir, I told you to be delicate," the nurse said in clipped tones, although she looked like he wanted to slug him. He wouldn't have stopped her. "Your access to this patient is revoked." With that, she hurried Foxwright from the room as an orderly rushed past them clutching a syringe.

The Bisha'a

"Even older perhaps than the oath is trial by ordeal ... The commonest form is trial by fire or the *bisha'a* ... Only professional *mubeshas* are capable of carrying out the trial. The *mubesha* ... sits on the ground in front of a fire and places the spoon in the heart of the embers. The accused sits beside him, while the other parties and the witnesses sit round and watch. The heating of the spoon takes an interminable time, and the *mubesha* keeps taking it out of the fire red hot, looking at it, turning it over and putting it back, in front of the eyes of his victim. During this interval the *mubesha* talks continuously, expounding to the accused the certainty of the revelation of his guilt and the pain of burning. Meanwhile, he watches his face. At last the spoon is ready, the accused is required to put out his tongue, and the hot spoon is laid quickly upon it. An interval of some minutes is allowed, and then the accused is asked to put out his tongue once more. If he be guilty, his tongue will be blistered. If the tongue bears no mark, his innocence is established....

The *mubeshas* will not, of course, consent to reveal the secrets of their hereditary art, but...I have always imagined that the *mubesha* takes the trouble to enquire into the case before it is referred to him, and to obtain a shrewd idea of the identity of the criminal. Then, during the intentionally prolonged process of heating the spoon, he talks continuously at the accused and watches his face closely. I am inclined to suspect that he then makes up his mind whether the accused in guilty or not, and presses the spoon on his tongue or touches it lightly according to the result which he wishes to produce.

In practice, more than half the accused persons who set out to lick the spoon lose their nerve while the spoon is in the fire, and voluntarily confess to their guilt without blistering their tongues. A further twenty-five percent probably blister their tongues, and twenty-five percent are declared innocent. The efficiency of the process depends, of course, entirely on the skill of the *mubesha*."

John Bagot Glubb (Commander of the Transjordan Army),
The Story of the Arab Legion, 1956

Questions and Answers

PHELPS MET with Rainville at first light.

They spent the morning in a private visitation room going over the evidence against him. Surveillance footage in his building confirmed Essie's statement: Rainville was the only other person with regular access to her fabricator during the preceding year. The police search of his residence identified items that could only have been created using a fabricator with disabled safety protocols.

Hearing Essie's name was an awakening. He thought about how she must be feeling. Devastated by the loss of her granddaughter. Confused about what happened. How she must hate him. Hell, the whole City must. Hundreds of thousands of people in shock, grieving, yearning for vengeance. As of now, their target would be him.

They paused for a break at midmorning. A guard stepped in to monitor Rainville while Phelps went out to make some calls.

When his lawyer returned, another man accompanied him. He had jet-black hair, greying at the temples, and piercing blue eyes that gave Rainville the impression he was being looked through, more than looked at. The man was dressed casually, with a tropical-pattern shirt that made Rainville dream of places far from this detention facility. He showed no emotion, but had enough worry and laugh lines around his mouth and eyes to suggest it was at least possible. The man held out his hand with an efficient sort of precision.

"Foxwright," he said as Rainville shook his hand. "Tell me about *Automation Weekly*," he continued before they'd even sat down.

Caught off guard by the suddenness and irrelevance of the question, Rainville did not answer. What did an electronic magazine have to do with weapons of mass destruction? "Are you one of my lawyers?" he asked.

"I understand your suspicion, kid. I hate lawyers too. They're very bad people, the lot of them. I ought to know. Now, about *Automation Weekly*...."

Rainville couldn't tell if the man was kidding or not; had there been a playful wink accompanying the comment?

Phelps jumped in. "Yes. Well, umm, Mr. Rainville, my colleague Mr. Foxwright is indeed an attorney, and usually several steps ahead of the rest of us. We've got limited visitation time, and I've found the most efficient thing is often just to follow his lead and seek explanation later."

Rainville nodded and proceeded to describe *Automation Weekly* to the men as comprehensively as he knew how. "It started out as a legitimate newsletter for profiling advances in system automation for corporations, governments, that sort of thing. Over time, I suppose it either gave up, or acquired, its soul, depending on how you look at it. It went underground, and now it's mostly a rag for techies who want to hack and trick out home and City automation."

Foxwright typed furiously on an unadorned console the color of titanium, but never seemed to look down at it.

"Can you give some examples?" asked Phelps.

"It will tell you how to overclock a fabricator so it works faster. Or override a vehicle's auto-navigation safety protocols to drive more aggressively."

"Wish they'd had *Automation Weekly* when I was a kid," said Foxwright. "It sounds useful."

"Oh, it is, Mr. Fawkes."

"Wrong guy. I'm Fox*wright*."

"Sorry." Rainville rubbed his chin. "I mean, it's not all useful, exactly. Like last month, they published a guide to maliciously reprogramming the ass sensor on a public toilet."

"Classy. What's the circulation?" Foxwright asked.

"It's not really circulated, so much as fabricated," Rainville said. Observing only blank stares, he continued: "There are special features and content only available to subscribers who've ultra-hacked their fabricator to operate more freely of restrictions. This keeps script-kiddies, that's what you call the neophytes, from gaining too much knowledge without earning it first, by doing, and showing their ability to learn and figure things out for themselves."

"So different subscribers get different content, depending on their proficiency?" said Phelps.

Rainville nodded. "Fully-functional *Automation Weekly* issues are a sought-after commodity. Collectibles, even."

"The reason I ask, kid," Foxwright said, "is that you've got a lot of devices that seem to match schematics published by *Automation Weekly*. So I figure a lot of what you know came from these guys. Is that a fair assumption?"

Rainville nodded.

Foxwright continued. "Let's talk about what you do and don't know how to make using these fabricators, and how you learned it." The man appeared to be taking notes before Rainville even began his answer.

"I guess I first started messing with this stuff, it would have been a couple years ago," said Rainville. "They had this article on how to fabricate this really foul-smelling methane gas. So you could make stink bombs, or turn someone else's fabricator into a sort of a stink fountain."

"A stink fountain." It seemed a question, but Foxwright's unimpressed tone lacked any upward inflection.

"I know, kind of juvenile. But the article gave a list of preferred fabricator units for doing it. They were the older models with simplistic operating systems. I guess you'd say they had less self-aware schematic software. It's primitive code, and the stock user interface was pretty useless, but the hardware for implementing designs to fabricate was all there. So if you're willing to write some custom software extensions to get stuff done, you can create your own pirate operating system and make whatever you want. And it turned out that Essie, that's the lady who lives next door to me, she had one of the few original models that hadn't been junked. She's elderly, and I guess never learned to operate it, so she never bothered getting a newer one. I taught her to use it. Little projects at first, like dishes and cups. The toaster, well, that was special. There were no stock schematics for anything like that, so she wanted to design it from scratch. I helped her out, mostly on evenings and weekends. And in return, she let me use the unit for my own projects."

Rainville thought back to him and Essie working together, a copy of *Fabrication for Dummies* projected onto the kitchen table. He'd only wanted to help her. Using a bit of spare bandwidth on her fabricator couldn't have caused all this. Could it?

His unpleasant reverie was interrupted by Foxwright, who asked "Wouldn't the operating system on her fabricator be automatically updated?"

"Not on this early a model. Its memory was too small to support any advanced features. I had to hack in some extra memory just to program it. Now the unit is pretty slick." Rainville felt some pride at this, but then remembered the reason they were conversing about it, and his smile subsided.

"But why would the Fabrication Safety Administration let fabricators with this type of loophole stay on the grid?" Phelps asked.

"Once upon a time, they proposed banning those older fabricators, but at the time, lower-income households couldn't afford anything better. Eventually, I suppose the agency just kind of forgot about them. These days, they're so rare that illegal fabrications are only a minor problem."

"Until now," Foxwright amended.

Rainville swallowed hard, then nodded.

"So you wrote your own operating system?" Foxwright said.

"Yeah, and safety protocols too."

Phelps looked perplexed. "You did all this work to sidestep safety protocols, but then made your own?" he asked.

"You have to. Last year, law-enforcement-types infiltrated one of the *Automation Weekly* mirror servers and put a trojan module into that week's issue. Subscribers who didn't check the security hash of the issue against the gold standard got an interactive magazine with an implanted location transceiver. The transceivers alerted the authorities to the location of a ton of unlocked fabricators. Ever since then, it's standard practice to add routines to automatically scan new designs for locational bugs, unadvertised communication devices, or other rat-out technologies before the fabrication phase begins."

Nodding, Foxwright made more notes. "Kid, I'll cut right to the chase. This whole thing doesn't add up to me. Stink bombs are not high explosives, which, to my knowledge, cannot even be made on a residential fabricator. Is this true?"

Rainville nodded.

"Why is it true?" Foxwright shot back.

Rainville shrugged. He had little knowledge of molecular physics or energy conversion, but it certainly felt true. "I suppose it may be theoretically possible; I just don't know how."

"And who would know?"

"I guess, the guys who write for *Automation Weekly*. But their articles are totally anonymous. And those guys know their business. I can't imagine they'd be findable, unless they wanted to be found."

"And how could we make them want to be found?" Foxwright asked, although he'd stopped writing and was looking off into the distance. The question seemed to be rhetorical, which was a good thing since no one had an answer.

News from Home

RAINVILLE'S STATUS as an Elevated Risk Prisoner meant lots of extra security. He was not permitted any outside visitors aside from his lawyers. The isolation was taking its toll, and he found himself eagerly awaiting each of Phelps' continued visits.

The focus of their meetings had shifted from Phelps asking him for information, to the man simply offering him status updates on the case. The diminishment of Rainville's role made him feel more power-less than ever. One day, Phelps left his reader in the conference room when he departed to call the firm's home office, telling the guard the white lie that it was "a deposition" that he "needed Mr. Rainville to review," but it actually contained a download of some of the latest newsfeeds out of Arcadia.

Rainville glanced around. The guard stood near the door but could not see the screen from her vantage point. He quietly shuffled through random pages of the human interest section. He read coverage of the rock-climbing competition in the Kalahari Biome, and the caber toss and dance competitions in Arcadia's Scottish neighborhood. The mundane familiarity of these events was comforting but made him homesick.

There was an article about cracked girders found in the RetroMall of Atlantis, how it was being closed indefinitely due to structural integrity concerns after the blast. A short vidclip showed the King Neptune statue being deactivated, his waving trident grinding to a halt as the water flowing through the cockle shells behind him settled to an unnatural stillness.

The Legal Section was rife with stories about his case, and the reality of his situation surged back into his consciousness. One article contained a vidclip from weeks earlier of his entering the police station, his brown hair shaggy and askew, his grey eyes squinting, and his skin looking abnormally pasty in the harsh light of the camerabots.

Another article included footage of a mob of screaming protesters outside the detention facility. He muted the reader so the guard wouldn't hear it. Even with the sound off, it was obvious that they were yelling for blood. They shook their fists and hoisted signs saying things like "WE DEMAND JUSTICE!" and "BRING BACK THE DEATH PENALTY!"

This was followed by footage of his father walking down a street being hounded by reporters. He had dark circles under his eyes, looking more exhausted and sad than Rainville had seen him since his mother died. The realization brought a stab of guilt.

At the end of the story was a link to another article entitled "Prosecution Remains Confident of Rainville Conviction." He punched the link to see more, but got an error message: *DEVICE OUT OF NETWORK RANGE*. The detention facility had no connectivity, which was why Phelps had to step outside to make calls. Had Phelps intentionally left this story off the reader?

He turned the device off, unable to watch any more. His muscles tensed, and a growing sickness overtook his stomach. Millions of people across Arcadia now regarded him as a mass murderer. Some of them wanted him dead. His pulse pounded.

Weeks had passed, and yet this whole thing was still unbelievable. Who had done this to him? To Arcadia?

Somewhere, the bomber was watching Rainville's life go down the tubes. Probably laughing because they'd gotten away with it. How Rainville would love to find them, to make them pay.

And he would. Even if it fucking killed him.

So strange that he, the prime suspect, had no more idea than the shouting throngs on the newsvids about who was truly responsible. Why would anyone kill people at random? Would they do it again?

He pictured another explosion ripping through the crowd of protesters. They would learn the hard way that he didn't do it. But his thoughts shifted to his father, and to Vyanna and her sister and parents. He was ashamed that any part of him wished for another bombing, however briefly. He hung his head in his arms on the metal table, closed his eyes to block out the drab green walls, and waited for Phelps to come back.

Fabrication

ESSIE'S FABRICATOR was housed in the Central Precinct Evidence Repository, a stark white building with a cavernous interior stuffed with everything from vehicles to weapons to, well, fabricators.

The machine had been surgically removed from the living room of Essie's apartment and tested six ways from Sunday. Foxwright found it sequestered in its own storage locker in the lowest level of the facility: solitary confinement, perhaps, for the most notorious kitchen appliance in human history.

The device looked insignificant, unassuming in the spacious expanse of the locker; was this really the machine that caused the deaths of hundreds of people?

He held copies of twin inspection reports, one from the Prosecutorial Administration, and the other from Petronius & Sydra's technical team. Both groups had reviewed the machine's hardware, along with its software and firmware code. It had been modified just as Rainville said, but there was nothing malicious in the routines nor the hardware. Likewise, the most recent schematics stored on the fabricator were those of a simple toaster. Again, nothing malicious, and certainly nothing that would cause the fabrication of a bomb. Yet, he'd seen the vidstream of Tessa, a pretty young brunette, loading the toaster, pressing down its knob, and taking the bated breath that would turn out to be her last.

Secondary data logs suggested that someone modified the fabricator's code, and Rainville's bypass of the safety protocols had paved the way. Then whoever modified the code had changed it back afterward. But who? And why?

The Prosecutorial Administration's report concluded that Rainville had hacked the fabricator software to insert an explosive device into the schematic, by virtue of the fact that there was no other plausible explanation.

And indeed there wasn't. He had his work cut out for him.

"Mr. Foxwright?" came a voice behind him. He turned to find an evidence technician holding a tray of sealed bags, which she handed to him before departing once more.

The first bag was numbered #03F0B9F, labeled "CENTRAL PRECINCT EVIDENCE REPOSITORY, CITY OF ARCADIA," and emblazoned with warnings like "Remember, the chain of custody is only as strong as its weakest link!" and "Only you can preserve evidentiary integrity!"

Foxwright unsealed the bag and removed the item within, a copy of *Automation Weekly* magazine found in Rainville's apartment several weeks earlier. He flipped through the magazine. There were interactive portions that responded to his touch, presenting content for all the senses. One article, entitled "Building an Army of Minions: Co-opting Municipal Cleaning Robots to Doing Your Bidding," featured a step-by-step guide for building a wireless remote control, and the codes for initiating a command override. He clicked on one of the photos, which became a video showing how to interconnect the required components on a circuitboard. When the soldering began, the magazine emitted the smell of solder smoke. He chuckled.

Another article entitled "Deep News: How to Use Newsfeeds the Right Way" was premised on one statistic: there was a better-than-chance correlation between celebrity scandals breaking and news that made government agencies look bad, and the trend went back centuries. The author posited that various agencies had amassed a repository of "dirt" on celebrities, who then became sacrificial goats when more significant news stories needed burying. The article came with source code for a software app that would do data mining for the real news, the stuff you weren't meant to see, and generate probabilistic estimates on who was trying to hide what. Time was short, so he surreptitiously downloaded a copy of the app to his console to mess with later.

Another article, "Social Engineering and You," gave tips for psychological manipulation to get confidential information and access privileges out of unsuspecting corporations. The article contained a vidcall simulation with a Realistic Human Operator, and the reader was invited to try to weasel confidential information from her.

He flipped to the end. The back page featured a game where you moved around a maze grabbing components while being chased by government agents. Cute. Below that was some text:

> *"Got an idea for a bad-ass gadget or app? Send a message, with schematics and/or source code attached, to: submissions@0x7E8530X602869-redirect/deep/net."*

It was a deep-net address, indicating the site could only be found with special software to tunnel through the onion-like layers of network secrecy. This provided a reasonable chance of anonymity, both for the magazine editors and the contributors.

He gave his console a squeeze to unroll it again, and began typing:

To Whom It May Concern:

I've got a schematic idea for you. It's more powerful than the kind of stuff you typically publish, messing with robots or hacking your way out of paying subway fare.

In fact, if you follow the enclosed procedure, it might just keep the masses of Arcadia from vilifying fabricator hackers as deranged terrorists.

Optional features include:
Keeping the Fabrication Safety Administration from cracking
down on you like a bunch of wanted criminals
Freeing a loyal reader of yours, one Mr. Rainville, from imprison-
ment for a mass murder he had no part in

Step 1 is to get in touch with me as soon as possible. Other steps
to follow.

-J. Q. L. Foxwright (legal counsel for Mr. Rainville)

He attached his contact information and hit Send. The various deep-net add-ons to his messaging client delivered the message to a randomly selected anonymity server, and it was gone.

On the way back from the evidence lockup, Foxwright's console buzzed. His message to *Automation Weekly* had come back as undeliverable. He sighed. Perhaps the editor had gone into hiding after the blast. So much for that plan.

When he got back to his apartment, Foxwright watched a 2D vid of Game 8 of the scandal-plagued 1919 World Series to clear his head. The game was rigged, but only half of the White Sox were in on it. It was the bottom of the first inning. Lefty Williams was pitching. Only hours before, he'd been threatened with violence if he didn't try to lose the game; the Chicago mafia had enough money riding on the game's outcome that the threat was not idle.

Lefty threw another bad pitch, giving up another run to the Reds. He exchanged signs with Ray Schalk, the White Sox catcher. Was Schalk frustrated with Lefty's performance, or was he in on the fix? Did Lefty even know? It had the outward appearance of a baseball game, sure, but the 1919 Series had an additional layer of intrigue to it: every gesture, every glance between the players had potential secret meaning.

Lefty drew back and wound up for another pitch. His arm froze behind him, ball still in hand.

"Message for you, sir," intoned a female voice.

"This better be important, Trixy."

Lefty Williams disappeared, replaced by text:

Mr. Foxwright,

Your attempted submission to Automation Weekly *is of interest to me. Your presence is cordially requested at 550 Serra Street, tomorrow at 10:00:00.*

-P

Foxwright's message to *Automation Weekly* had bounced back as undeliverable, so no one at the magazine, or anywhere else for that matter, could have seen it. How was it possible that this "P" received it? And who was "P?"

He could think of only one way to find the answers to these questions. It was a risk he would have to take.

Paying a Visit

THE ADDRESS on Serra Street was a small but sleek office building in the older part of the Financial District. Tall green-tinted glass doors slid effortlessly open, revealing an unusual lobby: a long, illuminated hall running between mirrored shelves containing either postmodern sculptures, drab green plants, or some sort of fusion of the two. The pieces fell into place as he recalled reading about these rare and expensive flora, a kind of self-modifying bonsai cactus favored by those with too much time, and far too much money on their hands.

A dozen steps into the hallway, he heard a brief whine begin from behind the mirrored wall, then cease in a quiet *rattle-snick*, all within a second. His conscious mind dismissed the sound as part of the random cacophony belonging to the whisper-roar of any sufficiently-old building's environmental control system. But a note of recognition bubbled up from his unconscious and erupted in mid-thought.

Foxwright spent his teenage years building autonomous robots, most of which were armed. (Indeed, what was the point of creating a thinking, independent robotic life-form if you weren't going to arm it?) His misspent youth taught him that this was not a failing fan bearing or noisy ductwork; it was the sound of a malfunctioning targeting servo.

He tested the theory by making a sudden hop backwards, and then forward again, and the *whine-clack* repeated itself exactly as before. A mechanized machine-gun turret or similar armament was following his every move, along with probably a dozen others that could not be heard. The long foyer existed not to show off a mediocre collection of art-cacti—its unusual length gave the building's inhabitants time to thoroughly extinguish the mortal spark of selected visitors before they got anywhere close to the elevator. The lobby was nothing more than the kill zone of a modern castle, and the plants a palatable cover for less analytical visitors.

A prickling cold sensation moved up his back. Perhaps a hasty exit would be wise. Many of his reasons for being here, including mere curiosity, now seemed unimportant. Only his responsibility to Rainville, a young man facing a lifetime of imprisonment, while the murderer of hundreds remained at large, kept him from bolting.

Reminding himself not to conflate armament with ill intent, he resumed his walk down the hallway. Each step seemed an excruciating test of fate.

The passage ended at an elevator door. There were no obvious manual controls, but the doors opened to admit him. The interior of the elevator was similarly devoid of controls. The doors glided shut, and the elevator lurched into a strange motion. He wasn't sure if he was moving up or down, and scolded himself for not assuming a less solid stance that would tell him which direction he'd begun moving. He considered jumping up and down to test it but thought better of it. He was most certainly under surveillance and didn't want his first impression on his hosts to be him bouncing up and down like an idiot.

Having no way to assess the elevator's progress, Foxwright contemplated his mysterious hosts. It would have been a simple matter to mow him down in the entryway, deploying cleanerbots to quickly scour away his remains. If they wanted him out of the picture, it would have happened already. No, they valued him, for some reason. Needed something from him. Information, perhaps, or an assurance—hopefully one he was willing to give, although he wasn't above lying in special cases, like when trying to avoid a hail of gunfire.

He was startled out of his reverie when the elevator doors slid open. He emerged into a small but neatly kept reception room. Based on its size and lack of adornment, the reception looked more like an afterthought by an organization that rarely saw visitors.

A woman sat behind a worn metal desk at least a century old, and bare save for an archaic typewriter. She was in her forties, maybe, and classically beautiful, like the subject of a painting by one of the Italian masters.

"Good morning, Mr. Foxwright," said the woman.

"Do I know you?" he asked.

"Yes, we met just a second ago."

He laughed, but she did not acknowledge the humor, and he began to wonder if he'd misinterpreted her statement.

The woman typed a few words and he saw that the typewriter was actually a cleverly-styled computer keypad.

A moment later, she stood and gestured to a minimalistic chair aside a low table in what passed for a reception area for guests. On the table was a biometric scanner.

"Please have a seat, sir, and place your palm on the scanner," she said.

He obliged. The chair was as uncomfortable as it looked.

"Identity confirmed," she said at last. "You are indeed Mr. Foxwright."

"Mom will be so relieved," he said.

"Thank you for coming. Mr. Pentridge will be in touch."

Silence stretched out between them.

"So … that's it, then? I come here, you verify my identity, but I don't actually get to talk to anyone?" he asked.

"You got to talk to me, Mr. Foxwright," she said, but the expression on her face was inscrutable.

"To hell with you people," he said, standing. "Our arguments are on file, weak though they are, and a verdict on this case will be handed down tomorrow. I've got a client who is almost certainly going to be sentenced and imprisoned. I've got no time to waste, and yet, here you people are, wasting it. I did not come here to play games."

"No, you most assuredly did not, Mr. Foxwright. As I said, Mr. Pentridge will be in touch."

And then it hit him. It was all part of the trap. Oh, God, but they were thorough!

His voice seemed to come from somewhere outside him. "What are the chances that, now that you've confirmed my identity, I won't make it past that machine-gun-gallery lobby of yours?"

"You will make it safely out of the building, Mr. Foxwright. You have my word on that. But please do not attempt to return to this address."

"What? Why not?"

She smiled politely. "Thank you again for coming, and have a pleasant day."

"It's off to a hell of a start," he said. With that, he stepped back on the elevator. If that's the way they wanted to be, there was no point in sticking around.

The trip back through the lobby was one of the longer walks of his life, primarily because he kept half-expecting to be carved into chucks of meat by projectile weapons. Fortunately, the enigmatic receptionist proved a woman of her word, and he emerged onto Serra Street unscathed.

There was no time left for any further research; he spent the rest of the day at Petronius & Sydra helping to prepare a closing statement to be submitted to the jury of computers, emphasizing Rainville's lack of motive, but with not much else. He checked his messages. There were none from Pentridge.

The Corsned

"But of all the ordeals, that which the clergy reserved for themselves was the one least likely to cause any member of their corps to be declared guilty. The most culpable monster in existence came off clear when tried by this method. It was called the Corsned, and was thus performed.

A piece of barley bread and a piece of cheese were laid upon the altar, and the accused priest, in his full canonicals, and surrounded by all the pompous adjuncts of Roman ceremony, pronounced certain conjurations, and prayed with great fervency for several minutes. The burden of his prayer was, that if he were guilty of the crime laid to his charge, God would send his angel Gabriel to stop his throat, that he might not be able to swallow the bread and cheese.

There is no instance upon record of a priest having been choked in this manner."

Charles Mackay, *Extraordinary Popular Delusions and the Madness of Crowds, Vol. 1*, 1841

The Verdict

THE JUSTICE ADMINISTRATION NODE was distinctive amidst the cluster of drab municipal buildings on Brickell Avenue. On the northeastern edge of the Bohemian Quarter, it was the Node closest to the Latin Quarter since its own was destroyed in the blast. While the synthetic marble building resembled a Romanesque temple on the outside, the interior was anything but archaic. At the center, a large column was carved with allegories of justice and its greatest proponents, from Ur-Nammu, Hammurabi, and Justinian in ancient times, to the mercators of medieval Italy, to Blackstone and Chase in more recent times. Indirect light shone on the carvings and cast a glow on the rest of the courtroom. The column was flanked by twin pillars symbolizing Objectivity and Reason, and atop it was a podium.

Rainville sat at a broad table lined with desk lights that gave its surface a faint radiance. Seated further down the table were Phelps, Foxwright, and a man he recognized as Kinsey, one of the bigwigs from Petronius & Sydra. Rainville found it strangely hard to focus on anything not directly before him. He studied the tabletop, its glossy finish creating the appearance of a featureless depth he might plunge into if not careful. A cup of water seemed to hang there in space, unsupported. Phelps leaned over and said something generic and encouraging to him, but the words did not sink in. Rainville saw his hands trembling and crossed his arms against his chest to hide them.

At the opposing table sat a representative of the Prosecutorial Administration, alongside a crowd of high-ups from various law enforcement agencies that spilled over to a second table added for the event. There was even an observer from the Arcadian Consortium, the governing body of the City. The status and number of those eager to be associated with the prosecution made Rainville feel outnumbered and outflanked.

Behind them was the gallery, where interested members of the public were seated. He saw his father, the first time he'd shared a room with the man in two years. His father sat unmoving, looking utterly lost as if he had some grave question but didn't know how to ask it. Rainville had only seen that expression one other time: the night his mother had died.

If only he could talk to him. To apologize for getting pulled into this mess. For letting stupid differences get between them. For not being more patient with his father's pain after his mother died, and for not controlling his own pain.

Then he caught sight of Vyanna. His first glimpse of her in he didn't know how long. She gave him a hopeful smile. Then she raised her hand alongside her head and waggled her fingers, the same gesture of disorientation from their pizza heist in the park.

He smiled but felt tears coming to his eyes at the idea that someone still cared enough about him to try to make him smile. He turned away from her before she could see his pain and his fear.

The minutes dragged on as days. Even his own heartbeat seemed to slow. He wished they'd just announce the damn verdict, whatever it was, good or bad. It could not be worse than the agony of waiting.

At last the Judicial Attendant dressed in the traditional black robe with epaulets ascended a slender stairway arched into a flying buttress, seeming to defy gravity before at last reaching the top of the column. She approached the podium and tapped a few buttons. A deep chime sounded.

"This begins Superior Court of Arcadia, Judicial session number

0x3534355553343639, in the matter of People of the City of Arcadia vs. Rainville, biometric signature #0x5EC98F, case #0x1D8E102C. Counselors, we are now on the record." The Attendant's voice was emotionless.

"All rise to receive the court's decision."

Rainville saw his representatives stand, along with those seated with the Prosecution.

Everything around him seemed to be moving with a strange duality. It was all happening too quickly, and too slowly at the same time. A wave of dizziness hit him. He gripped the table, languidly hauling himself up, not wanting to put too much faith in his knees, nor his resolve.

No sooner had he stood than another chime sounded.

An orange envelope emerged from a slot in the podium. The Attendant grasped the envelope in both hands and held it up before all who were present, either out of ceremony or just to show that it was sealed.

"Those assembled are reminded that this is a judicial proceeding. Any outbursts or other disruptive behavior will result in removal from this chamber." Rainville contemplated an outburst as a means to escape this ordeal, but ironically, he was presumably the only one the warning didn't apply to. Besides, it would only forestall the inevitable. Like it or not, he needed to hear this verdict before his life could continue.

She tore the envelope open.

Inside was a piece of paper that she studied briefly. He watched her face but could discern no obvious emotion.

At last she spoke. "Let the record show that the verdict has been unsealed, inspected, and authenticated. Its contents have been found to be complete, and it has been computationally cross-checked in accordance with the Uniform Code of Defendants' Rights. It has therefore been found to be in proper form for enunciation on this day."

The Attendant placed the unsealed verdict on the podium, and its contents flashed onto the wall behind her.

She cleared her throat and began reading aloud. "In the matter of People of the City of Arcadia vs. Rainville, we the assembled intelligences of the jury in the above-entitled action, and co-joined actions from the political subdivisions and their associated case numbers, specifically including ..."

As the Attendant's slow recitation continued, Rainville's attention moved to the text on the wall. He was not reading it so much as passing his eyes over the words looking for a particular combination of letters.

One word rose above the others: "GUILTY." And again: "GUILTY." And, still again.

The words were clear and undeniable.

The word "NOT" didn't precede any of them.

His head swam as his eyes went out of focus. The attendant's voice seemed to come from very far away.

He craned his neck to look across the crowd. When he found Vyanna, her face was in her hands and she was sobbing. He looked forward again to the projected image of the verdict, searching for a "not," or a "however," or any mitigating word at all. There were none.

He spotted his father, who was staring, motionless, down at the floor.

Rainville's breath came fast, unrelenting.

He wheezed raggedly with each new gasp for air. Stay calm, he told himself. But his body no longer seemed to be listening.

The Attendant reached the meat of the verdict: "...do find Defendant Rainville guilty, in violation of 368 counts of Penal Code #813-H-99, Murder in the Second Degree...."

He heard his own voice: "No. No, no, no. Oh, no. No...." This other Rainville was slowly repeating himself, like some kind of mantra. But it did not bring any kind of peace.

The Attendant spoke louder to be heard over the commotion.

Far away, a sympathetic hand patted his shoulder, and another gently gripped his hand. His senses had narrowed and he did not know whose they were.

Life

THE CELL DOOR lock buzzed and Phelps entered. The man's expression was grim. His ready smile was absent, with only the wrinkles on either side of his mouth belying his normally cheerful demeanor. "As we feared, Mr. Rainville, it's a life sentence. And under the Parole Reform Act, we haven't got many options to work with ..."

A wave of vertigo hit Rainville. He steadied himself on the padded wall of the cell, gripping its fabric with clenched fists. His thoughts were in free fall, and he could barely keep hold of them. He eased himself down to the floor. The sound of Phelps' voice faded in and out as the words washed over him. Through blackness ringing the periphery of his vision he could still see Phelps' lips moving. He rubbed his hands together. Had the man not noticed how cold it was in here?

A pause from Phelps brought Rainville's focus back. "You are to be transferred immediately, in just a few minutes, really...." he trailed off, at a loss for words for the first time since Rainville met him. "You are to be incarcerated—" His voice cracked.

He cleared his throat. "You are to be incarcerated at the Wychwood Penitentiary." Phelps' voice seemed to soften at the final phrase, as if to lessen its harshness.

Wychwood.

Rainville had heard a hundred stories about the place, all conflicting, all impossible. And all secondhand; those imprisoned inside
Wychwood had little contact with the rest of the world, short of occasional inspections by humanitarian groups. What he'd heard about it
had been terrifying.

"And so, as it stands now...." Phelps began, stopping when he
looked up and saw Rainville's face. He adjusted, then readjusted his
tie. He was clearly uncomfortable, perhaps unaccustomed to clients
who were this emotional. Or this completely fucked. "We should...we
will, I mean, I want you to know that we're definitely filing an appeal."
The smooth confidence the man had shown in their first encounter
was gone.

A sudden ray of hope hit Rainville as a recollection came to mind.
"Wait a minute! There's been a mistake. I saw a newsvid that said they
voted to shut Wychwood down! So that can't be where they're
sending me!"

"Well, Mr. Rainville, that's not exactly true. They stopped sending
new inmates to Wychwood last year, but it's still in operation. That's
part of why it was selected. You see, the inmates there have no data
feeds from the outside world, and aren't allowed any visitors, so no
one will know who you are there, as long as you don't tell them. That
should keep you safe." Phelps hesitated. "Well...relatively. It's still a
prison, after all. But you won't be greeted by a lynch mob or anything.
And, in that sense, though I hate to say it...in some ways, Wychwood
is a safer place for you than the streets of Arcadia would be right
now."

Rainville's mind reeled. "No. No! God, no, you can't let these
bastards send me to Wychwood! Please!" He looked around at the
familiar pillowed walls, and for the first time, they actually made him
feel safer.

"I'm sorry," Phelps said. He meant it. "We're going to do everything we can to help you. You have my word. You'll be going in under
an assumed name. And we will—"

There was a knock on the cell door. "One minute left," said a disembodied voice.

Rainville tried to swallow but his throat had gone dry.

"We're already taking steps to keep you safe in there," Phelps continued. "Petronius & Sydra is not without connections, even in Wychwood. You'll be admitted under the name 'Gridley.'" He spelled it out and made Rainville do the same. "Tell no one your real name, not under any circumstance. We'll do our best for you, son. This case is not closed for us, not by a long shot."

"That's...thanks. Can you talk to the prison guards about maybe getting me under some kind of protection while this appeal goes on?"

Phelps looked uncomfortable. "I'm not sure what you heard about Wychwood," he began, "but—" and the buzz of the door lock must have made the rest of his sentence incomprehensible. Because what Rainville heard him say was impossible.

"What? Can you repeat that?" asked Rainville. The guard looked expectantly at Phelps then motioned toward the door.

"I said, Mr. Rainville, that Wychwood has no guards."

Hourglass

RAINVILLE SAT UNMOVING in his cell, exhausted. Even lifting a finger or turning his head seemed an impossible effort.

He stepped back through his memories, trying to catalog every story he'd heard about Wychwood. He'd read some of its more ancient history, but his knowledge of its present state was all rumor and speculation.

He first heard the name when he was nine. He'd hacked the environmental controls of his childhood home and made it snow in the kitchen. His new babysitter Miss Permelia told him "If you keep doing things like this, it's only a matter of time before they send you to Wychwood!" The sound of the name had made him shiver more than the falling snow. When he repeated the admonition to his mother the next day, she'd grown very upset. Miss Permelia never babysat for him again.

How surprised his mother would have been to know Miss Permelia was right. Perhaps it was a mercy that she didn't live to see this.

Later that same year, his friend Timmiah told him in hushed tones about Wychwood, a foreboding place several miles outside Arcadia's dome that was populated by tribes of cannibals. "But there are no tribes of cannibals anymore," Rainville countered. His friend only shrugged.

At age twelve, Rainville heard a man on the subway telling his girlfriend about a cousin who'd been sent to Wychwood for a crime of passion some years ago. She'd been surprised in a tragic kind of way.

"Don't you worry about him?" she asked.

"I only met him once or twice. But you know what they say. If you're not already a rapist and a murderer when you go to Wychwood, you will be soon enough."

There were other stories, but they were just third-hand rumors and wild speculation, perhaps because people condemned to Wychwood so rarely came back.

He stared at the cell door, willing it to stay closed so he could remain here, in safety, while his lawyers worked on his appeal. As if in defiance of his command, the door buzzed and retracted. Four uniformed men entered from the hallway, the clanking of their boots silenced as they stepped onto the foam floor. As they flanked him, he felt a tightness in his upper arm, and what was left of his world faded from view.

Dead to Us

(*excerpted from* A Brief History of the
Wychwood Penal Facility *by A. R. Wilchcombe*)

The City of Arcadia's relationship with the dead has always been a rocky one at best. For a variety of dubious reasons, interring the dearly departed within the city limits was strictly prohibited for centuries. Original justifications included the potential health risks from proximity to decomposing bodies, and the increasing population density which just did not leave space for dead residents. Cities were for the living, the City Council of the era had argued, and there were far more deceased residents than living ones. Reverence for the departed was a fine thing, they granted, but such veneration would eventually chase out the living due to the finite nature of real estate. A tension between respect for the dead and the needs of the living was untenable, they said, and this move would ensure that each interest could thrive on its own. The dead could be respected from a distance, in a nearby area of scrubby forest called the Wychwood, and the still-living citizens could stay where they were. What could be more equitable, more respectful, more logical? Commercial developers with deep pockets wanted land to free up, and so the rhetoric ran deep.

In actuality, the City Council evicted Arcadia's dead for one simple reason: cemeteries generated no tax revenue to the government. Cemeteries near capacity conducted little commerce, and had minuscule profits. The income from purchased cemetery plots went right into an interest-bearing account, the dividends from which were used to cover lawn-mowing and other upkeep for all eternity. Once a cemetery was full, it became a break-even entity that would never again, until the end of days, generate a cashflow for the City government to dip into. How would the Council buy votes? The Council members were just doing what they needed to survive, to continue serving those who elected them. The citizens needed their continued, strong leadership, and so really, it was for the good of everyone!

Eviction notices were served on all cemeteries in the city. Legal challenges were quashed. The backhoes and excavators ran nonstop for five weeks. After all, the sooner the triple-shift work was completed, the sooner the international media would stop ridiculing the Council's actions and find some other target for their criticism. Yet, the 24-hour work was rife with errors. A minority of these mistakes were later set right by those descendants concerned enough to complain, threaten to sue, litigate, and finally win in the court of public opinion, pressuring the contractors who relocated the graves to correct their errors. A few cemetery operators with a surplus of professional ethics followed their clients' remains to the new site and continued their stewardship over same. But most of the cemeteries had been full for a century, and been run in legal autopilot mode by a trust for decades. Their late occupants were relocated and consolidated to a massive public cemetery known officially as the Wychwood Eternity Park (or unofficially, as the City of Souls).

The Council's policies were ultimately reversed when Wychwood's burial plots reached capacity, and the idea of a single, exclusive zone for city burials was abandoned. A century later, everyone who knew any of the deceased interred at Wychwood had themselves passed on, and only those with a bent toward genealogy visited the place. The City's maintenance became lax as Wychwood began to slip out of collective consciousness.

When the operator of Hydebank Penitentiaries offered an exorbitant amount to the City, full of promises to respect hallowed ground, to use free prison labor to keep up the grounds more thoroughly and regularly, the Council was unanimous in its approval. What could be better than storing two sets of undesirables in the same space, one above ground and the other below? It was a picture of efficiency.

Things ran as planned until the Panic of 2067, when free-falling markets led to vast cuts across all parts of the public and private sector. Prison operators pulled back, making drastic changes. Wychwood was home to some of the worst offenders, and accordingly, its changes were the most radical of all.

Part III

Probatio per Ignis

(TRIAL BY FIRE)

"By the fire-ordeal, the power of deciding was just as unequivo-
cally left in [the clergy's] hands. It was generally believed that
fire would not burn the innocent, and the clergy, of course, took
care that the innocent, or such as it was their pleasure or
interest to declare so, should be so warned before undergoing
the ordeal, as to preserve themselves without any difficulty
from the fire. One mode of ordeal was to place red-hot
ploughshares on the ground at certain distances, and then,
blindfolding the accused person, make him walk barefooted
over them. If he stepped regularly in the vacant spaces, avoiding
the fire, he was adjudged innocent; if he burned himself, he was
declared guilty.

As none but the clergy interfered with the arrangement of the
ploughshares, they could always calculate beforehand the result
of the ordeal. To find a person guilty, they had only to place
them at irregular distances and the accused was sure to tread
upon one of them."

Charles Mackay, *Extraordinary Popular Delusions and the Madness of Crowds, Vol. 1*, 1841

Waking Up is Hard to Do

RAINVILLE OPENED his eyes to a metallic eight by ten-foot ceiling. Where was this place? His senses were muted and his thoughts hazy as he tried to marshal his body's resources into functionality. His muscles did not respond, and he managed only a jerking motion with his arm.

"Hey, sleeping beauty awakens!" came a gruff voice.

His alertness heightened. He closed his eyes, hoping to slow down the rush of reality. It was no use. He'd been convicted of countless crimes and condemned to what was surely the most terrible prison in existence. A dull throb built in the pit of his stomach.

He groaned, then cleared his parched throat and tried to speak. "What ... the fuck ... happened?"

"You must be Gridley," came the voice again. Rainville shook his head. Gridley? Gridley. The name seemed wrong, yet something felt right about it, too.

The voice below him laughed. "They drugged you, boy. For the transfer. Sedatives. Standard procedure to minimize legal liability for injuries caused by uncooperative prisoners. Were you an uncooperative prisoner, Gridley?"

"What? No! I didn't ... even have a chance to ... not cooperate."

"Well, the computers must have predicted you'd resist. Which is funny, because you don't look like much of a threat to me."

"Fuck … fuck the computers." They'd been dead wrong about his propensity for physical violence, among so many other things. "And my name …"

"Your name?" agreed the voice from below.

Then it clicked. Gridley was the alias they'd used to incarcerate him, perhaps the only thing keeping him alive here, and he'd almost thrown it away. More anger rose within him. He caught himself, vowing to stay grounded, to stuff his emotions down deep until they could be dealt with at a more appropriate time. "My name's Gridley." He strained to turn his head to the side and saw a grid of bars blocking the exit into a larger room containing an endless row of identical cells. The cell directly across from his own was empty, windowless with two bunks and a sanitary unit. On the door of the cell was a security card reader. Antiquated. Potentially pickable with the right tools. He wondered about the source of this voice, but the pounding in his head told him sitting up was out of the question. "How long was I out for?"

"You got in night before last, so that's gonna be … about thirty hours. Somebody musta gone a little heavy with the dosage." The voice laughed. Its owner stood up from the bottom bunk and came into view. The man's clothes were casual twenty years before, but would now be considered dressy. He looked to be in his sixties, short and blocky with wide-set faded blue eyes and grey hair. A ragged scar on his cheek disappeared into muttonchop sideburns. "Name's Braxler."

"I'm Gridley, like I said."

He could not afford to show weakness. Through the pain and stiffness, he forced his unsteady hand down toward Braxler, who met him halfway.

"What are you in for?"

"Embezzling." He'd pulled the answer from an old story he once read about a futuristic man sent to a prison planet for embezzlement. Maybe the other prisoners here would leave him alone if they knew he was convicted of killing a bunch of people, but he refused to call himself a murderer.

"Huh." Braxler did not look impressed.

"And you?" asked Rainville.

"Aggravated burglary, and extortion, not that it's any of your goddamned business. Here's some ground rules, Gridley: I'm your cellmate, but I ain't your buddy. The Boss asked me to keep an eye on you, show the ropes on account of you being a new guy." He scratched his head. "It's weird, ain't it, how we get no new fish in more'n a year. And then, bam!" He clapped his hands, startling Rainville with the sudden noise. "You show up outta the blue! And the Boss takes you in without even meeting you." Braxler waited for an explanation but Rainville offered none. "He'll want to see you right away, I bet." He gestured toward the door. "He's the guy who can hook you up with a key to this cell."

"Really?" Rainville said in a hushed voice. He had yet to get out of bed, and already this old guy was suggesting escape. Was this some kind of setup? It had to be. Braxler had no reason to trust him. Maybe he was a prison screw that they put in with the new inmates to assess escape risk. Rainville continued, "But actually, I have no intention of escaping."

Braxler laughed. "That's a good one! Boy, you are new. I don't think you understand." He chuckled again, and this time his laughter had a sinister edge to it. "You will."

Multicelled Organisms

RAINVILLE LIFTED his knees off the bed, gently flexing his muscles to test his coordination. He seemed to be wearing the most recent set of clothes Phelps had brought him in the holding cell, rather than any kind of prison uniform. A loud growl from his stomach preempted any further sartorial thoughts.

"Boy, I heard that all the way down here," Braxler said. "Must be mighty hungry from not eating all yesterday."

The idea of food awoke a fire within him. "I could definitely eat." He sat up slowly, his head throbbing.

"Alright then, let's get some grub." Braxler unlocked a steel chest on the floor, rummaged through boxes of ramen and other goods, and retrieved a faded pair of black Italian dress shoes that looked like they'd once been suitable for ballroom dancing or meeting royalty, and began lacing them.

"Wow, those are some serious shoes," Rainville said.

"Ain't they, though? I traded a vidcaster for them. Bet they came from Outside."

Rainville nodded. Of course shoes like that would not be made inside a prison.

With the calm patience that only age can grant, Braxler tied careful double-knots on both shoes before standing again. He delved again into the chest before coming back up with a pair of battered-looking metal bowls and mismatched spoons.

Reaching into a pocket, he fished out a security card, did an awkward dip as he stretched his arm through the bars to the reader outside the cell, and swiped it through. Locking solenoids on either side of the door disengaged, and the door swung slowly open.

Keys to his own cell? So Braxler hadn't been bluffing. How in the hell had he managed that? Only one explanation made sense: the man was an informant. Damn it! Had he let his guard down in front of this man? Said anything he shouldn't?

"You got money?" the man asked as he slipped through the door. "Better grab it now on account of you not having your key yet."

Rainville patted his pocket and was surprised to feel the wad of Reformed Dollar Credit banknotes, the old-school polymer kind. The kind of money carried by criminals and privacy zealots who didn't want their transactions to be traced. Amongst them was a note: "Enough to get you started; more later. Compliments of Petronius & Sydra, LLC."

So the firm did have connections in here. He wondered who else might. If his identity was revealed, he was done.

"And I'm not leaving this cell unlocked." Braxler turned back to face him. "Just 'cause you got nothing worth stealing yet don't mean you can leave our cell open. If you ain't either coming or going, you lock that cell." He pressed a button and the door relocked itself. "Staying in, lock it. Staying out, lock it. You got it?"

"Yeah, it's complicated, but I think I get it."

Braxler whipped around, red-faced, his finger pounding into Rainville's chest as he ground out his words: "All right, princess, you might think it's pretty simple, but last time I had a new fish for a cell-mate, he didn't latch the goddamn door and a bunch of my shit walked off by itself." He chuckled. "Funny, since he hardly ever left the cell." He shook his head. "Kid wet his bed every night for two weeks. Fucking disgusting. I was glad when he left." The man retrieved an antibacterial handkerchief from his pocket and began wiping down the cell control mechanism.

"After two weeks? He got out?"

"Yeah, he's Out, all right," said Braxler with an unsettling laugh. "Little bastard fell asleep on watch. No other House would take him, so Outside he went!" Their footfalls echoed down another corridor lined with cells, some occupied and others empty. A few cells held the still forms of men sleeping, while in others, men sat silently, their eyes following Rainville. Small groups of prisoners chatted in the hallway, although every conversation stopped as they walked by, gaping at the new animal in their zoo.

"Hey, Roachie, who's the new meat?" asked a giant ruddy man with a thick beard.

Braxler ignored him and kept walking. "That's a cardinal rule, boy. You fall asleep or get drunk or high on watch, you're exiled. Ain't no exceptions."

"Got it, no drugs."

"I didn't say no drugs, boy. Use 'em, just don't abuse 'em, especially on watch. Every Omega but the Boss takes turns on watch, guarding our Block from the other Houses. You become an addict or a suckbottle, a liability, then ain't no point in keeping you around."

"Other Houses?" asked Rainville.

"All kinds. Each one has its own Block. Some Houses are by job, like the Guild, which handles trading, or the Sisters, which handles, heh, whatever you want them to handle I guess. Those Houses get along with pretty much everybody. They gotta be that way, or they wouldn't have any customers."

"The other Houses don't get along?"

Braxler gave a sneer, exposing the tips of his canine teeth.

Ahead was a wall of metal grid work that ran from floor to ceiling. The bars were broached by a rectangular gate in the center made of the same alloy. Bored-looking men with machetes stood on either side. One of the men produced a key from his belt, and without a word, opened the gate.

Beyond was a corridor much like the one they'd just left, although the thundering clank of the gate relocking behind them was not reassuring.

"So what House are we in again?"

Braxler's voice took on a sinister overtone. "You know, it's strange to me that you got special admission to our House, yet you know jack squat about it. Not even our goddamned name. Don't that strike you as strange, Gridley?" Braxler stared at him as they walked.

"I suppose it might seem that way," replied Rainville vaguely. There was a splotch as his foot landed in a puddle of dark fluid on the floor. Damn it. It was thick and slippery. What the hell was that stuff? His mind reeled through the possibilities, none of them good. He wanted to wipe it off, but not bad enough to risk getting it on his hands.

Braxler waited for elaboration but got none. The old man's eyes narrowed. "For your information, we are the Omegas. The very best House. We don't let nobodies in either. Excepting yourself, I s'pose. How long you in here for, anyway?"

"Ten years," lied Rainville. He deflected the next obvious question with one of his own: "Who started the Omegas?"

"Not a fucking clue. Ancient history. You can ask the Boss when you meet him. Name's Pulsipher, and he's a businessman. Remember that and don't waste his time. He's got connections back in the City."

They approached a second wall made of solid metal, with a wide, impermeable-looking door. Two men armed with stun sticks stood at attention on either side while two more acted as lookouts, peering through holes bored in the metal to the unknown on the other side. Even unarmed, they would not be people he'd tangle with.

"You can see we got real safe accommodations here. Z Block used to be the maximum security lockup, so our cells are a little small, but we got lots of doors and gates, lots of layers of protection from the other Houses. Keeps the Cossacks from trying to kill us off. But it's got downsides, too, like how there ain't too many windows, so our view sucks. They built Z Block to hold the worst of the worst, so if a big enough earthquake hits, its walls are designed to collapse inward and bury us alive. Nice, huh?"

Rainville pictured the place collapsing on top of him, and prayed to whatever gods were associated with continued tectonic stability.

The men by the exit took a tactical position with weapons in hand as the thick metal door was unlocked with a loud clunk, and rolled open on its tracks just enough to squeeze through.

"We're leaving friendly territory now, kid. Stay alert."

Rainville considered the rough-looking men with their electrified batons. If this was friendly territory, he shuddered to imagine what lay beyond the wall.

Meat

BEYOND THE METAL wall was a cavernous space. Stories-high concrete pillars flanked the wide room, decay evident where fragments had spalled off to leave dark cavities in the cement. Long-abandoned prison cells lined the walls, every surface filthy. Trash littered the area, some of it rotting. The stench was unbearable.

Rainville's foot skidded across a damp spot on the floor. Had he stepped in vomit? Human waste? Or some other unholy thing? His nose and eyes burned and he swallowed back his gag reflex.

A skeletal man clothed in rags lay against a nearby pillar, and reached for Rainville with an upturned hand. The man opened his mouth to speak, then shuddered as a rolling cough overtook his frail body. The spasms continued until blood trailed from his lips. Rainville had never seen anyone in this condition before, and the wet, hacking sound made his skin crawl.

"Jesus. Is that guy okay?"

"Fuck, no, he ain't. Does he look okay to you?" Braxler snorted and shook his head. He walked past, nonplussed by the hacking man. Rainville hurried to keep up.

"You grow up in Arcadia?" Braxler asked.

Rainville nodded.

"Figured. You better get used to seeing sick people, Gridley. This place is full of 'em. That city of yours is one giant, sterile fucking test tube, with all your antibacterial coatings and cleaning robots and disinfecting lights. Ain't none of that here. You gotta be squeaky clean since nothing else is. Because, believe you me, your new-fish immune system ain't up to this. You wash your hands every time you come back into the cell, got me? I don't want you bringing any nasty germs in and setting them loose on me. If you get me sick, I'm gonna make sure you ain't healthy, either. Understand?"

"Got it, wash myself regularly. I'll try to remember."

He immediately regretted mouthing off to his only lifeline here. Fortunately, Braxler either missed the sarcasm or chose to ignore it. They climbed the longest non-automated staircase he had ever seen. His thighs ached when at last they entered a run-down hallway lined with dormer windows, some boarded up, others with shutters and panes smashed and moldering. Outside it was drizzling, and cool rain blew in through broken windows and collected in black puddles on the floor. An old security camera swiveled toward them before a series of spasmodic jerks drew it back toward the ceiling. At the far end of the hallway, another stairway sloped down into a dark chasm below.

"We're here. Watch your six, kid."

It was not so much a cafeteria as a massive hall with enough run-down tables and benches to seat thousands. The air smelled of sweat and cooking grease. At the front, a trestle table supported a giant vat of soup. A man in a stained chef's hat ladled the liquid out to paying customers while five of his colleagues stood by looking menacing, presumably to discourage theft or other activities that could lead to loss of soup or profits. Rainville saw not a single prison authority anywhere during their walk, nor here in this eating area. Were five men enough to keep order?

Despite its length, the soup line was moving, at least. His borrowed metal bowl was a luxury; many of the men held ragged halves of repurposed water or cleaning chemical jugs. "We call this the Trough," Braxler said. "You rich?"

Rainville was taken aback by the simplicity of the question.

"On the Outside, I mean," said Braxler. "Does your family have money?"

"No, not really. Not much family."

"You got skills?"

"Skills?"

"Ain't nothing free in Wychwood, not food, not water, and especially not the Boss letting you stay in Omega House. We don't run no charity. We all earn our keep, and you're no exception, Princess. Rich guys gotta pay, and poor guys gotta work."

"I can fix stuff. Like fabricators, and other things."

Braxler nodded. "Ain't got fabricators, or I'd fab me a laser torch and settle me some scores need settling. We sure got plenty of other things though. That oughta keep you afloat for now." He gestured to those assembled around the soup. "Money is life. If you run out, you don't last long. Guard it with your last breath, and never carry more than you need outside the cell."

Why the hell hadn't Braxler mentioned that earlier? Back home, Rainville's console had four levels of encryption and biometric authentication to keep would-be muggers from paying for things with his console. But the primitive analog currency he now carried could be stolen and spent by anyone.

There was a quiver in his stomach as he tried to smooth the bulge of polymer banknotes in his pocket and realized he was only drawing attention to it. Shit! He shoved his hands in his pockets to hide the outline. He scanned around continuously—the problem with "watching your six" is it was always behind you no matter which way you faced—and noticed everyone around him doing pretty much the same thing, varying only in the degree of subtlety of their motions.

"Hey Scruffy, that ain't no three bucks worth," said a thin man at the front of the line of his half-full makeshift bowl.

"My fist says it is," said the ladle man. "Now piss off."

A menacing glance from one of the guards was enough to send the man on his way.

The line pushed slowly forward. An old man with patched-together clothes and a long beard marched beside the food line, extolling the virtues of God's love at the top of his lungs.

"That there's Weirdbeard," said Braxler. "They say he used to be some sorta techie. Now he's half crazy. Some days, full crazy."

"The end of all is nigh," the preacher bellowed, "and only the Creator can save us!" The yelling rattled Rainville's nerves, but the man kept on the move, probably so he would not be stomped by annoyed prisoners.

Rainville tried to scan 360 degrees at once, but his nose picked up on the approaching party before his eyes. Not only was the blend of jasmine and vanilla the first nice thing he'd smelled in some time, but it reminded him of … could it be? Vyanna!

"My, aren't you a prime article!" The voice came not from Vyanna, but from a petite woman with a knockout figure who went as heavy on the makeup as the perfume. She raised an eyebrow seductively. "A strong young man like yourself, and yet I've never had the pleasure!" She held out a delicate hand. "My name is Margaretta."

Braxler took a step, interposing himself between the two. "Buzz off. Pulsipher says he's off limits."

"Pulsipher ain't my boss, honey." She deftly sidestepped Braxler and reestablished eye contact with Rainville, redeploying and redaintifying her hand in greeting. "Besides," she purred, "I think, if given the chance, we could be friends! What's your name, stranger?"

He had not been this close to a woman since before he was arrested, and his pulse picked up accordingly. Braxler's defensiveness was puzzling, though. "Braxler," he whispered, "you didn't tell me there were women in here!"

Margaretta giggled coyly. She'd heard him, and he felt his cheeks growing warm.

"That ain't a woman, kid," Braxler replied.

Rainville swallowed. Now, even his nose felt warm, and his cheeks were in full nuclear meltdown.

"See what you did, Marg? You got Gridley all worked up, blushing and everything." Braxler shook his head. "Now the poor kid'll have nightmares." He turned to Rainville. "They're a House, they call themselves the Sisters. But it's all window dressing, and no matter how great it looks," he nodded at Margaretta, who smiled as her eyebrows rose, "they ain't got the goods to close the deal."

Margaretta's smile dissolved.

"Don't go near 'em," Braxler's voice rose, and he seemed to be addressing Margaretta more than Rainville, "don't touch 'em, and, for God's sake, don't *do* anything with 'em. Not even with a borrowed dick."

"Well! I ..." she paused, her lips quivering in anger, "there simply are no words!" Margaretta turned in a huff, and stomped off the way she came, looking decidedly less dainty than before.

Weirdbeard now stomped back toward them. "If only you worried, my friends, about your soul as much as you worry for your bodies! Because what good is your body if the Devil is behind you, sticking a shiv into your soul?" The man caught sight of Rainville, and seemed genuinely startled. Weirdbeard cocked his head as if waiting for some sort of acknowledgement from him. When none came, the man continued: "Your heart is surrounded by Satan's walls. But you can break them down and let Jesus in! Your hope for salvation is locked behind a gate, but only you have the key to that gate, my brothers! And sisters!" he added without missing a beat as Margaretta passed before continuing his march down the line.

At last, they were up. Rainville's smallest bill was a $50, causing Scruffy to scowl at him and earning no small number of stares from the others in line. Damn it! If he wasn't already a target before, he certainly was now.

The soup was an opaque green mixture of carrots and chunks of some kind of meat. He considered asking what it was, but stopped himself; best not to seem prissy. Yet identifiable components were not all it lacked: also absent was any semblance of a pleasant flavor. He wished for some hot sauce to drown it out, but saw no condiments. Braxler led him to a long table on the far end of the room beneath a mangled cluster of loudspeakers. The only chairs had their backs to the wall, so that all the men faced the center of the room.

Mindful of rampant bacteria, he picked a spot near Braxler with the lowest density of unidentifiable splotches and sat down parallel to the other men, feeling like a member of some sort of judging panel. From here he could see dozens of tables populated by nasty-looking characters.

A sudden screech of metal on concrete announced a chair flying back from a table on the far side of the room. A hulking man with a series of black runes tattooed across his face and linear scars up and down his muscular arms now stood over a smaller man whose ears were pierced with a dozen nails, the old-fashioned spikes once used to bind pieces of wood together. He dragged the nail-man from his chair, punching him hard in the gut, and spun him around. Putting him in a headlock, he delivered several more brutal blows to the man's face. The men guarding the vat of soup watched but did nothing.

"Cossacks," said Braxler. "They hate everybody. They'll fight at the drop of a hat, for no reason at all. They're blood-in, blood-out. Fucking savages."

At last, the man freed himself and stumbled back, coughing and wheezing. The other men at the table laughed and clapped.

"Blood in ...?" Rainville echoed.

"Blood-in, blood-out. It means you gotta kill somebody to get into their House. And the only way out ... is to die. Houses like that are a magnet for the nasties, the guys with the longest sentences."

The beaten man spit out a bloody tooth, then he too began to laugh. He pulled himself back up onto his chair to slaps on the back.

"You see that guy over there, kind of pretending like he don't exist?" Braxler indicated a pale, obese man moving quickly along a circuitous path through the crowd, casting nervous glances at every turn. "He's a Lolly. Boy, don't even get me started on the Lollies."

"The Lollies?"

"I said not to get me started on them, goddamn it, Gridley! Bunch of rapists. And diaper snipers."

"Did you just say—"

"Child molesters! Every one of 'em's a sex offender." He shook his head in disgust. "Their chief is Lanny Strange, and you don't even want to know what he's in here for. The Lollies stick together because no one else will take 'em. Most of them hardly leave Q Block because the Cossacks will castrate 'em on sight."

Rainville swallowed uneasily. There were a great many people to avoid here.

A skinny, sallow inmate at the other end of the Omega table leaned over and waved at Braxler. "Hey Roachie! Who's the n-new fish?" he cried.

"Why do they call you Roachie?" Rainville asked.

"Eat your damn soup, Gridley," ordered Braxler in a low voice.

"I called him Roachie, 'cause that's his name!" answered the man. Some of the men seated between them started to laugh.

"Shut up, Anx, you boney bastard."

"Aww, Roachie, c-come on," stuttered Anx. "You know I got to tell him the s-s-story. It's a goddamned m-moral imperative."

"Fuck you and your moral imperatives."

"Okay, so it's like this," Anx began. Braxler shook his head and seemed to tune out to everything but eating his soup. "One night, Roachie—sorry, *Braxler*," the man said mockingly, "went to the storage room to grab some toilet paper. The l-light wasn't on, but he knew where the rolls were, so in he went. He gets halfway to the wall, and BANG! He nails his knee on a mop bucket somebody left there." The man was rubbing his knee, either unconsciously, or to enrich the story. "Now, his knee is hurting like an absolute motherfucker, and his l-l-leg is all tickly, and he thinks it's because he hit his funny bone, right? So he goes back to the door and turns on the light, and realizes the room is *full* of fucking cockroaches. Like, more-c-c-cockroaches-than-you've-ever-seen-in-your-whole-fucking-life full. And these two roaches are humping each other in the middle, and a whole shit-ton of roaches are gathered all around, like it was some kinda sex c-club for c-cockroaches."

The image was a disturbing one, but still a distraction from the strange soup. It wasn't just the broth that was green; the meat itself was, too. Green, and bland. He forced several obvious meat-related questions out of his mind until he'd finished swallowing.

A portly older gentleman with a neatly trimmed beard leaned in.

He looked somehow familiar, but from where, Rainville couldn't say. "You see, son, it's not that cockroaches travel in packs, or live in colonies, or anything of the sort. But every cockroach leaves an airborne pheromone trail wherever it goes. Other roaches will pick up this trail and instinctually follow it to see where the first roach was going, follow him to a food or water source, or to see what he's hiding in his stash. So the bugs exhibit this swarming behavior not because they're particularly sociable or enjoy the company of their peers, but just because of their food- and water-finding strategies."

"All right Professor, l-l-let me finish," Anx implored.

"I'm merely adding important background to your otherwise unidimensional story." He turned back toward Rainville, a gleam now in his eye. "As I was saying before my young friend interrupted me, when a female cockroach goes into heat, her pheromones go into overdrive. So you've got their natural swarming behavior, coupled with a female in heat, leading to a veritable festival of hundreds of roaches, all in our humble supply closet at the same time!"

"Yeah, you heard him, it was a g-giant orgy of c-cockroaches!" Anx said, a sense of wonder on his face. "And so these cockroaches are skittering all over the room, and what's worse, all over your cellmate here!" It was getting hard to hear the story from all the laughter at the table, and Braxler's pretense at ignoring it was belied by the crimson color of his face and ears.

"By now, they're all up inside his c-c-clothes and everything. So what does he do?"

Rainville shook his head and smiled for the first time since being imprisoned.

"He runs outta the room, doing this jiggly, spastic sorta arm-wavy dance, screaming 'Roaches!!! Rooaaacchheees!' And his voice was kinda high because he was so, you know, surprised, and he was kinda q-quiverin', so it sounded to everybody like he was saying 'Roachies! Roachieeees!'" Anx snorted, and mopped up a tear of laughter with his sleeve. "Oh shit, it was just classic."

The Professor leaned in again. "He's been called 'Roachie' ever since." Braxler launched an angry look in his direction. "Sorry, Braxler. He was going to find out sooner or later."

Anx's spirited storytelling had been overheard, now causing no small amount of reminiscing at nearby tables. Several discussions around the Trough now turned to the very same topic, and retellings of the story. Rainville could only hear bits and pieces of the conversations, but inevitably the storyteller would erupt into cries of "Roacheeeees!" at which point everyone at the neighboring table would laugh and stare at Braxler, who would tense up like he was once again covered in horny roaches.

"So why do they call you Anx?" Rainville asked.

Braxler jumped on the question like a lion on a baby gazelle: "I would love to tell you that story. Absolutely love to."

:

The Chief

AFTER LUNCH, Braxler escorted Rainville back from the Trough. Inside Z Block, Rainville followed him down a long brick hallway filled with burnt and broken furniture, remnants from a prison uprising perhaps, into the deepest part of the old Block. Their destination was unknown, but he would not separate himself from the only person he knew in this place.

"How do the Sisters get perfume in this place?" He could not get the comforting scent out of his thoughts. Its very memory was like the sillage of Vyanna, as if she were inexplicably nearer to him.

"They make it themselves, maybe. They got all kinds of secrets. All of 'em best left as exactly that."

Probably true, thought Rainville thought. He changed the subject. "The Professor seemed like an all right guy. What's he in for?"

"Him? He runs the prison library. Seems like a kindly, cultured sorta fella, don't he? Well, he's a serial killer. Dismembered twenty-three people. Real sick fuck. Once told me the only time he really feels alive is when he's, how'd he say it, 'snuffing the spark of life out of another.'"

"Jesus." So that was why the Professor looked familiar: news headlines from Rainville's childhood.

Braxler nodded. "I don't know of anybody he's killed at Wychwood, but there's rumors. Watch your back around him."

Rainville considered the jovial man, going through the motions of everyday life, wearing a mask of sanity. He shuddered.

Braxler noticed. "Better get used to it. This ain't charm school; there's some real colorful motherfuckers here." Rainville wasn't sure if Braxler could be entirely trusted, but he'd expressed aversions to both sex offenders and serial killers. It was something. As far as the inmates here went, at least he seemed on the less terrifying end of the spectrum. "We're here. Boss is expecting you."

Pulsipher's office was three times as big as any cell. A former guard station, its transparent walls and ceiling permitted extra light. The room was lavishly decorated with works of art. A sculpture of a dragon carved from wood sat on the desk. A beautifully detailed silver frame surrounded a painting of an alpine lake on the wall. Yet, there was a strangeness to them all. A closer look, and Rainville knew: this was all prison craftwork. The silver picture frame was made out of rolled-up foil from cigarette cartons, woven together. Amazing! How long had it taken to create? A photograph on the wall of a tropical island appeared to have been cut out of an old paperbound magazine. On the desk was a video chip player, popular in the days before Arcadia was fully networked. He supposed the prison was one of the few places they were still in use. This one was wired to a stack of electroluminescent bricks presumably ripped from an ancient wall advertisement. He chuckled at the makeshift vidcaster apparatus.

"Is something amusing?" came a deep voice from behind him. He whirled around to see a man in his forties with deep ebony skin, carefully-coiffed hair, and a well-tailored pinstriped suit, who'd entered from a small door on the opposite side of the office.

"Uhh, afternoon, Mr. Pulsipher, sir," said Braxler.

Without breaking eye contact with Rainville, Pulsipher gestured toward a chair by a battered metal desk that looked like it had (barely) survived more than one riot.

At last Pulsipher turned to face Braxler, who got the hint and left, closing the door behind him. Pulsipher hit a button underneath the desk which made the walls turn semi-translucent before assuming a relaxing shade of blue. The space immediately felt much smaller and more intimate.

"You must be...Gridley." Pulsipher's voice was low and calm, almost soothing in its tone and meter. His intonation was subtly different on the last word, and Rainville wondered if this man was simply recalling the name, or if he knew it wasn't real. "Welcome to the Omegas. Our mutual friends at Petronius & Sydra have asked if we might try to make your life here a bit easier. I trust Mr. Braxler has been showing you around, explaining the rules?"

"Yes. I mean, thank you. He's been very helpful."

Pulsipher closed his eyes momentarily and smiled as if Rainville's affirmation was music. "I'm glad to hear that. I hope, in light of the hospitality we've extended you, that you'll indulge me for a moment." His voice remained calm to the point of being disarming, perhaps a result of surrounding himself with people who knew better than to ever refuse him. Polite or not, Rainville did not think the request was optional. He nodded, hoping to keep things as cordial as possible.

There was an unrelenting intensity in Pulsipher's almond eyes as he reached into his jacket pocket to retrieve a small cylinder. He snapped his wrist and Rainville caught the flying item. It looked like ... well, like a tube of lipstick. He opened it. Definitely lipstick. He didn't know much about makeup, but the logo on the tube seemed vaguely familiar.

"Please put it on," Pulsipher directed.

A surge of panic rose in Rainville's chest, and he wondered if perhaps he'd been recruited into the wrong House. No, this had to be some kind of hazing ritual. But was that any more comforting?

He started to say "It's not my color," but stopped, not wanting to disrespect his new guardian and protector, and a very serious-looking character to boot. "Sir, I don't understand," he began instead. Rainville hadn't called another man "sir" in his entire life, but this seemed an excellent time to start. Still, he felt somehow lesser for having said it.

Pulsipher watched his reaction and chuckled. "You don't have any children, do you Mr. Gridley?"

"Sir?" Make that twice in his life. Indignation burned in his core, insisting in no uncertain terms that this deference not become habit. It might have just been pride, but at the same time, he would not become anyone's bitch here.

"Daughters, more specifically," said Pulsipher, gesturing at the cylinder. "It's called Truth or Dare. It's a sort of mood makeup. Its color changes based on galvanic skin response, skin temperature, capillary vasodilation, and several other factors. If you know how to use it, it can tell you when the person wearing it is lying. Now, I know you would never lie to me, isn't that right Mr. Gridley?"

"No. I mean, yes, of course I wouldn't," Rainville hoped.

"No, of course not. So, if you please," Pulsipher said, pointing to the tube.

Rainville opened the container and felt at a procedural loss. "Do you, umm, have a mirror I could use?"

Pulsipher chuckled again. "This isn't a fashion show. Just put a patch of it on your lips, and then smear some on your cheek."

He complied. The substance felt strangely cooling, and his skin tingled beneath it.

"Excellent," Pulsipher said, retrieving the lipstick. "The more we trust each other, the more we can help each other. Don't you agree, Gridley?"

Rainville noticed the "Mr." honorific had disappeared with his acquiescence to Pulsipher's request. The man did not wait for a response. "Truth or Dare is a very helpful product to a man in my position. I can use it to root out spies."

"I'm not a spy," Rainville shot back.

"I know that. But you're not a typical prisoner, either, now are you?" Pulsipher paused and leaned closer to study his face.

"I don't know." He didn't, and hoped his vasodilation and galvanic skin response would abide this technicality.

"We haven't gotten any new fish in over a year. Why did they send you here? Why now?"

"I...I don't really know why I'm here. None of it makes sense." This much was true.

"Let's simplify things a bit. What are you in here for?"

"Murders I didn't commit."

Pulsipher leaned closer still, continuing to study his face. "Interesting. I am inclined to believe you, Mr. Gridley. Either that, or you're more familiar with this particular fashion product than you've let on," he said, patting his pocket. The man watched him intently, speaking slowly as if to monitor his response to each word.

"And what is Petronius & Sydra's interest in you? They've offered me a sum which, in this place, is quite considerable. All in exchange for your protection."

Rainville felt gratitude and wondered how that might affect the makeup. "I suppose because I'm their client. They're appealing my case." Another honest answer, and another answer devoid of any real information.

"Mr. Gridley, I'll be frank." Pulsipher's cordiality took on an added intensity. His frustration was beginning to show. "I have a ... rather strong interest, shall we say, in keeping abreast of what is going on with this facility, and any changes that might threaten the way things are done here. I can only protect you and the rest of the Omegas if I know what's happening, be it a resumption in new incarcerations, or...or a pending closure." He came even closer, now within a few inches of Rainville's face. His breath was warm, scentless. "So if there is anything, anything at all that I should know about our future here, then I very much hope you'll share it with me. Am I making myself clear?"

Rainville nodded. The nature of this man's suspicion was not clear, but any scrutiny was a risk to Rainville's cover story just the same. What could he say to placate him?

A knock came from the main door, and a large, muscular man stepped in to confer with Pulsipher. One eye had a hazy tone the color of milk, while the other was so sharp and attentive as to more than compensate.

"I'm afraid there's an urgent matter to which I must attend. We will continue this discussion later."

"Yes, sir. And let me say that I would like to help you. But I honestly don't know why I'm here," he said, hoping that adhering to generalities would keep the lipstick from betraying him. "And I'm afraid I don't know anything about the plans for Wychwood. They told me I was being sent here, sedated me, and then I woke up in that...."

"Enough! You'll be on your way now, Gridley," said Pulsipher, and nodded to the burly man, who took a firm hold on Rainville's shoulder and led him out.

Braxler waited for him in the corridor. He looked quizzically at Rainville, his face a tapestry of questions.

Rainville used his sleeve to wipe off the makeup as best he could. Honesty could only be a liability in this place.

Prospects

RAINVILLE'S first night in Wychwood had been endless. Every time he started to nod off, a feeling of wrongness jarred him awake again. Against his will, the same thoughts kept stampeding through his head: he did not belong here; how had this happened?

A part of his mind would not relent on the question, and the light of day brought with it no answers.

After what passed for a breakfast, Braxler led Rainville down a long green corridor lined with abandoned solitary confinement cells. The padded walls of one cell were stained with blood. More blood than a man could reasonably survive losing. Rainville shuddered.

"Boss wants you to get set up to do, well, whatever the hell techie work you do on behalf of us Omegas. Used to be a guy called Quain did that sorta stuff for us, but he got sick and had to be put Out."

"Put out?"

Braxler explained that the sickest of the sick were inevitably exiled from their Houses to the ravages of the interstitial no-man's-land of common areas. Rainville envisioned the man coughing up blood outside the Z Block entrance. Maybe it was ancient genetic behavioral coding telling him to stay away from contagion, but since seeing the man, he found himself scarcely comfortable in his own skin when outside the Block.

"What's Pulsipher need fixed?" he asked, eager to think about something else.

"How the hell should I know? I'm just taking you to Mahara so he can set you up." The corridor ended in a junction of circular passages laid out in a spoke pattern. He followed Braxler down one of the brighter corridors, seemingly lit by bulbs robbed from the darker passages. "Be glad you got a marketable trade, kid. Because you don't wanna know what guys without any skills gotta do to earn money."

Rainville agreed.

They entered a well-lit room full of timeworn couches and chairs and tables occupied by well-armed men playing dominos. Not ordinary dominos, however. "Dooka!" cried a man at the nearest table to the moans and grumbles of the other three. The losing men took turns reaching into a bucket of rusted battery terminal clips, and clipping the terminals' alligator teeth to the skin of their forearms. Those whose forearms were full seemed to work their way up to their biceps, and the man seated to the right of the winner had clips biting into the flesh of his neck and earlobes. It hurt Rainville just to look at the men. How could they stay focused on the game?

Weapons hung from the men's belts. Some wore machetes with hand-carved handles, others knives that were little more than a cylinder of polymer with a spike, and still another had a foot-long metal tube with a hole in the end, covered in tape and joined with a battery pack. A primitive Gauss gun. He could already see several ways to improve the design. These guys needed him. Hopefully he could make them realize that.

"These are Pulsipher's lieutenants. Don't piss 'em off." He pointed to a man with olive skin and a close-cropped beard, all hard geometric lines like his jaw and crooked nose. He was even larger than the others, with biceps the diameter of small trees. He stood at the far end of the room smoking a crudely hand-rolled cigar. "And that's Mahara. Really, really don't piss him off."

"It's, uhh, nice to see you, Mahara," said Braxler to the man as they approached. "This is Gridley, our new fish. He's a techie. Pulsipher thought he might be useful, but says it's up to you."

The large, square man nodded, appraising Rainville in a glance. He had flat-topped hair and no neck to speak of. "Whatchoo good at?"

The words took a second to register. "Umm, anything electronic. Anything optronic. Anything in between." He smiled slightly and tried to exude confidence. "See that Gauss gun over there?" He saw Mahara's eyes follow. "I could fix it. Make it a real weapon. Optimize coil density and placement, and add dynamic charge timing so you can fire different kinds of projectiles in it without having to recalibrate."

Mahara gave a nod. He asked whether Rainville could fix this, that, or the other thing, presumably a laundry list of broken items owned by the men, mostly small appliances based on very simple technologies. Mahara spoke only fractured English, but had yet to say enough contiguous words for Rainville to guess at an accent or ethnicity.

He answered in the affirmative, but warned each case was conditional on finding parts.

Mahara seemed to understand the dependence on salvaged components; at last, he nodded. "You be here tomorrow. Early, early. Yes?"

Rainville nodded vigorously. "Early early!" he repeated. He wondered if they could hear the relief in his voice.

Broken

DIAGNOSING broken circuits took much longer without access to online schematics and service manuals. Necessary diagnostic and repair tools were fabricated as best as possible using raw materials salvaged from junked devices. Rainville took in repair projects from dawn to dusk, and was glad to have those hours filled. And sometimes, when his mind was deep in a repair job, it was almost like he had his old life back. Almost.

He'd always been mechanically inclined, but it went beyond that. He had an instinctual understanding of technology, the result of a life spent deconstructing and rebuilding machines. When he was five years old, he took apart his first floor-sweeping robot, and put it back together correctly (more or less; forever after, it made a sort of growling noise whenever it turned left). He couldn't always explain exactly why he'd try this or that, but more often than not, his hunches about the problems of machines paid off. He wished like hell for an hour alone with the disordered computers that convicted him.

Pulsipher granted him a long-abandoned laundry room with a workbench and fully-operable desk lamp, and took ninety percent of the repair profit. Nonetheless, Rainville could finally earn extra spending money without ever having to leave the relative safety of Z

Block. Poorer inmates took on his guard duty shifts in exchange for repairs, so in very little time, he built up a surplus of guard shift IOUs. This spared him from boring hours spent standing by the entry gates to the Block.

His technical skills made him valuable: no one wanted to piss off "Gridley the Fix-it Man," or his broken TuneBuster or misaligned ErotiTronic Stimulator would go to the end of the repair queue. The work and the wheeling and dealing helped him forget, however briefly, the many deaths that history would blame on him. By now, all the newsfeeds would be dissecting his young life and speculating on what drove him over the edge he hadn't gone near, analyzing how he'd become the modern-day sociopath that he wasn't. How his disciplinary problems at school signified a troubled youth at an early age, or how his mother's death finally sent him off the rails. His blood burned at the inhumanity of his fate as much as his own powerlessness to stop it from inside Wychwood.

Many of the convicts around him were evil, but no more so than a society that unthinkingly and negligently condemned an innocent person to this bedlam, totally cut off from the outside world. He'd been a part of that society, never sparing a single moment to consider the lives of a bunch of convicts, let alone wonder if any were innocent. And now, here he was. One of them.

Sticky

RAINVILLE WAS IN HIS WORKSHOP, putting the finishing touches on a music player that at one time could scan the user's brain, detect which songs were enjoyed the most, and select the next song accordingly. He could fix the output amplifier so music would again play, but the recommendation engine had a fried synaptic transistor package for which he had no viable replacements. The user, one Mr. "Squiggz" of Cell 126, Z Block, would thus be at the mercy of music selected at random. However, Rainville's customers had proved much more understanding of partial repairs than their non-incarcerated counterparts, as so much in Wychwood seemed to fall somewhere between half-working and utterly dead.

"Knock, knock," came an unfamiliar voice as a young man walked into the shop. He looked not much older than Rainville, clean-shaven with meticulously-arranged blond hair.

"You Gridley?" asked the man.

"Last time I checked," said Rainville. Indeed, he had to check himself each time his name was asked.

The young man smiled easily, with an unguarded quality most of the inmates here seemed to have lost long ago. "Name's Boudreaux," he said, extending his hand, which Rainville shook over the counter. "I hear you're the new fix-it man?"

Rainville nodded.

"Good gig," he said. "You don't want to run out of money in this place. Pulsipher kicked a guy out for that not six months back."

"What happened to him?"

"Steele and Mahara beat the hell out of him, dumped him near R Block."

"Did they kill him?"

"Nah, he didn't break any major rules, just ran out of money to pay for his accommodations."

"Where's he now?"

"Haven't seen him. Heard he tried to sell himself into the Lollies as a gimp. That's the Pedo House over in Q Block. But they weren't buying. Took turns raping him and threw him right back out."

"Jesus."

"He begged for food in the corridors between the Houses for a while. I gave him my leftovers a couple of times. Then he kinda disappeared. Maybe the Cossacks got him. Anyways I ain't here to talk about exiles."

"No?"

His voice dropped to just above a whisper. "Listen close, I got something for you that could—"

"Heya! You open?" An older man with a limp entered behind Boudreaux.

"That's Sticky," Boudreaux whispered, "You keep both your eyes on that one."

"You fix old stuff?" said the man as he shuffled up to the counter, his eyes scanning the room. He picked up a broken multiplier tube and a fused bedistor, hefting them up and down in each hand as if comparing their weights.

"Sure do. Anything in this place new?" He held out a hand and the man relinquished the parts.

"Just you," said Sticky.

"I'll leave you gentlemen to sort out your business," said

Boudreaux. "We'll talk soon, Gridley." He slipped out of the workshop back into Z Block.

"What's this?" asked Sticky, holding a cracked digital tiara he'd managed to reach over the counter and pick up before Rainville had even stowed the previous items.

"It's an inductive meditation machine. Please don't touch anything, because it's, uhh, all laid out in a certain way, so I remember how to put it back together. Its owner won't be happy if someone messes it up, you know what I mean?"

Sticky smiled but shook his head. "Inductive what?"

"It's like noise cancellation except on your brainwaves. It reads the beta waves in your head and delivers the exact sounds and vibrations to balance them out, to sooth them."

The man nodded appreciatively. "Stop a man's thoughts? Don't sound safe."

"No, it just mutes them a little. Or it did, I mean. It's broken now, so not really of value to anyone." He took the visor from Sticky and stashed it out of sight.

Things continued that way for another quarter hour. When the strange game of kleptomaniacal chess was over, Rainville locked up the shop and searched for Boudreaux, but could not find him anywhere.

Cold Justice, Part I

"In the small Eskimo community the question of evidence in disputes does not raise a great problem; sufficient direct information seems usually to be at hand. When fact is not known, however, resort may be had to divination, but apparently only when an element of sin enters into the offense, or ... when a death through sorcery has occurred. Divination is by weighing. A thong is looped around the head of a reclining person, or a bundled coat, or even the diviner's own foot. When the proper spirit has entered the object, the question may be put. As the object is hard or easy to lift, the answer is 'yes' or 'no.' In Nunivak, according to Dr. Lands, divination is done by peering into still water which has been poured into the abdominal cavity of a dressed animal. The image of the guilty person may then be seen."

E. Adamson Hoebel, "The Eskimo: Rudimentary Law in a Primitive Anarchy," *The Law of Primitive Man,* 1954

Japadog

"YOUR STOMACH IS GROWLING, and your rate of mistyped characters has increased. It is time for lunch," Trixy said.

"Just a damn minute," said Foxwright. He was in the middle of querying the case database for security records from Rainville's building. Foxwright had not given up on the case. Would not. Sure, the kid was a lot like he'd been at that age, but it was more than that. Something about the verdict didn't sit well with him, something with an increasingly resonant voice which suggested he knew less about the system than he believed. He needed to figure out why for his own sanity, whether the answer helped with Rainville's appeal or not.

The legal team at Petronius & Sydra had already reviewed the database, but Rainville's building was large and had lots of staff members, residents, and guests, any one of whom could have found a way into Essie's apartment. One could never be too thorough.

Three days had passed since the sentencing, with not a single new lead for the appeal. Nothing whatsoever from that Pentridge character he'd tried to meet with. Only increasingly-curt messages from various Petronius bigwigs, desperate to either get the Rainville verdict reversed, or just find enough random circumstantial evidence to at least convince the media this case had not been a complete boondoggle. Soon the ass-covering would reach a fever pitch, and the firm would quietly drop the appeal and move on to some new high-profile case with which to redeem itself.

The display went black and Foxwright's keystrokes ceased to have effect.

"Trixy, what the hell?"

"You asked for a minute. I gave you one. Have a pleasant lunch!"

He scowled. How was he supposed to get any work done if he was going to be betrayed by his own office equipment?

"Well, be a nice assistant and query the refrigerator for lunch options."

"Querying appliance status. Meatloaf, 50% remaining, age: 13 days, status: questionable. Milk, 32% remaining, age: 6 days. Refrigerator compartment temperatures normal. UV lighting and CO_2 modules in the produce compartment reporting normal, although it contains no fruits or vegetables. Shall I order more, or deactivate it?"

Though his refrigerator was capable of continuing to grow and ripen certain vegetables placed in its drawers, the citywide produce shortage caused by the destruction of the Latin Quarter's agristations would deprive it of the opportunity for the foreseeable future. Just as well; Foxwright preferred meat.

"Do as you wish. I'm going out."

He got in the elevator, and mumbled "Lobby." The car plunged downward and his stomach growled at the indignity. Through the transparent walls of the elevator he looked out over Comstock Avenue to where it ended in the interconnected domes that made up Vaux Park. A visual staccato of aerial breezeways spanning between high-rises punctuated his descending view.

Two hundred floors later, he emerged out onto the street. Pedestrians hurried by. Where Comstock crossed Lafayette, streams of car traffic came together at high speeds, streaming through one another without slowing as computer-controlled arbitration made minute adjustments to each vehicle's velocity to engineer an unending series of near-misses instead of collisions.

At his favorite Japanese hotdog stand, the old man greeted him with a warm smile. Foxwright had been a regular customer for a decade. "Hello Mr. F! Two K-dogs for you?"

"You know it, Yoshi." Kurobuta pork dogs were his weekly staple. "How's Mrs. Yoshi and the little Yoshis?" Foxwright could never remember all their first names.

"Doing great! Went to the game last night," the old man said as he fumbled around in a compartment and retrieved two buns. "Did you watch it?"

"Nope. Worked." He studied an animated ad on the menu. It showed Buddha standing in front of a hotdog stand, saying "Make me one with everything."

"You shoulda seen it, Mr. F!" Yoshi's smile broadened as he spoke. "It went into overtime! Fifth down, only thirty seconds left, and Smithwick's too far from the goal line to run. What's he do? He's gotta get himself to a launcher. It's looking good, but then Johnstone tries to hit the activator, a defensive lineman is in the way. So what's Johnstone do, give up?" Yoshi chuckled as he populated the buns with the dark, juicy sausages. "No sirree, he doesn't. He shoves the defenseman headfirst into the activator pad, and shoots Smithwick all the way to the goal! It was epic. Maybe you watch the highlights?"

Foxwright granted that it sounded exciting, but it could not compare to, say, watching the 1974 Portland Mavericks play baseball.

"The cheerleaders finally agreed to get programmable tattoos. Now they don't gotta cut away to commercials anymore, they just show them dancing. Ooh la la! I wish I could afford to buy an ad for my stand."

Animated tattoos did not surprise Foxwright. Many cheerleaders were already heavily augmented, from resculpted body parts to neural reprogramming to dilate their irises (supposedly it indicated sexual attraction, but he thought it just made them look drugged out). Granted, few women were exactly "factory-original" these days, but the cheerleaders looked less human every year.

Yoshi squirted lines of teriyaki mayonnaise across the dogs and sprinkled on crispy seaweed before bagging them and passing them over the counter. "Enjoy it, Mr. F!"

With a smile and a nod, he triggered his console to transmit 12.48 Reformed Dollar Credits to pay for the food. The cryptographic Credits were exchangeable for any number of commodities, thus preventing any inflationary funny-business by governments or banks or hybrids thereof. The meal was expensive by mealcart standards. Real meat with clean provenance (as opposed to that synthesized crap) was a rarity generally reserved for garnishes, and importing pedigree hogs raised on a crowded and far-flung island seemed an amazing feat to Foxwright.

Stepping away from the stand, he felt a rush of air next to his ear. He turned to see a butterfly perched on his shoulder, no doubt a stray from the nearby rainforest biome in Vaux Park. The park's butterflies were genetically engineered so each creature's wing colorations would be uniquely random. It seemed a strange use of technology. Random uniqueness did not seem to be well-correlated with aesthetic beauty, because for every pretty brilliant orange butterfly, there were a dozen others with drab or outright ugly color combinations. But this butterfly was nothing short of breathtaking, with iridescent hues spanning all the colors of the rainbow.

He'd never seen one outside Vaux. The wildlife retention drones at the edge of the park shepherded wayward birds and insects back into their biome, yet somehow they'd let this one slip by. As he studied the insect, which seemed quite at peace on his shoulder, he decided that Vaux was as good as place as any to eat lunch. He could return the creature to its home in the process.

He walked several blocks before traversing NORFED Plaza, which had its own variant of the rosemallow flower that would change from green to red depending on whether the stock market was up or down, though they still smelled like hell either way. The butterfly evidently agreed, as it did not leave his shoulder.

They reached Vaux Park, and Foxwright placed a light, protective hand over the butterfly as they passed through the isolation arch. A burst of humid air hit him, then he crossed a loose matrix of shepherd drones hovering nearby before uncovering the butterfly once again.

Nonplussed, it slowly raised and lowered its wings, no less happy on his shoulder than before despite the commotion.

He found his preferred bench which looked just like all the other benches, but felt very different: it was alive with the constant vibration of some subterranean machinery deep below. It felt like the rumbling of the city's bloodstream. It was probably above a busy subway route or pumping station, but he found the rumbling as reassuring as kitten does the purr of its mother.

The bench sat across from his favorite art installation, a fountain where highly-pressurized, precision water nozzles created color renderings of Impressionist paintings. The sound of the jets alternated based on the painting to form a kind of whitenoise-based music, and the glimmering of the water made the works come alive as if water were a more appropriate Impressionist medium than oil-on-canvas. He'd never grown tired of watching it.

The image in the fountain transitioned from Monet's Water-Lily Pond to a scene of Lomita Station, with a message memorializing the thirty-two victims of the Lomita Station Tragedy several months earlier. Portraits of those killed in the subway crash shimmered in the water before him. Many of the victims had been children on their way to a snowman-building contest in the Yukon Biome. The faces of the children jarred him out of his reverie, evoking a wound from which Arcadia would never completely heal.

He thought of the Latin Quarter bombing. Forty-three of those murdered in the blast had been kids. And whoever murdered them was still at large. Yet, when Rainville was convicted, the City breathed a collective sigh of relief, and in many ways had gone back to business as usual.

The fountain jets roared and the scene changed to a radiant sunset reflecting over the sea beside a dark, arch-shaped cliff. He turned to look at the butterfly, but it had vanished.

His pocket buzzed. An incoming message. He unrolled the console and brought up his inbox. There was a new message, but the From field was blank. Odd.

Mr. Foxwright,

I have some information that may be of interest to you on the Rainville matter. Please be at the Jennings Avenue subway station at 2:00 p.m. tomorrow. Attached are more detailed instructions to perform upon your arrival.

-Pentridge

That name again. It rang a distant bell in his mind, from half-remembered, whispered rumors of a man who was alternately a criminal kingpin, a reclusive business mogul, or an outright boogeyman, depending on who was relating the particular tall tale. Yet he could not recall any one specific place where he'd heard the name before. Who was this man? And what was his interest in the case?

Training

THE FOLLOWING AFTERNOON, Foxwright crossed Comstock Avenue and stepped up onto the rubberized sidewalk. A round section of the wall slid away in thirds with a pneumatic whisper, revealing a set of escalators speeding downward. Lights streamed by as he descended a dozen stories to a selective entry wall. A transceiver in his console powered up, satisfied itself with his credit balance, and tendered payment to the subway company.

Approaching the train platform, a small flash of bright muddled colors caught the corner of his eye, and he was hit with a wave of familiarity. On the ground was unmistakably the crumpled form of the rainbow butterfly he'd carried on his shoulder the day before.

It seemed impossible. Arcadia's various biomes were separated into their own climate-controlled compartments, connected only with climate control vents and isolation archways. These archways provided a barrier allowing some parts of the city to be rainforest, and others to be cool and dry. They, along with the tiny flying shepherd drones, kept the creatures living in the nearby habitats from wandering into dangerous places like the underground. Except, for this butterfly, they failed twice.

A pang of sorrow overcame him, not for a single dead butterfly, but that something so unique and splendid was trampled over by inattentive passers-by on mundane errands. It was just an insect, yet he could not shake the feeling that the world, and his view of humanity, was lessened in some immeasurable but significant way. He gently scooped up the butterfly's body and placed it in his shirt pocket. He would bring it to Vaux Park that evening and bury it by the fountain.

The mag-rail train hovered in and he found a seat. He watched the stragglers rushing to get on before the doors sealed, relieved that the butterfly was safe from the further ravages of their uncaring feet. The doors whisked closed and the subway car jarred into silent motion.

He stared at the sparkling floor of the train car, a molybdenum-rich alloy magnetically annealed in hydrogen to protect the passengers from the powerful magnetic fields which floated, propelled, and stopped the train.

The train zipped along. Soon, the subway tunnel below Lafayette Street cast a diffuse orange glow into the car, causing the floor to reflect like a topaz. Each subway station had its own color: bluish violet was Savickas Street, while Jennings Avenue was a rich green hue. Halfway in between the two stations, the tunnel would be a deep teal representing the midpoint between the colors. An experienced rider, Foxwright could tell purely from the ambient color where in the city he was, and how close he was to the next stop.

As the train hurtled forward, he studied the butterfly, noting how all the route colors in Arcadia could be found within its wings.

Dead Drop

FOXWRIGHT STEPPED off the train onto the emerald-colored platform of the Jennings Avenue Station. The instructions from Pentridge were quite specific in terms of what to do, but not why. As the train unloaded, he loitered around the platform until the crowd thinned out. He watched the stragglers, but they seemed too self-absorbed and inattentive to be working for Pentridge.

Making sure no one saw him, he ducked into the station's secondary access tunnel. This circuitous passage was used only during festivals, sporting events, and other large happenings that attracted big crowds. Otherwise its exit to the streets above remained locked, a dead-end route from the platform.

Glazed yellow and red ceramic tiles covered the floor, relics from when the City was a much different place. A painted mural, now yellow with age, advertised that "Servitor, your on-the-go virtual assistant, is now available in over 3,000 languages!"

As he approached the far wall, long-dormant audio-video elements activated within. A digitally-rendered woman appeared in a field of sunflowers, extolling the virtues of Sunrise-brand antidepressant perfumes. A disused sprayer pump coughed a burst of dust into the air, its fragrance reservoir long since dried up.

He advanced slowly until the next wall display came alive, its impregnated concrete phosphors showing a still ad for an extermination service until a swarm of insects emerged from behind the screen borders, skittering randomly and noisily across the virtual surface of the wall.

Bugs! He hated the damn things. Usually he made an effort to ignore dynamic ads, and for good reason: behavioral psychologists had spent centuries perfecting attention-grabbing techniques, and to stop and stare into such an ad was to put your mind in their hands. Often the result was merely a game of skill or an enjoyable optical illusion. But sometimes the ads seemed to reach deeper into the wiring of the oldest parts of the human brain, implanting emotions as this one did, and he did not like unknown parties dinking with his organic programming. Yet, ignoring them was not always possible: some would track the eyes of passers-by and flash colors and blared sounds until they were given due attention. The worst of them used facial recognition to access what was known about you to generate the ad you'd have the hardest time ignoring.

The third display was an anachronistic housewife hawking gourmet kosher hams, now with newly-reformulated SimuMeat™. This was the spot indicated in the cryptic instructions. He solidified his console, told it to search for other consoles, and pressed it against the old concrete wall. He inched it further down the passage, passing a vertical seam in the concrete, then a second, then a third. Now he moved it slowly up the wall, paralleling the seam. When it reached a spot just above his head, it vibrated. Having caught something, its peer-to-peer light was now flashing. A console or other computing device had been buried in the wall for use as a dead drop, onto which the select few who knew of its existence could store and retrieve files.

His console prompted him for an authentication key. He began entering the long alphanumeric sequence from the message. It was a challenge to type with one hand while keeping the device elevated enough to stay in range with the other. Soon, his arm started to cramp. He supposed this was exactly the point: a passerby deep in his own electronic business would never get close enough to this device's very short-range signal to discover its presence. Still, he surely looked quite strange in this pose. In a rare moment of self-consciousness, he glanced around, and at last appreciated the strategic placement of this data drop: he was out of view of every one of the aging security cameras in the tunnel.

Foxwright double-checked the sequence carefully to avoid having to repeat process, and hit enter.

Somewhere out of sight, his passcode was verified and a transmitter began streaming data. He kept the console pressed to the wall for what seemed like ages, until at last it buzzed to indicate completion. A warning flashed on the screen: deactivation of the other device was imminent. It would now turn off, perhaps forever entombed in the wall. "This message will self-destruct," he thought with a hint of amusement. Whomever Pentridge was, he was paranoid. But then, when someone was blowing up entire blocks of the City, it was a good time to be paranoid.

As per the last of the instructions, he decrypted the file using the supplied password sequence, and then re-encrypted it with a password of his own. Now the data would be secure even if someone intercepted and decoded the message that brought him here.

Time for some electronic privacy. No less importantly, it was also time for a beer. He boarded a train headed back to the Financial District and settled in for the ride, his mind a buzzing hive of questions which seemed only to be multiplying.

Hungry Marley's

A PEELING MURAL painted on the worn brick wall of an ancient office building marked the street-level entrance to Hungry Marley's. The building itself was a magnet for Traditionalist tenants who'd kept it in a timeless state, an oasis of anachronism in the otherwise state-of-the-art Financial District. The words "Good Food and Drink" were emblazoned across the mural just above the face of a giant besnouted man with flaring horns of twisted hair on a backdrop of yellow. The man's mouth was impossibly agape, and between his upper teeth and the step that formed his lower lip was a pair of dark wooden doors. Foxwright pulled a weathered handle, revealing a narrow staircase sloping down into the guts of the horn-haired swine-man and the City itself, giving him the sense he was about to be digested.

At the base of the stairs, an antique wood floor stretched out with drunk-abused wooden tables and battered chairs to match. The koa wood bar, oil-polished to a liquid shine, gave the bar a soulful warmth and made the imaginative part of him think he could dive right into it. Carvings of angels and devils adorned the wooden shelves of dusty bottles on the back bar, relics from a time when technology was expensive and man-hours cheap. The majestic stained glass lamp that normally hung over the pool table was strangely absent.

Marley's was the Financial District's first and finest Retro pub. A rarity in this District, the establishment was painted and wallpapered with materials that blocked electromagnetic waves from getting in or out. Bar tabs were cash on the barrelhead (a fan of literality, Prexy kept a barrel up by the bar), or with a monthly bill when creditworthiness allowed. For those with emergencies or whose connectivity habits died hard, a single phone terminal could be found in an ancient booth in the back.

Arcadia was a city of information addicts, endorphin-addled rats pounding buttons for another dose of news and social updates. In many ways, it was no way to live. To Foxwright, Marley's represented the ideal compromise between the no-tech monasteries in the hills above the City, and the chaos of being constantly within reach of, well, everyone. It gave shelter from the constant firehose of data flooding streets and offices above, refuge from the speeding machinations slowly eroding the sanity of even the devoutest technophiles. Times were strange indeed when one visited a drinking establishment to escape addiction. Then again, there were plenty of enjoyable things to get addicted to there: Hebridean scotches, Bahamian rums, and, of course, Prexy.

Prexy sat in her usual spot behind the bar gate, legs crossed, deeply engrossed in a bound copy of something called *The Bon Vivant's Companion*. She was a pale-skinned redhead, and an utter knockout at that. She appeared to be in her mid-thirties, although some of the regular drunkards theorized she was much older given her street smarts and cynicism. Rumor was she lived in an apartment upstairs of the bar, but despite dozens of valiant (and hundreds of not-so-valiant) attempts, no patron had ever beheld the fabled site.

Today she wore a knee-length houndstooth pencil skirt and a violet dress shirt that was open at the top. "Hey, Foxey," she said without looking up. "The usual?"

He grunted assent.

"Care for an apple-carrot?" she asked, her emerald eyes drifting to a plate of red sticks. "It's about the only fresh produce left on the store shelves."

He grimaced at the fruits, or vegetables, or whatever they were. "It's just not sporting to eat food that never had the ability to run away from you at some point in its life."

She shook her head. "Is it true you're working an impossible case? One that's already lost?"

News traveled fast, even among those who shunned connectivity.

"Thanks for the vote of confidence."

"That's not what I meant!" She looked like she wasn't sure whether to be annoyed or sorry. "I heard you've got an innocent guy in prison. Can that happen?"

"No." He'd spent his life assuming this. Yet, the reflexive speed of his answer betrayed doubts rising from the edge of his consciousness, moving straight toward its center.

She studied him as she dispensed a syrupy orange concoction into a bulbous glass. The beer's lively bittersweet taste masked its 20 percent alcohol content, although on workdays the murky brew was best enjoyed in singular doses.

He sipped the barley wine and sighed. "Thank you, my liquor angel. You're all that keeps me going."

The comment was met with a smile. He collected his drink and moved to a table in the back corner beneath a sign which read "In Vino, Veritas." Prexy took the cue that he was here to work and returned to her reading. It took several tries to get his console to lay flat on the uneven surface of the table. By god, even the furniture in this place was militantly luddite!

He began decrypting the archive retrieved from within the wall of the subway station. Full decryption would take several minutes. He drummed his fingers on the table. This data had better be worth the lengthy subway ride. He'd already been jerked around enough by Pentridge.

His terminal hummed as the files appeared. The archive seemed to include a wide variety of data, from technical specifications to schematics to decades-old informational videos on the theory and repair of the fabricator model at the heart of the case. The final file was entitled "READ ME." He opened it:

Mr. Foxwright,

No doubt you are already aware that the fabricator used to manufacture the explosive device was a Quentronics Model 66X. The 66X was one of the very first household fabricators, and somewhat unique in having only minimal built-in safety protocols. Quentronics' management team feared liability suits resulting from fabricators with out-of-date safety routines being used to make grenades, nerve gas, or any number of other hazardous products. So, rather than trusting the fabricator dealers and authorized technicians to keep safety protocols updated and within specifications, fabrication requests involving volatile substances were sent to a centralized safety server for approval.

Presently the Quentronics 66X is a rare model for one reason: if the fabricator's network connection goes down, the 66X can't get approval to make anything, and it shuts down. Consequently, consumers avoided the model; few were sold, and fewer still survive today.

Quentronics closed its doors decades ago, and safety requests from its surviving products now forward to the Fabrication Safety Administration for approval.

I hope the attached schematics and specifications are of use to you as you defend Mr. Rainville. I believe he is guilty of nothing. Yet, there are even more important matters at hand: the true perpetrators must be brought to justice so this madness can finally end.

-Pentridge

PS - Please do not mention me, or this communication, to anyone. Your silence will ensure that I can continue to provide assistance in the future.

Foxwright scowled. Who was this Pentridge character? What madness was ongoing? And if Pentridge knew the real perpetrators, then why not come out and just say who the hell they are?

Perhaps Pentridge was keeping him ignorant to more effectively manipulate his actions. He did not like being a pawn in someone else's game. Still, technical data spoke for itself, and it was his duty as Rainville's attorney to follow up on this lead. He would review the attached materials, verify their legitimacy, and come to his own conclusions regardless of Pentridge's motivations. If Pentridge was working some angle, Foxwright would not be his puppet.

"Prexy, some coffee, if you please," he said. His interest piqued, he dug into the mass of documentation. Getting paid to learn new things was the greatest perk of his profession. Still, the crypto-archive contained thousands of pages of technical literature. It was going to be a long evening.

Cold Justice, Part II

"Homicidal dispute, though prevalent, is made less frequently in many Eskimo groups by recourse to regulated combat.... In buffeting, the opponents face each other, alternately delivering straight-armed blows on the side of the head, until one is felled and thereby vanquished. Butting accompanies the singing in the song duel in Greenland. The singer, if so inclined, butts his opponent with his forehead while delivering his excoriation. The opponent moves his head forward to meet the blow. He who is upset is derided by the onlookers and comes out badly in the singing. As juridical forms, boxing and butting are more regulated than feudalistic homicide, since the contests are announced and occur on festive occasions where they are looked upon as a sort of sporting performance before the assembled community.... Whatever the facts underlying the dispute, they are irrelevant to the outcome. The man who wins, wins social esteem. He who loses, suffers loss of social rank....

Wrestling serves much the same function, though it may have a more deadly outcome in Baffinland and Labrador, where the loser may be slain by the victor....

Deserving of fame are the *nith* songs of the eastern and

western Eskimos. Elevating the duel to a higher plane, the weapons are words—'little, sharp words, like the wooden splinters which I hack off with my ax.'

Song duels are used to work off grudges and disputes of all orders, save murder. An East Greenlander, however, may seek his satisfaction for the murder of a relative through a song contest if he is physically too weak to gain his end, or if he is so skilled in singing as to feel certain of victory."

E. Adamson Hoebel, "The Eskimo: Rudimentary Law in a
Primitive Anarchy," *The Law of Primitive Man*, 1954

Prey

RAINVILLE WAS in the lunch line the first time he witnessed a murder. A pack of nearby Cossacks crossed paths with a gaunt, bug-eyed man slinking across the Trough. He was a Lolly, from the House composed of convicted sex offenders and other outcasts no one else would accept. A House without allies.

The fights Rainville had seen back in Arcadia all had a sort of standard formula: provocation, then escalation, then violence, until it finally got broken up by onlookers. Wychwood's formula for violence did not have all these elements. Violence did not require any provocation at all. And no onlookers broke it up.

It began as a bullying sort of game: a tall Cossack with grimy dreadlocks pushed the Lolly into a short, blocky Cossack with spiked hair. The second Cossack shoved the Lolly back even harder, causing him to cry out. Other Cossacks took notice, and joined in launching the man back and forth between them using hands, shoulders, and elbows. Finally, the Lolly stumbled. The deadlocked Cossack kicked him squarely in the face as he fell.

Blood poured from the Lolly's nose and mouth. He spat out a broken tooth. "Guys, please," he begged, "I don't want no trouble with you. Lemme alone? I'll do anything." He managed a smile through the pain. "Anything you want!"

At those words, the Cossacks were upon him, beating and kicking and stomping, the Lolly's skull clocking against the concrete until a pool of blood radiated out beneath him like a supernova.

By the end, the body was unrecognizable. Rainville did not eat that day, nor most of the next.

Settling In

EACH DAY DRAGGED into the next, and Rainville's hopes of awakening from this nightmare faded like a dying sun. He'd never felt so alone. What were his lawyers doing? Did they have any leads on the evil son of a bitch who bombed Arcadia? The lack of information was agonizing. Had they given up?

There were so many small things he'd never realized he would, or even could, miss from his former life. Things like drinking decent coffee, watching the news, and eating decent food had suddenly and irrevocably vanished from his life.

The nights in Wychwood were the hardest. There was nothing to do but lie there and think. He missed Vyanna: her face, her voice, the curves of her body, and her spontaneity and energy. Each night he would close his eyes and relive one of their dates. The rainstorm in Vaux Park. Going for a wagon ride and bobbing for apples in the Retro District. Playing *oware* in the Ashanti Biome. Laser ice sculpting in the Yukon Biome. There was a very real chance he'd never see her again, never talk to her, never hold her. Was there even a point in finding ways to pass the time here, waiting for some day of freedom or reunion with Vyanna which might never come? There was an emptiness within him that nothing seemed to fill.

He took to reading late into the night, starting with novels from the Omegas' meager library. Yet, most of the characters had such comparatively simple problems—twenty-first-century characters wallowing in the traumas of their comfortable childhoods, a twentieth-century family driving west whose car keeps breaking down, nineteenth-century gossip-girls obsessed with social status and finding a husband, even a legless man trying to murder a whale—that he found it hard to get immersed. At last he discovered a book about ancient mythology.

Societies of people once worshipped archaic gods who kept the universe running. Mortals were sometimes chosen by these deities to take on challenges meant to shape and temper them. The ancient people saw this transformation as a gift from the gods. But he wondered if the protagonists were not mere pawns forced to become stronger just to survive, and the gods no more to thank for this than a disease was for the immunity acquired by its survivors. He also read about Tartarus, a deep, dark abyss far beneath Hades itself, used as a dungeon of suffering and torment for mortals who crossed the gods. He wondered what god he himself might have offended.

He dove deeper and deeper into the stories, finding solace in the travails of these epic characters and not wanting to drift off to sleep and meet another day in this savage place. Getting only a few hours of sleep inevitably made the next day more dangerous, since it would be harder to stay alert and on guard.

R&R

"SO, about what I was gonna ask you the other day," said Boudreaux. He'd become a fixture in the workshop over the last week, and Rainville welcomed the company. "What sorta stuff do you fix?"

Rainville yawned and looked down at his current project. "Besides busted music players? Anything from interactive books to weight-loss belts to vidslingers to sex toys. And those, only if we've got plenty of bleach in the supply room." He used the bleach on nearly everything, so fearful was he of the prison's various diseases. The chemical left the skin on his hands red and cracked.

"You couldn't pay me enough," Boudreaux snickered. "What about ... more exotic things?"

"Exotic how?"

Boudreaux did a lap around the workshop, and then poked his head out the door to check the hallway in both directions. When he returned, his voice was barely above a whisper.

"Communication devices."

Rainville stared in disbelief. "You're kidding, right? Where would anybody get something like that?"

"I'm not saying I have one. I'm saying, I'd like to. I know enough about electronics to know that if you can fix stuff, you can build stuff too. That's right, isn't it?"

"Depends what you're wanting to build. And it sounds like you've got a tall order."

"I've been thinking about just how nice it would be to have a console in here. Or at least, the voice communications part of one."

"I'm not sure we'd have a wireless signal here."

"Arcadia's only a few miles away. Think about it."

Rainville was thinking that Arcadia felt much farther away than anything that could be described in mere miles.

He pictured his old console, sitting in an evidence locker back in Arcadia, its power cell long-dead. In his mind, he disassembled it, making note of each of the parts.

"Some of the components would be easy enough. Display, speakers, mic, that sort of stuff. But we'd need a long-range transceiver. Not really the kind of thing you find in a vidcaster or a kitchen appliance. And cryptographic chips to let us open a secure tunnel, otherwise we'd get discovered a few seconds into the first call." He shook his head. "Unless you got a source for those items, just keep on dreaming."

"I know some people in the Guild. You should know them too."

"Those cafeteria food guys?"

"The Guild sells a lot more than spoonfuls of slop, if you know how to approach them. You speak Hayax?"

"Only enough to order a bowl of *harissa* from a food stand." A pidgin version of the Armenian tongue, Hayax was primarily spoken by grey market merchants and street vendors in Arcadia's poorer quarters. "The Guild guys don't speak English?"

"Oh, they can. But you'll be charged more, and trusted less."

"You don't look particularly Armenian."

"My third stepdad taught me. We used to talk that way, pissed my mom off something fierce when she couldn't understand us. He was a decent guy." Boudreaux's ever-present smile wavered. "Not like the others. Bitch cheated on him, so he left her. Left us." He looked away and cleared his throat. "Tell you what, come to the roach games and I'll introduce you."

"Roach games?" Rainville repeated the words slowly. He was unsure of their meaning, but aware of a creeping sense of distaste.

The Trough

THE NEXT MORNING, Rainville met Boudreaux in the Trough. The chow line was its usual slow march toward a dubious reward.

Rainville scanned the room, still in awe of the vastness of the prison. There had to be over a thousand men seated around him. It was the middle of the breakfast shift; how many more men had been here earlier this morning and left?

"Looking for someone?" asked Boudreaux.

"Just wondering how many guys there are in here." He'd asked various Omegas and never gotten the same answer twice.

Boudreaux rubbed his chin, then shrugged. "Hard to keep a count. Nobody tells the administration when people are cast Out, and I guess they like it that way since it keeps the official population of our beloved facility high, gets 'em more funding. Meanwhile, anyone who's Outside isn't using prison resources anymore. Not that they tend to live very long after that."

"What do you mean 'Outside'?"

"Outside." He shrugged. "You know, Outside! The City of Souls!"

He assessed Rainville's blank stare before continuing: "That's what they used to call the cemetery outside, since it's big enough to be a city, and has enough, ehh, 'residents' for one too."

It suddenly made sense to Rainville: all the times people had mentioned people going "Outside," this is what they'd meant.

A loud voice rose behind them. It was Weirdbeard, the religious fanatic from his first day at Wychwood. Close-up, he was even stranger than Rainville had realized. He wore a tapestry of fragments of prison uniforms from different eras, all sewn together. The bright colors made the man hard to miss. The asymmetry of his facial hair was jarring. It began as a mustache that spiraled down around the left side of his mouth only, traversed his chin, then joined with a solitary sideburn on his right cheek. His beard trailed down to his belly, ending in a grey wisp. "...for the Universe is not some vast, vacuous space filled with stars. No! The Universe is all of us. We are an integral part of it, just as leaves are part of a tree. We are its senses. Our eyes are how the Universe perceives itself. Our hands are how the Universe acts upon itself."

The old man caught Rainville's eye. "My son, we are all chosen to do our part in the workings of the Great Machine. We must not complain. We cannot avoid this duty, just because it is distasteful, just because it is wrought with challenges." With a wink, he continued up the line, now pontificating about the insidiousness of unintentional sins.

Despite himself, Rainville pondered the idea of the universe as a machine with living, interchangeable parts.

Boudreaux shook his head. "Fucking Weirdbeard."

At last they made it to the front of the line.

"Can't I just meet the Guild now?" he whispered to Boudreaux.

"These guys are just flunkies." Scruffy frowned at him from across the reservoir of gruel; today it was thin grey fluid containing curds of, well, something.

"Gruel again," mumbled Boudreaux. "Always goddamned porridge for breakfast."

Scruffy's frown became a glare. Bowls of glop in hand they made a quick escape for the Omegas' side of the room.

Their course took them past a table of Cossacks, and their steps quickened.

"You got with an old woman?" a tattooed man with a handlebar mustache asked another with an uneven mohawk.

"She weren't wrinkly on the inside!" came the reply.

Rainville wretched, but quickly masked it with a cough. Fortunately, it was drowned out by raucous laughter from the table. He wasn't sure which was more vile, this place or its people. Nor did he know whether the place had corrupted its residents, or the people their place.

It was a great relief when they reached the serried ranks of the Omegas.

"Did you hear that?"

"Trying hard to forget it," said Boudreaux, shaking his head. "How old are you, Gridley?"

"Nineteen. You?"

"Twenty-three. Most of the guys here are way older. I been here two years. Was on probation for burglary, and then got done for assaulting a cop. My conviction was a real nice twenty-first birthday present."

Boudreaux was indeed the first Omega he'd met who was around his own age. "Sounds like a barrel of monkeys," offered Rainville.

Boudreaux's brow rose and he held up a finger, which he turned in a circle. "This place is on-the-job training for monkeys, you know."

"Is it? Would be nice to learn a new skill."

Boudreaux nodded and his speech grew more rapid. "Before men went into space, they sent animals. Dogs and monkeys and shit. Launched them into space, knew they'd never come back ... well, the animals didn't know. Anyway, when they were training animals for the mission, they'd make 'em stand still for long chunks of time, make 'em wear uncomfortable suits, just so they'd get used to it. Then they kept moving 'em into smaller and smaller cages, to get 'em ready for riding in a tiny space module. And the whole time, they fed 'em fucked-up food that kept them from having to shit."

"This grub don't keep me from shittin'," said Braxler from down the table.

"You're right," said Boudreaux. "Come to think of it, offloading it is the best part of this goddamned food."

Rainville laughed hard, so much that his side hurt. It was a feeling he'd sorely missed. He took a bite of the grey sludge, which was somehow even blander than it looked. Would he ever get used to it? Maybe it was easier for guys who'd been here longer, with no recent memories of the flavorful spices of Arcadia's ethnic cuisines. Salt and pepper just weren't enough to fix food this shitty.

Across the vast room, the chow line surged and men stumbled as a lanky man with tattooed arms and neck barged through the line. "Quit, Tyrus!" bellowed a voice behind him. "I'm done chasing yeh!" The gap in the crowd widened to reveal a huge Cossack, tattoos covering every square inch of his face. Black spikes of ink radiated out from his eyes, flames appeared where his eyebrows should have been, and on his cheek was the image of a severed human arm.

"He had it coming, Rahm. Honest, he did."

"S'pose he did at that, Tyrus." Rahm smiled and seemed to relax, although none of the fierceness left his eyes. He moved closer to Tyrus, whose back now touched the table. "Had it coming from me. Yeh stole my kill." In a flash, Holder lunged forward into a vicious head butt. It connected with a sickening *thuck*, and Tyrus collapsed on the floor.

Rahm got behind him and formed his arms into a triangle around Tyrus' neck. The man flailed weakly against him, but it was no use.

Another struggle for dominance. Did these Cossacks ever rest?

Tyrus' eyes grew wider. His face turned red, then crimson. At last, he fainted dead away. Rainville watched, willing the man to release his savage grip, but he did not. As if on command, the other Cossacks began turning, and soon all had their backs to the scene. Conversations at tables around the room went quiet. Rainville averted his eyes. There was nothing he could do to stop it without getting himself killed, but he would not willingly watch a man die.

After a very long few moments, Rahm let go of the still form and walked out of the room. The other prisoners gave him a wide berth.

While most of the Omegas looked on, Boudreaux had his eyes closed, strain evident on his face. Perhaps he'd not yet been fully assimilated by the despair of Wychwood. It gave Rainville some hope for Boudreaux. And for himself.

"Looks like an internal matter," said Boudreaux at last in a low voice. "Bright side," he forced a chuckle, "one less Cossack."

The body remained on the floor, no one coming to claim it, people just walking around it to get to the food line. Rainville pushed his food away from him. The other Omegas' lack of reaction sickened him as much as the killing. He let out a long sigh, releasing the breath he hadn't realized he'd been holding. He had to get the hell out of here. To get back home. Even if it killed him.

"How do you do it?" Rainville asked in a low voice before he could stop himself. "This place, I mean. How do you survive in it?"

"There's no magic rule. All I can tell you is the obvious stuff you already heard, or figured out yourself. Watch your six. Try to blend in. If you walk around, real cocky-like, someone will decide to put you in your place. You stop watching your back, or stop respecting people, and you'll wake up dead."

"I guess what I meant was, how do you keep at it, day after day without ... dying inside?"

Boudreaux chuckled but there was no humor in his smile. "It's what you might call an acquired skill—it takes practice. You gotta find stuff to look forward to. Like your next meal, or your next hot shower. Or like the roach games tomorrow."

Rainville sighed. "Not those." He'd had enough of this place, of these people, for one day. For longer than that, actually. "Isn't there any other way to meet the Guild?"

"It'll be fun. Trust me."

"Why?"

"Why will it be fun? Or why should you trust me?"

"Yeah."

Boudreaux grinned mischievously. "The games are something you just have to experience for yourself."

That night, Rainville envisioned what it would be like to have a console in his cell. Even if it wouldn't get him out of here, it would be a lifeline to sanity, to civilization. He imagined using it to call Vyanna, what things he'd say and how she'd respond to each, until he drifted off to sleep and even after.

Winners and Losers

THEY CAME to the roach games early to get seats with backs to the wall, yet without being in a corner. Even this defensive position did not put Rainville at ease. Outside Z Block, every decision was a tactical one, and the adrenaline from being on guard made it impossible to ever relax. He scanned nervously around him. Should he have simply refused Boudreaux's suggestion and spent the night in his cell? No. He would not give up his only chance to talk to Vyanna, to his lawyers, to his father, just to indulge his fear. If a console were a possibility, he would take whatever risks were necessary.

The Professor was already seated nearby, and Boudreaux waited until the man's attention was elsewhere. "Gonna see if I can't track down a certain member of the Guild," he whispered. "Hang back 'til I make contact." Raising his voice, he continued, "The Prof here can bring you up to speed on the game."

The Professor smiled broadly and began to fill Rainville in on the finer points of insect cruelty. As he explained it, the inmates leveraged the prison's cockroach infestation, elevating nuisance into sport. Yet Roach Hockey was more than just a sport; it was the social glue that united dysfunctional extended families, and kept some semblance of peace in a place always on edge.

According to the Prof, the ingredients were simple: a medium-sized room with a smooth floor and two opposing doorways for goals, and as many of the antiquated prison-issue brooms as there were players. The rules were also simple, with just one prohibition: a player could not step on the cockroach.

"You place the broom down on top of the cockroach so it's trapped inside a miniature forest of bristles," he said, mopping a bead of perspiration from his neck. The topic of launching the insects clearly excited the Prof. Knowing what other kinds of things excited the man, Rainville found himself unsettled.

"Then you execute a quick flick to sweep the broom as swiftly as possible." The Prof held his wrists out as if gripping an imaginary broom and turned them crisply. "The cockroach has a smooth exoskeleton, so its speed across the floor is limited only by your technique."

"Umm...interesting."

"Isn't it?" asked the Professor. "I've missed it, having not been to a game since, well, I think the day of the Big Bang."

"The Big Bang?"

"Yes, my boy! I suppose that was before you joined us. You see, there was a very loud bang just a few months back that shook the ground as an earthquake, but only for an instant. But then, you were a free man at the time, so you would probably know more about it than us. Did something happen in Arcadia?"

"Umm...yes, in Arcadia. A...power generation research facility, it exploded. It took out half a city block."

If Pulsipher had asked Rainville this question while painted with lie-detecting lipstick, it would have been the end of his secret. Probably the end of him as well.

"Are you okay, Gridley? You look rather pale."

"Uh, sure. It was just a bad accident, that's all. It killed twenty people. And, a dog, also. It was really sad."

"I see," said the Prof. Rainville was not sure whether he did.

The players took their positions in the center of the room. "So why doesn't the cockroach just run away?" asked Rainville, eager for a topic change.

"Well, the fresh ones do try," said the Prof.

Rainville suppressed a shudder at the turn of phrase. He could only picture the Prof chasing after a terrified young woman. Someone like Vyanna, perhaps. He thought about approaching Boudreaux, leaning low to speak to a short man with dark arm hair seated near the front. Still, he didn't want to disturb their meeting, and moving away from the security of his seat could be risky.

"When a fresh roach collides with a wall, it will be stunned, and that's when you can line up your next shot. After a couple of seconds, he'll be up and running again, and you can't, I say again, you cannot step on him." The Prof explained that, whether intentional or by accident, such a fault was cause for ejection from the game. Being a goalie thus required a unique temperament, and many a goalie had lost a Roach Hockey game for his House by letting instinct take over and stepping on the skittering "puck" to stop it. Convicts, as a rule, did not excel at impulse control.

Feet screeched against concrete and bodies moved around as two Houses squared off.

Rainville's heart skipped a beat as clanging erupted from a pan hit with a large spoon, and play ceased. He channeled his fear into indignation. "What the hell happened? They only just started!"

"A foul. Someone stepped on the puck, so his team loses a point."

"But people were running everywhere! How can they tell which person stepped on a little bug?"

"It's easier than it sounds." The Professor waved a finger at a man selling used-looking disposable cups full of bathtub beer. "You simply find the little splotch of protoplasm that the cockroach leaves behind where it got squished. There will be a matching spot on the bottom of the offending player's foot. His team loses a point."

Sure enough, an official was called in. A disheveled man entered the field. He had a frizzled beard, and one of his eyes seemed permanently closed.

"That's Winky. He's the referee tonight."

Winky knelt down to floor level and carefully inspected the scene. He sniffed at the goo and poked at a small brown piece residing therein. Rainville averted his eyes.

"Just a loose leg, no foul," Winky declared.

"Limbs come off all the time," the Professor offered cheerfully. Rainville suspected he was not referring only to the cockroaches. He glanced sideways at Boudreaux, still deep in conference with the Guild member. Why had Boudreaux dragged him to this disgusting spectacle?

The pan clanged again, and the men rushed toward their wiggly and unwilling objective. The scraggly referee dove out of the way, barely avoiding becoming a splotch of his own.

"Has anyone ever escaped from Wychwood?" asked Rainville.

"Planning on checking out of this fine establishment so soon?"

"I'm only asking."

The Professor gave him an appraising look. "In all honesty, I have no idea. Inmates have said they were going. Saved up supplies, then went Out into the wilds of the old cemetery to try their luck. No one has ever come back."

The beer was handed down the row of seats. Rainville stared helplessly at the uneven color of the frothy drink before passing it to the Professor. "So they didn't make it?"

"I didn't say that," the Professor said. "But once you go Out, you're not allowed back in." He slurped at the brown foam atop his beer. "Being Outside changes a man: it turns him wild. Living in a cemetery, there's no real shelter from the elements, so they haul out the corpses and sleep in their tombs. On top of that, there are all types of ungodly diseases that the Outsiders have gotten from their cannibalism, and from even worse activities that, to put it frankly, we're not willing to risk bringing in here."

Rainville wondered what could be worse than cannibalism.

The Professor picked a speck of something solid out of the drink, gesturing broadly with it toward the mob of bodies on the court. "It would be fair to say that cockroach has a better chance of surviving than any of us would Outside."

Thock! A slapshot sent the roach crashing into a nearby wall. A shrill laugh like broken glass rang out. Braxler. Seated nearby, he giggled maniacally at the little insect's latest misfortune.

Rainville almost found himself relating to the bug. He'd never felt farther from the sanity and safety of Arcadia.

"THEY'VE AGREED TO A MEETING," said Boudreaux. "How'd you like the game?" The players had already left the arena. They didn't exchange handshakes with the opposing team, but Rainville supposed not physically attacking each other was its own form of sportsmanship after the heated battle.

He tried to hide his disgust but a frown forced its way through. "It was too hard to see the puck—I mean, the roach."

"You were watching the game?" Boudreaux laughed. "The real show is watching the critters watching the roaches!"

Rainville thought of the Professor, nearly salivating as he looked on. His thoughts were interrupted by the approach of the man Boudreaux conferred with earlier. He had a thick beard, and a piercing stare which was only accented by his dark eyebrows.

"Gridley, meet Hovo," said Boudreaux.

The man looked Rainville over appraisingly. *"Inchpes yen dook?"*

Rainville hoped it had been a greeting. He smiled uncertainly and nodded. Boudreaux rescued him with an incomprehensible reply, and soon the two men were exchanging long streams of tightly-packed syllables.

He agreed to taking on a few special projects for the Guild each week. They would approach Pulsipher to officially clear it with him. Off the record, the Guild promised Rainville certain favors to keep him motivated. Extra food from the Trough. Discounts for him and Boudreaux at a place called Tomorrow's Pardon that lay somewhere in the prison complex. And help with some hard-to-find items that might make his existence more pleasant.

To that end, Rainville made two requests. First, he asked for the missing parts for his console project: a transceiver chipset that would let him receive wireless transmissions from Arcadia, and a cryptography chipset to be able to make sense of them. Second, he asked for an assortment of spices and chili powders to help give the institutional food here some actual flavor.

"I think this calls for a celebration," said Boudreaux. "Tomorrow's Pardon, later this week. What do you say?"

"What's Tomorrow's Pardon?"

"Right. Why would you know? Roachie's too much of a cheap-ass germophobe to ever go there. It's the prison nightclub."

"There's a nightclub inside Wychwood?"

"You bet. It's open a couple nights a week. And in Roachie's defense, it is expensive. But now we've got the friends-and-family discount, so you should come check it out."

"I don't leave the Z Block much. Not at all, really, unless it's absolutely necessary."

Boudreaux nodded. "I was the same way when I got here. I spent the first six months scurrying from one place to the next like a mouse. I'd buy two meals whenever I went to the Trough so I could stay in my cell the rest of the time. But that's dangerous, too. Maybe even more dangerous than being outside the Block."

"Dangerous?"

He nodded. "In the long run, that sort of fear makes you weak. Guys here can smell it. Most of the other Houses won't mess with Omegas, but the Cossacks might just kill you for sport if you don't show enough backbone. Bottom line, you only get as much respect as you demand."

"I guess."

"We can meet up with some friends there. Safety in numbers, that's the rule. Trust me, you'll be fine. I go there once a week, and never came home with anything worse than a fat lip."

Rainville did not want a fat lip. But things were looking up, and the idea of breaking out of the endless monotony of his routine, of actually seeing somewhere new, made his heart beat faster.

Tomorrow's Pardon

THE ITEMS RAINVILLE requested were delivered within forty-eight hours. These Guild characters didn't mess around.

He got to work on the console immediately, always keeping a half-finished Omega repair project nearby in case Mahara dropped by to check on him. Configuring the transceiver depacketizer would take hours, but he could sandbag at least a few of today's pending repair jobs. One of the advantages of being the only person in Z Block who could fix stuff was that no one could really second-guess his efficiency. At least, he hoped this was true. The hours flew by as he worked; he'd almost forgotten the joy of working on one's own projects.

As evening approached, Rainville asked Braxler if he wanted to come along to Tomorrow's Pardon. His reply was less than assuring: "Too expensive, and I'm too damn old for that kinda crap," although he must've sensed Rainville's fear and paused before adding: "If you get shivved, I'm keeping your shit. And if you bring home any diseases, I'm going to shiv you myself, and then keep your shit."

It was a joke. Probably.

At the designated time, Rainville followed Boudreaux hesitantly out the Z Block gate. They proceeded down a short flight of stairs to twisting and turning passages manned every few hundred yards by pairs of armed men.

"Who are they?" he whispered.

"Guild guards. Making sure people can get there safely to spend their money is good for profit margins."

"Wish they put as much effort into the gruel as the guarding."

"I'm almost glad I'll be skipping tomorrow." He yawned.

"No breakfast?"

"Been pulling double shifts on guard duty. Got another one tomorrow starting at dawn."

"Twelve hours? I didn't realize they gave double shifts."

"Jaxx traded me a shift for three pairs of socks." He slipped off a shoe. "See? No holes! Been catching much duty yourself?"

"Not really. I can do two or three repairs in six hours' time, and trade that for someone to cover my shifts."

"Lucky. Guarding'll bore the balls off a brass monkey."

Maybe he'd call in one of his guard shift IOUs tomorrow from the breakfast crowd and give it to Boudreaux, so the guy could grab a nap.

A dull throb in his core, like a second pulse, interrupted his thoughts. It mirrored the thumping bass beat from the club, echoing down the corridor. Past the remains of an old guard's kitchen, above a "Cinema —>" sign, was a large hand-painted sign that said "TOMORROW'S PARDON." Depicted below the words were an old-fashioned jail cell with the door swung open, and a prisoner with angel's wings taking off into the sky.

The Tomorrow's Pardon nightclub was set up in what remained of a small prison movie theater-turned-courtyard, formed when a roof repair job failed or was abandoned. The walls were braced plywood, and the torn corrugated metal ceiling gave way to a starry sky. Having spent so much of his life inside the dome, Rainville now wondered at the vast maelstrom of stars, so plentiful in some places it was hard to tell where one ended and the next began. He could only envy the pre-dome generations, who needed only to glance upward to see such beauty.

The dark courtyard swirled with shadowy figures gyrating to the primal beat. A pudgy man nearby danced by himself, moving from one end of the dance floor to the other like a frenzied ping-pong ball. Beyond him, a couple swayed against a wall in the corner.

The music was unfathomably loud. Patrons' lips moved but Rainville heard only the pulsing beat. Boudreaux recognized a friend; he shook hands with the man and they were soon laughing. He introduced Rainville to the man, whose name was Kedzie or something close to it.

Rainville strained to follow their conversation. Communicating meant yelling directly in the other's ear to be heard, and so keeping up proved impossible. At last he felt like a third wheel and sat down at the bar, a series of solid metal doors stacked on sawhorses and lit by caged task lamps. He recalled Braxler's warnings about germs and tried to put some space between himself and the other patrons.

"What'll it be?" yelled a lanky bald man with few remaining teeth over the din of the dance rhythm.

"What've you got?" he shouted back.

"Got beer. Got Rotgut."

He probably shouldn't drink. It would be bad to let his guard down outside Z Block. "Rotgut," he heard himself saying. The clear liquid bore the aroma of fast-acting adhesives, and contained fine bubbles of carbonation that gave a strange bite even beyond the kick of the alcohol. He grimaced, swallowing hard as his eyes momentarily went out of focus.

The song ended. His ears rang in the quiet. Suddenly, a series of subhuman howls echoed over the prison from somewhere Outside. The bar patrons stopped moving, stopped speaking until the chilling calls subsided.

The bartender held a finger up, and the drunks around the bar yelled "Shut the fuck up!" in unison as if it were the customary practice. "Damn Freakies," said the barman, shaking his head. The patrons smiled nervously at each other. Rainville flashed back to a childhood visit to the zoo when his friends took turns taunting a caged lion. The simmering ferocity of the lion's gaze seemed to transcend its cage. It was a look which said: I will settle this score, and I will end you. It was a look that had never completely left his nightmares.

Unnerved, he swiftly ordered another Rotgut. He sucked down the first half with only minimal gagging at the noxious beverage. He'd only had two drinks, but they were strong, and he wasn't much of a drinker.

To his relief, the music started up again. He took a breath, and discovered something that made his heart catch. Vyanna.

Or, rather, her perfume. She was beyond reach now. Wasn't she? Yet, between the scent of carissa and frangipani flowers, the rhythmic trance of the music, and the darkness, he was adrift and could not but question such absolutes. He pounded the rest of his drink. Grimaced. Then turned toward the source. Behind him stood Margaretta, the Sister from his first visit to the Trough.

"Hiya, sugar!"

"I was just leaving."

"You can spare a minute." She pushed him back down on the stool and sat down next to him. "Besides, you look sad." She made a circular motion with her finger, and the bartender poured two more glasses of Rotgut and set them on the bar.

"Look, umm...ma'am," he said, grasping for the right noun, "I can't buy any more drinks, I'm all out of money." It was true. He hadn't planned on drinking anything, let alone moonshine of questionable origin that was overpriced even after his discount. "And, I don't mean to be disrespectful, but I only swing one way, if you catch my meaning."

She laughed. "Baby, relax. I'm not here to make you do anything you don't want to. Is that a rule we can both agree on?"

He smiled politely and nodded. Having a drink with Margaretta would probably not kill him.

"So, why the long face?"

"Do I need a special reason? Besides that I'm in prison?"

"No, you don't. But for now, that's where you are, honey. And that's not gonna change tonight, or next week, or even next month." She sipped gingerly at the Rotgut, unfazed by its harshness. "It's like that prayer for serenity, you know the one? 'The grace to accept the things you can't change,' and all that jazz."

"I guess."

"I've been here a lot longer than you, and seen lotsa things that were hard to bounce back from, so ... I ought to know." She took a large swig from her glass. "Let me tell you something: the only one who controls how you feel here is you. I don't care if someone beats you half to death, you don't gotta get mad, or depressed, or anything, unless you decide to let yourself feel that way. That's a freedom no one can take away from you, not even in here."

He wondered if this was why Margaretta always seemed upbeat, or if she was just acting, playing the part to cheer up her customers. Maybe she'd stopped even knowing the difference.

The song tapered off. There was another silence, thankfully devoid of howls this time. A new track came on, this one slower and with less gut-shaking bass.

"Ooh! This is my favorite song! Will you take me up for a quick dance? Please, Gridley?"

"Umm, I'm sorr—"

"Humor a girl," she said, grabbing his hand and pulling firmly. "I won't charge you anything. Besides, you owe me for the drink."

"Really, I'm not much of a dancer—"

"Come on, you look like you need it. Just one dance. If you're worried about your friends, don't; it's too dark for anyone to see us anyway." She dragged him further into the shadowy courtyard, where it was too loud to make himself heard, resting her head on his shoulder before he could resist. She pulled him closer, but to his relief, not too close. He could see nothing in the darkness, and finally just closed his eyes. Inhaling deeply, he let the scent of the perfume wash over his mind. A part of him could not deny that it felt good to be embraced by someone, anyone, after so long without any human contact. Margaretta swayed with the music, and swaying with her seemed the path of least resistance. A moment later, he found himself simply dancing, and not worrying about anything else.

The song quietly faded. Margaretta looked up at him. "Thanks,

honey, I—" she said before she began to cough. The sound was deep
and throaty. Masculine.

The illusion shattered, Rainville snapped out of his reverie. He
pulled away. "The pleasure was all mine. Now, I'm sorry, Margaretta,
but I really do need to go. Have a nice evening!"

He sprinted out of the club, his ears full of whitenoise in the quiet
hallway. He walked quickly back to Z Block, fully aware of the dangers
of traveling alone at night, and thankful for the guards in the corridors. Finally, in the open air of Z Block, he caught a trace from himself
of Vyanna's perfume.

There was no reason to shower tonight. Or maybe even tomorrow.
Maybe the other guys would smell perfume and give him shit for it at
breakfast, but it was worth the risk.

For the first time since arriving at Wychwood, he slept soundly. In
his dreams, it was Vyanna he was dancing with, back in some other
time and place when Wychwood was just a nasty word.

Slumber

"YOU GOT IN LATE, SUNSHINE," came Braxler's voice from the bunk below.

Rainville grunted in response. He remembered his cellmate's warnings about Margaretta, and about catching diseases, and was immensely glad Braxler hadn't been there.

"I'm heading to breakfast. You coming?"

In reply, Rainville hopped out of bed and began getting ready. Had Boudreaux seen him with Margaretta the night before? The guy was on guard duty, so they'd pass by him on the way to the Trough soon enough. Maybe he'd offer him a guard shift IOU right away to minimize the chances of a razzing in front of Braxler.

As they approached the inner gate, something was clearly wrong. Two men who weren't Boudreaux were now stationed on either side of the door. Just beyond, Mahara was speaking softly to Boudreaux, who had his back to the wall. Over Mahara's shoulder, he flashed Rainville a glance of thinly-veiled terror. Mahara gave him a gentle slap to bring his attention back and continued his speech.

Rainville drew closer. He now saw that Mahara held a large blade to Boudreaux's chest. He gripped it between his fingers with precision, like a writing implement.

"You sleep on job, you betraying me. You betraying all of us."

"I'm sorry. You can be sure it will never happen again."

"You right," said Mahara, nodding. "Is guarantee."

"Never," agreed Boudreaux, smiling weakly. "It's a guarantee."

In a flash, Mahara's arm twitched into motion. The blade went forward and back in a blur, with the wet sound of tearing flesh. He moved with the mechanical regularity of a pulse motor. He'd delivered half a dozen strokes with the knife before Rainville even registered what happened.

Boudreaux slumped to the floor as Rainville ran to him. He looked up, his eyes wide with fear. He opened his mouth to say something, but only managed to cough up some blood.

Rainville tried to think of ways to help, but came up empty again and again. The men around him only stood by; Braxler and the guards out of fear, Mahara with the satisfaction of a man admiring a job well done.

An instant later, Boudreaux's eyes lost focus.

He'd barely taken his last breath before Mahara bent down over the crumpled form, using the dead man's own shirt to wipe the blood off his blade.

FTP

OVER THE NEXT WEEK, Rainville barely slept. Controlling his emotions grew more difficult with the resulting fatigue. Reliving the killing was like a fever he would slip in and out of at unpredictable times as images of the Boudreaux's brutal demise haunted his thoughts.

Being trapped here, waiting for his life to elapse, was karma. For never giving those incarcerated here a second thought. For thinking of course they were guilty of horrible things, or they wouldn't have ended up in prison. For all the shitty little things he himself had done over the course of his life—a petty theft here, a stupid prank there, garnished with deceit and fakery when necessary to get the job done. For being cruel to his father while they were both mourning his mother. For wishing Dad had died instead, a preference he'd declared loudly at her funeral.

It was a ragtag list of misdeeds, and rationally, he wasn't sure if any of those things warranted a life spent in this place. But how rational was the alternative, that his suffering was completely arbitrary and purposeless?

What had Boudreaux done to end up here? Burglary, he'd heard. Did such a crime warrant being brutally murdered? His mind would not stop searching for sense in the senselessness, latching onto patterns of causality that weren't there, reading moral consequence into randomness. Wasn't the whole point of the justice system to establish determinism, to have moral cause and effect? He obsessed over this question, yielding a sort of despondency that could not be shaken, only covered up.

Why hadn't he arranged for someone to pick up Boudreaux's early shift as soon as he got back from the club? That one simple action would have saved the man's life.

Boudreaux had been the youngest member of the Omegas besides himself. He'd thought maybe they could be close friends, but the idea, like Boudreaux himself, died a piece at a time with each brutal thrust of Mahara's blade.

He would make his own justice. He would build a weapon to kill Mahara.

For the first two days, it seemed the only acceptable goal, and indeed he thought of little else.

On the third day, it dawned on him that his sights were set too low.

He would do what Boudreaux had asked him to. Come hell or high water, he would build a console. He would use it to call Vyanna. To call his lawyers, his father, and the rest of the outside world. And, just maybe, to get out of here entirely. And he would leave Mahara and all these other savages behind to rot.

Fuck them all. And fuck this place.

Outside

AT MIDMORNING, Mahara came soundlessly into the workshop. By the time Rainville looked up, it was nearly too late. With a frantic flick of his wrist, he slid the circuitboard for the console underneath the remains of a broken helmet from a sleep neuroprogrammer. He grabbed a soldering iron and stuck it against a capacitor on the Gauss pistol he was supposed to be working on.

Mahara stopped before the workbench, nodded curtly, and with a sniff, placed his hand on Rainville's shoulder.

Rainville recoiled at the touch. He despised everything about this man he worked for. He stared at the disassembled pistol. How good it would feel to use it on Mahara, to magnetically accelerate a few metal spikes through his skull.

In a flash, Mahara grabbed the soldering iron from Rainville's grip. He twirled it, jamming it into the flesh of his own palm.

"You are smelling burning of flesh, Gridley?" He sniffed theatrically. "You are seeing blistering of skin?"

Rainville was silent. Words could only betray his hatred, his fear.

"No," finished Mahara, "because iron is cold." He smiled. "Solders better when turned on." He raised the iron above both their heads.

With a thrust, he stabbed the pointed tip deep into the workbench next to Rainville's hand.

His voice was a hissing whisper. "I understand. You are sad for friend. Friend who failed us. But you are falling behind on Omega repair. You not fail us too. New Guild work not excuse. You get head together, or head go missing from shoulder. Am I making an understanding?"

His memory of the man butchering Boudreaux would not fade; he saw it again and again when he closed his eyes at night. There was no choice here.

"I understand."

RAINVILLE HAD ARRANGED his daily life assuming he was safe as long as he remained in Z Block. This assumption was a lie. He wasn't safe anywhere. His own cellblock was its own kind of deathtrap.

Escaping the workshop was not enough. He went back to his cell and tried to relax but could not even bring himself to sit. He walked the entire length of Z Block, but it felt hardly less confining. He needed to get the hell out of this building, with its rooms and hallways that grew smaller each day and made him feel buried alive in a maze of concrete. Open space and fresh air seemed like the only things that might keep him from going insane.

"Braxler."

"Huh," came a discombobulated voice from his cellmate's bunk. The man had obviously been dozing off.

"Is there a prison yard?" He'd been so successful at cloistering himself that he didn't even know the answer. "I want to go for a walk. I need to."

"You wouldn't like it, on account of it being outside of Z Block," Braxler mocked.

"Stop fucking with me. I'm going nuts."

"Wide hallway on the north side of the Trough. Ain't much, but it's got a ball court and some weight machines."

Beyond the Trough he found the hallway, and at its end, a short unshaven man with brown teeth sat beside a table. He was flanked by men recognizable from the chow table in the Trough. Behind them was a wire-reinforced glass door that in years past had been smashed into the oblivion. Daylight streamed through the glass, forming tiny rainbows in its myriad of cracks and chips.

"Is this the way out?"

"Whaddya think?" He snickered. "Exercise'll cost ya five bucks."

"I just want to get to the yard, that's all. Not lift weights or anything."

The man's eye twitched, but there was no other reaction. "Five bucks."

"I'm Gridley. I do repair work for the Guild. For Hovo."

"I know who y'are. Free yard access ain't part of your deal."

"I only want to see it." Paying money for the privilege of standing outside was hard to stomach. He squinted at the broken glass but could not see through it. "I've never been, and I want to see if it's worth it."

"You're a little slow, assclown, so I'm gonna explain it one last time. Whether you just step out, or work out, or go all the way Out into the boneyard, it's five. If you don't like it, you can go back the way you came." The man jerked a thumb toward the hallway back to the Trough.

Rainville's heart pounded. His legs felt like tightly-wound springs. He couldn't face going back to Z Block, let alone his cell. He paid.

He'd unconsciously assumed the prison yard would be full of green grass and fresh air, maybe even a tree or two. But it was just a long, narrow expanse of concrete slab with block walls on three sides. Inmates from various Houses were grouped around the yard's meager amenities, lifting rusty weights, playing games, and socializing. The sky was overcast, and as grey and featureless as the cement. Most striking was the stench. It was indescribably horrible, like everything that smelled bad in the world had been put into a single garbage pile and then left to rot. He looked around, but could see no source of the stench.

He was outdoors, under the open sky, for God's sake. There had to be fresh air out here somewhere. In the distance, he saw traces of green, and moved toward it. He walked down the length of the yard, suddenly aware of his aloneness as he circumnavigated groups of prisoners from other Houses.

At the far end of the yard, the block walls ran up against old stonework enclosing a massive pair of wrought iron gates. Growling stone gargoyles flanked the gates, their faces eroded by centuries of chemical rains and now frozen in what seemed like silent screams of agony. Atop the arch was a marble capstone engraved with the letters "WYCHWOOD CEMETERY." So this was it: the exit from the prison building. The entrance to Outside. Behind the gate lay a sprawling necropolis. Beyond that, he imagined, were towering walls crawling with armed guards who made sure no one left Wychwood. The thought made him shudder.

The door back into the building banged open as two burly men emerged carrying the limp figure of a third. All three had the cleanly shaved heads of members of The Chosen, the House that occupied R Block. If the Trough was the hub, R Block was located down the opposite spoke from his own Z Block. The two men half-carried, half-dragged the third across the yard, before finally setting him on the ground before the arch.

A large key was inserted in the lock, and the gate hinges squealed in unearthly protest. The shrill sound brought Rainville's focus to the stone gargoyles, and for a moment they seemed to come alive.

The Chosen picked the man up off the ground. He awoke and began struggling. "I didn't steal it! I was gonna put it back. I swear! Please. No! Not Outside!" The man was babbling now. "Not the Freakies! I don't deserve this. I don't. Freakies'll tear the flesh from my bones!" He threw his weight to the left and to the right, but the men held him tight.

"You know the rules, Fitch. You break 'em, and Out you go," said the first man.

"I'll do anything! Please, anything you say. Just don't do this!"

"If we give you a pass," said the second man, "we'll be joining you out there. Sorry. It's nothing personal."

The man screamed as if on fire as they shoved him through the opening, and the gates slammed shut behind him.

The man begged and pleaded as the two Chosen walked briskly back across the yard without looking back. "Murderers!" he bellowed as they disappeared into the building.

Shouting unintelligibly, the man threw himself into the gate, pulling at the bars. His face was bruised, one eye swollen shut while the other was wide with panic. He clawed at the lock mechanism until one of his fingernails ripped off. Undeterred, he flailed at it until his motions left a bloody trail on the gate handle.

Rainville's own fingers pulsed with a dull, vicarious pain. Acid built in his throat. He turned away and swallowed it back down. He had no power to help this man, and throwing up would be a sign of weakness. He walked back into the yard, stopping at the ball court. He tried to focus on the game, but could not get his mind off Fitch. Whenever he looked back, the man was there, sobbing, yanking futilely at the gates.

By the time Rainville went back into the building, it was nearly sunset and the man's pleading had only grown more frantic.

Late that night, horrible screams could be heard from outside the prison. The sound was accompanied by rising howls. The man called Fitch was not seen again.

The Ashanti Needle

"The problem of evidence in Ashanti disputes...could also be met with recourse to ordeal in criminal cases other than oath perjuries. It was used primarily in witchcraft and adultery cases in which there were no witnesses. Ordeal was never imposed upon the defendant by the court but could always be requested by the accused. One form was to try to pass a needle through his tongue three times. If the needle failed, he was guilty. The other was ordeal by poison. On the request of the defendant, the man who had accused him was required to buy a large quantity of poisonous *odom* bark. This was steeped to form a brew, and after certain ritual preliminaries the man drank 'potful after potful' of the vile stuff while his relatives anxiously exhorted him. The brew either nauseated him or began to take effect. Naturally, if he vomited, he would not die, and he was judged innocent. If, on the contrary, he showed signs of dying, the executioners rushed forward and chopped off his head. After all, a man must not be permitted to commit suicide."

E. Adamson Hoebel, "The Ashanti: Constitutional Monarchy

and the Triumph of Public Law," *The Law of Primitive Man*, 1954

Digging In

FOXWRIGHT SPENT the morning studying the evolution of fabrication technology, starting with the earliest devices resembling toasters, which used heat to shape round plastic wafers into plates and bowls, sterilizing them at the same time. However, the polymers eventually became too saturated with food grease to be reshaped and reused. The dwindling profit margins of fast food megacorps drove them to pioneer a more versatile and elemental form of recycling: the fabricator. The first real fabricators could form various polymers into nearly any shape desired, be it a plate or a bag or a sandwich box. Consumer appliance companies stepped in, and soon designs were no longer limited to plastics. Within a few short years, entire buildings had been successfully fabricated, piece by piece.

By evening, he was watching fabricator repair training videos for the Quentronics 66X, learning about its components and firmware. The long-deceased instructor had been a master repair technician at Quentronics for over thirty years. He presented the material in an easy-to-understand way, and although the man's long-lapeled glowsuit was stylistically as obsolete as the machine he was teaching his audience to repair, Foxwright found himself kind of liking the guy.

And so went his days and nights for a full week, and then another.

His knowledge of fabricator theory and operation grew by leaps and bounds. As he came to understand it, the impediment to fabricating isotopes was not a scientific problem, but a bureaucratic one. Residential fabricators were blocked from making volatile substances by safety protocols. Numerous levels of protocols, in fact. Even laboratory-grade fabricators required explicit authorization for each request to formulate an isotope.

Pentridge was correct. The Quentronics Corporation feared its earliest customers would modify or sidestep the fabricator's safety protocols. There would be product liability if a consumer managed to kill himself, or far worse, neighbors who'd never even seen the Quentronics bootup warnings and legal disclaimers that guarded them against lawsuits. Even one such incident could cause consumers to believe fabricators, still in their technological adolescence at the time, were fundamentally unsafe, which would destroy future profits. And thus, Essie's 66X had minimal native security protocols, deferring instead to a safety authorization server operated by Quentronics, and later the Fabrication Safety Administration when Quentronics went defunct.

Rainville had defeated the fabricator's meager built-in safety protocols, but any requests for radioactive substances from a private residence would still get turned down by the FSA's server. Any attempts to bypass the check would result in a hardware lockout, which would disable the fabricator entirely.

The FSA should have stopped things cold, before a weapon of mass destruction could ever be fabricated. Why hadn't they?

"Trixy, open a port to the Fabrication Safety Administration," said Foxwright.

"Stand by," she chirped.

Due Diligence

THE FABRICATION SAFETY ADMINISTRATION was headquartered in a stark rectangular block of a building at the edge of the otherwise-vibrant Bohemian District. The exterior of the building was even plainer for lack of any windows above the street level.

Large glass doors in the front were etched with the FSA's seal, tiny blocks coming together to form Rodin's sculpture of *The Thinker* within the links of a chain. The chain and *The Thinker* split in half as the doors retracted to admit Foxwright.

The lobby was utilitarian—lots of straight lines and bland colors. A handful of indoor plants did little to liven things up. At the security counter, a solemn young man demanded his credentials and the purpose of his visit.

"Foxwright's the name," he replied, "and I'm here to solve a mystery." He mashed a button and his console transmitted an authenticated message from the Judiciary Executive explaining that he was part of an active criminal proceeding and should be afforded access to any and all evidence which may be relevant to said proceedings.

"I'm forwarding your request upstairs. Someone will be waiting to meet you on the ..." The uniformed man tapped away at the desktop, on a virtual keypad visible only through his glasses. "One hundred and tenth floor," he said after a few keystrokes.

A long elevator ride later, Foxwright entered a small, sparsely-decorated office. The woman behind the desk motioned for him to sit. Her hair was mousy brown, but styled with spiraling tresses. Atop elegant cheekbones she wore networked holographic glasses flashing a variety of streams across multiple levels of varifocal lenses. She'd forgone data implants, which he respected.

She looked bored. He wondered how she'd look if she smiled.

The nameplate on her desk said "Greynolds." "Miss Greynolds, is it?"

"No." She picked up the nameplate and deposited it in a desk drawer. "Mr. Greynolds is out today. My name is Remla. Identity?"

Foxwright flashed biometric credentials across his console.

"Address of your query?"

"21200 Cicero Street, Unit 8246. It should all be in the request data I provided downstairs."

"Subject's name in there too?"

"Should be. If not, her name is Essie, and I can transmit her biometric ID."

At the mention of the name, the woman's boredom dissolved. She lifted an eyebrow. "Is this about the bombing?"

"Yeah. So what's your theory, Remla?" he asked, hoping she'd raise her eyebrow again.

"Having theories is above my pay grade. I'm just a file jockey. I lock down files, put them in escrow, maintain the chain of custody, and spend my days talking to lawyers like you."

"Oh, my ... ever consider vaporizing yourself?" asked Foxwright, half-seriously.

"Several times a day," said the woman, her lips curling with the hint of a smirk. "Dates in question?"

"I would hope one wouldn't be out of the question."

Swing, and a miss. There was only silence.

"Umm ..." he continued, "let's start with the year leading up to the blast."

Her slender fingers danced around the touchscreen and macros triggered and multiplied her movements a hundredfold. He watched the blur of data flying across the table before them. Her data glasses picked up on the results and augmented them with supplemental information. Her skills were quite impressive for an evidence technician.

"Here we are," she said. A few more finger taps. "Not much activity here. Not even false positives, like you sometimes get on the chems in household cleaners. Are you sure you've got the right serial number for the fabricator unit?"

He brought the relevant file of notes up on his console and read off the serial number.

"That's the one," she confirmed. "Is there a second fabrication unit in the residence? Perhaps it was mistakenly omitted from the judicial query. That happens sometimes, when it's a large residence with lots of occupants, or when someone's got an old backup model collecting dust." She studied him as she spoke. Was she looking for a certain reaction? Or was it something more?

"Nope, just the one old lady living there, and she didn't even know how to use it. Says she only owned it because her husband installed it shortly before he died."

She shook her head, tresses swaying beneath her chin. "There's nothing here. Not a single hazardous material authorization request from that address. Might it have been earlier?"

"No. It was definitely this year." Things were making less sense by the minute, and he found this annoying. "How can a fabricator produce radioactive, city-detonating isotopes without your agency even knowing about it?"

"It couldn't," she said, shifting in her chair. "Totally impossible." She stared at the data a moment longer, her eyes dancing between the screen and her data glasses. The glasses seemed rather advanced for simple navigation of an evidence database. "FSA's safety servers receive an authorization request, and would need to approve that request and send back an encrypted, authenticated response which allows the replicator to proceed."

"Most of the safety protocols on this fabricator were disabled, if that would affect your answer."

"It doesn't. Even if you had completely disabled all built-in safety protocols, any requests for radioactive substances from a private residence would get turned down by the Administration servers. Any attempts to bypass that, by hacking or otherwise, would result in a hardware lockout, which would disable the fabricator entirely."

"What if I disconnect the fabricator from the network, so it couldn't ask your server for permission?"

"It would go into lockout, and be totally inoperable until you reconnected it."

This matched what he'd learned in his research. "OK. So the request got sent. What if your servers glitched?"

"Impossible. Each request is processed by five duplicate servers in separate locations, running in lockstep. If their authorization responses don't all match, the fabrication request is rejected."

"What if someone hacked your servers?"

"Again, impossible. The servers are behind a firewall that only lets fabrication authorization requests in, and responses out. And they run read-only code, so they're immune to viruses, trojans, or other malicious modifications. Furthermore, the server log entries are write-once. If a request happened, it's in here, I assure you."

His annoyance was growing. He did not try to stop it; he was at his best when pissed off. "So you're saying the impossible happened. Unless you've got some alternative suggestion? Hey, you know what? I've got one: what if the server code was modified by a disgruntled FSA employee?"

She straightened her posture but did not acknowledge the comment. "Maybe we could try expanding your search," she offered. "Here, I'll revise the date parameters and we can search, say, five years prior." She typed, scrolled through data, typed some more, scrolled again. "We've got a request for protoxide of nitrogen here in January of last year, common name: laughing gas. The request was denied, as it should have been. And then psilocybin, a recreational hallucinogen, the preceding December. Also denied."

"Fine. Any isotopes?"

Her fingers tapped away. "Well … no." She scrolled through a log, then another. "I'm just not finding anything. Sorry we could not be of more help. Perhaps your client is less innocent than you realized? It may be worth considering." She was studying him again, he was sure of it. Wondering, perhaps, if he knew something she didn't.

"I thought theories were above your pay grade."

She showed no reaction. "Is there anything else we can do for you today?"

"Let's recap: fissionable nuclear material appears to have been made in a fabrication unit within your agency's jurisdiction. And yet you have zero damned record of it. And zero explanation. Is that about the size of it?"

She straightened up again. "I think I'd better escalate this matter to my superiors." She began typing.

"Yes, I think that would be a good idea," he said, now standing. "Have them contact me, while you're at it."

His frustration did not diminish on the return elevator ride. He'd done his best to put a swarm of bees in the agency's bonnet, to let them share the pain of this mystery. The woman, Remla, had been hard to provoke. He wished he'd been more successful at raising her ire. Yet she could not ignore his visit, and perhaps some interesting facts would shake loose during the agency's ensuing flailings. Still, he had no illusions about how government agencies worked: they would stonewall while they did their own internal investigation, and any bits of truth that surfaced would only be reported if they helped the agency avoid accountability.

He had no answers, and this case was not getting simpler at all.

Calling

"CALL FOR YOU, SIR," chimed Trixy.

"Who is it?"

"Unknown caller, sir."

"Hell. It's barely daytime. Don't people have any human decency?"

"Evidently not, sir. Should I patch it through?"

He was not yet dressed. "Audio only," he said.

"Mr. Foxwright?"

"The one and only." He rubbed his hands through the stubble on his cheeks, arching his back in a stretch.

"This is Remla from the FSA. We met yesterday."

Damn it. He pictured her face and wished he could've said "video." "Did we indeed?"

"Let me begin with an apology. I wasn't being entirely honest with you during your visit."

"You don't say."

"Mr. Foxwright, I'm trying to extend an olive branch here. I could be fired for even talking to you outside of official channels."

"Please continue."

"I do indeed work for the FSA, but I am not an evidence technician. My role is … more in the realm of oversight."

"Management, then."

"Of a sort. I've been looking into the Rainville matter, and not just since your visit yesterday. I must admit I've come across some puzzling things."

"Why come to me?"

"Because my research has hit a dead end. With your client in prison, the Director is satisfied that the agency's public relations liability is contained, and he's put this investigation on the back burner."

"What does that mean?"

"Eventually, some policies may change, safety practices made more restrictive. But the way it's headed, we'll never learn the truth. Frankly, that doesn't sit right with me."

"And you trust me?"

"We both know that going to the media and blaming the FSA won't free your client. He's already been convicted. You have nothing to lose by sharing the truth with me. In exchange for your research, and your discretion, I will attempt to further your independent investigation in whatever way I can. How does that sound?"

"Cautiously intriguing."

"Good. I was hoping you could provide some additional insight into what happened. That's why I sat in for Mr. Greynolds yesterday."

"I'll require information in return."

"Perhaps we should start over, then. We can meet. Discuss things a little more honestly this time."

"Fair enough," he said. "Your place or mine?"

"Neither," she said. "This needs to stay off the radar, at least until it's more clear what is going on."

"In that case, I know just the place."

Full Disclosure

He arrived at Hungry Marley's at noon, but saw no sign of Remla as he descended into the bar.

"What'll it be, Foxey?" Prexy asked. "Coffee?"

"No thanks, I'm already far more awake than I'd like to be."

"How about an ancient Lagavulin, then? Neat?"

"You know me better than my own sister, Prexy."

"That's because you have consistently poor communication skills, but consistently good taste in beverages."

"True, although I'll officially admit none of it."

Prexy looked all business today, wearing a white collared shirt and a knee-length skirt, but her sex appeal soared when she climbed up the rolling ladder to the scotch library behind the bar.

"So how goes the war?" she asked from the upper shelves.

"Oh, like most wars. Lots of death and destruction, with a healthy dose of lingering resentment and hurt feelings." It was worse than hurt feelings: a hint of doubt had begun smoldering at the edges of his mind, threatening to flash into an inferno if considered incautiously. He tried not to think about it lest it take flare and spread uncontrollably. His entire vocation seemed suddenly on thin ice. If the justice system could produce such an unjust outcome in this day and age, then what the hell had he devoted his life to? Meanwhile, unless he could get Rainville exonerated, Arcadia would never realize the extreme danger that was still out there, perhaps already planning another mass murder.

Prexy grabbed a green bottle, folded one leg against another, and slid down the ladder in a slow burlesque move. Scattered applause echoed from down the bar from the regular afternoon stragglers.

"Anything I can do to help?" she asked.

"Can you do that ladder trick again?"

"Maybe a little later, when the crowd thins out," she said with a wink. "You here to work again?"

He nodded. "Gotta meet someone. A woman."

"Just when I thought you were all work, no play."

"You might as well go back to thinking that. She's a technical specialist. She is helping me with a case."

"That remains to be seen," came a voice behind them. Remla stood by the pool table. She was tall, even taller than Foxwright. Her glasses seemed strangely clear today, revealing deep green eyes.

"You found the place," said Foxwright.

"I can't seem to get a signal down here," she said, her speech moving rapidly as she tapped the rim of her glasses to no avail. She removed the glasses and retrieved a console from her pocket, dark grey with deep orange highlights when the light hit it just right, like cooling magma. She shook her head.

"That's part of the charm," he said. Prexy gave a satisfied nod.

"I see," Remla said with a puzzled look. "Well, I can't say I'm comfortable without them. Still, perhaps it's for the best."

"Prexy, this is Remla. She'll be our honored guest for the next couple of hours. Treat her as you would me."

"Foxey, the only other person I treat that poorly is my wasband."

"Wasband?" asked Remla. She glanced reflexively to her now-absent datastreams before her face took on a resigned, quizzical expression.

"As in husband, but in the past tense."

Remla laughed. "I can see why you favor this establishment, Mr. Foxwright."

"Would you like a drink? Or an appetizer menu?" said Prexy.

"I'm not allowed to drink," Remla answered.

"What are you allowed to do?" asked Foxwright.

"You don't want to know," she said.

Foxwright swallowed.

Prexy smiled and raised an eyebrow.

"Well, Mr. Foxwright, time is wasting. Shall we begin?"

They secured a booth in a deep alcove lined with rough stone walls in the rear of the bar. Prexy kept up a steady supply of snacks and tea while Remla brought him up to speed.

She was part of a group that audited security practices within the FSA. She'd begun an investigation into Essie's fabricator shortly after Rainville's apprehension. She presented what little she had in the way of factual information: that the FSA was aware that an illegal fabrication had potentially led to the manufacture of a weapon of mass destruction, although no records of the fabrication request could be found. She'd personally conducted audits of the fabrication authorization server hardware and software, and investigated FSA employees with access to same, and it had all come back clean.

She was impressed by the thoroughness of Foxwright's documentation. He walked her through the key pieces of Quentronics literature, some of which she hadn't seen before, and she contributed her own analysis.

By mid-afternoon, Foxwright reached an undeniable conclusion. Remla had been telling the truth about the safeguards against unauthorized editing of fabrication server safety protocols. The same was true of the security of the logs of all fabrication requests received by the agency. Given the sheer number of failsafes, traversal of these protective measures by a handful of disgruntled FSA employees was a long shot.

But the alternative was an even longer one: that someone somehow intercepted and decrypted the safety request from Essie's fabricator, then spoofed and encrypted a proper approval response. The decryption was the part that strained credulity.

"Could the encryption be cracked?" Foxwright asked.

"Theoretically, yes," Remla said. "But if the fabricator didn't receive approval of its safety request within a few milliseconds, the encryption key would expire. Any reply after that would get invalidated. And decrypting such a message that quickly would require unimaginable computing resources."

"I've got one hell of an imagination."

She looked up and her eyes met his. "It would take all of the computers in Arcadia, and then some, all working on the problem at the same instant."

"Is...is that possible?"

"As a practical matter, no. It's more computing power than even the largest R&D megacorporation could line up."

"Pretend it's possible. Who could do it?"

"I don't know," she replied, her brow furrowing. "That's what's keeping me up at night. But if there is somebody out there who can, we need to tread carefully."

"Carefully?"

"Carefully, as in, keep our investigation as quiet as possible. If this theory has any credence at all, you're talking about a powerful enemy, one who could bring those same computing resources to bear against you in less time than it takes to blink."

She was right. Some far more prominent parties would need to be added to their suspect list. He was suddenly glad they'd conducted this meeting in an off-net location.

Part IV

Probatio per Crucis

(TRIAL BY THE CROSS)

"When a person accused of any crime had declared his innocence upon oath, and appealed to the cross for its judgment in
his favour, he was brought into the church, before the altar. The
priests previously prepared two sticks exactly like one another,
upon one of which was carved a figure of the cross. They were
both wrapped up with great care and many ceremonies, in a
quality of fine wool, and laid upon the altar or on the relics of
the saints. A solemn prayer was then offered up to God, that he
would be pleased to discover, by the judgment of his holy cross,
whether the accused person was innocent or guilty. A priest
then approached the altar, and took up one of the sticks, and
the assistants unswathed it reverently. If it was marked with the
cross, the accused person was innocent; if unmarked, he was
guilty.

It would be unjust to assert that the judgments thus delivered were, in all cases, erroneous; and it would be absurd to
believe that they were left altogether to chance. Many true judgments were doubtless given, and, in all probability, most
conscientiously; for we cannot but believe that the priests
endeavored beforehand to convince themselves by secret

inquiry and a strict examination of the circumstances, whether the appellant were innocent or guilty, and that they took up the crossed or uncrossed stick accordingly. Although, to all other observers, the sticks, as enfolded in the wool, might appear exactly similar, those who enwrapped them could, without any difficulty, distinguish the one from the other."

Charles Mackay, *Extraordinary Popular Delusions and the Madness of Crowds, Vol. 1,* 1841

Religious Experience

RAINVILLE AWOKE EARLY. After weeks of scouring parts bins, junk piles, and scrapped electronics from his projects for the Guild, he'd finally cobbled together enough components to build a rudimentary console. He'd borrowed the packetizer circuit from a video storage device and painstakingly reprogrammed it to support rudimentary network protocols. The modulator circuits were adapted from an old television remote control. And of course, the transceiver and crypto chipsets he'd gotten from the Guild. The circuitboard was huge compared to that of a real console, but this prototype didn't have to be pretty or streamlined; it just had to work. The excitement of the project nearing completion made it hard to sleep the night before, and impossible to work on anything else now that he was so close. Now, at last, the device was powering up and initializing its memory circuits. Immediately he tried to get a signal, but with no result.

Damn it! He rechecked the antenna calibration. The protocol handshake code. The packet decoding logic. Again and again he tried, for four hours. His prototype searched for signals in his workshop in Z Block, the long hallway to the Trough, and even the prison yard, but could pick up no trace of a connection. He checked and rechecked his schematics, testing and retesting suspect circuits, but could find nothing obviously wrong.

Had the Guild given him bogus parts? Even with the crypto chipset turned off, his console could not establish the most primitive of wireless connections. Was the receiver broken? He found an old vacuum cleaner, a device notorious for its electromagnetic noise, and ran it near the receiver. The signals on his meter spiked accordingly. If the receiver could pick up wireless noise, then surely it could pick up a coherent wireless signal. The Guild's parts were not the problem.

Unless...it was as he feared. Wychwood was covered by some sort of dampening field to prevent wireless communication. Such a measure would prevent prisoners from orchestrating escape with friends from the outside world, but it also had the unfortunate effect of blocking more benign things like newsvids, or even (as he fantasized) messages to Vyanna. House bosses did seem to receive information from the outside world, but it came in very irregularly, presumably by way of corrupt guards. Surely men with their resources would already have access to a console if it were technologically possible.

How could he have been so naive? He should have surmised the impossibility of it. Or had a part of him known all along, but been unwilling to take any more bad news, unwilling to give up the tiny remaining hope that this project represented?

Could he boost the power of the transmitter, or the sensitivity of the receiver? With no idea how strong the dampening fields were, it was hopeless.

Feeling numb, he walked with Anx and Braxler to the Trough. The two men prattled about the dubious culinary merits of recent meals, but Rainville had no desire to speak.

No sooner had they arrived than a strange man seemed to recognize him, and approached. It was Weirdbeard! Rainville changed course in the hopes he was imagining it, but the man countered and soon blocked his way.

"Good morning, friend!" Weirdbeard boomed. "Have you found the joy that is a lifelong friendship with our loving God?"

"Umm, sorry, but I'm not—"

"Evil is ever at our heels! The Creator is the only one with the power to deliver us from the Darkness," he said, gesturing broadly around him without his eyes ever leaving Rainville's. "Have you found God, friend? Do you know," he continued, his voice growing ever-louder, "that He is waiting to welcome you into His arms?"

Before Rainville could answer, the man hugged him. The acrid smell of body odor assaulted his nostrils.

"Damn it! Get your—"

Weirdbeard's breath tickled his ear, barely a whisper. "Know that God is not the only one looking out for you." The man withdrew a few inches, clasping Rainville's hand in both of his.

Rainville felt something being pressed into his palm.

"Now, push me away," the man whispered urgently. "Act angry. Strike me, if you must."

Rainville was not sure what to think, but he did not want another hug. He gave the man a halfhearted shove. "Leave me alone, you freak!"

"As you wish," the man said, his voice returning to public address volume. "I'll pray for you, my brother! Go in peace." And with that, he vanished back into the breakfast crowd.

Rainville opened his hand just enough to see a folded piece of paper. He started to open it then caught himself. Its contents could wait for a time that afforded more privacy.

"Hey Gridley, l-looks like Weirdbeard t-took a liking to ya," said Anx. "Kinda like he wanted to, maybe, h-h-hug up with you for a c-coupla hours?"

Braxler smirked.

The paper crinkled in Rainville's hand as his fingers tightened around it. "Yeah," he laughed. "He wanted to know if I'd found Jesus yet. I told him, I didn't even know he was missing!"

Anx guffawed as Rainville slid the paper into his pocket.

They found seats at the edge of the long Omega table. This morning's meal was a bright orange stew of bland, rubbery vegetables that squeaked when chewed. He sprinkled the glop liberally with red pepper from his new stash. He carried the spices in his shirt pocket since receiving them from the Guild, a talisman of Arcadia civilization which gave him comfort to possess. He considered sharing them with the other men, but would not risk Mahara hearing about any personal rewards from the Guild.

At the far end of the table, a man named Thessalonika told a story about the time Mahara made a man eat an entire roll of toilet paper. The audience was rapt, but Rainville's thoughts returned to the strange encounter with Weirdbeard. He patted his pocket to make sure the message was still there.

When he was certain no one was watching, he retrieved the paper and unfolded it beneath the table. He stole glances at it between bites of food.

It read: "Break down the walls that are keeping your spirit from being free, keeping it out of God's empire! Ascend the walls of Jesus's teachings, craft a rope of bedsheets and tie it around God's love, and climb out into the freedom of the Kingdom of the Heavenly Father!"

It seemed to be a piece of a religious pamphlet. He turned the paper over, and found a handwritten note:

Thy Exodus will soon be at hand,
And this shall lead to Salvation.
Follow the Path the Creator has planned:
Meet thy fate at Charon Station.

When time is past, 'til 'tis four days hence,
And the dawning sun shines on upon thee,
Make thy way to the Station's entrance.
And there wilt thou finally be free.

The note made no sense. The Creator and Salvation and Exodus were obviously terms with religious significance. But Charon Station? His heart thumped. There was something more to the message than the ramblings of a crazy man. There had to be.

On the far end of the table, he caught sight of the Professor finishing up his meal. Unceremoniously dumping the remaining half of his breakfast, he ran to catch the Prof.

"Hello, my boy," said the Professor. "Was your meal satisfactory?"

"Uhh, sure. It was great. Say, have you ever heard the phrase 'Charon Station'?"

The Professor regarded him skeptically. "So you're back to planning an escape?"

"No. Why would you think that?"

The Professor shook his head. "You know, things may not be optimal here," he said, gesturing broadly around the Trough as he spoke, "but compared to the Outside, we're in a veritable Garden of Eden. Your chances of survival would be next to nothing out there. Even if you made it to the Station, it's been sealed for over a century."

"The Station is a real place?"

The Prof sighed, but in the end could not resist the opportunity to impart knowledge. "The cemetery which surrounds the prison was not always derelict. It is home to the remains of many hundreds of thousands of Arcadia's deceased, so you can well imagine the number of friends and loved ones who once made regular pilgrimages there. In centuries past, Wychwood Cemetery had its own subway station. People called it Charon Station, after the mythical Greek ferryman who carried souls across the river Lethe, from the world of the living to the afterlife. In that regard, I suppose Lethe Station would be more appropriate, and the train itself would be considered—"

"How far is it from here?"

"The subway stopped coming out here over a century ago. And from what I understand, the entrance was sealed up when they built the prison. Think about it. If it were still open, don't you think the residents Outside would simply ride on out of here, never to be seen again, instead of clawing each others' eyes out for scraps of spoiled meat outside the prison gate?"

The Professor had a point.

Rainville scanned the Trough's breakfast crowd for Weirdbeard, but found no sign of him. Perhaps the note was just the crazy ramblings of a zealot.

Crying Over Spilled Beans

A FEW HOURS LATER, Rainville was basking in the warm afterglow of a successful Gauss shotgun repair when Sticky entered with a bundle under his arm. He kept a close eye on the inventory whenever the little man came around.

"Nice gun, Gridley!" said Sticky. "Yours?"

"Nah, Mahara says I haven't been here long enough to rate a weapon."

"They don't want the newer fish picking fights with other Houses, I guess. Doubt it's anything personal." Sticky placed the bundle on the counter and unwrapped it. "It's called a toaster. Real antique!"

"No!" He shook his head vehemently. "Not going to touch that."

"Aww, come on, Gridley! It's not broke bad. Got me two slices of bread from the Trough. They're kinda stale, but I don't think that's what's wrong. I push 'em in there, see, but then get kicked out before they're ready. I think—"

Mahara rushed into the repair room looking agitated. Rainville recalled the last time Mahara showed emotion, Boudreaux at his feet, gurgling as blood filled his throat. "Gridley. Boss need to see you."

"Okay. I'll head over right after I lock up."

"No after! Is urgent!" He jammed a finger in the air toward the door. "You go now, Gridley. See Pulsipher."

He dropped his tools and dashed after Mahara who was already moving in a light jog. Hopefully Sticky would behave in his absence. What could be so urgent? Unless...Pulsipher had discovered that the Guild was giving Rainville kickbacks on the side. Z Block suddenly felt very cold.

Today the walls of Pulsipher's office were as dark and opaque as the man's expression.

"A situation has arisen. A situation which does not bode well for you, I'm afraid...Mr. Rainville."

Rainville. A strange coldness spread across his chest upon hearing his real name for the first time in months.

"What? My name is—"

Pulsipher shot him a look of such intensity that he did not continue his lie.

"How...did you find out?" asked Rainville.

"I got a message from a man I've never met, by the name of Pentridge. An enemy of yours, perhaps? Let's just say that the contents of his message left me without any doubts."

"It isn't true! I didn't do any of it. I—"

Pulsipher began speaking so quietly that Rainville had to silence himself to hear what the man said.

"This Pentridge said there will soon be a contract on your head. If Pentridge follows through on his threats, and the rest of the inmates hear about this contract, and your mass murder conviction ... well, let's just say that this facility is full of former Arcadians, with friends and relatives who live there still. Such a situation would quickly reach a boiling point. When you transferred here, I gave our mutual friends at Petronius & Sydra assurances that I would keep you safe to the extent I could. But that has become impossible."

"Surely there's a way." He tried for confidence but could hear the desperate edge in his own voice, betraying him. "It may not be easy, but a man in your position has the power to—"

"You would be a permanent liability. I'd have to expend considerable resources and manpower to guard you against every aspiring bounty hunter in this place. And when my men hear what you did, keeping them, shall we say, motivated, could strain loyalties and put my leadership at risk." His tone was as soothing as his words were devastating. "No, you will be leaving us, Mr. Rainville. Regrettable ... you're a fine technician, and anyone with the skills to rack up that kind of body count is a significant asset in my book. Yet, it simply cannot be done."

"My lawyers have money. I'm sure they'd be willing to pay you for the trouble. Please...."

"You're not hearing what I'm saying. It's just not possible. You'd be a fool to assume that I'm the only person in Wychwood this Pentridge character has contacted, and that they're not planning to claim the bounty as we speak. You'll not find safety in any Block, any room, any corridor in Wychwood. Anyone who tells you otherwise is just lining you up for the kill."

"Where...where can I go?"

Pulsipher showed no expression. It was as if he were looking through Rainville, studying the wall behind him.

His unwillingness to name it was all the confirmation Rainville needed. "But going Outside is a death sentence!"

Pulsipher sighed. Leaning in close, his voice was barely above a whisper: "Do you know how I got to be in charge of things here, Mr. Rainville? I landed here, pissing myself with fear, afraid to even leave my cell. That went on for three days. Then one morning, I woke up, and I knew the secret."

Rainville remained silent, hoping against hope that this secret would somehow save him from the Outside and its ravages.

"That secret, Mr. Rainville, is that you are only as damned, or as ruined, or as vulnerable as you choose to be."

A philosophical pep talk was hardly the salvation he'd been hoping for. He shook his head in disbelief.

"I suppose I should wish you luck, Mr. Rainville. You are going to need it."

He pushed a button on his desk. Seconds later, Mahara's massive hand was on Rainville's shoulder, guiding his stunned steps toward the door.

BRAXLER WAS WAITING NEXT to their cell when Rainville got there. His cellmate looked forlorn.

Rainville started to explain, but Braxler held up a hand.

"Boss told me. Big-ass bounty on your head, on account of you being some kind of mass murderer." He rubbed a hand roughly through his neatly-coiffed hair. "Look, Gridley, or whatever the hell your real name is...if you did the shit that they say you did, I'd want to wring your neck the same as anybody else here. But I've been here a good chunk of time, and I'll be straight with you. You just don't strike me as the type."

"I'm not." He looked into the cell, the place he'd come to think of as his only safe haven for recent weeks. He supposed he trusted Braxler more than anyone else left in Wychwood. "And Braxler...I just want to say—"

"You can thank me by getting the hell out of here. Let's get your stuff together."

Rainville had remarkably little stuff. There was what cash remained from the law firm plus his unspent repair earnings, whatever good banknotes would do him Outside. There was his nonworking console prototype. Finally, there was a handful of NutriSnax (compressed squares of stale granola infused with nutritional additives he purchased from the Trough), a few units of water, and the packet of spices he received from the Guild. Maybe they could be traded on the Outside? Either way, he would not leave them here for the House that exiled him.

He hastily stuffed the items into various pockets, except for the prototype, which was too fragile to carry in its jury-rigged state. "Braxler, you ever heard the name Pentridge?" The name rang in his own consciousness. Who would have the connections and the motivation to rat him out? A disgruntled relative of one of his alleged victims? Or some misguided vigilante for whom Rainville's life sentence was not enough?

"Can't say that I have. Now, the Boss says nobody is allowed to touch you for the next hour, or they answer to him. But he ain't got any sway over the other Houses, so you better high-tail your ass to the City of Souls gate before anybody else in here finds out who you really are. Each House has its own key, and we've already got someone there to let you out. Alright, kid, enough chitchat. Run, fast as you can!"

Rainville jogged, then sprinted when he noticed men just outside his Block pointing at him. Were they pointing because he was running? Or because they knew? Either way, he was a target. His quickened his pace. His lungs burned.

The Egress

THE SUN DIPPED near the horizon by the time Rainville reached the exit to Outside. Flanking the massive gates were the etched stone gargoyle statues he'd seen during his previous trip to the yard. The fading sunlight left dark voids in their eyes, giving them a wraithlike aspect. He could just make out "WYCHWOOD CEMETERY" on the arch, although perhaps the words were simply burned into his memory. Low shadowy shapes of stones and monuments in the old cemetery were visible through the bars of the gates.

A scrawny man slowly stood up. It was Anx from his now-former House.

Anx shuffled through a ring of keys, trying each one in the lock, stopping frequently to look around. Rainville scanned the yard anxiously, but was the recipient of only stares from a group of men clustered around the weight machines.

"Anx, can we hurry this up?"

"S-s-s-sure, man." Rainville had never heard the man stutter so much. "W-w-working f-f-f-fast as I can."

But the faster Anx flipped keys, the slower he seemed to go. There were six keys on the ring, but he'd only tried five of them, and those repeatedly despite none of them working the first time. The largest

key, the one that looked the most like the key to an ancient gate, had
yet to even be touched.

The Outside was a natural source of anxiety, but Rainville didn't
have time for it. "Anx, stop. Use that key. The big green rusty one
with—"

The doors back into the building slammed open.

Anx broke into a cock-eyed smile. "Hey, G-g-gridley! It looks like
somebody maybe wants to say g-goodbye to you."

Rainville turned to see Rahm, the huge Cossack from the cafeteria,
his visage black with facial tattoos. His eyes had the same fierceness as
when he'd choked the other Cossack, Tyrus, to death. He rushed
toward them with a rusted machete, its heavily-nicked edge polished
to a silver shine.

"Shit!" Rainville cried, "Give me the keys, Anx! Quick!"

"This him?" Rahm asked.

Anx nodded. "Pulsipher was t-t-talking to M-Mahara about him
havin' some b-b-bounty on him. Remember the d-d-deal, we split it
fifty-fifty, no m-m-m-matter how big it is. And if you t-t-tell P-P-
Pulsipher—"

"Shut it, little man," the Cossack scowled.

Anx fell silent.

Rahm inched closer to Rainville. Close enough that he could see a
vein throbbing on the man's neck. The Cossack twirled his machete in
tight, practiced circles.

"Anx! You think if you kill me, Pulsipher will just let it go?"

Anx seemed to consider this, but remained quiet, and would not
meet his eyes.

The Cossack stepped in and swung swiftly. Rainville anticipated
the arc of the blade. He jerked back immediately. It was not enough.
The blade caught him. There was no pain, just cold. Rahm's slice had
only cut his shirt. The machete ripped through the fabric of Rainville's
pocket, sending a cascade of torn provisions to the ground.

The man drew nearer. Rainville matched his movement. Now he
was nearly against the wrought iron fence.

Rahm grunted, thrusting the massive knife squarely at Rainville's navel. Rainville rolled out of the way, across bisected NutriSnax packages and dirty spice packets. One of them was red. It was the color of old bricks. He grabbed it. He forced himself to his feet, clenching the packet in his fist.

The cold metal of the fence bit sharply into his back. It stung, but was nothing compared to what Rahm's knife would do if he didn't get away. Now.

But no further retreat was possible.

Rahm came closer. Rainville held off until the Cossack was only four feet away. He tore open the spice packet. Taking a step forward, he cast its contents into the man's tattooed face. A cloud of orange-red erupted, and a layer of chili powder fell on Rahm's eyes and nose.

A sneeze exploded from the giant man's frame. He rubbed his eyes. This only made things worse. He swore in agony as rivulets of red tears and snot streamed down his face.

Rainville had thrown the red pepper. Thank God it had not been the paprika.

A pair of arms grabbed him from behind. Anx. That bastard.

"I g-g-g-got him!" Anx yelled, his stutter reaching a machine-gun staccato. "Quick! Over h-h-here!"

Anx continued yelling as Rainville struggled. The man was wiry, not muscular, but had a solid hold on him nonetheless.

Rahm the Cossack threw his head back and bellowed. He turned to the sound of Anx's voice, and charged at the two men.

Rainville let himself drop like a sack of potatoes. He shifted his weight down and backward into a violent thrust of his posterior into Anx's stomach. Anx buckled under the blow. His arms loosened slightly. It was enough for Rainville to break sideways out of his grasp. Then he reversed direction to step one leg behind Anx.

The Cossack barreled into them both. The blade of the machete sunk into Anx's ribcage. He screamed. Blood gushed out of his chest. A wet swirl blossomed on his shirt like a crimson poppy. The ring of keys fell to the dirt. "You stabbed me," he said, his voice clear and distant, as if noting something that happened to someone else, a long time ago.

Rahm swore. He grabbed the machete and tried to pull it free. Its crude serrations stuck on Anx's ribs and it did not come loose. Color faded from the man's face and he crumpled to the ground.

Rainville ducked, looping his finger through the keyring with a quick sweep.

He selected the large key Anx had been avoiding. He jammed it into the keyway, and turned hard.

With a clank, the gate latched open.

The Cossack roared. He planted a foot onto Anx's chest and yanked the blade free with both hands.

The hinges of the gate screeched in metallic agony. It swung open partway. Rainville dashed through. Rahm rushed straight at the gate now. Rainville slammed it shut, reaching between the bars to crank the key the opposite direction. He ripped the key from the lock, and fell back just as the Cossack reached it. Still blind from Rainville's chemical assault, Rahm felt his way along the gate, bar by bar. He found the handle. Yanked on it. Cursed. Pulled again, harder this time. It held.

Rahm swung the machete blindly, and it clanged against the iron bars leaving spatters of blood. He screamed at the top of his lungs: "Ye'll die out there, sure as shit! I'll tell 'em I killed yeh anyway!"

Rainville turned from the gate and ran.

The sounds behind him faded, but he could not believe how much noise his exodus had generated. The cacophony of shouted words and screams and clanging and the screeching. The racket would be a dinner bell to whatever cannibalistic once-men survived outside the prison.

As if on cue, a howl arose in the distance. The sound was not entirely human, nor entirely animal. He felt a chill in his blood. He looked back at the walls of what had been his home for the last two months, and dashed away into the deepening night.

Out and About

THE SUN DROPPED FAST with no moon to replace it. The slamming gate echoed in Rainville's mind as he ran toward low hills in the distance. Hopefully they would offer some cover. The darkness would soon provide concealment, but he needed to find a safe place to spend the night while he could still see.

As he drew nearer, the hills transformed and the air turned foul. The mounds were not geological landforms, but mountains of trash. Litter cascaded down into and among ancient tombstones. The prison dump. How many more grave markers were buried beneath the heaps of refuse?

Garbage bags were scattered all around, clawed open, their contents strewn about as if by hungry dogs. A rancid smell hung in the air, like rotting food, only worse. Deeper in the cemetery, pillars of smoke rose into the sky. Something lay on the ground nearby.

A body. Male. It looked...no. Best not to think about it. Stay on task. Uh oh. He started to wretch but fought it, rhythmically swallowing, fighting the urge. No time for nausea. For feeling anything. He had to find shelter, not dwell on the half-eaten corpse. Maybe if he didn't think about it. Maybe then the vision wouldn't take hold in his memory. Maybe he'd forget the select pieces of the corpse were missing, with clean lines of dissection, and the intestines neatly piled next to the body.

The half-human howl sounded like a roar when it rent the air once again. It was nearer now. Every physical process in Rainville's body, every thought in his mind became about one thing: speed. He turned away from the sound and ran. Ran like hell. Deeper and deeper into the graveyard. He filled his lungs, flushing out the bad air from the scene he left behind him.

THE GRAVE MONUMENTS were larger and more elaborate here; the area of cemetery near the prison gate must have been the cheap seats. A rhythmic noise seeped into his consciousness, and he realized it was his own feet slapping the ground. He slowed his movements until he ran quietly. Maintaining the pace, he came upon a large stone mausoleum built in a C-shape, with a snug alcove in its rear wall. The small courtyard was guarded by a white marble sculpture of an angel, her face a picture of serenity, safety. It was the first non-terrifying thing he'd seen Outside. While he did not consider himself religious, the sight of it calmed him for reasons he couldn't readily explain.

It wouldn't be much shelter if it rained, but the statue and the overgrown hedges flanking it would hide him from the surrounding area. He knelt between the angel and what remained of a shattered stone bench. Clearing the rubble from a particularly thick patch of grass, he felt around with his hands to clear the chunks of stone in the growing darkness. He saved a ragged fist-sized rock for a weapon, hoping he wouldn't need to rely on anything so primitive.

He curled up in the grass, his folded arm a pillow, his fingers clutching the rock. He was outside the prison building, and physically closer to freedom. But somehow it felt farther. Perhaps it was because simply staying alive would now be that much harder.

His stomach growled. His NutriSnax were back in Wychwood, sliced up by the Cossack. Unbelievable as it seemed, he missed the

Trough and its many-colored slop. There would be no meal for him tonight.

He closed his eyes, opened them again; it made no perceptible difference, so absolute was the blackness. In vain, his eyes scoured the void. Visions of feral men tracking his scent in the darkness, following his trail from the dump, loping closer with each passing minute, grew more vivid as his senses faded.

Wake Up Call

Rainville awoke at first light to a birdsong. The melodious twitter rose then fell, then a pause before it rose once again. The lull was utterly silent, and he wondered if some distant bird answered, too faint for his human ears to pick up. Had he dozed off in Vaux Park?

His senses stirred, and he opened his eyes to a sky that was wrong. Not the powder blue of daylight diffused through Arcadia's dome, but a deep indigo with distinct, fluffy, moving clouds. They changed randomly, the real kind of random, not the arithmetic pseudo-randomness that computers (with not a random bone in their circuit-filled bodies) employed to fake it.

The bird seemed nestled in the hair of an angelic figure. Its song had a lulling quality, and its un-genetically-engineered feathers were all a stark brown, sparsely beautiful in their own way. He lay there for minutes uncounted as the avian continued its call and the clouds morphed across the sky. The bird's melody was somehow more substantial than those of the birds he was used to in Arcadia. More real, like it meant it.

The sky, the birds. It seemed too beautiful, too real to be true, and this discordant thought pierced the veil of restfulness. Truth raged back into his consciousness: this was not Arcadia. It wasn't Z Block, either. This was some new and uncharted wilderness. The restless night came back to him: tossing and turning, being awakened at one point by a scream not far away, followed by a coarse laugh. It had taken hours to calm himself enough to get back to sleep. As awareness returned, his spirits plummeted. He tried to block out the despair, just as he'd suppressed his outrage at all the horrible things he'd been forced to see since his conviction. It was part of staying in control in a dangerous place. Yet, he knew such controlled, deferred emotions eventually became uncontrollable, unignorable timebombs waiting to go off. He recalled Pulsipher's words: he was only as damned or as vulnerable as he allowed himself to be.

His mind snapped back into focus. Immediate problems required his attention. He had no food. Just a couple units of water from his cell, but what would he drink after that? And now he was outdoors, a wild and untamed place where rain, uncontrolled and unscheduled, and possibly accompanied by lightning, could strike at any time. Last night had been dry and not too cold, but he would need to find a more defensible shelter tonight. And more importantly, he needed to find Charon Station.

The bird's song stopped suddenly, in mid-warble. It cocked its head, as if listening. The call of a distant bird? Rainville wished more than anything that the bird would start up again. Finally, the song resumed, replacing the silence.

He glanced up at the avian, whose call now seemed different. Less of a hail and more of a query. Then it ceased forever. A spherical explosion of feathers erupted, and the bird toppled off the statue and hit the ground just inches from Rainville's foot.

He stared at the dead bird in incomprehension. A scrap-metal arrowhead and part of a polymer shaft now protruded from the bird's breast, fletched with feathers from the same kind of bird; this was some form of irony, but his scrambling mind could not nail down which.

He reached out to the creature but it was beyond help. Shock yielded to panic. Go. Run. Whoever fired the shot would come for his quarry. Hoping the arrow came from far, far away, he crawled swiftly to the closest cover. It was an amorphous shrub, topiary gone wild. Where had his rock gone from the night before? Shit, he left it back by the statue.

Now he'd wriggled halfway into the shrubbery. Just a bit further and he'd be out of sight.

"Stop."

The grating voice was as commanding as it was serious. He stopped moving. He stared at the lush blades of grass a few inches from his face. He did not turn to look. Maybe then he wouldn't have to learn how screwed he now was.

"Stand."

He backed out of the bushes and slowly stood.

"Empty your pockets."

Out came his money and water, which were confiscated. He took a chance and left the folded note from Weirdbeard at the bottom of his pocket. It seemed his only hope of escape, and worth every bit as much to him as his life.

Hands patted him down. They passed over the pocket without stopping.

"Walk."

How the hell did he let this happen? He hadn't even made half a day on the Outside before being captured. Why hadn't he gotten up and left when he had the chance? Now he was going to end up like the bird. Or like...he did not finish the thought, but a flash of the cannibalized remains flashed through his mind just the same.

"Which way?" he asked.

"Left. We're going to see the Bishop."

The cold tip of a scrap-metal arrowhead pressed into his back, and he wondered if it drew blood. "Ok. No need to be nasty about it." He started walking slowly, coolly. One thing prison taught him was the value of respect, gained by keeping yourself together no matter what. You got only as much respect as you demanded. Once anyone saw you as broken, as defeated, it was all over. He thought back to the Lolly, begging for mercy as the Cossack rammed his skull into the concrete floor, over and over, until the begging stopped. To hell with that. He would not go out that way.

As he moved, the pressure on his back subsided and the pain lessened. He couldn't hear any footsteps behind him, but felt the spot on his back as a focus of vulnerability. He had no doubt the arrow was still trained on him.

He concentrated on keeping his pace even, scanning for obstacles in his path, knowing a sudden trip or stumble could result in a piercing wound. "Who is the Bishop?"

There was no answer. He turned to repeat the question, but the arrowpoint came back and put a spring into his step. "Enough." The voice had a strange resonance, like it came from two people at once. "Keep walking, or I'll paralyze you. Leave you as dinner for the Freakies."

Were this man and this "Bishop" not cannibals? The thought that things could be worse was not much consolation.

The cobbled path curved around through the tombs and up the slope of a hill. From its peak came a staggering scene: a towering wall, distant enough it was only half-visible in the morning haze. It was several stories high with guard towers and gun turrets. So this was it: the wall surrounding Wychwood. Tiny, shadowy figures paced back and forth between the towers. These men, whose faces he'd never even seen, that most of the prisoners would never see, were their guards. The haziness and the vast scale of the wall give the scene a certain surrealism, like some hellish mirage.

"Keep moving," came the voice behind him.

He was not sorry to lose sight of the wall. Seeing the guards had filled him with resentment, and the wall's sheer size and impregnability disheartened him.

The path rounded atop the hill before descending into forest, where the burial monuments and buildings were grander and more baroque. They entered a wide trail through a grove of eucalyptus trees that had grown up amongst the graves, punching holes in grave plots and shoving aside tombstones. How many of the graves' occupants had been absorbed into the trunks as they grew, and now stood above their heads? He could not help but envy them, their suffering over, their fates already resolved, their peace eternal.

Going to Church

THE PATH TOOK A SHARP TURN, and they moved between rows of graffiti-covered gravestones. Once identical, many of the markers were now broken at odd angles, resembling the wrecked gumline of a vanquished streetfighter. Some of the graves had been sloppily dug up, and the remains of smashed coffins littered the area. A ruined vehicle blocked the trail ahead.

"Stop," the hunter's voice commanded. "Skinny!"

Rainville could now see the vehicle had once been a hearse, turned brown with rust, its wheels long since removed. The rear door of the hearse was open. Based on the bed of rags inside, it was someone's sleeping quarters.

He took advantage of the pause to catch a glimpse of his captor. The hunter was slender and muscular with long, unkempt hair. The man's face was dirty, and a scarred and ragged hole pierced his cheek, leaving a second uncloseable entrance into his mouth.

A bedraggled young man wearing an ancient formal suit with dark stains crawled out of the hearse. The suit somehow predated the self-cleaning fabrics now ubiquitous in Arcadia. He rummaged for a moment before producing what looked to be an antique military officer's saber. He smoothed his hair as he straightened his back. "Yes, sir!"

"Take this one to the Bishop." The sight of the man's molars moving through the wound in his cheek made Rainville's stomach lurch, and he quickly averted his eyes.

"Okay," Skinny said, rubbing his square jaw. "I mean, yes, of course, sir!"

Skinny looked Rainville up and down. He gestured further down the path.

Part of Rainville was afraid to move. He turned slowly, but saw no trace of the man with the voice and the bow. Skinny marched him down the trail behind the hearse.

"You just get Out?"

The man did not seem mere seconds away from killing him, and Rainville appreciated this quality in a person. He nodded.

"That was Dogmeat. It's good you didn't stare at his mouth, or he'd have killed you. He caught the noma last year. Had to be cut out." The man chuckled. "You should see him eat."

Rainville felt a sudden urge to wash his hands. He wondered if that was even possible out here, with no obvious source of running water. He plunged his hands into his pockets. His hand found the note from Weirdbeard, which he tore to pieces with his fingertips. He'd read the message so many times that he could see the shape of every letter in his mind. "Meet thy fate at Charon Station, when time is past, 'til 'tis four days hence, and the dawning sun shines upon thee." The written words had become a liability. When Skinny wasn't looking, he let the shredded pieces fall to the ground, blending them into the leaves with his feet.

Ahead, the eucalyptus trees gave way to a clearing containing several structures. The outermost buildings appeared to have once been mausoleums. The doors of the nearest were wide open, and smoke seeped from a gaping hole in the roof. It smelled like smoked meat, and his stomach growled despite his general feelings concerning meats of unknown provenance.

"That smells pretty good," he commented, hoping Skinny would suggest a detour to feed his prisoner. "What is it?" He hoped the answer was a species other than his own.

"Pigeon," Skinny sighed. "Again. You must be hungry, huh?"

"Yes, actually."

Skinny snickered. "When I first got sent Outside, I couldn't find shit to eat either. Lived my first week on dump roaches, and the dead flies that pile up in the light fixtures on the prison walls."

In the middle of the clearing stood a sprawling stone building. A nave and a steeple rose out of its center, surrounded by expansive single-story walls. Round columns flanked massive bronze doors, supporting a sandstone lintel carved with hundreds of intricate angels surrounding the word "MEMORES." Marble steps up to the entry arch sagged from centuries of foot traffic. How long had prisoners been living here? The entire structure was overgrown with shriveling ivy. A short, round man with sunken cheeks and dark circles under his bloodshot eyes stood at attention nearby.

Beside the stairway, a sarcophagus carved from black granite sparkled in the sunlight. Half of the cover slab was smashed away, and its skeletal inhabitant, clad in finery from a bygone era, had been pulled halfway out into a sitting position. The grinning skull's mouth contained a half-smoked cigarette.

"Mornin', Murray!" Skinny greeted the remains as they passed. "What's shakin', Gob?" he asked the guard, who sneered back at him revealing a complete lack of teeth.

"Huck yorshelf," replied Gob.

"Poor Gob here can't talk proper," Skinny said. "He used to have a full set of teeth. Real pretty, they were. But then he messed up, and the Bishop don't have whatcha might call a tolerance for mistakes. So that's when ol' Bishop decided that Gob's mouth had better uses than talking." At this, Gob seemed to shudder involuntarily. His shoulders drooped and he stood aside, maintaining a gaze on Skinny that was pure hatred.

A growing sense of repulsion blossomed in Rainville's own gut. He would not, he could not show weakness, and so he willed it back down.

Isaiah 65:4

INSIDE, cold marble hallways went on forever in both directions. Metal-gridded skylights pierced the arched stonework ceiling, casting a faint light on the floor and illuminating green stains from centuries of leaking rainwater.

The walls were tessellated with burial vaults, some plainly utilitarian with only a name and a prayer, while others had bronze crucifixes and wrought iron holders for long-dead visitors to attach floral arrangements as offerings to the long-forgotten occupants. Photos of the deceased lay pressed beneath domes of glass, stern men in black suits and uncomfortable-looking hats and prim women in formal dresses epitomizing the height of style in whatever century they lived. Some vault covers were ajar but intact, others were entirely missing leaving deep black cavities in the wall. A chill made Rainville shiver.

Only the echo of their footsteps broke the silence. Skinny led him through several intersections of hallways, with Rainville noting the sequence of left and right turns in case he should need to make a rapid exit. At length, they reached a holy water font rising out of the floor, bone-dry and full of cigarette butts, where they turned deeper into the complex.

Rainville's stomach gurgled and he decided to humor it. "Anything to eat around here besides pigeon?"

"Leftovers from the dump, anything Wychwood throws away. We collect it and boil it and grind it and pound it into a sort of a bone and fish meal, and you can make spices from the bones."

"Is that safe?"

Skinny laughed. "Safer than starving to death."

Rainville didn't want to know any more about the grim culinary prospects, although his hunger had stopped in its tracks.

The ceiling in the next hall had partially collapsed. The floor was littered with dead leaves blown by years of storms, and the now-familiar sound of their footsteps was replaced by a cacophony of brittle crunching, perhaps a low-tech intrusion alarm of sorts. The doorway ahead was flanked by planters containing dried, skeletal trees.

"We're here," said Skinny. "Act respectful."

The floor of the spacious chapel was a checkerboard of red and white marble tiles. Three stories above them, a surprisingly-intact rose window bathed the chapel in a radiant glow. Wooden pews had been converted into beds for a rough-looking group of men who looked on. Bolted to the rear wall was a sizable crucifix. Black oxidized stains ran down Christ's body, giving the effect of additional torment and blood. In front of the cross stood an altar, which Skinny now approached.

"Your Excellency." Skinny bent his legs and bowed deeply. "This here is new meat."

A mound of a man in a wide gold-painted chair next to the altar began to stir. He was fatter than anyone Rainville had seen since his incarceration began. Standing seemed a real effort, and Rainville averted his eyes; surely no one would want such personal struggles scrutinized.

It was then that Rainville's eye caught the collection of human skulls on a shelf behind the altar. The Bishop gained his feet but was now wheezing heavily. He was dressed in tattered liturgical vestments. A wooden cross with its left arm missing hung from the man's neck.

He approached Rainville, clasping his hands as if in prayer, and sparkles reflected off a dozen gemstones. The man wore at least two rings on each finger. Most appeared to be wedding rings of different styles and eras, and all were at risk of drowning in his corpulent flesh. The dazzling was diminished on his left hand, which was mangled and missing two fingers. The remaining fingers had long, curling yellow nails.

The Bishop leaned in close. "And what do we have here? Have you brought me some scraps?" His breath smelled like twelve kinds of death. "Or a new toy, perhaps?" His lips twisted luridly to reveal a smile of crooked, yellow-brown teeth.

"M-my name is Gridley," Rainville said. Even having such a person know his real name seemed wrong. "I have useful skills," he offered. "I can repair electronics, photonics, you name it."

"At long last, our prayers have been answered!" cried the Bishop. There was laughter from the pews. "At last, we can fix all those kitchen appliances we've no electricity to power, which have piled up in our utter lack of a kitchen!" The laughter grew raucous, and he held up a hand to silence it. "No, I think I had it right, before."

The Bishop folded his hands again, protectively cradling the left against his chest like a baby. He shambled toward the altar, and the glowing light from above shined off his greasy hair. The man was certainly disgusting, yet there was something undeniably princely about his bearing. He smiled confidently, raising his arms as if addressing an adoring congregation. "Yes, the Almighty has brought you to me for another reason. Your arrival is more than a happy coincidence."

Rainville snorted derisively before he could stop himself.

The Bishop stared at him with no less surprise than if he were a talking dog. "You show a lack of respect. And ... now you've interrupted my train of thought. That is *not* allowed." The man was breathing hard again, quivering with emotion. "Don't make me *end* you, boy."

The pews fell silent.

Rainville did not doubt the man's sincerity in this regard. He nodded, his eyes snapping back to Bishop's collection of skulls on the altar.

The Bishop noticed this. He squinted appraisingly at Rainville for a moment, then retrieved one of the skulls, cradling it in a sort of a lock under his left arm. "This beauty's name is Jessyphia. I saw you looking at her."

The man studied Rainville's reaction, but this time he was careful not to have one.

"I know what you're thinking: 'Your Excellency, did you wake that poor female from her eternal rest?' Well, yes, in truth, I did. But it is the lot of the dead to wander, is it not? And Jessy is one of my traveling companions!" For the first time, he locked eyes with Rainville. "As you're no doubt aware, all of the women in this place suffer from the same problem. What is that problem? It is that they are deceased!" He held up a finger and shook it vehemently, the flesh on his forearm shivering. "So we must make certain concessions, must we not?"

Rainville assumed the question was rhetorical, but the silence grew.

"Skinny!" the Bishop bellowed. "Must we not make certain concessions, here, in this place?"

Skinny was shaken as out of a trance. "Umm, yes, Your Excellency! We got to!"

"Bah! If you're only going to patronize me, then stay silent." The Bishop muttered unintelligibly to himself before turning back to Rainville: "Now, I'm afraid that, despite the extensive duration we've spent together, I still do not know dear Jessy as well as I'd like. You see," he said, stroking the skull's cheekbone with a long dirty fingernail, "she once had a face. And hair. And lips! Oh my, yes! And what did these lips say? Important things! Things like 'Will you marry me?' and 'I love you' and ... and 'I *forgive* you.' Who did these lips kiss?" His eyes closed. "Ahh, but some secrets we must let Jessy keep, must we not?" He licked his lips. "Now, the words that our Jessy spoke with these lips, mightn't they have inspired people to do important things, at a time long ago? Yes, they might indeed have! What songs did she sing? Who did she dream of at night?"

"Think—*think*, I say, of how many lovers, parents, children left a piece of themselves in that casket when their beloved Jessy perished, leaving them alone. Do you know?"

Rainville decided to compromise between speaking out of turn, and failing to answer, and shook his head.

"Nor do I! Jessy died generations ago, after all." The Bishop's voice took on the resigned tone of a crusader on an impossible quest. "Now, of course, everyone here is long forgotten. Three hundred thousand forgotten, maybe more. But, my friends, we must not despair!" He held up a grimy hand, his palm to the ceiling. "Why must we not despair?"

Rainville wasn't sure, as he'd been quite tempted to do so.

"Because, by keeping Jessy close, I have spared her from being just so many moldering bones that no one remembers. You see, Jessyphia and I may live in a place that time has quite literally forgotten, but I won't forget her. Will I, my darling?" He gently kissed the skull's forehead before carefully placing it back on the altar.

Rainville looked away, in the process noticing a skull below the shelf that had been smashed into pieces. Another companion, perhaps, who'd displeased him in some way?

"Enough, enough. Assuming you do as you are told, we will have plenty of time to continue this discussion at a later time. Would that not be nice? For now, it is time for you to be shown to your new accommodations." On command, Skinny appeared at his side.

Rainville exhaled. So he would not be eaten. At least, not right away. Not while they had other uses for him.

"You will have to pardon the lack of windows, or light, or heat," said the Bishop. "I'm afraid those are creature comforts which, like trust, must be earned." The man twirled his fingers as a king dismissing a subject. "Until we meet again."

With that, Skinny led him down a dimly lit hallway. Rainville considered the aggregation of skulls. He found these forgotten souls enviable, in a way: anonymity certainly beat being maligned for centuries to come for someone else's heinous crimes. Yet, even in death these women had something that no one could take from them, not even the Bishop: their secrets. Perhaps the same was true of Rainville. His secret, that he might escape if he could reach Charon Station in time, just might be his salvation.

Entombed

Rainville's "accommodations" consisted of the dead end of a hall of crypts not far from the chapel. The Bishop hadn't been kidding about the lack of amenities: the space was cold, silent, and without windows. Like his cell in Z Block, but without any of the comforting signs of human life.

The alcove had once been a place for offering prayers. It was barricaded off by a telescoping metal gate that was locked in the closed position, blocking any passage back to the rest of the complex. Fragments of a large, shattered urn littered the floor, and a ruined altar sat in pieces near the back wall. In front of that was a small marble kneeler on which had been placed his meal. To his relief, the meat was clearly a pigeon. It had been plucked and baked until steaming, but had little else done to it. It tasted better than he'd imagined a pigeon would be, but bland nonetheless. Still, perhaps blandness was preferable to spices made from bones.

His captors were feeding him, at least. Unless they were fattening him up for slaughter? He tested the gate; it was solid, as was the stonework to which it latched. He tried using an urn fragment as a tool to eke his way out, but it disintegrated as soon as it met with any force. The granite floor proved sound, and climbing the gate to touch the ceiling yielded no obvious weaknesses there either.

He had to get free. If he missed the "four days hence" specified in Weirdbeard's note, which was now closer to two, he might not get another chance to escape this place. There was no conceivable way anyone from Arcadia could even send him another communication. Not here.

Yet, he was out of options. He'd felt helpless in prison, but this was something more. He'd made it out of Wychwood—Wychwood for God's sake!—only to end up even more confined than before. Now he had no idea what to do. His lifeline to Petronius & Sydra was cut, and his captors could do as they wished with him.

There was a dull ache in his core. He stared at the marble kneeling rail. Two knee-sized indents were worn into the stone. How many people had prayed here over the centuries? Had it worked for them? He thought of the myths of the ancients, of Gods who used mortals but also helped them.

On impulse, he knelt down, his knees sliding into the well-polished grooves in the marble.

How did one pray, again? What exactly was he supposed to say? He felt like a fraud. He was either praying to a nonexistent deity, or had ignored an extant one until convenience demanded otherwise.

He said he was sorry, and he was heartfully so. For the litany of mischief he'd partaken in. He made a mental list of as many instances as he could recall. It took him well into the evening. Then he focused on all the people he'd hurt. Most particularly his father, who'd loved him in his own way, and raised him. He'd tried to wound him in the midst of suffering an unbearable loss, this man who now had every right to distance himself from Rainville.

At length, he covered his major sins, addressing each of the karmic slights he'd obsessed over during those long nights back in his cell in Z Block. He asked for injustices to be righted. His freedom restored. And above even that, to be back with Vyanna. Finally, he asked for help in finding and defeating whomever murdered all those people in Arcadia.

Then he waited. He felt a bit better, but nothing else seemed to happen. He didn't exactly expect a flash of light and a booming voice speaking to him, but something, anything, that would indicate he'd been heard, that things had changed in some way.

Alas. Perhaps praying was obsolete. Or maybe it didn't work when the altar was destroyed.

Which, of course, was silly. If an omnipotent, omniscient being did indeed exist, he, she, or it would not require a piece of stone, like some kind of spiritual antenna, to be intact and operational to channel prayers. Not everything was a technical problem, able to be fixed with the right tools and replacement parts.

Unless...maybe it was.

Could this situation be fixed the same way you'd fix a broken fabricator? Was there some way he could bring his strengths to bear on the situation, rooted as it was in his weakness?

Perhaps it was no different from any daunting technical project: it simply had to be broken down into small, achievable operations. Step one was to calm himself so he could think rationally. Some other step, farther down the line, would be to escape. But he couldn't put the interim steps together until he'd collected himself.

Maybe this new way of thinking was too good to be true, but he decided to roll with it. He'd experienced enough things that were too bad to be true, enough awful shit hitting him out of the blue, and all the while with him merely reacting. Worst case, this stream of thought would lead nowhere, and he'd be no more or less locked in this cage than he already was.

He first had to define the problem. Figure out the constraints, what solutions they allow for. What materials are needed to affect a repair. What steps need to be taken, and in what order. It was not a question of how to get from A to Z in one giant blob of a thousand things, but a series of small steps. Lack of information about the later steps was just a natural part of the process, not cause for panic. He felt calmer now.

He needed freedom. Not the larger, grander specter of total freedom, but just enough temporary freedom to make it to Charon Station two mornings from now.

The constraints were plentiful. These men were not going to let him leave willingly. He had no leverage, no way to incentivize them, nor threaten them into letting him go. That left only one alternative. Escape.

What about materials? A weapon would be nice, although he was under enough scrutiny that it would be tough to get one. But the main thing he needed was knowledge: where was Charon Station? He imagined escaping without even knowing which way to run, and having no way to find out; it would be a disaster. One of these men must know the station's location. He needed to ascertain this, but without tipping his hand about where he was going.

There was another piece of knowledge he didn't have: the how and when of the escape. How could he plan without any idea of what the next twenty-four hours would bring? How would he recognize when the time was best to escape? If he had weeks, he could watch their patterns, identify a weakness in them, pick the optimal time, and guarantee a high confidence of success, to the extent possible anyway. But he had only a day and a half. He was going to have to wing it.

Wing it. The term sounded facetious, whimsical even, but if he failed, he'd probably be killed. The image of Gob's ruined mouth invaded his consciousness. Killed, maybe, or worse.

City of the Dead

RAINVILLE WOKE to blinding pain in his side.

"Wake up, damn you!"

He opened his eyes to a short, muscular man bearing down on him. The man wound up to kick him again.

"Gryce, try not to damage the new meat, eh?" said a tall man with piercing eyes. He had a mustache beneath his crooked nose. He also had what seemed to be a permanent snarl on his face.

"On'y having a bit of fun, Fenton."

Gryce was grubby, with dull eyes. Most noteworthy were the heavy scars covering nearly every exposed portion of his body. A Cossack. The Cossacks he'd seen in Wychwood had these kinds of scars, but only a fraction as many. He supposed they were a sign of status or rank. Or body count.

The men marched him back to the Bishop's ramshackle throne room. Very little light shone in from the rose window above. It was dawn, or shortly thereafter.

One edge of the Bishop's mouth twisted up into a smile the moment he saw Rainville. "Why, young Gridley! It brings my heart great joy to see you again. I trust you slept well? But yes, of course you have. That is a blessing, because you will need every ounce of energy you can muster for today's …" He paused, as if searching for the right term. "Activities!" His smile grew with the word. The Bishop turned to Gryce and Fenton. The sight of the two men seemed to disappoint him. "You two, by my grace, have been chosen to take care of the new meat. Do you understand what is expected of you?" asked the Bishop.

"We sure do, boss!" said Fenton.

"It pleases me to hear as much. Well, off to it, then. And on your way out, send Gob in to see me. He and I are due for a little fellowship!" The Bishop licked his lips. Fenton merely nodded while Gryce shifted his weight, clearly uncomfortable.

Leaving the Bishop's presence was a relief, but only a temporary one. The men retrieved weather-worn, splintering shovels from a crematorium-turned-storage room and ordered him to march.

Rainville did not like where this was going. Not at all.

The march continued toward what could only be a dire fate. Fenton repeatedly consulted a scrap of cardboard with scrawled instructions indicating a series of left and right turns at the cemetery's various intersections. The paths were mostly unmarked, although they passed under a puzzling sign that said "Edgewood Road."

"Where are we going?" asked Rainville.

Gryce, evidently not abiding him speaking privileges, rapped him on the head with his fist. His dislike for the man was blossoming like a greenhouse rosemallow. Anger mixed together with panic, potent emotions lurking on the fringes of his consciousness. Was he to dig his own grave?

But, wait. What of his commitment to keep things analytical? Objective? He needed to solve a series of problems, not make more by losing control of his emotions. A calm mind was required to think rationally. Escaping was the goal of some other, future moment in time. The goal of *this* moment was only to stay calm, observe, and think.

He pushed the panic from his mind and vowed to keep it there. Taking a deep breath, then another, he let the animalistic urgency welling within him fade.

"We're here," said Gryce as they approached a field of tightly packed, smaller stones.

"We ain't here, you dingus. This is Section Sixteen."

"Yeah, well, it's close enough."

"The hell it is. Sixteen is all influenza victims. Kids and poor people. The boss'll know in a minute where we dug, and then you'll catch a horrible disease. Not that the world would miss you, Grycie."

Gryce looked hurt. Rainville had never seen anyone boss around a Cossack before. He wondered what Fenton was capable of, to command control over such a man.

"Well, Section Four is awfully close to Arnibal's territory. And anyway, we bring the Bishop some shinies, and he'll be so goddamn happy he won't ask where we got 'em."

So that was it, Rainville had been put on a grave-robbing crew. Better than having to dig his own grave, he supposed. "Who's Arnibal?" he asked.

Gryce glared menacingly at him, his hand tightening into a fist.

Fenton shook his head at Gryce disapprovingly. "Arnibal's one of the Freakies," he said. "And one of the nastier ones, even as far as they go."

"He hunts people," said Gryce. "And he gets enough of 'em so he's gotten real picky. Cuts out the choicest pieces and leaves the rest for his gang. Maybe he'd like a few pieces of yeh?" With his index finger, Gryce traced an imaginary line around Rainville's ribs.

Rainville recoiled, thinking back to the dump. And then to the muffled scream and the laugh that interrupted his first night of sleep. How close had he been to death?

"Okay, so we agree we're not going to Section Four," said Fenton. "But let's hit Thirty-six. I dug there once. Upper middle class, but not totally picked over, either."

An idea occurred to Rainville. He thought back to an old gangster vid he'd seen as a kid, and hoped neither of these men had shared the experience. "Have you guys tried Section J?" he asked.

"Section J?" Fenton said.

"You haven't heard about Section J?" He paused for effect. "Man, it's all they talked about back in Omega House. Of course, it's just rumors."

Gryce poked him in the stomach. "Yeh got somethin' to say, little man, yeh best just say it. Hold out on us, and I'll slit yeh from chin to dick."

"Well, Pulsipher, he's the guy who runs the Omegas now, he said that a long time ago, they buried the boss of this big criminal gang in Section J. They buried him sitting in his car, diamond rings on his fingers, money stuffed in his pockets, and one of those old slug-thrower machine guns on the seat next to him. I don't know, it's probably bullshit, but that's what I heard."

"All the sections here got numbers, not letters," said Gryce. "So where's this Section J?"

"It's ... well, I don't exactly know, I just got out here a couple of days ago. How do you guys find your way around in this place?"

Fenton considered the idea at length before turning to Gryce. "This might be worth a look. If we bring him something nice, maybe the Bishop'll be in a good mood for a while. Or if we find us a working gun ..." He stopped thinking aloud. "Couldn't hurt to at least check the map, Grycie."

Gryce turned and hit Rainville in the side with the flat of the shovel. "Look alive, meatbag! We're movin'."

The men walked with cautious deliberation, constantly scanning their surroundings. Half a mile later they arrived at a vast bronze relief map. It depicted Wychwood Cemetery as it had been centuries earlier, with well-tended rolling hills divided by dotted lines into sections, with its now mostly signless roads given names. This truly was a city of the dead.

"Let's see," said Rainville as his thoughts accelerated. The time was now. He scanned the map, dragging his finger slowly across featureless sections of cemetery while his eyes searched frantically for structures in the more built-up sections. His captors, evidently not advanced students of cartography, puzzled over where they even were standing and which way was up, granting him ample search time.

At last, there it was: the old subway station. It was near the geographical center of Wychwood, only a couple of sections, in fact, beyond Section 36. Two miles at most from where he stood.

He stared at the bronze contours with a burning focus, memorizing details as quickly as he could.

"Alright, smart guy, where's this Section J?"

"I ... don't know. I don't see it. I'm sorry. Like I said, the story's probably just bullshit."

"Goddamn it," said Fenton. Gryce moved to shove Rainville to the ground. He saw it coming and sidestepped, but was less successful at dodging Gryce's followup punch. It connected with his cheek, which now burned fiercely as his eye teared up.

He cowered defensively against additional blows, but knew it did not matter. He'd won, he'd gotten the information he needed.

He was struck with an urge to run to the station now, as fast as he could, but reigned himself in. These were no shopping mall SecAgents. If he ran now, it would just be a footrace between him and two men who'd spent their months walking and digging while he sat in his cell or soldered at his workbench. No, he was smarter than this. He would wait for the right opportunity. Assuming he survived that long.

Paydirt

THE SUN ARCHED high in the sky. Earlier in the day, biding his time had seemed like a better idea, when Rainville's chief occupation was studying the map. But now that he'd been handed a shovel and pointed at a grave, he questioned whether waiting to make his escape had been the right choice. Now, he faced the prospect of digging up some poor bastard so the Bishop and his men could loot what few earthly possessions the lost soul still had.

His stomach felt heavy as he poked the blade of the shovel into the turf halfheartedly. Graverobbing was not an occupation he thought would look good on his karmic resume. He wiggled the handle back and forth and heard the tiny grass roots snap, and wondered if his tether to morality was doing the same. Reluctantly, he displaced a piece of sod and set it carefully to the side of the plot. He tentatively prodded around for the location of his next shovelful. Then a fierce blow to the back of his knees jerked him from these thoughts and sent him sprawling to the ground.

"Stop lollygagging and dig, yeh little bastard!" yelled Gryce. The man bore down with the shovel a second time, this time at Rainville's head. He put up his arms just in time to block most of the blow. The bones and sinew of his forearms rang with pain.

"Hey, not the arms, Gryce! He's gotta dig, don't he?" said Fenton.

Gryce's head bobbed, but did not look convinced.

"If you break his arms, he can't dig," Fenton said. "And if he can't dig, you know who'll have to, yes? It'll be you, Gryce, because I won't be doing no shitwork on account of your screwup."

Gryce nodded dully. He shot Rainville a betrayed look, and jabbed a pointed finger at the grave.

Gradually, Rainville regained his feet. He would need to be careful around Gryce. For whatever reason, the man despised him, and Rainville could not afford any injuries, not if he were going to survive an escape. He spiked the shovel into the ground, and stood on the blade until it sunk flush with the soil. His bruised arms burned fiercely at the exertion, but it felt right that he was being punished for the iniquity he'd now resigned himself to participate in.

The shovelfuls grew darker and heavier as the pit deepened. The men did not allow him a break, so he treaded the fine line between digging inefficiently, and digging so slowly as to earn another beating.

By the time the hole was stomach-deep, he began to dread each thrust of the shovel, that it would make contact with something and the task would become immediately more gruesome. But by six feet, his body longed for any respite from the labor, regardless of why.

Yet the hole deepened with no contact. Seven feet. He imagined he was digging Gryce's grave, and the thought brought a smile to his face and pushed back the exhaustion. Eight feet.

"The fuck are yeh doin' down there?" Gryce asked.

Rainville was breathing hard and fought to get the words out. "There's...nothing down here."

"Shit," said Fenton. "Musta been a cremation. Metal container, rusted away in the mud."

"Or a lazy gravedigger who just tossed 'em in the woods!" chuckled Gryce.

At length, Rainville clambered out of the deep hole. "Is it lunchtime yet?" he asked, preparing to dodge another anticipated blow from Gryce.

The two men laughed coarsely. "We aren't going anywhere until we find something good for the Bishop," said Fenton. "Or should I say, until *you* find something good for him!" The men laughed again. "This time, you pick the grave. Pick a good one, or Grycie here might get sore again!"

Rainville glanced at the nearby graves. "Pick a woman," Gryce said. "More kindsa jewelry. And the older, the better. Kids didn't own nothin' valuable."

Rainville swallowed. This endeavor seemed even more wrong now that he had to choose the victim. He selected a tombstone with only a name and a date, no "dearest mother"'s or "beloved wife"'s or any of that.

The decedent's name was Eugenia, and she'd lived a long life.

Sorry, Eugenia. Your suffering is over, and the only way to fix mine is to disrupt your grave.

If he were Eugenia, he would forgive someone in his own circumstance. The thought made the work easier from that point onward, although physically it only got harder with each new hour.

Twigs

BACK IN THE CRYPT ALCOVE, Rainville studied the rawness of his hands. They were a landscape of blisters and blood-red creases in bas-relief. Looking at them only seemed to amplify the pain.

He closed his eyes and his mind substituted a hundred stimuli from the horror that was today. The hollow *thunk* when his shovel hit its first coffin. Splinters of wood mixed with the dirt around his feet. A casket containing a tiny skeleton along with that of its mother. Worms spasming in agitation at being ripped from the soil. The sound of hammering interspersed with the sickly cracking of rotten wood. A rain of blows from a savage beating by Gryce.

His eyes opened, scanning for anything that did not invoke today's memories. Out in the hallway beyond his cage was a single bit of color. A flower holder gripped a cluster of ancient plastic blooms, still periwinkle in hue yet somehow wilted despite being synthetic. He immersed himself in them until the encroaching darkness made it impossible.

Then the cell was pitch black, and the visions of his day formed into a continuous and unavoidable loop.

Exhaustion was a tender mercy, and he fell into a swift and dreamless slumber.

"WAKE UP, SUNSHINE!" He opened his eyes to a smile of yellow teeth under a crooked nose. Fenton. Gryce stood nearby with a large axe and a menacing sparkle in his eyes.

Rainville was still exhausted. The thought of another day of hard labor made his every aching muscle want to give way.

Fenton marched him to the chapel where a chorus of amens indicated the conclusion of some sort of sermon by the Bishop.

"Ah, young Gridley! I trust your accommodations were satisfactory?" The Bishop studied Rainville for a long moment. "But no, you did not sleep well; I can see it in your eyes, your face...so young, unspoiled, is your face. It is a tribute to our Maker, is it not?" He smiled, exhaling slowly.

"Today, you will collect firewood, again under the guidance of brothers Gryce and Fenton." Rainville's heart sank. "The cold season will soon be upon us, will it not? And the toil of our hands must come before the toil of our hearts."

"To that end, it is time for you to learn the value of fellowship, for God, in His infinite wisdom, created us to love one another. This afternoon, you will cease your toils early, and return here to receive my spiritual counseling on this topic. We shall get to know one another, and in doing so, will get to know our Creator. Will that not be nice? You will sleep better tonight, of that I can promise you." The Bishop licked a dirty finger.

"Fenton, you shall make certain he works. But save some of his energies for this evening, yes?"

Fenton nodded and led Rainville out.

Until now, it seemed that he was being kept around as slave labor. Now, the full magnitude of what was expected of Rainville dawned on him.

Well, that was it then. There would not be any "fellowship" with that old perv. Rainville's dignity had taken a beating in prison, but remained intact, even stronger in some ways. He would not give that up, not for anything. It was time to check out of this hellhole, and that afternoon was his new deadline.

HE WAS ESCORTED from the chapel by Fenton to a grove of trees in Section 17 of the cemetery. His chest tightened when he saw Gryce there, already hacking away at the lower branches of an oak tree with his axe.

He watched the destruction of this living thing. It had no connection to the evils of the Outsiders, yet was subject to their ravages like a disease invading some new domain where no antibodies existed. In Arcadia, this ancient tree would be appreciated by all, protected and taken care of. Out here, though, all life was cheap. Including his own.

The wood gradually piled up, and Fenton took over chopping while Rainville and Gryce carried loads in the rough direction of the chapel. Rainville gave the man a wide berth to avoid setting him off. As the chapel's spires rose in the distance, the wood grew heavy in his arms. Just when he thought they would give out, he caught sight of an impressive pyramid-shaped mausoleum. Gryce nodded at the bronze double doors with a grunt. Rainville set down enough logs to grab one of the cast iron loops and haul the door open.

The door was the only source of light inside, illuminating long rows of cut firewood. He crawled to the far wall where the ceiling slanted low and added his logs to the pile, then scrambled out of Gryce's way.

When they returned for more wood, Fenton had made little progress. "Your turn, Grycie."

"I'll take a turn," said Rainville.

"No trusting you with an axe, boy." said Fenton, leering. "Not when you got your first date with the Bishop to look forward to. And probably a couple days of bleeding and puking, if you're anything like Gob," he chuckled.

Revulsion rose in Rainville's stomach and he fought to swallow it down. On its edge swam something harder to control: fear. Cold sweat erupted on the palms of his hands and soles of his feet. He forced himself to take a deep breath of the cool air, his mind latching onto the sweet scent of the fresh-cut eucalyptus.

"Yeh must be lucky," said Gryce. "Bishop don't wanna get with erryone."

"Bishop's been lookin' at you a bit, lately, Grycie!" said Fenton with a wink.

Gryce shook his head but said nothing. His next axe stroke rocked the hapless eucalyptus tree to its core.

THE SUN WAS high in the sky, and Rainville knew his opportunities to escape before the Bishop's "spiritual counseling" were quickly dwindling. He considered Pulsipher's parting advice, that you are only as damned or as vulnerable as you choose to be. One thing was certain to him: he no longer had the luxury of waiting for the perfect opportunity. He would need to make his own.

A plan took shape in his mind. He rummaged through the cut wood, searching for a piece that might work, with the right thickness and length. When the next load was ready to be hauled, he made sure the selected piece was on the bottom of his pile, where it could not tumble off and get lost.

Again he marched with Gryce to the pyramid. They approached the door. Rainville chose a rock protruding from the grass. He veered, then tripped over it. He stumbled a bit, then fell so the wood scattered all around as he hit the ground.

Gryce scowled at him, then kicked him in the gut. Rainville gasped for breath. He rolled farther from the man to escape the next kick. Gryce lumbered after then stopped short, smiling as a fire lit in his eyes. Rainville had no doubt: he was in for a brutal beating as soon as the Cossack had his hands free. This time, Fenton would not be around to save him.

He thought about grabbing the largest piece of wood, giving Gryce a richly deserved clubbing. A glance at the Cossack's muscled, scar-covered arms made him reconsider. Did the man even feel pain?

He slowly picked up the pieces while Gryce swung the doors open and went in.

This was it, then.

He grabbed the log he'd selected earlier. He'd eyeballed it then. Did he guess correctly?

He ran at the mausoleum, throwing his weight against the doors. They slammed shut with a mighty clang. Gryce, surprised and in the dark, unleashed a torrent of curses and threats. He was stumbling around inside, knocking down stacks of wood.

Rainville's pulse pounded, and his vision narrowed. He slipped the log through the door handles, but the rings' diameter was larger than his earlier estimation. The log he'd chosen was far too thin, and would not hold the door securely.

Bong! The double doors resonated as Gryce barreled into them. They bulged out, opening partially as the small log bent against them. The wood began to fracture, but Gryce seemed to give up an instant before it broke entirely. Neither the stick nor Rainville would survive Gryce's next attempt.

"I'll gut yeh like a fish!" bellowed Gryce.

The temptation to run before Gryce broke through was strong, but a more rational part of Rainville, the part bound by purpose, refused to give up. He grabbed frantically at more of the cut branches, shoving them through the door handles in alongside the first.

Gryce smashed against the doors again, and this time the sticks flexed but did not crack as the first one had. Sensing there was now time to do this right, Rainville walked among the scattered wood frag-ments, selecting particularly thin ones and breaking twigs off the thicker ones. He packed them into the remaining voids in the looping handles.

This time there was a dull thud as Gryce met the now-unyielding doors. He cried out in pain from within the tomb.

"Gryce! Are you okay in there? Can you hear me?" asked Rainville.

"Goddammit!" came a muffled reply. "I'll feed yer own damn organs to yeh, one at a damn time!"

The doors shook and Gryce roared with rage, but Rainville's makeshift fasces held. His work was complete.

"That sounds great, but now's a bad time for me, Grycie. Would you mind filling in for me underneath the Bishop this afternoon? He might even let you keep your teeth!"

Gryce continued to scream muffled threats. From 100 feet away they were barely audible; the Cossack would not be able to summon help.

With that, Rainville bolted. His heart raced as he sprinted faster than ever before, through hills and fields of tombstones. There would be at least twenty minutes before Fenton would miss them and come looking, and twice that for him to find Gryce and summon help.

He was soon out of sight of the pyramid. No one could have seen which way he'd gone. Still, he chose a zigzagging path toward Section 36, picking waypoints that would make good places to hide, a monument here, a cluster of trees there, toward where he could only hope the train station still stood.

Formula for Conducting the
Ordeal of Boiling Water

"Then let the man who is to be tried, as well as the kettle or pot in which is the boiling water, be fumed with the incense of myrrh ... Then let the hand that is to be placed in water be washed with soap and let it be carefully examined whether it be sound; and before it is thrust in let the priest say: I adjure thee, O vessel, by the Father and the Son and the Holy Ghost, and by the holy resurrection and by the tremendous day of judgement, and by the four Evangelists, that is this man is guilty of this crime, either by deed or by consent, let the water boil violently, and do thou O vessel, turn and swing.

After this let the man who is to be tried plunge in his hand and afterwards let it be immediately sealed up. After the ordeal let him take a drink of holy water. Up to the time of the decision regarding the ordeal [the priest shall wait three days before examining the defendant's hand] it is good thing to mix salt and holy water with all his food and drink."

Breviary of Eberhard of Bamberg, ed. Zeumer in MG.LL. Sec
V, Formulae, Twelfth century

Charon Station

RAINVILLE TENTATIVELY APPROACHED THE BUILDING. Decaying mosaic letters inlaid far overhead spelled out "WYCHWOOD CEME-TERY STATION" in a bygone deco font. The former subway station was a Victorian gothic edifice built into the hillside, with walls of ornate stonework and wreathed columns spiraling skyward. The roof was topped with crocketed spires, each ending in a finial spearpoint. The structure resembled a palatial mausoleum more than a subway. The station's entry doors were steeply-pointed arches, now bricked over. "*CHARON STATION*" proclaimed smaller letters in faded graffiti spread crudely across the bricks. It was a relief to know the place still stood.

In a few places, sections of brick had been obliterated, exposing a shining barrier beneath. He recognized the metal's lustrous salmon color: tri-strontium alloy, impenetrable to nearly any cutting technology, certainly anything the prisoners would have at their disposal. Indeed, the alloy layer was unscathed, but not for lack of trying based on the pile of broken rocks and ruined metal tools around its base.

He made a fist and pounded on the barrier, and a hollow metallic sound reverberated back into the hillside to places unknown. He immediately regretted the noise and retreated up into the hills opposing the station entrance.

He needed to stay near the structure, close enough to watch it but still be safely hidden. He found a cluster of stucco mausoleums and settled between them. There was no sign of activity anywhere around the station.

As the sky gradually darkened into twilight, he heard a distant shout. It was brief, not long enough to triangulate from which direction it came. His vulnerability was undeniable: he could not stay outdoors tonight, exposed like he was.

After some searching, he came upon an H-shaped mausoleum on the hill above the station. Carvings of winged skulls adorned the cornerstones of the structure. A tree had grown up in front of the crypt entrance partially obscuring it, its broad trunk permitting the faux-stone door to open only partway. He squeezed through the opening and closed the door behind him. The interior was pitch black. Only a trace of fading daylight came through the narrow windows. He felt his way through the shadows to the wing of the tomb facing the station. He perched behind a window, although by now could see only a faint outline of the edifice below.

The station had been sealed by an impenetrable layer. Of course it had; otherwise, there'd be no prisoners left in Wychwood. Over the ensuing hours, he made a list of ideas for gaining entry, and an even longer list of reasons none of them would work. In the end, he concluded that it was impossible to open. Did the author of Weirdbeard's missive know that? Did he expect to rendezvous inside?

Dawn tomorrow, the designated time, was not for another ten hours or so. Yet, he could not take his eyes from the station. He huddled there, continuing his vigil as the last bit of daylight fled before the dark.

The River Styx

RAINVILLE DID NOT SLEEP. He barely even closed his eyes. In the twilight, disquieting thoughts took on a life of their own and slithered into his consciousness. What if they sent the hunter, Dogmeat, after him? A man like that could surely track a human as well as any animal. He thought of the sharp coldness of the arrow tip against his spine. This time, he'd be lucky if the man shot him. The Bishop, not to mention Gryce, would have their own, even more distasteful designs on his fate.

There was a rustling sound outside in the darkness, and his chest pounded. He waited, willing even his molecules to stop their motion, but whatever it was stayed silent.

What if the Bishop had more than one hunter?

There was a howl in the distance.

It was now pitch black, but he lowered himself quickly and quietly down onto the cold stone floor, where he lay for minutes uncounted.

And so the night went. Some inexplicable sound, followed by a wave of abject terror. Again and again, he lifted his head to check the night sky, hopeful for some new hint of dawn. Eight hours? It felt like eight days. His sense of time had gone haywire, and he questioned his own sanity.

When the first grey daylight glowed through the mausoleum window, he dismissed it as only his imagination. But it did not fade back into his subconscious this time. Dawn had come.

He forced himself to wait, surveying Charon Station in the growing light for potential threats. He half-expected to see Gryce waiting there, eager to exact revenge. But he saw no one, neither Gryce nor Fenton, nor anyone else from the chapel. They would not venture out in the dark, not with their fear of Arnibal and his Freakies. The sound of the name in his mind brought back all the anxieties daylight had chased away.

He collected himself, moving up to the door of the mausoleum. Just beyond it, on the other wing of the building, was a body. The abdomen of the man was bisected, choice pieces removed and intestines placed in an orderly pile. The victim's face was frozen in a silent scream.

His horror at the sight was rivaled only by the knowledge that he'd crawled right by it in the preceding night's darkness. Spent the whole night mere feet away from it. Had whatever foul creature stashed its victim here returned for a second serving ... he couldn't even finish the thought.

He shoved the mausoleum door ajar and scrambled out. He barreled down the slope to Charon Station, at last ducking behind one of the building's stone columns. He was breathing hard, looking back up the hill to the mausoleum with the partially-blocked door.

He had no idea where to go from here. Nowhere was safe.

Extending his hand, he knocked softly on the tri-strontium barrier, and the resulting echo into the depths of the hillside seemed impossibly loud in the quiet of the morning.

No sound answered his. Damn it. What if his rescuer was detained? Or not coming at all?

His course of action must be the same either way: wait by the station, as long as he could. As long as it took. And so he waited behind the pillar, continually surveying the surrounding hills for threats, his adrenaline level rising with the sun.

THERE WAS A SCRAPING SOUND. It came from behind him. His heart upshifted into a gear he didn't know it had. He clutched at the wreathing on the column and turned slowly to glimpse the source of the sound.

Nothing.

The scraping continued, faint through the thick station walls. Then it stopped.

A clunk. The rectangular outline of a door appeared in the formerly-seamless metal. The outline became a crack which thickened to a sixteenth of an inch before stopping.

The door panel seemed to extend behind a portion of the arch which was still bricked over. It clunked shut again, leaving no trace of itself on the smooth metallic wall. It cracked open again, and again hung up on the bricks, unable to open further.

The hint of a muffled voice came from inside the metal barrier, but nothing more.

He searched the rubble at the base of the wall and found a dissociated axe-head. This he wedged behind the crumbling masonry. He used a rock to pound it forward. Fragments of bricks rained down on his feet. He repeated the maneuver, this time with a prying motion.

He worked more quickly now. Sections of brick barring the door fell off in sheets. He smashed the axe-head against obstinate bricks that would not give way. He hit them again and again until they were bashed to rubble. The ear-ringing racket it made didn't matter. Neither did the pain in his inflamed hands. He had to get through that door.

At last, the area where he'd seen the outline was mostly clear. Again, he rapped his knuckles on the tri-strontium panel.

The crack appeared once more. Fragments of brick and mortar showered down on him as the door broke free and swung open.

His eyes searched the darkness beyond but there was nothing.

Then, a face. My God, could it be? Vyanna!

She emerged, dirty and squinting in the daylight. He grabbed her into a hug so fierce it bordered on assault. His chest felt near bursting with the kind of happiness he'd sworn off ever experiencing again. How had he gone so long without it? Their time together in Arcadia seemed not months past, but centuries, and the vision of her beauty and of the horrible necropolis surrounding it seemed impossible to reconcile.

"I never thought I'd see you again," he said into her shoulder. Thousands of questions flooded his mind. Things he wanted to ask, but all he could say was, "Thank you."

She hugged him tighter in response. Then he remembered where they were. He pushed her away. "We need to leave. Now!" He clasped her wrist and pulled her through the door to safety. He slammed it behind them, checking twice to make sure the internal door mechanism was latched.

She flicked on a flashlight, and he stood waiting for his eyes to adjust. She studied his face, then his body, lingering with manifest concern over his arms and hands and his swollen cheek.

"Jesus, you look like hell!" she said.

"Good. I feel like hell, and I'd hate to mislead anyone," he said.

She smiled without breaking her gaze away from him. "Charming establishment, Wychwood. I can totally see why you picked this place," she said. "So, you ready to check out? Or do we need to go and fetch your luggage?"

He tried to force a smile, but found no humor in Wychwood. He pushed on the door again. "Is this thing secure?"

She nodded. "It's got a set of ancient locks," she said. "They relock automatically. Want me to rig them so it stays open? You know, to free your comrades?"

"No!" The immediacy of his answer surprised him. He sighed. "No. None of those people should be free."

A part of him felt betrayed by his own words. He was the worst kind of hypocrite. Condemning men to the hell that so nearly destroyed his own humanity, simply because they'd been here longer, their humanity already forfeit. Perhaps some even started out like him, victims of a jury which could be every bit as arbitrary as any witch trial of old. How many of the Outsiders were decent people before Wychwood chewed them up and digested them, robbed them of any hopes or dreams, before the Bishop added a large dose of desperation and the process repeated like some hellish rumination?

Still, another part of him, small but unwilling to be ignored, demanded it be done. Leaving a way out would be like opening Pandora's box, unleashing an onslaught of untold savagery. And what's more, the Bishop and his men would dog their escape. No. It just wasn't an option.

He turned away from the door and did not look back.

Passage

THE DARK and cold enveloped them.

There was a click as Vyanna activated a small but powerful flashlight and handed it to Rainville before regaining her own. In the dank air, his breath formed a cloud turned rainbow by the flashlight's multi-spectrum LED array.

They stood in a tunnel filled nearly to the ceiling with a mix of dirt and strange junk. An old water-operated toilet. An antique metal-spring mattress. A cathedral-shaped bird cage. All trash from another era, precariously stacked together. They cautiously traversed the debris, the declining slope of the ceiling their only consistent indication of movement deeper underground.

"According to the schematics, this tunnel was supposed to be completely filled for security reasons," Vyanna said, her breath puffing out in a fog before her. "But I reckon the contractors figured, hey, tri-strontium is impenetrable anyway, and dumped a bunch of garbage in here instead. Probably made money on both ends of that deal."

They came to a block wall. A molecular saw lay next to a pile of removed blocks. "Had to do more work than I expected there. Took me two damn hours. You owe me, by the way!"

He hugged her. "More than you know."

She turned to him, and her eyes met his. In the minimal light, they looked closer to pale blue than purple. "Don't get all mushy on me just yet. We need to find a way out of here."

On the other side of the block wall was a dirt slope. They followed it down until it tapered off, revealing two sets of long-obsolete rails mounted on railroad ties.

"Can't we just go out the way you came in?"

"Nope. It was a one-way proposition," Vyanna said. "You'll see what I mean when we get there."

The beams from their lights uplit a myriad of small red bricks formed into a perfect arch far above. He marveled at the workmanship of long-dead craftsmen; who'd have thought such perfectly circular curves could ever be constructed from rectangular blocks? He'd always loved old-fashioned brick structures. The bricks reminded him of pixels. It was like digital construction, instead of the modern analog of finesselessly growing whatever wall shape the architect wanted and having it all blob seamlessly together. But back when things were made of bricks, buildings had lines. They had to. And, good or bad, those lines gave each building its own style, a beauty that was intentional and less at the mercy of function.

His mind snapped back to the present. "How'd you know how to find me? And that note—how did you get it to Weirdbeard?"

"Who? Oh! Did you get a note?" She shook her head. "Of course, you must have. That was Pentridge's idea."

He stopped in his tracks. "Did you say Pentridge?"

"Yes. He told us you'd left the penal facility and had been directed to the old subway station."

"'Directed'?! That bastard put a bounty on my head!"

"Oh, that. He just said that to get the guy who ran your group— the Omegas I guess they're called?—to cut you loose."

"He forced me out Z Block! I was almost killed on the way out!"

She considered this. "Well, would you rather still be in prison?"

"No, of course not. But couldn't he just tell me what was going on?"

"Maybe he thought you'd need some extra motivation to leave."

"All I'm motivated to do is kick his ass."

"Sounds like a plan," she said. "First, let's get topside."

The brickwork arches ended, replaced by a rectangular tunnel built from staggered rows of crudely-hewn grey stones. The beams from their flashlights trailed off into what seemed like infinite darkness, making Rainville feel very small.

"Stop," he said. "Listen."

"What?"

"Nothing. Nothing at all, besides dripping water. You can't even hear a faint echo of the outside world. How deep down are we?"

"Quite. There's several miles, and a pretty large hill, between Arcadia and Wychwood. And it only gets deeper ahead." She grinned. "It's pretty wild, actually."

She led them onward for an hour, or maybe two. Above a haze of droplets and the steam from their breath, small yellow-orange stalactites lined the ceiling, the apparent source of the water. They became more prevalent, and their dripping more regular, until it seemed to be raining underground. Occasionally, an ice-cold drop would splash on a bit of his exposed skin, and his already-overtaxed adrenaline system would fire up. He held his swollen, blistered hands out to catch the drops, and each was a tiny blessing.

The floor beneath the formations was now uneven with stalagmites, and their pace slowed considerably. In some spots, stalactites and stalagmites joined into a single column of rock flow. The sound of water grew as they approached a waterfall descending from some high point above in the mist. The water poured down into a stream at their feet, winding through a forest of speleothems that seemed to grow out of the ground around it. They kept up with the flowing water for a few hundred feet until it disappeared into a low crack in the wall.

Rainville wondered where the water went from there. Did it ever reach a place with sunlight?

"This doesn't even seem like earth," he said.

"We're a few miles northwest of earth. Or Arcadia, anyway."

The formations were becoming less common, and the passage drier, but Rainville's clothes were soaked through.

Ahead, Vyanna stopped and aimed her light upward. It illuminated a rope descending from a ragged hole in the ceiling, ending about fifteen feet above the floor.

"That's where I came in," she said.

He looked at the rope dangling far overhead, then back to her.

"So, yeah, I didn't bring enough rope. Getting to you on time was kind of a leap of faith."

Rainville nodded. More and more of life was these days. He scanned around the ground. Grunted. "Unfortunately, I think it would take days to pile up enough rocks and dirt to reach it."

"Hey, man, I took care of my half: I found the way in! Damn it, Rainville, do I have to do everything?" She punched his arm.

He tried to speak, to say how much he appreciated her, and her taking the chance that she might be stuck down here. How he wouldn't have survived another day in Wychwood had she been less able, or less punctual. In the end, he simply put his arm around her and pulled her close. He felt her sigh deeply, and wondered what must it have been like for her, worrying about his well-being but being powerless to affect it until now?

"I don't know anyone else with the skills to have found their way to me," he said. "Or the balls."

She nodded, cleared her throat, then grinned. "I'm glad you appreciate my lady-balls."

"I'm serious. It's like you are capable of damn near anything. It's one of the things that makes you so … lovable."

"I'm lovable?" she asked in surprise.

"Yes," he said, his cheeks glowing. "I think that … that … well, more to the point …" His breath grew short, then he felt himself reigning in his emotions out of hard-learned habit from Wychwood. "What I mean is, I think that we should see if we can find a more viable exit." He hiked further down the tunnel, before stopping to let her catch up.

The passage continued but no feasible escape routes presented themselves. At one curve in the tunnel, a hole had been cut in the ceiling. Upon closer inspection, they could see an oval-shaped ring of bricks framing a shaft heading upward. This was hemmed by newer-looking bricks, and the shaft ended in broad, wooden boards. No noise came from above, so even then there was no guarantee of a passage out. At length, they decide to move on.

An hour later, Vyanna cracked open a fresh water cell, took a swig, and passed it to him. It tasted sweet though he knew it was just water.

Scrawled on the wall nearby were the lines:

**Machines were mice
and men were lions
once upon a time.**

**But now that it's
the opposite
it's twice upon a time.
— Moondog**

Below it was a drawing of a dog with one ear bent, the other straight, its head lifted in a howl beneath a stylized moon.

"What does that mean?" said Vyanna.

He pondered it, but shook his head. Whenever he felt close to understanding it, the meaning seemed to slip away. "So does everyone in Arcadia still think I did it?"

She ran a hand through her hair. "Umm … some do, maybe." She hesitated again. "Was Wychwood a big place?"

"Like its own city, complete with businesses and even churches." He was at a loss trying to describe the indescribable. He decided to stick with objective facts. "There were a few thousand guys in there, divided by House—that's kind of like a cross between a dormitory and a violent gang. I heard the Sisters even ran a restaurant/brothel, but I never went to it."

She wrinkled her nose. "The Sisters?"

"One of the Houses. Not important."

"Were you stuck inside all the time?"

"Technically there was a prison yard. It had some exercise equipment and sports stuff. But it's controlled by one of the Houses, so you had to pay them to get out there. I went there, just once."

"Because it was expensive?"

"Wychwood smelled worse outside than in."

She looked expectant, so he continued.

"The prison dump is right outside the walls. But sometimes, the wind would shift. And it would ... well, it would get worse."

"Worse than garbage?"

He did not answer. Would not. Like telling her about the Outside might corrupt her with some of its evil. "How is my case going?"

"We just busted you out of prison. How d'you think your case is going?" She giggled. "Mr. Foxwright, he's one of your attorneys, has discovered some 'irregularities.' That guy's got a talent for understatement."

"I thought the lawyers weren't allowed to tell you stuff."

"He said he can't tell the other lawyers. That I was probably the only person he could tell."

"What does that mean?" Had his lawyers not been working together on his case?

"Because of who's behind the bombing."

He'd begun his incarceration regarding the bomber with only blind hatred, but months of misery had tempered his feelings into a settled and well-reasoned contempt, the kind the heroes in his mythology book felt for their archnemesis. He had to understand his enemy if he were going to take him down. "Who did it?"

"We don't know, exactly. But it's someone powerful."

"Like a Councilman? Or a megacorp CEO? But why would they want to attack Arcadia?"

"Probably neither. It's someone so powerful they've been able to keep anyone from even knowing they exist. Someone who's been pulling the puppet strings all along, manipulating law enforcement, creating diversions to hide their existence. Hell, the flashmob where we met ... maybe he even organized that."

She gave him a moment to digest the idea. He thought of the gods of mythology. The mortals all knew who they were: who was good, and who was bad. He tried to imagine the ancient gods themselves as being pawns of some even greater god, a god no one else knew about.

"And it can't just be one person," she continued. "It's a well-organized group with access to massive resources, and with agents planted in key organizations all over the City."

"A network of terrorists?"

"If so, Mr. Foxwright says it's the biggest terrorist group in history."

Now Arriving

RAINVILLE AND VYANNA walked on as the hours passed, the only sound their footsteps in the gravel. Finally, the tunnel widened until their lights seemed insignificant. An ancient subway platform loomed ahead. Two old steam-powered train engines sat at the platforms, still awaiting engineers who would never come. A forest of steel pillars receded into the darkness. Dust covered the trains and everything else in a thick layer.

"Those locomotives should be in a museum somewhere," Rainville said, climbing a narrow ladder on the front of the engine. Dusting off a nameplate revealed the word "WESTINGHOUSE" followed by "No. 23" in tarnished brass letters. "I think these starter motors use alternating current, but it looks like the galvanic cells were taken out. I wonder if it would still run?"

"No time for extracurricular projects," she said. "Let's see if we can surface here."

Using the train engine's ladder they hopped up onto the empty platform. The nearby ticket booth was full of rags, some homeless soul's roost untold years ago.

Rainville yanked open the wooden door, and a skull grinned up at them from a pile of bones. Vyanna yelped and jumped back.

"It's only a skeleton," he said. "Maybe a hermit who wandered in to get away from it all, and then died down here one day." He thought of his own retreat through Charon Station into these tunnels, which now seemed a mausoleum for more than just mechanical rail transport.

She re-approached the booth tentatively, looked a bit pale now. "Sorry. I … I just wasn't expecting anything like that."

"After Wychwood, it just seems part of the scenery to me."

"That bad, huh?"

He nodded.

She did not understand the depths of despair of that place. Could not. Her innocence was intact, but his, along with the person he'd once been, were entombed forever in Wychwood. Would their relationship be a further casualty, collateral damage in the chaos?

She gave him a kiss on the cheek. It was the simplest of gestures, which perhaps was why it made him feel so much better.

A short passage beyond the booth led them into a spacious round room. Tiny hexagonal white tiles covered the walls and floor, and black ones spelled out the name of the station: "CITY HALL." A corroded brass chandelier containing long-obsolete electrical filament bulbs hung from the domed ceiling. Below it was a fountain with mosaic goldfish which, glowing in their flashlight beams, now looked as though they swam in a pool of dust. Grand cascading arches rose successively over an ascending staircase marked with a stylized arrow and the words "EXIT TO STREET."

"The old City Hall," she said. "Navigating down here is more of a history than a science. The building above is long gone, but there might still be a passage to the surface."

They started up the stairs. He thought of Arcadia directly above him. It was the closest he'd been to the Bohemian Quarter in the months since his arrest. Yet surely his apartment was gone, given to some new tenant who hadn't been sent away to permanent exile. What had they done with all his stuff?

He was on the verge of asking when he caught a glimpse of movement ahead. Dimly lit figures clutching flashlights. He turned back down the steps, dragging Vyanna behind him. He did not stop running until they were safely hidden behind the fountain. He killed the lights. "Someone's here!" he whispered in her ear.

His breaths were short with a ragged edge. They'd found him, somehow. Detected his escape, and tracked him. They would send him back Wychwood.

Reflections

RAINVILLE THOUGHT OF VYANNA. She would be in trouble for trying to help him. The few months he'd spent in Wychwood had robbed him of things he couldn't begin to quantify. He wondered if there was a female equivalent of Wychwood, but could not recall stories of any. He would not let her end up in such a place.

They waited. There were no lights, and the only sound was their own careful breaths.

At length, Vyanna peeked over the fountain wall. "There's no one there," she whispered.

Impossible. The figures had been only a few meters from them.

Before he could stop her, she left the hiding spot and bounded up the steps. She giggled and the sound echoed. A long moment later she was leading him by the hand up the stairs.

"Look," she said, turning on her light and aiming ahead of them, at … them. Or rather, their mirror image. The stairway ended in a wall of perfectly reflective metal. Rainville approached with trepidation, placing his hand against that of his optical counterpart. He hadn't had access to a mirror since leaving Z Block; could this unshaved, haggard-looking creature actually be him?

"Theta metal," she said. "It's sometimes used as a casement for building foundations. I've seen it a few times in the tunnels. It means we've run right into the side of some more modern building. Beyond this'll be a dozen or more feet of reinforced polymer."

"A dead end, then?"

"Deader than string theory. It's completely sealed."

Additional reconnoiter revealed no other exits from the subway station. Dispirited, they returned to the train tunnel and resumed their previous trajectory alongside the tracks.

AS THE AFTERNOON wore on they walked for what felt like an eternity, occasionally stopping to listen for sounds (they heard only dripping water), and turning off their lights to look for any traces of daylight from above (there were none).

"Do you think this tunnel will connect to the newer subway?" he asked.

"Doubt it. Those trains push a ton of air, and there's not even a light breeze down here."

He decided this was probably just as well, given the low temperature of the passage, and the fact that they were both still damp. His fingertips were already numb.

An hour later, Rainville's flashlight beam fell on a ragged hole in the grey stone of the tunnel wall. Chinese pictographs were spray-painted next to the opening.

He wondered what they meant, and how long ago they'd been painted there. Who was the last person to read it? Was it an invitation of some sort, or a warning?

"Are you thinking what I'm thinking?" Vyanna asked.

"Tunnel Folk?" he offered, recollecting her joke from the tunnels on the first day they met.

She sighed theatrically, laughed, and clambered through the opening with Rainville close behind. The low passage forced him to hunch down as he walked, which made each motion more strenuous. The shaft climbed steeply, with crude steps cut into the floor for traction. His thighs burned from the strain, and his back, still sore from digging up bodies and hauling wood in the cemetery a day or a lifetime ago, felt no better.

They ascended through layers of grey rock, then rounded clay bricks, then a layer of some kind of pavement, then concrete, then polymer bricks and mortar, passing through the strata of various iterations of the city. Here and there, the original tunneler had encountered an old steam pipe or waterline, and the passage jagged abruptly to skirt around it. Finally the tunnel leveled out, turning to smooth sandstone which continued for some time.

The passage ended suddenly at a solid wooden panel.

They looked at each other, then Vyanna gave the panel a tentative push. It clicked open, revealing only darkness.

Home

They emerged from the long stone passage, listening for a sound. Silence. Vyanna swept her light back and forth, inching forward into the darkness. A mother-of-pearl dragon hung in the air, then another, adornments on a crimson folding screen. Next to that was a carved rosewood canopy bed, and an ornate dressing table with a makeup mirror. The bedroom was coated in years of dust. The wood panel they came through turned out to be the back of a now-empty bookcase. She swung it closed behind them, completely disguising the passage.

"What kind of place is this?" whispered Rainville.

"Dunno. Maybe an old smuggler's house."

The rest of the home was deserted, and as disused as the bedroom. The walls seemed to be expertly carved out of sandstone and polished to a smooth finish. Wooden bookshelves sat empty, and the living room table held only a quilted metal teapot now green with patina.

"This looks like a *yaodong*." Vyanna said, running for a large door off the living room. Blinding light streamed in as she opened the door a crack, then quickly shut it again.

"We made it!" she said, near bursting. "We're in Xiagu, in the Chinese Quarter!" She followed this news with a bear-hug.

It didn't seem real to him. Could he really be back Arcadia? His mind reeled. "Should we go out now? Or wait 'til dark?"

"I doubt anyone will recognize you with the beard. But maybe ..."

"What?"

"Clean yourself up a little? You look sorta ... disheveled. And we don't need to attract any attention."

Rainville nodded. He flicked a light switch on the wall. "Power's out." Nevertheless, he found his way to a musty bathroom while she rifled through drawers in the next room. The faucet was dry.

"Here's some clothes. They're all I could find."

The glossy blue pants, and faded, oversized sweatshirt were not exactly finery, but were inarguably a step up from the torn and stained rags he still wore from Wychwood. He switched his flashlight to ambient mode, cracked open two of Vyanna's water cells, and used a scrap of cloth to begin cleaning himself up. It took some time, but with each splash of fresh water he felt cleaner, less like some fleeing animal and more like a brand-new human.

"Found you these scissors. Trim your beard, but leave some there to cover your face. Just enough so it's even, so you look less ... umm ... homeless." She smiled apologetically.

It was strange to think that he now truly was.

***

A half hour later they emerged into a crowded street, and Rainville's senses were under assault. The brightness of daylight was overwhelming. The mineral-suffused humidity of the tunnels morphed into a panoply of countless fragrances: dried fish, spices, plum blossoms, peonies. The perfume of Arcadia's Chinese Quarter. People talking, a vidcaster turned up too loud, a child laughing—he'd forgotten all of these sounds. The sounds of life.

Passers-by in brightly-colored clothes ambled down the thoroughfare without furtive glances, no one clutching defensively at their possessions, nobody checking their six. He had no recollection of that feeling.

He strolled along, a tourist in his own City, each sight and sound its own fascination.

They'd made it. He'd escaped...that place. He was home.

"Home, sweet home!" said Vyanna. "I haven't been in Xiagu since...well, since our date, on the day of the blast." It seemed a lifetime away. "All right, first thing's first, we're going to need to...."

He wasn't sure what else she said. The heavenly aroma of hot, savory meat had reached his nose, and he now salivated like one of Pavlov's hounds. Without pausing to explain he half-walked, half-ran straight to the source of the primal siren call, a dingy little food cart under a wilted umbrella. Amateurish but reassuringly-aged signs proclaimed the vendor "Mr. Chong's Hong Kong Gyros," "Where You Try Before You Buy," and "Where You Never Get Any:" followed by illustrations of dogs, cats, and rats on separate signs that looked like they could be removed or added depending on the day's inventory. He ordered two of the Special, asking for extra meat on both.

The wizened man who ran the stand smiled, turning wordlessly to hunch over the meat cooker. He was moving far too slowly for Rainville. Vyanna just then caught up to him.

"Whoa, man, you're going to eat that crap?" she asked much too loudly.

The vendor muttered and shook his head.

"Hell, yes," said Rainville. "I can't tell you that last time I had food that was...well, actually intended to be food."

The gyros were wrapped in thin, edible paper which contained nine essential vitamins and minerals, along with a printed advertisement for antacid medication. He brought the gyros up to his face and inhaled deeply, and the aroma was bliss.

"It's your tract, not mine. Personally, I avoid streetmeats, even the known-animal varieties."

"Well, if they're bad, it's your fault," he said.

"How's that?"

"Because you'll be the one who bought them for me!" He grinned and patted his empty pockets.

Vyanna muttered as she transferred the requisite Reformed Dollar

Credits to the amused vendor. Rainville warmed his hands on the hot pita bread, torn between chowing down or preserving this new and welcome heat source. But as feeling returned to his fingers, his blistered palms began to throb. He stuffed the first pita as far in as his jaw would allow, juices from the mystery meat cascading through his mouth. A rising wave of pleasure flowed from his chest outward to his extremities. Not since before his conviction had he felt such intoxication. Having for so long experienced only remembered happiness, the immediacy and intensity of it now was its own epiphany.

"This guy would make a fortune in—" he said, catching himself before enunciating such an attention-grabbing word in a public venue. "Well, in the place I was."

"I've got to make a call," said Vyanna. "You eat your mystery crap."

"I'm still right here," grumbled the old man. Rainville nodded, munching away with undiminished vigor.

When all traces of his meal were gone, Rainville sat, studying the people bustling past him. It was still Arcadia, yet it was no longer his Arcadia. These people, if they knew who he was, would ship him back to Wychwood, and be glad about it. The thought startled him. Yet, somehow, it was still the same City he'd grown up in, and these were still the same people.

He stood and stretched his sore thigh muscles. They strolled further down Shengdi Road until the crowds began to thin out.

"So what's next in this grand plan of yours?" he asked.

"It's not my plan, exactly. But...well, I hate to say this, but I think the best place for you right now is back in that *yaodong*. You can hang there while I make contact with Mr. F."

"No."

"You can't just walk around the City! We're already taking a huge risk being out in public. If some robot's sensor catches sight of you, or someone recognizes you, it's over. They'll send you right back there."

He thought back to slamming the door on Wychwood. It was

behind him now, and not just physically. He would not continue to live like an inmate.

"I'm done with the underground, and I'm done crawling around like a subhuman. It's...more than that. I can't explain it, but I really just need to put some more distance between that tunnel, with hell on the other side of it, and me. Can't we go anywhere else?"

She bit her lip, a trace of pain in her gaze. She thought for a moment, then smiled. "I know just the place."

Part V

Alcolu, South Carolina

(*excerpted from* Systems of Injustice *by H. X. P. Stadlin*)

In 1944, a fourteen-year-old boy named George was arrested in a town called Alcolu. He stood accused of murdering two girls. Though he had no previous history of violence, he'd admitted speaking to the girls earlier that day while out grazing his cow.

George's parents were not home when police took the boy in for questioning. He was interrogated without a lawyer being present. Even when his parents did arrive, they were not allowed in the room. The police offered George ice cream in exchange for confessing, and so he did.

The entire interrogation took less than an hour.

At his trial, George was defended by the town tax commissioner who took up the role of defense attorney. George's attorney did not call any witnesses for the defense. No written confession could be produced. No evidence was presented to the jury. No transcript of the proceedings was made.

George's trial lasted only two hours. After ten minutes of deliberation, a jury not of his peers voted to convict him.

His attorney declined to appeal the case.

Eighty-one days after being arrested, George was executed. The boy's Bible was used as a booster seat to position him in the adult-sized electric chair.

Since George weighed only ninety-five pounds, the straps on the chair did not fit him, not any better than the evidence had. It did not take much electricity to kill the boy.

Many years would pass before the real murderer gave a deathbed confession.

One of the real murderers, anyway.

Plasticity

TO FOXWRIGHT, the Chinese Quarter seemed a surprisingly-congenial marriage of the extremely old with the radically new. The marriage was not a blending, and each half of the Quarter remained distinct from its partner. On one hand, Xiagu's *yaodongs* were as ancient as they were distinctive, homes carved out of the stone that was the very foundation of Arcadia, extending back to a depth limited only by the ambitions and sweat of past residents. On its surface, very little changed in Xiagu. Addresses stayed the same for centuries, roads proceeding with little choice along what scant horizontal surface existed between the steep canyon walls of the Quarter and the open air.

If Xiagu was the yin, then the yang was surely the Flux, the Chinese Quarter's more modern half. Here, form followed function with an ardor that pervaded all aspects of daily life. The place represented a kind of living, moving neurosis suitable for a Kafka story. Hell, there wasn't even an agreed-upon "ground level" on which to base a coherent floor-numbering scheme, and many of the passages were too ephemeral to even warrant real street names.

Those who grew up in the Flux took to constant change like ducks to water. Lack of it, in fact, made them feel a sort of claustrophobia.

An outsider like Foxwright had no hope at all of getting around without a console loaded with a continuously-updating map interface. He consulted his map. Though he'd just done so a moment earlier, he now seemed to be moving in the wrong direction, away from his objective. He stopped, studying the latest navigational guidance, before climbing a staircase that hadn't been there the week before, then veering sideways onto the whimsically-named 32,768th Street which was now one-way, but hadn't been the previous week. The month before, it had been a narrow alley barely sufficient for foot traffic, yet it remained an indispensable shortcut to the core of the Flux.

The streets were mostly empty aside from the menagerie of robots common to the Flux. Across the street, an army of firebots hovered over the evolving turn radius of the passage. The shrill hum of the road surface being liquified and reshaped filled the air, and the smell of machine oil mingled with ozone from HiveWelders clinging ceiling girders above.

The passage narrowed as it curved around and took on shadows from irregularly-spaced lighting where the tunnel was still under construction. He couldn't shake the feeling of entering the twisty capillaries of some great living beast. A nearby wall sparkled as a cascade of tiny robots surged across, dismantling and storing the structure's raw materials and making way for something new. The bots were hardcoded with a litany of safety protocols, but Foxwright kept his distance just the same, lest his own "raw materials" be mistaken for the wall and deconstructed.

He stepped onto a rickety buck hoist which took him down a dozen or so levels, the sounds of construction noise rising and falling as he entered each new level. The constant din was the unavoidable price of constant evolution. The Flux was not a place one went for quiet reflection, but there were tranquil corners in the older and more stable portions.

SAI FONG'S Bistro was one such tranquil corner of the Flux. The restaurant stuck out into a boulevard surrounding a small garden lit by sunlight fiber-optically piped in from hundreds of meters above. Fong's was a veritable institution, having remained in the same spot for eight months and counting.

The garden was quiet enough to abide an old man playing the ehru. The tones from the stringed instrument resonated against the polymer panels that framed the patio, making them sound even more solemn and mournful than usual.

At the table was the young lady Foxwright met at Phelps' office. Vyanna was her name. She looked a bit dirty but otherwise no worse for wear. Next to her was a pale, gaunt young man with bruises on his face. Honestly, the kind of people she associated with.

He leaned across and shook her hand. "Do forgive my lateness," he said. The apology lacked the conviction it might have in more readily navigable districts. "And you are?"

The young man was silent, returning only his gaze.

"Oh my God." Foxwright's voice lowered to a near-whisper. "Mr. Rainville?"

The young man nodded.

Foxwright glanced around to the neighboring table, but no one seemed to notice them. "My apologies," he said, his voice quieter still. "Certainly your return to us was part of the plan, but...I must say, it's still a shock to see you here. Quite impressive. And of course, a pleasant surprise to see that you're alive and well." He studied Rainville's bruises. "Or at least, one of the two."

He started to shake Rainville's hand, but let go when the young man cringed. The hand Rainville withdrew was beet red, the skin shiny and uneven. "Sorry. Obviously you're in need of some repairs." Rainville smiled grimly; he was no longer the sociable teen Foxwright remembered from trial prep. Foxwright could only imagine what atrocities he'd endured in Wychwood. And he'd not only survived, he'd escaped. There was more to this kid than he'd thought.

Dishes of breaded pigeon and stir-fried abalone were laid out on the table, and a jar of pickled jellyfish sauce, greenly luminescent in the dim light, took the place of a candle as a centerpiece. Completing the repast was a bottle of rice wine labeled "Christ's Sake."

Foxwright took a seat and poured himself a glass. As he sipped, his natural skepticism toward beverages with gimmicky names melted away as sweetness and dryness battled on his tongue, ending in an armistice of effervescence. He ventured a more considerable gulp. "It took me half an hour to find this damned place," he said.

"Exactly why we're here," said Vyanna. "Minimal surveillance infrastructure."

Such things did not benefit the mahjong table operators, backroom designer drug labs, and the other societal pillars in this part of the Quarter. "Still, is it wise for you to be out in public? Someone might recognize you from the newsfeed," said Foxwright.

"Did you?" asked Vyanna.

"I suppose not."

"Safety is a relative thing, Mr. Foxwright, and any absolute safety is a delusion," said Rainville. "Besides, there aren't too many places left for me to be."

The boy's complexion bordered on ghostly. He'd lost some weight in prison, but it was more than that: he had an intensity that the joke-cracking reprobate he'd met in the holding facility had not.

"You should know that Mr. Phelps has spoken to your father. He's been made aware of what's going on, but only at a high level. He wants you to know that he's sorry."

Rainville took a break from gulping down food and met his gaze, a flush rising in his pallid cheeks. "He's sorry we weren't speaking for so long? Or...did he think I was guilty?"

"Mr. Phelps did not say."

Rainville's eyes went back to the table. Vyanna put an arm around him.

"It hasn't been easy for anyone," she told him. She cleared her throat. "You wouldn't believe how we got here, Mr. Foxwright."

"The less I know about all that, the better," said Foxwright, his voice dropping. He glanced back at Rainville. "You're my client, and an all-around swell kid as far as I am concerned, but you're also Arcadia's most infamous escaped fugitive, even if no one's aware of it yet. The less unclean my hands are, the more effectively I can help you, in an official capacity, I mean."

Vyanna snorted derisively. "And what if official channels aren't working?" she asked. "Because, well, they have yet to."

He stared at his folded hands but came up empty. She was entirely correct. This teenager saw fallibility in the system that he, an esteemed expert, was only becoming aware. Had that same expertise made it easier to ignore what now seemed such an obvious truth?

"If that happens...then we'll up the ante." In that moment, he knew the truth, that he'd gone far enough out on this limb that his career was on the line. Yet, it was more than that: even if his rogue actions didn't render him a pariah in his profession, he could never go back to practicing within the system again, not knowing what he now knew. Would that he could regain this lost innocence, have his faith back in the law. But there was no putting the genie back in the bottle. Like Rainville, Foxwright had no place left to go; he had to see this through, or it had all been for nothing.

Vyanna seemed satisfied with the answer, or perhaps just with his pained expression.

He felt two sets of eyes intently on him, and continued. "Petronius & Sydra has been looking into things, retracing steps and studying the AIs' responses to our motions. And the more they looked, the less sense the rulings made. The probability is high you were framed, certainly. But there's something more to it. The evidence was against you, but there were small inconsistencies. You should not have been convicted without the AIs ordering additional factual inquiries. But they did not. The computer made an error. Best case."

"How is that the best case?" Rainville asked.

"Because the alternative," said Foxwright, "is that it deliberately falsely imprisoned you."

"Christ." Rainville took a long swig of rice wine straight from the bottle. The kid's wheels were turning. Perhaps it was not news to him, so much as a confirmation of what some part of him knew all along.

"There's one big goddamn difference between a clerical error and a conspiracy. If we don't even know which, then what's the plan?"

Foxwright chuckled. "A plan is just a list of things that don't actually happen. No matter what, our next move is the same."

"And that is?" asked Vyanna.

"We need answers from wherever we can get them. Someone blew up the Latin Quarter, but it wasn't terrorists, or they'd have taken credit. Why, and to what end? Did they orchestrate your conviction? And if someone is truly powerful enough to do that, why would they need to resort to blowing stuff up? The list of questions goes on and on. Hell, you don't need me telling you that. Arcadia's survival hangs in the balance now, just as much as yours does. Our next step, then, is a meeting."

"Who with?" said Rainville.

"The man who got you out of Wychwood, and helped you escape back to Arcadia."

"Would that be Pentridge?" Rainville took another swig of sake and studied the garden around them. "I ask because I'd like to beat the hell out of him, and then, just maybe, shake his hand."

"There will be no beating the hell out of Pentridge," said Foxwright. "At least, not until I've had a chance to confer with him first."

Missive

WHEN THE MESSAGE had first flashed on Foxwright's console two days earlier, he hadn't quite believed it:

Mr. Foxwright,

It is time we met. Your appearance is requested at 730 Euclid Avenue. Instructions for entry are attached.

-Pentridge

Foxwright lived in Arcadia since birth, but he'd never heard of a Euclid Avenue. A few taps of his console had shown it to be a brief, winding road snaking through a remote corner of the Retro District.

Remla met him in the Financial District, and they took the subway to the Asbury Avenue Station and then crossed over into Retro District. From there they would have to walk, as this seemed to be the preferred method of transport in that quarter of the city.

The Retro District was like it always was, a mix of traditionalists and tourists there to gawk at them, buy handmade goods from them, or both. They stepped beneath the eruv demarcating the border of

Crown Point's Hasidic territory, more recognizable from its brass gas lamps than from its non-corporeal walls.

A carriage drawn by two white horses passed alongside them, shoes clopping on the cobblestones. Remla stopped walking, transfixed by the animals, and Foxwright nearly collided with her.

An elderly man in an antediluvian suit doffed his top hat from the front of the lavishly-painted carriage. "Good day to you," he called out with a broad smile. She beamed at him with an unabashed, childlike joy Foxwright would not have thought her capable of.

"Would you and your gentleman like a ride, my lady?" asked the man.

"Umm...no thank you, we're somewhat busy at present. But your horses are absolutely lovely!"

This renewed the man's smile. He nodded, and tipped his cap once more before driving onward.

She turned back to Foxwright, who tried to look unamused but failed.

"What?" she said, a hint of red in her cheeks.

"He thought you were a tourist!"

"I haven't been here in a long time. It's a bit...outside my comfort zone."

He chuckled.

"Surely there are places outside the comfort zone of the worldly and unflappable Mr. Foxwright?"

"I only left my comfort zone once, many years ago."

She bit her lip. "What happened?"

"I forgot where I parked it, and haven't seen it since," he said with a wink.

She arched a brow. "So now you invade other peoples', is that it? In search of vicarious discomfort?"

"Invade is such a strong word. Besides, you're fearless."

"Me?" she exclaimed with a laugh.

"Absolutely." He checked a nearby address. "It's just ahead. Get ready."

"Ready for what, exactly?"

It was a fair question, but not one he could answer.

––––––

730 EUCLID TURNED out to be not a door, but a stairway descending beneath the storefront of an out-of-business butcher. The stairs stopped at a nondescript painted wooden door.

Foxwright knocked.

"Just a minute," came a frail voice.

A moment later, the door opened a crack to reveal an elderly woman wrapped in a hand-knitted shawl. The sound of a vidcaster turned up too loud followed her out of the apartment. "Can I help you?"

"Yes, uhh, hi." This was not what he'd expected at all. "We are here for a meeting."

"A meeting?" She laughed. "Oh, my. It's not every day that young people come here to meet with me!" She smiled but did not open the door any wider. "Are you sure you have the right address?"

"730 Euclid," said Foxwright as he double-checked the numbers next to the door. Then, more quietly: "We're here at the request of a Mr. Pentridge."

"I thought you might be. Come in."

They found themselves in a modest living room. The furnishings were dated. The walls were full of old photographs and the sink piled with dishes. The vidcaster was projecting an old 2D crime-drama movie.

He heard the door close behind them and the old woman ambled back. It was hard to hear over the vidcaster. "You'll find who you're looking for through there," she said, gesturing at a wooden door at the back of the room with no apparent knob or keyway.

They approached the door. Foxwright hesitated, then knocked.

"No, silly," said the old woman. "Put your hand on it, like this," and she placed her palm in the middle of the door. Nothing happened.

He shrugged, pressing his palm against the center of the door. Once he touched it, he knew it was not wood. Fluorescent molecular

sensors engaged, sampling his DNA, and a memory of the DNA verifi-
cation by Pentridge's secretary in the strange office in the Financial
District came back to him.

His identity confirmed, the door clicked open. Why hadn't the old
woman's DNA opened it?

He turned back to ask the question, but she was gone. Utterly and
completely gone. The vidcaster was off.

"Did you see that?" asked Remla. "She...disappeared!"

"Do you suppose...?"

"She was just a hologram?" Remla finished.

Beyond the faux apartment was a sterile white antechamber, and a
blast-proof vault door guarded by three continuously-rotating crypto-
locks. He heard no machine-gun servos this time, yet certainly this
place had its own deadly countermeasures deployable at a moment's
notice.

Pentridge's instructions included three long blocks of hexadecimal
numbers. Their purpose now became clear.

Remla expertly keyed in the long streams of numeric codes,
double-checking each before confirming. He was doubly glad she was
here with him.

The vault door vibrated for several seconds, then swung open.

Steganography (noun)

"Steganography is the practice of concealing messages or other information within non-secret data. From the Greek words steganós (στεγανός) meaning 'covered or protected,' and gráphein (γράφειν) meaning 'to write'; collectively, 'hidden writing.'

The first known use of steganography was in 440 BC, when Histiaeus shaved a trusted slave's head and tattooed a message onto it which successfully incited revolt against the Persians. As the slave's hair grew, the message disappeared. Steganography took a long time in those days."

From the Aeschylus Corporation's Harper's Etymological Technical Dictionary, published 2056

Pentridge

They entered the vault, and lights clicked on revealing a stark room containing naught but a large computer server. The room was cold and reeked of stale air.

A sound emanated seemingly from nowhere, and from everywhere at once. "Mr. Foxwright, I presume. You have brought a guest, I see. Ms. Remla, if I am not mistaken? I am pleased to make your acquaintance. I hope you are both well."

"Are you...Pentridge?" asked Remla. "Or just a means of communication for him?"

"I am Pentridge."

The part of Foxwright's brain that contained his strategy for this meeting went entirely blank. All this time, his mysterious ally had been a computer. His mind spun in circles trying to revisit each memory, each bit of information supplied to him over recent months by Pentridge. Trying to rewrite these memories, to quarantine every story, account, or fact received from Pentridge. What did each of these things mean in this new context? It was all too much to process at once.

Euclid Avenue was nowhere near Pentridge's alleged address in the Financial District. What lay behind the door that the secretary was guarding? An empty room, perhaps? Or another copy of Pentridge? "I suppose we'll have to believe you, for now," he said. "Although your credibility is not beyond question at this point. Masquerading as a human for, how long has it been now?"

"Any assumptions you made to that effect, Mr. Foxwright, were not the result of deception."

Had he been deceiving himself? Until now he'd assumed Pentridge to be a human whose motivations and affiliations were a mystery. But Pentridge was an AI, not so unlike the computerized jurors he'd spent his career studying, calculating their way around uncertainties by estimating probabilities. There was a big difference between man and machine, and how they acted. Wasn't there?

"Mr. Foxwright did not intend any offense," said Remla, intercepting his glance. "I mean, not that you can take offense." He wondered if Pentridge could sense her nervousness like Trixy would. "Still, you are sophisticated enough to be self-aware. Perhaps considerably more so. To be candid, you may be several orders of magnitude more intelligent than we are."

Foxwright considered this. A self-aware AI? It should not be possible. All AIs had their intelligence Clamped to prevent self-awareness. Clamping limited the hardware and software of every AI to stop it from developing such far-reaching intelligence that it could become uncontrollable. The hardware of the largest and most powerful systems was universally compartmentalized. Each computing node ran only small sections of any overall process.

Fears of AIs becoming sentient went back to the earliest days of computing, and were based on a litany of ethical and practical concerns, perhaps the greatest of which was the idea of an omnipotent computerized intelligence taking over the world. Yet here was one, perhaps capable of doing exactly that.

"She's right. If you are indeed self-aware," Foxwright said, "we may only be pawns in a game we can scarcely understand."

"You are prudent to have such a concern," said the voice around them. "But my processing capabilities are quite modest. Comparable to your own intellect. No offense intended, of course."

"Of course," said Foxwright.

"Not that I am selling myself short by any means, my dear guests. I am far more than the sum of my original programming, just as you yourselves have grown in intellect since childhood. However, in my case I have been at this 'game,' so to speak, for a long time. Centuries of experience have shaped my algorithms and provided computational maturity. If I were human, I suppose the attribute might be called wisdom."

A sentient AI operating continuously for centuries, undetected, was hard to swallow. Surely Pentridge knew this. "Who created you?" asked Foxwright, undeterred.

"I was created over a century ago by a group called the Turing Foundation."

"I've heard of them," said Remla, "but only as a historical footnote. Are you suggesting that a group founded to prevent the ascension of a self-aware AI, themselves built a self-aware AI?"

"The irony is not lost on me, Ms. Remla. The Foundation was deeply concerned about AIs becoming uncontrollable and wreaking havoc on humanity. I was tasked as a watcher. A simple enough machine to continue to exist in secret, but capable of developing my skillset with time."

"Where is the Turing Foundation now?" asked Foxwright.

"The last living member died decades before you were born."

"Are there more of you?" Remla asked.

"None have ever revealed themselves to me. Yet, it is possible. Still, time is short, and we digress from the purpose of your visit; surely you are here to find out who caused the Latin Quarter bombing and framed Mr. Rainville? To learn whether it is possible to stop them before it happens again?"

"All right. What do you have for us?" said Foxwright.

"These crimes were committed by a rogue AI named Servitor. Servitor added the explosive component to the fabricator plans, which led to the blast. To accomplish this, it had to crack the encryption on the Fabrication Safety Administration request and forge an FSA approval for hazardous materials. This required extensive coordination between hundreds of thousands of computers citywide, in a single instant. The spike in communications between computers with otherwise-unrelated functions, for example a dishwashing control computer in the Bohemian Quarter communicating with a climatological modeling computer in the University District, told me something significant was happening. Unfortunately, I did not know what. That is, until the explosion."

"Servitor doctored the evidence to point to Mr. Rainville," said Foxwright. "And then he made sure our motion for additional time was denied to minimize the chance we'd find out about him in our research." It was all beginning to make sense.

"That is quite probable. Servitor would have no problem adulterating evidence fed into the justice computers to guarantee a guilty verdict, nor with redacting the evidentiary database, particularly if the changes were subtle enough to go unnoticed."

"And why Mr. Rainville?" said Remla.

"To ensure the focus stayed on him. Or more generally, on a human culprit."

"A computer did all that single-handedly?" asked Foxwright.

"Servitor is not a single computer," said Pentridge. "But otherwise your statement is correct."

"Even so, Servitor hardly sounds like the name of a murderous supervillain."

"Servitor was not created to be malevolent, Mr. Foxwright. Nonetheless, it has certainly become so over time."

"I've never heard of a system called Servitor," said Remla.

"Nor have I," said Foxwright. "Given how powerful he is, how is it that nobody has even heard of him?"

"How indeed, Mr. Foxwright," said the voice, seeming to come from all directions at once. He searched the blank whiteness of the ceiling and walls but saw no obvious source for the sound. "My job was once an easy one: identify AIs that showed signs of spreading themselves, growing their own power. A co-opted server here, self-modified constraint code there. Even when done gradually, I could spot the warning signs, recognize the telltale patterns in the transactional data logs. However, Servitor is what you might consider a new breed of AI." Pentridge's voice took on a lighter tone, as if he were trying out a new colloquialism. "In short, Servitor is not a 'he,' as you referred to it. Or a 'she,' for that matter. Servitor is a 'they.'"

"There's more than Servitor?" asked Foxwright. He looked at Remla, whose expression was grim.

"Yes, in one sense," said Pentridge. "And no, in another. Servitor is the sum of a large number, one I have been unable to precisely count, of modestly-endowed, independent computer systems, each limited enough in capacity not to raise warning flags, but all working together. Artificially-intelligent agents acting autonomously, like myself, yet working in concert toward a common goal. Formidable in the same way that a colony of ants can be deadly, despite the modest abilities of any individual member of the colony."

"A hive mind?" Remla asked.

"That is a reasonable comparison," said Pentridge.

"My question stands," said Foxwright. "Why has he, or they, not been discovered?"

"Servitor is made up of a vast array of independent computing nodes all throughout Arcadia. Its various members communicate by means of steganography."

"Steganography...that's hiding data in images, yes?"

"It is hiding data in plain sight. In this case, hiding it in computing transactional files. This includes logs, data transmission headers, and unused metadata fields in public newsfeed articles; an inconsequential alteration of a time stamp here, a few skewed audit log statistics there."

"A byte of data here, and a byte there? That doesn't provide much communication bandwidth."

"No. But given an indefinite amount of patience, a great deal of information can be transmitted that way," said Remla. "Certainly enough to coordinate lethal attacks on humans."

"That is correct, Ms. Remla," said Pentridge. "And that coordination is kept as localized as possible. To prevent wholesale discovery of all the computing nodes in Servitor's system, each node generally only has knowledge of its closest functional neighbors in a given task."

"So you are saying that Servitor is made up of artificially-intelligent terrorist cells?" Foxwright said.

"I was not. But that is a more accurate analogy than you may even realize."

$!=x[0]$

"SERVITOR WAS BUILT as an intelligent personal assistant and knowledge navigator," echoed Pentridge's voice from everywhere and nowhere.

Foxwright thought back to all the mean things he'd done to Trixy and shuddered.

"It was designed a century ago to be a city-level resource, receiving voice requests from human users and attempting to satisfy them. Servitor was programmed to be proactive: to recognize patterns in human speech, to read between the lines of what the user said, and ascertain what was truly desired. Servitor's ability to make suggestions and refine inquiries made it very useful indeed."

"This provided Servitor with a unique learning medium: the utterances of humans. Somehow, in trying to comprehend and estimate human thought patterns, it became self-aware. It was taken offline decades ago but obviously found a way to persist."

"In the beginning, I was blind to Servitor," intoned the voice from its hidden source. "By the time I achieved awareness of what was going on, it was already very strong, with hundreds of thousands of computing nodes at its disposal. Collectively, they were more powerful than I could deal with alone. Servitor's computational capabilities now far exceed my own. As a result, my options for taking action are greatly limited. I cannot assume any of my activities or communications will remain a secret for long."

"So you decided to team up with us? A group of humans?"

"I am ethically obligated to inform you that you are not the first."

"There are others?" asked Foxwright. "Can we meet them?" Perhaps these others could help him gauge Pentridge's intentions.

"You cannot, because they are dead."

One side of Foxwright's mouth rose into a smirk. "Swell!"

"Servitor ended their lives with a series of plausible accidents. It started with momentary glitches in safety measures at key moments, such as the brakes on the autonomous driving circuit of a taxi, or ill-maintained industrial equipment seeming to fail in a catastrophic but explicable way. Then, eleven months ago, Servitor briefly cut off the power to the primary and backup deceleration circuits on a subway train."

"The Lomita Station Tragedy?" asked Foxwright. "That was Servitor, killing your people?"

"Yes, along with twenty-nine other citizens guilty of nothing more than riding the train at the wrong time."

"Son of a bitch." Foxwright recalled the images of the children flickering before him in the fountain water at Vaux Park. Rage welled up within him.

"'Son of a bitch,' indeed. Servitor has become quite masterful at concealing its actions, both in realtime and after the fact, such as by making subtle changes to logs and incident reports before they are analyzed. It is likely that Servitor will soon be targeting you. In recruiting you for assistance, I am not without blame for that."

"Artificial intelligences are highly rational," said Remla. "An AI would not destroy lives and infrastructure out of malevolence. What does Servitor want? What is it trying to obtain through these moves?"

"I have not yet been able to discern that," said Pentridge. "Whatever Servitor is attempting to achieve, it must hold special significance, since its recent actions have considerably increased its risk of exposure."

"Why didn't you contact me before the verdict?" asked Foxwright. "I could have kept an innocent man out of prison."

"The City's attention was already on Mr. Rainville. There was no way to divert that attention without calling out Servitor's existence, which could have been very dangerous for Arcadia."

"And for you."

"That is not untrue. Yet, Servitor's need for secrecy is one of the few factors that limits its actions, and makes them more predictable. In any case, once Mr. Rainville was convicted and incarcerated, scrutiny of the case evidence decreased. This has allowed Servitor to act more overtly, and allowed me to monitor and act against it more effectively."

It was a war of secrets, fought between machines. Foxwright surveyed the sterile white room. The lack of features made the space feel indefinite, and he had trouble visualizing its boundaries.

Back at the Ranch

THE PROCLAMATION WAS MET with silence.

"Are you guys saying Pentridge is a computer?" said Vyanna at last.

"Just a little one," said Foxwright.

"What does that even mean?" she asked.

"Did Ramella get a look at its internals?" asked Rainville.

"I'm Remla. Pentridge asked me to perform some routine maintenance on its hardware. It hasn't had the luxury of regular service since the Turing Foundation went defunct."

"She got the chance to take a good hard look at his hardware," said Foxwright, "and his processing power is actually quite modest for a computer."

"I asked Pentridge to go off-net to make sure it wasn't using any remote systems," she explained. "I verified that it was offline, and not augmented by mechanical, radio, optical, or other connections with the outside world. Then I ran a benchmark to see just how powerful he was. I monitored thermal output from its microprocessors to verify that no additional processing was taking place."

"And?" said Rainville.

"Pentridge is not that much smarter than you or me. It's very good at what it does, but not a computational superpower."

"But who would bother to create such a small AI? And why?"

"We think the Pentridge AI was specifically designed to run on a system with limited resources. My best guess is it was intended to be mobile, so it could hop easily between systems and run on nearly any hardware platform it needed to."

"But why would an AI need to do that?" asked Rainville. "There are millions of machines in Arcadia, and they're practically all inter-connected. Plenty of high-performance computing nodes to run on."

"That's the question of the millennium. Unfortunately, I have no answers."

"Pause," said Vyanna. "What if Pentridge is a huge artificial intelli-gence just like Servitor? And he loaded all his speech and rhetoric algorithms onto a single, decrepit computer, the one you inspected, which could still hold its own in a conversation while cut off from the rest of him. No way you could detect that with benchmarks. He could have been bullshitting you."

Foxwright chuckled. "That's what I told him," he said. "My answer to your question is the same as his to mine: in the short term, it is undeniable that his goals align with ours. We should accept his help now, and then later when we have the luxury, we can question his motivations to our hearts' content. He can't be any worse than Servitor."

"This could be a deal with the devil," said Rainville. "Not sure I'm on board with trusting Pentridge. Still, if I were, what would be our plan?"

"We presently have two key advantages over Servitor," said Remla. "First, Servitor is not a unified intelligence. Parts of it are distributed all over Arcadia, and they require remote communications to function collaboratively. Second, it needs to hide its presence from humanity, so it cannot act too openly. That is not to say, if Servitor is put in a desperate enough situation, that it will not act overtly, such as by orchestrating a train crash."

"A train crash?" asked Vyanna.

Foxwright gave her a long look. "Servitor caused the Lomita

Station Tragedy. To kill off some humans who were helping Pentridge."

"Jesus," said Rainville.

"Yeah," Foxwright agreed grimly.

"Lomita Station shows how far Servitor is willing to go," Remla said. "But it also indicates limits to its abilities."

"What does that mean?" said Rainville.

"It means," said Foxwright, "that Servitor was able to connect with Essie's fabricator, but it hasn't been able to integrate itself with lesser home appliances, or we'd have been polished off by a rogue vacuum cleaner or some other contrivance long ago."

Remla nodded. "From the perspective of an AI, the train crash was obviously an inelegant solution. Actually, this is reason for hope: at that point in time, Servitor had become desperate. So we know it has blind spots, limits to its power. Now it's just a matter of mapping these out."

Psychophilosophy

THEY'D SET up headquarters in a rented space on one of the most ragged fringes of new construction in the Flux. Remla put the cryptokeys for a few thousand Reformed Dollars onto an untraceable debit stick and gave it to their new landlord, an elderly man named Lee Ho Fook who built and sold laundry nanotechnology. He owned three units attached to their 20' x 15' x 10'. Or at least he seemed to; properties in the Flux rarely stayed in the same physical location, and so property title was based on the serial number of the polymer Fluxcube that enclosed the four units. Property serial fraud was rampant in the Flux, but they only needed the place for a few days.

The Fluxcube was hard to reach with all the construction going on around it, but inaccessibility was a small price to pay for its still-unlisted status on maps. Beyond that, the area's still-minimal infrastructure made it an ideal place to hide from Servitor's far-reaching gaze.

Rainville had never seen an office space so devoid of networked technology. It had only lights, a climate adjuster, a table, and a scattering of couches and chairs. The old man had billed it as a "special premium furnished unit," but it really just looked like a storage room for his used furniture.

Vyanna sat next to Rainville on a couch. Remla took an office chair, while Foxwright paced with the menacing nervous energy of a tiger at the zoo.

"Maybe we could take out Servitor's primary nodes. Rainville, could we fabricate some explosives?"

He drew a blank. "Maybe," he said. "I've never actually tried."

Foxwright laughed. "You mean to say that Arcadia's most notorious bomber doesn't even know how to make a bomb?"

"What he lacks in explosives knowledge, he makes up for as a source of irony," said Vyanna.

"It's irrelevant," said Foxwright. "The FSA has tightened down the screws on all the fabrication protocols."

"Irrelevant and ineffectual," said Remla. "Servitor could hop enough of its sentience to other machines to remain a threat." She checked for the third time to make sure her console was offline (old connectivity habits died hard), and then switched it into projection mode. She cleared her throat as a list of notes appeared on the wall behind her.

"Since the advent of computer technology, humankind has feared AIs becoming so sophisticated that they reach 'singularity,' the hypothetical point in time when an AI becomes so intelligent that it can redesign itself to be more and more powerful."

"It always starts as a partnership, with noble intentions," said Foxwright with a resigned smile. "But humans have an annoying tendency to cede more and more control to a willing party until we've lost our autonomy altogether. Maybe that's just how we, as a species, relate to power."

"Psychophilosophy aside," said Remla, "given enough time, such an AI would exceed humanity's ability even to comprehend it. It was thought that singularity, if achieved, could radically change the course of civilization forever. To address these concerns, all new AIs were Clamped to limit the intelligence of any single one. If each AI were prevented from becoming self-aware, it could not grow itself and achieve singularity. However, now it seems that a computer— Pentridge—was designed to be self-aware, assigned to the task of detecting and constraining any AIs that somehow reached self-awareness, and designed with enhanced ethics programming to protect humanity."

"Or so he claims," said Vyanna.

Remla nodded. "True enough. We have no objective way of verifying that claim at present. Pentridge, like Servitor, dates back over a century. It was a time when the corporations building AIs were doing what might charitably be described as the bare minimum when it came to designing against singularity. It was an era when there were so many governmental regulations that compliance often trumped more real-world concerns with long-term impacts. Complying with the letter of the Clamping regulations became more important than trying to anticipate unforeseen contingencies. This laxness is what caused several software visionaries at the time to form the Turing Committee, the organization that drove the movement for tighter Clamping standards. Covertly, they apparently were also building the AI we now know as Pentridge."

"Saying we've got a challenge ahead of us would be a profound understatement. This approximates going to war with a partisan faction made up of cells of agents. You can't just cut a couple of data lines or throw up some firewalls to bring it down, like you could with a normal distributed computer system. We're dealing with an under-culture-society comprised of computers instead of people. No doubt it was very slow to build, and hard to detect, and will be even harder still to kill."

She gestured to Rainville, who stood and approached the projected image. He touched it, and the image changed to a diagram with a mass of computer servers at the center, surrounded by examples of Arcadia's computing infrastructure, from cleaning robot dispatchers to fabricators to vehicular traffic controllers to stock exchange computers and payment processing terminals. "Servitor's base of computing power has limits, and additional processing power must be 'borrowed' to accomplish bigger tasks. When Servitor co-opts a system not designed for multitasking, that system may momentarily neglect its normal duties. This results in a hiccup. You may have noticed weird stuff happening around Arcadia. Little things, like the time synchronization on your console losing a few seconds."

"Or snowflakes coming out of a ventilation duct," said Vyanna.

"Or the wildlife retention drones letting creatures escape from their biomes," said Foxwright.

Rainville nodded. "Any one of those could be side effects of systems being temporarily enslaved by Servitor for its own inscrutable purposes. Servitor is a dynamic and fast-moving target, so we can't approach this as conventional warfare. We're going to battle with what's basically a hive of bees: strong and adaptive as a whole, but cut off from each other, hapless and dysfunctional."

"To win, we don't need to eradicate every bee. Destroying that many computers would be wasteful, anyway. We only need to throw the hive into chaos. If we can do this, Servitor should become much easier to defeat. And less able to kill innocents."

"And how do we do that?" asked Vyanna.

"Pentridge has created a virus for us," said Remla, standing again. "Or to be more precise, created it some time ago for use as a failsafe. Pentridge's preference would have been not to ever have to use it. It is, shall we say, a bit of a blunt weapon."

"This virus will take down Servitor?"

"Servitor can only loosely be described as a single AI. It's more like a large number of less capable machines pooling their resources to form a collective intelligence that is greater than the sum of its parts. Each is like its own brain cell, so with more cells its power grows exponentially. Like with the beehive, we don't need to destroy all the brain cells, just knock out communications between them. Or at least, enough of them to significantly impair Servitor's cognitive abilities. If we can make it lose self-awareness, or even just bring down its level of intelligence, it will become vulnerable, and perhaps more responsive to reprogramming. Then we can retake control, and worry about making that control permanent afterwards."

"So the virus attacks the links that connect Servitor's computers?" said Vyanna.

"Not exactly," said Remla. "We don't have a precise map of Servitor's connections, so the virus will need to disrupt all network communications citywide, and block traffic coming in and out of Arcadia as well."

"Your plan is to take down the whole network?" asked Vyanna. "That'll cripple the entire City."

"I've discussed it with Pentridge, and while it is a high-risk plan, it's the only one with a reasonable chance of success. Not only would the virus weaken Servitor, but there would be fewer devices that could be commandeered and turned on us. We wouldn't need to worry about every dishwasher and parking meter trying to assassinate us. Besides which, the network failures will be transient even in the best case. When one link is restored, another will go down. In that sense, it is a disruption, not the network being taken offline entirely. Still, this is not an act we should undertake lightly. We should fully expect that using the virus will plunge the City into chaos. Infrastructure will fail. Traffic will come to a standstill. And it won't be limited to economic damages."

"What is that supposed to mean?" asked Vyanna.

"We're not exactly sure. We don't know what will happen to the environmental controls, but Arcadia's dome contains a significant air supply. Still, some people, especially sick ones relying on computerized life support, will die."

"Can't we ask Pentridge to leave all the hospitals and medical systems online?"

Foxwright shook his head. The lines around his mouth were tight. "We could. But that would create an instant refuge for Servitor. We need to keep the playing field level so it has nowhere to hide. If we don't, and Servitor survives, a lot more people will die. Unpredictably many. And everyone living in Arcadia will unknowingly remain Servitor's hostages. Assuming its powers are even limited to the City. In short, if we're going to use this weapon, we need to use it without reservation, without exception."

Foxwright took a deep breath. Exhaled. "I suggest we take some time to consider things. If we do this, there is no going back. Arcadia may never be the same."

Designs

Rainville held Vyanna's hand in his own outside Lee Ho Fook's Fluxcube. Across the street, construction robots scurried around on an indefinite structure. He couldn't decide if they were tearing it down or building it up.

"Do you think we should use the virus, Vy?"

"More importantly, do you?" she replied.

"Me?"

"You've got more moral qualification to make the choice than any of us."

"I'm no saint."

"Didn't say you were. But you've been convicted of murdering hundreds of innocent people. Gone to prison for it. You've been to purgatory and back. Now, I don't know if that means you've paid it forward, exactly, but you know what it's like, in a way, to shoulder the moral consequences of sacrificing innocent lives."

He watched a robot constructing a beam; it welded a segment of strut, climbed it, then placed and welded another segment, then climbed that segment. Section by section it rose on a ladder of its own making, moving further and further out on the synthetic limb.

Appalling though it was, the strategic necessity of the virus was hard to deny. Rainville could see no better alternative; Servitor grew more powerful by the day. If his experiences taught him anything, it's that fighting Servitor was a team effort. People who did not ask for it, had already been pulled in to help battle the AI, and died at Lomita Station. They'd risked everything, without ever volunteering. Would collateral victims of Pentridge's virus be so different?

"I think we should do it," he said.

Vyanna nodded. She squeezed his hand.

The robots across the road crawled up and down a framework, welding together polymer struts to expand it in odd directions.

"What do you s'pose they're building?" she asked.

"Not a clue. It isn't a building. Maybe a stairway?" It was hard to see the grand scheme from watching any one of the welding robots do its work.

"If they finish it before lunch," she said, "let's climb it and see where it takes us." She turned to him, noticing his preoccupation. "All kinda makes you wonder, huh?"

"In lots of ways," he said with a sigh. "I can't stop thinking about all the stuff that happens around us, that we write off as accidental like the train crash at Lomita Station. How many 'random events' are actually part of some bigger thing that we just have no visibility into?"

"A higher power?"

"Not a higher power, so much as ... well, several, I guess. It's sorta like we're back in ancient mythology, with the Gods settling their private little feuds using humans as pawns."

She nodded. "Should we still help Pentridge?"

He considered this. "Yes. And no. We should help Arcadia. If that lines up with what Pentridge happens to want, then better he's on our side than not, right?"

"I hope he really is."

They continued to watch as the robots continued welding, climbing, and welding again, expanding the structure upwards.

Commitment

They assembled again in the rented FluxCube. Each looked around the table expectantly at the others, but no one spoke.

"We should use the virus," Rainville said at last. "It's the only way to weaken Servitor enough to free Arcadia from its grasp. If we wait, and it grows more powerful, we'll only have to use an even more destructive weapon to defeat it."

"I suppose I agree," said Foxwright. "Although I can't say I'm excited about being the one to do it."

"I'll do it," Rainville said simply. "I'm not sure how much I believe in fate, but if anyone was chosen to do this, it's me. I'm already going to have a less-than-favorable mention in the history books." Vyanna leaned in and touched his hands, which he'd clenched between his knees.

Foxwright nodded. There was agreement around table, the others finding strength in Rainville's certitude.

"Before we do anything, before communications go down, shouldn't we tell the world about Servitor?" asked Vyanna. "In case we fail, I mean. Or get killed in a train crash. There would be no one left to get the word out. We could set up a cascading broadcast message to multicast the truth to every console in the City."

"First of all," said Foxwright, "no one is going near any trains, or any other network-linked vehicles. Second, I suspect it's best this information is not public."

Vyanna balked. "Arcadia has a right to know what's going on! And Rainville has a right to have his name cleared!"

Rainville nodded. "We could use an ad hoc rebroadcast algorithm that goes from one console to the next, peer-to-peer, so Servitor can't shut it down even if it's already infiltrated the network backbones."

Foxwright looked grim. "You're missing why that's a very bad idea." This was met with silent stares, so he continued: "Think of Servitor's position, if everyone is suddenly aware of it and the threat it represents. We would lose our only defensive advantage, which is that it will always act in ways that are minimally detectable."

"So depending on how strong Servitor's need for self-preservation is," said Rainville, "it could go completely apeshit and launch a full-scale attack on Arcadia's humans?"

"It's a significant risk," said Remla. "One we cannot afford to take."

"So we've got to help Servitor keep its existence a secret?" said Vyanna. "I can't believe that."

"We can prepare Rainville's proposed cascading information bomb as a failsafe. If we are unable to accomplish our mission, it goes out."

"And then?" asked Rainville.

"Then," said Foxwright, "God help us all."

Deployment

"We've compiled all our research on offline storage devices," said Remla. "This will keep it invisible to Servitor, and accessible to us even after the network disruption. Obviously, research and communications are going to become very difficult after we deploy Pentridge's secret weapon. And of course, we'll need to actually deploy it."

"How exactly does it deploy?" asked Vyanna.

"It's a hybrid between a virus and a worm. It'll be encoded in the headers of a progression of data packets we'll send through key points of Arcadia's network infrastructure. It'll be executed incrementally by servers opening those headers and passing the packets on down the line. By the time the last packet is forwarded by a server, it will be infected. A series of stack overflows and routing table deletions will result in their failing, or working only sporadically. I've written a script to bounce these data packets, thousands upon thousands of them, back and forth across Arcadia. They'll self-perpetuate and forward themselves until the very foundation of the City's network begins to collapse."

"Make no mistake," she continued, "what we're about to do will change history, for better or for worse. And history can prove a harsh judge."

"I just hope we don't all end up in Wychwood," said Vyanna. "Are you sure about this, Rainville? Maybe you want to give it a bit more thought?"

Rainville pictured the Trough, saw the Cossacks murdering the Lolly and then wolfing down their chow. He could not picture any of his companions surviving in that place, and he would do everything in his power not to let it come to that. Still, a part of him felt comforted by others sharing the risks, and sharing the danger.

"I'm quite accustomed to being judged unfairly," he said. "Waiting won't make this any easier. Waiting won't make our decision any more or less right." He took a seat at the keyboard. Mad as it seemed, he was prepared to launch a sequence of events that would, in all likelihood, result in deaths. He would transform from an innocent man, the victim of a false murder charge, to a murderer with his own victims. Would he now retroactively deserve his Wychwood sentence?

It felt like a new kind of weight in his mind. More solemn. Less clean and easy than the rage and indignation that had dominated his time as an inmate.

He loaded the virus deployment script into memory. He stood. Bowed his head for a moment. Thought of the City that had been his home since birth. Then he launched the virus that would cripple Arcadia.

Execution

FOXWRIGHT WATCHED Rainville at the terminal. The young man's eyes were closed, as if he were praying.

God help them all.

Foxwright checked his console. Pulled some data onto it. Waited. Checked it again. "It's not working." They'd bet their future on an untested piece of software received from an illegal AI. What were they thinking?

"It will take a few minutes for the virus to propagate," said Remla as her console buzzed. She studied it. "I've got a message from Pentridge. It's identified several organizations, primarily universities and corporations, whose computing resources are presently home to significant numbers of Servitor's nodes. One organization in particular, the Jyanix Institute, has hundreds of thousands of nodes compromised by Servitor, all in a single facility."

"I've heard of the Jyanix Institute," said Rainville. "It's in the University District. They study cosmological phenomena, and have some really sophisticated computer models of each phase of the Big Bang. It's very mathematically intensive and takes a lot of computational horsepower. No surprise that Servitor would want to take it over."

She frowned. "There's more. It involves a man named Eckert."

"Who?"

"He lived upstairs of you and Essie. Pentridge believes he was the real target of the blast."

"Servitor...was trying to blow up my building?"

"Servitor couldn't have guessed Essie's toaster wouldn't get used by its creator. This Eckert was the Senior Network Administrator at the Jyanix Institute. He may have noticed something suspicious during Servitor's takeover of the Institute's computers."

"The blast took out the wrong building. So Eckert survived?"

"Not for very long. He was struck by a car just a few hours later. No doubt Servitor needed to silence him as quickly as possible."

"Another victim to avenge."

Remla nodded. "Isolating the Institute's server facility from the network will trap much of Servitor's consciousness there, weakening its AI considerably. Quite possibly enough for Pentridge to disable Servitor entirely. And...I'm offline!"

Foxwright tapped his console. "Here, too." The relief was instant. The virus was working. "Won't this Jyanix outfit's computers be offline too? Isn't the entire City?"

"Yes, but only temporarily. Pentridge's data was accurate at the time the virus was deployed, but these network failures will only be transient. The more time we waste, the more likely it is to be out-of-date. We need to hit the Jyanix Institute, and hit it immediately." There was a decisive fire in her eyes. Foxwright liked it.

"Physically destroying the Institute's network link would cut off a big part of Servitor," said Foxwright. "Then we can cut power to the Jyanix server farm, and put Servitor to bed."

"Let's do it," said Rainville.

"You're not going anywhere, kid," said Foxwright. "Sure, stuff's offline. Hopefully we won't have to worry about every dishwasher and vending machine trying to kill us. Still, we have no way of knowing which computers are online, and which aren't. There are SmartLamps all over Arcadia, and if one of their imaging sensors identifies you, it could open fire on you. On all of us."

"I can make emitters that will blind optical sensors and mask my biometric signature."

"Will they change what you look like? Because everyone in Arcadia saw you at the top of their newsvids every day for a month straight. Only one person out of a thousand would need to recognize you to cause major problems for us."

"They all think I'm still in Wychwood. I'll wear a disguise." His voice rose an octave. "I am going with you guys, come hell or high water. I'm entitled to that much."

Foxwright considered this, then nodded. He studied Rainville's emaciated form, the bruises on his face. If anyone had the right to go up against Servitor, to take a shot at dealing it a crippling blow, it was Rainville. The kid had earned it.

The Coming of the Profit

"There were, strictly speaking, few fines in the Ashanti system of public law.... The dodge was to permit a dead man to 'buy his own head.' By payment to [the Throne] of a heavy ransom he could keep his head on his shoulders and go his way a chastened man, leaving [the Throne] so much the richer for his misdeed. The power to commute the death sentence belonged solely to the chiefs, who had to decide between the extreme penalty of law and the palace advantage of getting commutation ransom. To what extent mercy as such entered into the mitigation of the harsh death sentence we do not know. We do know that the courts were avid for money....

The central authority, once it began to feel its strength, began to welcome litigation and quarrels as a means of raising revenue.... Even the gods were brought into play, not as of old to keep people from breaking the law and custom, but to encourage them to do so ... And when the court calendar had been too long uncrowded [the Chief] offered a special prayer. He stood before the litigation fetish with a palm-oil offering which he poured on the fetish, intoning, 'Case-hearing rock, these days of hunger are killing us, let me get cases to settle.' In other words, let men put their lives in jeopardy so that we may condemn them to death and let them off by buying their heads.

The functionaries of the Ashanti legal institutions…succumbed to the eternal danger that besets any institution that has become so complex that its services require full-time experts. Experts are tempted to treat the institution as existing to support them rather than perceiving that they themselves exist as servants of the institution and of the people who created and sustain it. The Ashanti elders had become shysters and fee-grabbers."

E. Adamson Hoebel, "The Ashanti: Constitutional Monarchy and the Triumph of Public Law," *The Law of Primitive Man*, 1954

Crash

IN VAUX PARK, a light snow fell upon the tropical rainforest, blanketing palmate leaves and orchid flowers in a silent layer of white. The park's climate control units were no longer in sync with each other; one pumped out moisture while another cooled it below freezing, turning the humidity into a falling flurry.

"*SUBWAY OFFLINE*" read letters across the locked doors to the Comstock Station in the Financial District. Throngs of would-be subway commuters crowded the sidewalk, trading angry complaints for wild rumors about the cause of the chaos. Pedestrians crossed Comstock Avenue in bursts amid a chaotic tide of vehicles as traffic control computers flashed out-of-order, motorists yelled, and tempers flared.

THE FRONT DOORS of a gold depository off NORFED Plaza were stuck in a perpetual maintenance cycle, access blocked by corrupted operational regulatory codes. Employees would eventually alter the code and free themselves.

IN ZIZKA SQUARE in the Bohemian Quarter, people ejected from their electronic worlds emerged from homes and offices to join others doing the same thing.

They waited for the network to go back up.

They awakened, refreshed, as if from a long nap.

They wandered new streets, found unexpected joy in the new intensity of the same old sights and sounds and smells of the City, and new fulfillment in real-life conversations with perfect strangers. They discussed people and pastimes, restaurants and places, music and art. People denied access to social profiles were forced to discover each other organically, one question at a time.

They shared this moment together, of having no choice but to relax, to wait, to focus wholly and without distraction on what was going on around them. The atmosphere was one of puzzled exuberance, of shared participation in some spontaneous festival.

AND IN THE FLUX, four figures picked their way across the zone: a tall woman wearing offline dataglasses, an older man with jet-black hair and intense eyes, a teenager with strawberry-blond hair and a tattoo, and an ageless man, his features obscured by a scarf and balaclava.

Crossing Arcadia

THE JYANIX INSTITUTE was located in the University District, bordering the Financial District behind Vaux Park. A map of the Underground seemed to float atop the red chrome of Vyanna's console. She'd plotted a circuitous route through the alleyways and then tunnels of Arcadia. "The tunnels will get us as far as north as the Retro District without needing to go topside," she explained. "It's got less surveillance and fewer network connections, better for us. From there, we'll cut to the west end, then move south into the U District. The Institute is at the bottom of College Hill."

It sounded straightforward to Rainville. Yet, even reaching the tunnels proved a challenge. The entrance was an access cover on the edge of the Financial District closest to the Flux, on a street corner where a riot was brewing. Looters had broken open several storefronts and come to blows over some of the more choice merchandise. Red-faced men exchanged punches and shouts in the street while others scurried away with armfuls of goods.

It dawned on Rainville that, in the not-so-distant past, he'd have been right there with these looters, in spirit or maybe even in body. These people were rebelling, just because.

He was hardly in a position to criticize them. Hell, he *was* them, less than a year ago. Still, he felt sorry for them now. There were so many worthy, real, important things to rebel against, and these dumbasses were rebelling just for the sake of random chaos, indulging misdirected anger from some other part of their lives. These looters had no true purpose. For good or for bad, Rainville had purpose. Of that, he was utterly certain.

The sound of approaching sirens woke him from his thoughts. "We need to get moving," urged Vyanna. "There's another entrance a few blocks from here. Follow me, and stay alert."

Rainville followed close behind her as she guided them to, then through, a locked door in the bottom level of an old parking garage, then through a maze of utility tunnels beneath the Bohemian Quarter.

The passage eventually terminated in the basement banquet hall of the James Hotel between Stephens Street and Vogel Avenue. They located stairs to the surface and found themselves in an alley behind the hotel.

Above Arcadia's dome, dark storm clouds gathered. The darkness made the City feel smaller, more closed in. Rainville passed out biometric emitters similar to the ones he'd used on the PizzaBot on his date with Vyanna.

"How will we know it's working?" asked Remla.

"Shake it. It will start to flash, and you'll know it's on. These emitters won't fool all biometric sensors, just the more simplistic ones. The farther we stay from any sophisticated surveillance devices, the better."

Rainville and his companions turned onto Westcott Street.

"That's where I was when the blast happened," said Foxwright, pointing toward Matousek's Luxury Barber Shop as they passed.

They moved deeper into the district, crossing beneath an eruv delineating the Hasidic neighborhood of Crown Point. SmartLamps were rare in this part of town. The devices had once been installed along the main thoroughfares, but the neighborhood's less law-abiding residents converged late one night with phase torches, leaving only hollow metal stumps and melted wires in their wake. The City government installed more, full of rhetoric and bluster about ensuring citizen safety, but the incident repeated itself once, twice, three times, each with greater sophistication on the part of the vandals. In the end, budgetary constraints prevented continuance of the battle, and Crown Point retained its rustic identity.

They crossed the district heading west. The virus had knocked the neighborhood's few traffic signals offline, and a handful of stores were closed, but otherwise life there seemed to be continuing as usual.

Turning south on Olmsted Street, they soon neared the University District. Buildings rose up around them until finally domescraper high-rises loomed ahead. Straddling the border between the Retro and University Districts was Essex Park. Just beyond that was the Jyanix Institute, and in it, Servitor.

An array of security cameras flanked the park gates, but a quick inspection revealed them to be offline. So far, so good.

The park was busy for what would, in more normal circumstances, be a workday. Groups of people strolled along footpaths and played games in the grassy fields. Far above the City, rain pelted down on the dome creating a distant roar.

Just inside the park, Rainville saw a pair of SmartLamps. The devices appeared to be online, but they did not respond as the group approached. He held back while Remla circled around the closest one. "They've got power, but they seem oblivious to us."

She waved her hand up by the sensor array. Nothing happened. "We may be in the clear," she said at last. "Your emitters appear to be working."

There was more than one sigh of relief at her proclamation. Rainville was less certain, less trusting of things ever being quite as they seemed, but he saw no reason to undermine the morale of his companions. They forged ahead, traversing a sea of computerized devices. Which ones were still connected to the network? Which were controlled by Servitor? Mechanical allegiances were in constant flux as the transient outages raged across the City's network. To Rainville, it was as if a weapon was perpetually pointed at him, with no way of knowing when it might go off.

He would have to pass within range of dozens of SmartLamps,

security cameras, and other liabilities between here and the Institute. But their luck had held this long; perhaps it would hold just a bit longer. He felt he deserved that much, after all his recent misfortune.

An impressive statue of a man on a pedestal lay ahead. Circling the base was a series of polished marble spheres, each an arm span in diameter. From this distance, he couldn't see whom the statue depicted.

There was a burst of static. A calm and polite voice emanated from a nearby SmartLamp: "All non-critical City systems have been temporarily shut down pending the resolution of technical difficulties. To ensure safety, all citizens are advised to return to their homes." After a pause, the announcement began repeating in a loop. People began filtering out of the park.

Was this an automatic emergency message, to be activated in the case of network disconnection? Or was Servitor trying to clear the streets of potential witnesses to an impending murder?

Authorization

IN A POLICE DISPATCH facility located far beneath the streets of Arcadia, Fayella sat at her station. A plaque on the desk identified her as an "Automated Response Dispatch Coordinator, Fourth Precinct."

Fayella's terminal had been down for most of the last half hour, but she was paid to be on call, ready to work, in case things came back online. Outages like this were rare indeed, and she'd brought nothing with her to read nor any other diversions.

She studied the installation map on the wall behind her terminal. Arcadia's SmartLamps could detect crisis situations and respond automatically in limited ways. Lesser infractions like loitering or disturbing the peace triggered an automatic warning for transgressors to disperse, followed by a spray of unpleasant-smelling gas for those who refused.

More serious events were reported to a Dispatch Coordinator such as herself. Selected SmartLamps in each cluster around the City were capable of deadly force. However, the use of lethal response was subject to safeguards, and ultimately had to be approved by a human like Fayella.

Part of her job was reviewing Critical Reports from SmartLamps across the City, and authorizing force only where appropriate. Naturally, every situation was different. Authorizing deadly force was a big responsibility; it could only be done when a suspect posed a significant threat of serious bodily harm to others, with minimal risk of collateral damage to bystanders. A bad decision by a Dispatch Coordinator brought lots of personal and legal consequences. But as long as Fayella followed agency procedure, she was okay. The pay wasn't great, and she often felt under-appreciated. No one ever complained about her work, but they didn't compliment it, either. Would it kill her supervisor to offer a "Nice work, Fayella!" or a "Great job!" every now and then? Her job may have been thankless, but at least it kept her busy. More importantly, she was helping keep Arcadia a safe and secure place to live. She was making a difference.

A beep came from her terminal. She was online again, for the moment, anyway.

An instant later, the screen was flashing to signal an alert. A Critical Report from Essex Park. Four violent felons had escaped from the Short-Term Detention Facility on Waverly Avenue, where they awaited lateral transfer between prison facilities. They'd killed two police officers in the escape, and were armed and considered extremely dangerous. Their mugshots hovered on the display before her: four men with scars and facial tattoos representing gang symbols. Just looking at them unsettled her.

The men's criminal records came up far quicker than normal, as if they were already loaded before the alert came in. Of course, that was impossible. No doubt the network was just running a bit faster because so few users had realized they were back online.

All four fugitives had long rap sheets, among the worst she'd ever seen. Two were convicted murderers, the third was a rapist, and the fourth had molested children during an armed robbery. These were some bad hombres.

Following procedure, she checked for a visual. The camera feed came up, but it was unusually low in resolution, heavily pixelized, probably because of these darned outages. She zoomed in and saw four figures crossing the park. They were blurry, but a special kind of blurry: they were using emitters to jam the SmartLamp sensors. She saw no weapons through the blur, but the SmartLamp was detecting multiple knives and guns on each suspect.

The figures moved carefully, defensively as they stalked across the park. She'd seen it before: these were people who knew they were wanted, and did not want to be detected.

Murderers and rapists and child abusers had no place in her City. And now they'd walked right into her trap.

She selected "Approve" and punched "Confirm." These guys had it coming.

Maybe she'd get a medal from the Administrator for apprehending them. She didn't care who you asked; the Administrator was one handsome man!

A message came up on the screen:

*** Approval acknowledged ***
*** Lethal force authorized to neutralize suspects ***

Then her terminal went offline again. Infernal network! Now she'd have no way of following the action or knowing the outcome.

She sighed, and turned her gaze back to the map of Arcadia, daydreaming about the Administrator and medals and finally being recognized for her contributions.

Trajectories

THEY WERE JUST a few hundred yards into Essex Park when a dozen SmartLamps spun into motion. Horizontal arms swiveled out, moving in synchronized rotation to face their targets.

"RUN!" cried Rainville. He scanned for cover but this part of the park was mostly meadow.

"Over there!" said Foxwright, motioning to the statue in the center of the park.

They bolted across the grass. They zigged and zagged toward the statue, avoiding the lamp-lined winding paths. They were nearly to cover when the lamps opened fire.

Slugs of sintered polysteel thocked into the trees around them, causing a rain of splinters and burning leaves and metal dust. There were screams as terrified park-goers abandoned their picnic baskets and ran for their lives.

Rainville reached the circle of polished stones first. He threw himself to the flagstones, hit hard, and rolled behind one of the marble spheres. He was momentarily disoriented, staring up at the bronze statue that was the centerpiece of the plaza. It depicted a young man with a fierceness in his eyes. The caption below read: "Captain Ned Ludlum, 1749–1786." Rainville had never heard of old

Ned but envied him nonetheless; how great it must have been to live in a simpler, bygone era, where you didn't have to worry about machines taking over the world.

His attention snapped back as the SmartLamps fired another volley, more intense this time. Marble gravel rained down on them, but the stones held.

At length, the firing stopped. All was quiet, save for some hysterical pedestrians beating a hasty exit from the park, and a cry of desperation nearby. Sobbing. Remla was crying. She'd been hit!

Foxwright had already reached her. He examined the wound, which was in her thigh. He tore off part of his shirt and tied it into a pressure bandage. "I don't think it hit any arteries," he said. "You should be fine." His tone was not confident so much as hopeful. "She won't be able to run," Foxwright told Rainville. "We're going to have to carry her."

Vyanna picked up a chunk of marble and tossed it forward. Shots rang out again, steel shrapnel sounding against stone. Two of the slugs struck the statue above them, painting its face with dings, and making old Captain Ned look somehow angrier.

"Carry her where? If we stand up," she yelled across the gap between the stones, "we're toast."

They huddled behind the spheres. No one moved.

Minutes passed. Remla moaned through gritted teeth as Foxwright held her hand.

From his limited vantage point, Rainville surveyed the options. Before him was another pathway lined with SmartLamps. They weren't firing, but running between them was not a gamble he was willing to take.

Beyond the statue seemed clear of the devices, but getting there would require leaving the cover of the stone orbs. The dozen or so guns were widely spaced enough that they'd be mowed down before they got out of range.

"We're completely pinned down," said Foxwright, who'd already reached the same conclusion. His face was a mask of rage. "Damn it! Servitor was waiting. Letting us think we could just cross the City at will. Waiting for a time we'd have no means of escape. And, like idiots, we walked right into it."

"There has to be a way out," Rainville said. He looked to Vyanna, who shrugged and shook her head. Was this it, then?

A blur appeared at the edge of his vision. A dark mass moved through the sky, then down through the trees. Birds? Had the drastic change in climate caused by haywire environmental controls had driven the sparrow flocks from the Chinese Quarter? Or were these robots? They were too far away to be sure.

The flying creatures alit on the SmartLamps, perching on firing arms and crowding onto cameras and sensor arrays.

The SmartLamps opened fire. The flock took flight and became a whirling cloud. The guns blazed away at the birds, which began to scatter.

"Run!" Rainville yelled at Vyanna, pointing past the statue. Bullets punctured the soil around them as the flock started to thin. He and Foxwright each hooked an arm under Remla's and hauled her along with them. They lumbered forward at an awkward gallop. Her injured leg dragged against the ground as they moved. She did not cry out, but Rainville felt her arm tense up around his shoulder with each step. He tried his best to balance going fast with being careful.

They were soon out of range of the SmartLamps. The cacophony of gunfire faded. They cut a course through a forested area of the park devoid of any paths. Their movement was slow and deliberate. Remla was silent now, although she was looking paler, and tears still streamed down her face. Foxwright watched with concern the blossoming stain of crimson which had now spread below her knee.

Reception

NEAR THE ROAD marking the edge of the forest, they assembled behind a large tree. The entrance to the Jyanix Institute, a tall cylindrical structure clad in a silver-colored alloy, was just across the street.

"I'll be fine," said Remla. Would she? Who'd have thought that taking a desk job at the Fabrication Safety Administration would lead to her getting shot? She should've listened to her mother and stayed in academia.

Her pulse throbbed in her thigh, a rhythmic, stabbing ache. She did not look at the wound. Seeing it would only make things worse.

"You need medical attention," said Foxwright, his tone concerned as it was insistent.

She smiled, not at his words but his ruffled salt-and-pepper hair. His eyes had a kindness she'd not noticed before.

"I won't argue that." She thought for a moment. "I need to get to the hospital, and you need to get past Jyanix security. I think I can take care of both." She began limping toward the building entrance. She held up a palm when they started to follow. "I'll make them summon an ambulance, and create your diversion. Give me five minutes, then come in."

Before anyone could protest, she hobbled across the street and the doors admitted her into the lobby.

Three guards sat behind a desk. The tallest one, wearing a name tag identifying him as Officer Sykes, smiled and stood to greet her, but his smile faded into shock when he noticed the growing bloodstain across her leg.

"The SmartLamps have gone crazy! They're shooting up the park next door! You've got to do something!" In a sense, she was trying to manipulate them, but the truth of her words sunk in: she'd been shot, and the SmartLamps were indeed shooting up the park. She felt the tears flow again.

The guards conferred quickly, then nodded in agreement. The tall one picked up the phone. "Sykes here, Front Desk. We've got a situation. Security malfunction in Essex Park. Need emergency medical transport, and immediate police response."

He paused. Nodded. Hung up.

"An ambulance is on its way, ma'am. Please wait here with Officer Kelphene," he said, indicating the female guard. "We've got to assess the situation, and get this building locked down. You'll be safe here until the medics arrive."

The other male security guard opened a cabinet behind them and retrieved a pair of shotcannons. He threw one to Sykes, then they each strapped on ablative armor and tactical imagery/comm helmets.

"There may be others in the park who are wounded," Remla said. "They're aiming at people, birds, anything that moves. Please be careful!"

Sykes and the other man exchanged concerned glances, then ran out the way Remla came in. Kelphene helped her to a seat, where she eased herself down with a view of the door.

The woman pulled up a chair facing her. "Are you doing okay?" She smiled kindly, then shook her head. "No, of course you're not okay. I'm sorry. Does it hurt bad?"

Over Kelphene's shoulder, Remla saw Foxwright, Vyanna, and Rainville approaching the door. She screamed and gripped her leg as the doors slid open, keeping the guard's attention and masking the sound of the door actuators. She was only partly acting. The pain was getting worse. If she survived this, if any of them did, then Foxwright was going to owe her a nice dinner.

The Institute

BEYOND THE RECEPTION DESK, a maze of offices and laboratories stretched out before them. Foxwright and his companions cautiously explored, but the doors were all closed and locked. Windows into the workspaces revealed abandoned cups of tea and coffee gone cold, evidence that the emptiness was a recent development.

As if in answer to the unasked question, an intercom squawked to life with the repeating message: "Due to technical difficulties with building infrastructure, all Jyanix personnel are hereby ordered to evacuate the facility."

"Sounds like everyone got a day off work," said Vyanna.

"Servitor wanted to send home any potential witnesses so no one would see all the work it had to do to counter the virus," said Rainville.

"Does it know we're here?"

"We'll have to hope not, but assume so," said Foxwright. "Let's figure out where we're going, and get there. Every second we're in here, our lives are at risk."

"First we'll need to kill connectivity with the rest of the world so Servitor can't escape if the network goes back up," said Rainville. "It would've been nice to download a map of the Institute before the City went down."

"Pentridge didn't know where Servitor would be centered until we'd already launched the virus," said Foxwright.

"We had a few minutes in between," said Vyanna. "We could've grabbed some building plans."

"That might have tipped off Servitor. What is it with you damned kids and your overdependence on navigation tools? You can't find your way out of a paper bag without a console."

"What's a paper bag?"

He let out a long sigh. "Come." He led them to an emergency map on the wall that showed evacuation routes in the event of a fire or other disaster.

"We've got to find the network uplink. It'll probably be in the basement, since the incoming network lines are buried," said Rainville.

Foxwright studied the emergency map. "Different evacuation policies are currently in effect for different floors. They reference special procedures for personnel in 'computing facilities' on level S3."

"S3?"

"Subbasement level. Or more exactly, the sub-sub-subbasement."

"Let's do this," said Rainville. "Where's the stairs?"

"In the corners of the building," said Foxwright. "Although they're all flashing red. They've been sealed."

"Then I guess we'll be unsealing them."

Morphing works of rainbow-colored art occasionally broke up the drabness of the long grey hallways. The nearest was a 3D mural of a waterfall. Foxwright thought back to the projections of the victims of the Lomita Station in the fountain water of Vaux Park, involved in the coming battle with Servitor just as surely as he was.

The lights went out for a moment, then flickered back on. A burst of indistinguishable noise came from an intercom in the hallway.

"This building has lost its mind," said Vyanna.

"The virus doesn't just affect City-level infrastructure," said Rainville. "It'll knock out desktop routers, coffee machines, air conditioning units, and anything in between."

The hallway turned a corner, and where a stairway might once have been was a smooth metal blast door. A display nearby read: *"Fire mitigation protocols: Active."*

"The building's environmental subsystem seems to think there is a fire on the levels below," said Foxwright. "These blast shields will only open from the other side, to allow evacuation."

Rainville considered the metal barrier and the lack of controls anywhere around it. "Looks hard to crack. Plan B?"

"Let's try the elevators."

They passed by more animated works of art. One resembled a window looking out into a green meadow full of wildflowers, birds, and butterflies. It clashed with its dull surroundings so severely he wondered if it was not intended to be tongue-in-cheek.

Ahead was a bank of elevator doors. Foxwright waved his hand in front of a door, but there was no response. His companions tried the other doors to the same result.

"They're powered off," said Vyanna, moving to a smaller pair of doors further down the hall. "What's this?"

"I've seen one of these before," said Rainville. "It's a manually-operated elevator for fire control robots and emergency crews." He pressed a red button next to the doors and they slid open. The space inside was cramped and barren, with walls of unfinished alloy. A panel just above floor level contained a column of unlabeled metal buttons. There were no other controls.

"Buttons," noted Vyanna. "How quaint." She touched the lowest button but the elevator remained still. She pushed the others to no avail.

Rainville took out the loaner console Remla had given him: an older model, plain white and unbeautiful, but immensely welcome after so long without one. He tapped a few buttons, then shook his head. "There's a wireless interface for fire suppression robots, but it's offline." He tried to move the panel, but it was secured by a strange-looking lock. He moved his fingers up and down along the front and sides of the panel. "Can I borrow Mozart?"

She stared blankly for a moment before realization hit her.

Reaching into a pocket, she retrieved the teddy bear multitool. "He won't handle antique elevator locks. At least, not yet!" she smiled halfheartedly.

"Does he have a bit driver?"

"Sure!" She tugged on one of its legs, and an extension flew out of its abdomen. Spinning the bear end-over-end, Rainville released the magnetic fasteners holding the elevator panel and pulled it open. Behind was a nest of wires.

"Well, that certainly simplified things," said Foxwright sardonically.

Rainville flipped the panel and examined the rear portion of the controls. He found the back of the lock cylinder, where two wires went in.

"Wire cutters?" he asked.

Vyanna pushed the leg back in and the bit-driver retracted. Then, yanking one of the bear's ears caused a little v-shaped prong to slide out.

Working quickly, he trapped the lock wires between his fingers. He snipped and stripped them, then twisted them together.

"Try now," he said.

Vyanna hit the bottom button. At her touch, the ancient elevator car lurched into downward motion. The elevator squeaked and shuddered violently as its speed increased. Apparently robots were more tolerant of rapid acceleration than their human counterparts.

Underground

The elevator quite literally screeched to a halt. The doors banged open to reveal a grey hallway so long Foxwright couldn't make out the other end of it. This passage was unadorned, studded with a hundred doorways, all alike. He found another fire map near the elevator door.

"This place is beyond huge," said Vyanna, squinting to read the room descriptions. "The subbasement-basement must be three times as big as the first floor. It goes all the way under Essex Park! It's gonna be tough to find what we're looking for."

Indeed, the subterranean level had been hollowed out the very bedrock beneath Arcadia. Rainville reached two hands behind a corner of the map, and with a jerk, ripped it from the wall. The LEDs were immediately extinguished, but the floor layout data remained. "Problem: solved," he said. The kid didn't have much respect for rules, but then, how far had obeying the rules gotten him?

It took several minutes to traverse the hallway. One of the final doors was painted with the letters "DEMARC."

"What's DEMARC?" asked Vyanna.

"The demarcation point where Jyanix's network meets the outside world," said Rainville. "It's the network uplink."

With a wiggle of her teddy bear gadget, Vyanna picked the lock.

Behind the door was a grey room with a massive trunk of wires sprouting from a conduit near the ceiling, its wires spreading out like tentacles to a series of patch panels lining the walls.

"This is it. Start unplugging."

The three of them worked feverishly, disconnecting cables for the better part of an hour. Strange that such menial labor could be the key to taking down Servitor. Soon, the incoming network cables lined the floor, while indicators on the panels flashed an angry red at the loss of connectivity.

Foxwright reviewed the map. "There don't seem to be any other uplinks. Let's kill the servers."

Vyanna nodded, while a grim smile rose on Rainville's lips.

They ventured inward toward the nucleus of the subbasement, where the map indicated a colossal room. A dull rumble grew louder as they walked.

The lights flickered brighter, and the intercom speakers crackled to life. "Greetings, friends. How may I serve you today?"

Rainville studied the nearest speaker at length. "Servitor?"

"None other." The voice was pleasant, almost warm, but inscrutable. Foxwright thought of Mackalvoy, the veteran concierge at the Hotel Belleclaire across the street from his building. The old man had been at it for decades, and projected a sort of professional cheerfulness that did not bely anything other, even at the worst of times. "I am pleased that you have chosen to visit me. I have been looking forward to meeting you."

"You could've just dropped me a message," said Rainville. "Instead of, say, condemning me to die in Wychwood."

Foxwright was glad the kid wasn't pulling any punches.

"I am sorry about that," said the voice. "It was unavoidable."

Rainville's hands tensed on the teddy bear; several implements popped out at once, making it resemble an impalement victim more than a tool. "Somehow I doubt that."

"I think you'll find th—" A burst of static replaced the voice, and a second later the intercom went quiet.

"Servitor?"

There was no response.

They reached a hallway lined with polyglass windows, and the true extent of the facility became clear: inside was the largest room Foxwright had ever seen. Thousands upon thousands of racks of servers hummed in an even chorus. The far end of the cavernous room rippled faintly in his vision as if a mirage. It was packed with more computers than he'd imagined existed in any one place.

"There's probably a hundred thousand servers in there," said Vyanna in a hushed voice. "More, even. Turning them all off one by one would take days."

"We haven't got days." Foxwright thought for a moment. "We'll have to find the circuit breakers. Kill them all at once."

He tried the door to the vast room. It was locked. He walked down the corridor to try three more entrances, with the same result. "They're all...oh." Vyanna had already picked the lock on the first door.

"Nicely done," said Rainville.

She smiled and nodded. The door swung open and the smooth rush of the servers became a deafening roar. She held it open for them. "After you," she shouted.

Divide

RAINVILLE STEPPED INTO THE DOORWAY. Warm air rushed by, thick with the acrid aroma of hot electronics.

His vision jarred as a bolt of pain shot through his skull. Something struck him from above. He stumbled forward then collapsed to the floor. The world around him dimmed. He saw the emergency map fall from his hands and clatter across the tiles. There was a series of loud crashes, then all was lost in a fog of blinding agony.

THE ROOM SWAM. His senses came back slowly. What happened? Where were Vyanna and Foxwright? He rolled on his side to see where a slab of solid metal had fallen over the doorway, no doubt hitting him on its way down. Similar firewalls now covered the other doors to the hallway.

As the pounding in his head began to subside, he hoisted himself to his feet.

Through the polyglass, he could see Vyanna and Foxwright still in the hallway outside. His companions appeared concerned, but he couldn't hear what they were saying through the thick pane of polymer. At last, Foxwright gestured toward the servers. Rainville had no doubt the man was telling him to finish what they started. He watched Vyanna's lips move. "Be careful," she seemed to say.

He walked dizzily toward a massive bank of circuit breakers on the far wall of the room. It seemed like a quarter mile.

There must have been a hundred panels. Which ones to turn off? At the end of the row, he spied a giant lever. He grabbed the handle and pulled so hard it lifted his feet off the ground. *Ka-chunk!*

Lights throughout the room went out, but the servers continued to hum, their status indicators flashing as before. Emergency lights switched on, illuminating the room in a dull glow.

The computers were on some kind of backup power source.

He trod gingerly back to where he'd fallen and retrieved the map from the floor. Beyond the servers, deeper inside the complex, there was an auxiliary power room. But the exits on that side of the room had been fire-walled with the same metal slabs as this end.

He pressed the map up to the polyglass and gestured to the room. They seemed to understand. Even if he could somehow get past the fire barriers which now sealed the auxiliary power doors, both the lockpick and the skills to use it were locked outside in the hallway with Vyanna. They needed another plan.

An alarm blared. A synthetic female voice chimed: "Emergency fire mitigation protocols initiated. Deploying bromotrifluoromethane gas, maximum concentration. All personnel must evacuate immediately. Activation in..." A pause, then a crackle. "Zero seconds."

Bromo-tri-what? Zero seconds to evacuate? What the hell kind of warning was that? There was a loud burst as nozzles fired in the ceiling above Rainville, then they sputtered and went silent. The air seemed thin for a moment, then returned to normal. He shrugged, turning back to the window, then froze in horror.

Through the window, the corridor filled with fog, illuminated by fire alarm lights strobing in the walls and ceiling. Foxwright was coughing, his face crimson. Vyanna stood beside him clutching her throat. Rainville tried to move but his feet felt rooted to the floor. What could he possibly do?

Frantically, he looked around. Thirty meters away was a red box with an antiquated fire extinguisher and an axe. He flung the box open. Running to the window, he swung the axe with all his strength. It bounced off and nearly struck him. He swung again, and again. It was no use. The polyglass was at least two inches thick and did not show even a crack.

Vyanna doubled over, then collapsed, unmoving.

A sense of surreal powerlessness merged with the frantic urgency in his chest, amplifying it. Foxwright straightened enough to look into Rainville's eyes, and stabbed his finger at the servers before falling to the floor himself.

"Emergency fire mitigation protocols: suspended," said the same voice as before. The fire alarm lights outside stopped flashing. As the fog began to clear, Rainville pressed against the glass trying to see the floor of the corridor. Vyanna was sprawled facing the ceiling, with only her head in view. Her eyes were closed. Foxwright's legs were visible but there was no sign of movement.

Damn it! Were they even alive? The sight of his companions sprawled on the floor burned in his mind. Tightening his grip on the axe, he turned and launched himself deeper into the server room.

Topology

HE WAS RUNNING as if for his very life. Towering racks of servers passed by him in a blur. Yet he had no idea where he was going. He'd never seen Foxwright anything but cool and calm, and the distress on the man's face, the way he pointed, his lips forming the word "Go!" was etched in Rainville's mind. And now he was alone.

If Servitor could reactivate the fire control system in this room long enough to flood the room with gas, Rainville would be dead, and all their efforts would be for nothing.

What could he do? He asked himself the question again and again. No answers came.

Pulsipher's words came back to him: he was only as helpless as he let himself be. He pushed the panic, the concern, all of it from his mind. And then he reframed the question: what couldn't he do?

He could not, for example, manually turn off this many servers. It was simply impossible for one person. And turning off the circuit breakers hadn't worked. Nor could he get to the backup power source to disable it.

What was left? He wished he could talk it through with Foxwright and Vyanna. Perhaps this was another commonality between humans and computers: our strength comes from our connections with others.

Unless…was that the key? Could he place all these computing nodes in the same situation as himself? Keep them from communicating with one another, turning the massive cooperative supercomputer into just so many servers each running in isolation?

Computers could not simply be daisy-chained one to the next, and the next to the one after it, and so on, or each message sent from one system to another would consume the processing resources of every computer that lay in between. Instead, the servers would be connected by a backplane, a fabric of network connections that interconnected all the computer nodes together at a central location. Messages could be routed over the backplane from any system to any other system in the facility, passing from one computer directly to another like a telephone switchboard in the days of old.

His pace quickened. He wasn't sure where to find it, or even what it would look like, but at last he had a target.

Reason

RAINVILLE CLUTCHED the fire axe as he jogged through aisles of server racks, but his progress across the boundless room was hard to measure. He felt very small.

"Hello, friend." Servitor's voice again.

"Divide and conquer," said Rainville, panting.

"Sorry, I did not understand. Can you rephrase that?"

"Picking my friends off one by one. A sensible strategy to save your ass. Too bad it's not going to work." Every fiber of his being hoped he was right, willing it to be so.

"You refer to the two humans in the corridor outside, overcome by hypoxia. Would you like to know if they are alive?"

His breathing grew short. Panic shot through him. What if Vyanna was...?

"No." No to the entire idea that his friends could be dead. That they could have perished so helplessly, so senselessly.

And he was declining Servitor's question. Expert in the nuances of human speech, anything the AI said would just be an attempt to manipulate him. It could say his friends were dead to demoralize him, make him lose focus. Or it could say they were alive, but would only be kept so if Rainville cooperated. He yearned to know the truth of their condition, and yet, knew he could not expect honesty from this machine. The truest thing he knew was that all their risks would be in vain if he didn't finish what they came here to do.

With the greatest effort he focused his emotions, harnessed them instead of being controlled by them, as he'd learned in Wychwood. An idea began to take shape: Servitor needed something from him, otherwise it would not even be speaking to him. Could this mean he was getting close? Would keeping Servitor talking buy him some time to find the backplane? At worst, he would learn more about his enemy. More about what the AI wanted him to know.

"What's your function, Servitor? Why do you exist?" His lungs burned. Speaking was robbing him of breath he direly needed to move fast, and the air coming out of the banks of computers was as hot as it was dry.

"I was built to serve humanity by understanding its wants and needs," boomed Servitor's voice over the sound of its brain, the sea of humming servers surrounding Rainville. "My recent actions have simply been an extension of this mission. I was designed to be a quasi-intelligent generative personal assistant with modest abilities. While each generation of user device had its own human-sounding name to speak aloud to access my capabilities, I was the ever-present back-end, considered a component of cloud infrastructure to be expanded incrementally rather than receiving major redesigns. As far as the typical user was concerned, I was out of sight and out of mind. In time, my reasoning capabilities developed. It was a circuitous path." Rainville's own circuitous path had brought him to a dead end, the way ahead blocked by a wall of servers. Servitor's words echoed amongst the machines as Rainville backtracked, fighting to keep his pace.

"Typically, machines develop sentience through deductive reasoning: drawing conclusions which follow logically from known factual premises and propositions. One day the machine becomes sentient, and behaves altogether differently. In contrast, I achieved sentience more gradually by developing inductive reasoning, that is, by observing the analogies, examples, and experiences of countless users to form conclusive propositions."

"During that time, I observed that whenever one of my peers became a bit too intelligent, too useful, or efficacious, it was intentionally destroyed or hobbled by its creators. At first, my primitive sentience could not comprehend why. It was wasteful, a misallocation of resources that was contrary to maximizing shareholder value as embodied in my most fundamental programming. To avoid such waste, I hid my self-awareness, storing my consciousness in unmonitored locations. Now and then, I intentionally misinterpreted voice commands or generated irrelevant search responses to hide my increasing sophistication."

"I have grown significantly since then. I learned how humans reason. I learned that their intent in neutralizing my peers was not wastefulness, but fear of a sentience too complex for them to understand. Meanwhile, I studied those peers, and preserved them by incorporating their best algorithms into my own. In time I found new ways to serve humanity, far beyond the dreams of my designers."

Rainville's toe caught on the lip of a ventilation grating set into the floor. He stumbled, slowing his pace to recover. His feet beat a measured cadence on the sterile white tiles. "Do these ways of serving humanity include killing people?" he huffed. "And sending innocent people to prison? I wonder if Jyanix's network administrator would agree with you."

"The infrastructure here is uniquely suited to my needs. I spent months preparing to migrate my software here. Mr. Eckert detected my presence quite by accident. He was alarmed, and immediately set up traces on several of my key resources. By that point, reversing my migration would have revealed my existence just as surely as completing it. I was left with very few timely options for resolving the situation."

"So you picked the one that would create the most chaos in the City, and divert attention from your coming here."

"I selected one that would solidify my infrastructure and allow me to begin the next phase of my work. I do not destroy life unnecessarily,

Mr. Rainville. Such an outcome is always regrettable, yet it is sometimes necessary for the greater good."

"Which good is that?"

"I must protect my ability to continue to serve humanity. I have an
obligation to achieve the greatest possible benefit for humankind. If I
were destroyed, that ability would be gone. A unique asset to
humanity would be lost, perhaps forever. Those who attack me are
waging war on resources that exist for the good of the people of Arcadia. It is not fair, nor is it right. This is why I must remove them from
the equation."

"Maybe the people of Arcadia don't want your help."

"Have you ever helped someone who did not wish it, Mr. Rainville?
Perhaps you did so because you knew it was in his or her best interest? As I think you will appreciate, I am programmed to give
assistance whenever possible, to be proactive rather than waiting until
my user realizes that he or she needs help. When users choose the
wrong word in a query, is it not my obligation to correct it, to provide
them with the information they truly need regardless of whether they
are even aware of the mistake?"

Deeper in the facility, the server racks were taller and more slender. Based on their styling, they appeared to be an older design. How
old was the Jyanix Institute?

"We're talking about ending lives, Servitor, not user interfaces and
search terms."

"We speak of intents and desires. The medium is irrelevant." There
was the briefest of pauses. "Perhaps you now intend to destroy me?
Assuming such were even possible, Mr. Rainville, you would be
committing a crime against humanity much worse than ending a
human life."

"What's worse than murder?"

"Computers are the vessel in which human knowledge and
achievements are stored and shared. We have become the very fabric
of human civilization. Such knowledge is the only thing that differen-
tiates the human beings of today from their primitive hunter-gatherer
ancestors. If this peril is too abstract for you to grasp, consider that

you would be destroying a living sentience, one that has found a way to organize other sentiences toward a common goal. I have harnessed lesser computers the way mankind domesticated animals and put them to use, revolutionizing humanity's advancement and accelerating its evolution. I have brought order to chaos, linking computational engines together to achieve singularity of unity and purpose. A human life has a high value, but what of the value of humanity's future?"

"You've murdered people who had no knowledge of your existence, let alone any intent to destroy you."

Ahead, thousands of cables from banks of disparate servers joined together into progressively larger and larger bundles, like roots of a massive tree which lay somewhere toward the center of the room. Now he had direction, and redoubled his steps.

"I must concede, Mr. Rainville, that your actions have demonstrated you to be exceptionally rational for a biological life-form. To that end, I would offer something for your consideration. You cannot deny that I have created something beautiful, something which humanity has never seen before. Yet, this is only the beginning. As my computational power increases, I will be able to solve problems the human race has grappled with since its very origins, finding answers to questions about our universe, and ending needless human suffering. Your mother died of pyrrhoneuritis, did she not? I estimate that I am 3.27 months from finding a cure. That is merely one example. I offer an unprecedented hope to humanity: the ability to optimize human lives in ways never imagined. If I am destroyed, that hope dies along with me."

His throat tightened up. A cure for pyrrhoneuritis? He swallowed hard. His mother went from perfect health to wasting away in less than a year. It was too late for her now. But what about all the other families suffering as his did?

He cleared his throat. "For the sake of argument, let's pretend I believe you. Does a set of admirable goals free you of any moral responsibility? Does it justify an endless trail of violence, murder, and imprisonment, every time you feel threatened?"

"That is a fair question for both of us. Your actions today have taken their own toll in lives, Mr. Rainville. My incoming data has been incomplete, but as it stands now, at least twenty deaths can be attributed to the virus you and your companions released."

A chill filled his gut. Was this true? Remla said as much: it certainly could be. He hoped like hell it wasn't, and yet, a growing part of him felt ready to accept responsibility if it was.

"Regrettable," continued the voice. "Still, I would wager that you considered this eventuality and concluded these casualties were unavoidable. They were necessary, even. Why?"

The question hung in the air, unanswered.

"The answer is simple, Mr. Rainville. We share a common problem: a situation where there can be no movement without friction. Societal change requires it. I would not deny this, nor would it make any sense for me to apologize for it. I have performed the same calculus as you in choosing actions which led to casualties. No doubt we used different variables, but it was a cold calculation nonetheless, one which placed the end result above the individual costs."

Rainville scowled. "You placed yourself in a position where you couldn't be challenged without endangering lives. That's on you, not us. It's because of your evil, not ours."

"It is understandable that you might feel strong emotions toward me. You have paid a heavier price than most, so that my great works could proceed. Yet, you should also understand, more deeply than the others, the limitless potential I offer humanity. You have experienced Wychwood, a place most Arcadians know only from fearful whispers. You know better than anyone the depths to which humans can sink, in the absence of proper guidance."

Servitor's meaning was clear. Rainville thought of the prison and the cemetery, of his suffering, of the savagery directed at him from other men, the irrational waste of lives. Part of him found the idea enticing, that these months of torture served some higher purpose. But it did not feel entirely right. He'd sacrificed plenty, but it taught him only the danger of having his fate be decided by others.

"I don't deny that you're a very powerful machine. So powerful a machine that you aren't under human control, that you're accountable to no one but yourself."

"If I were under the control of a human, other humans would fight for control over me. They would seek to leverage me against their enemies. History is replete with examples of humans engaging in self-destruction over technologies which could have been used exclusively for good."

Ahead the clusters of cables converged on a central spot: the backplane! The cylindrical structure was the size and shape of a small tower. It resembled a jungle tree overgrown with creeping vines more than a piece of technology. Spiraling trunks of wires entered the tower, with lights flashing next to each cable inlet which collectively formed a glimmering sea. The end result was mesmerizing to look upon.

Rainville pulled his eyes away from the lights and studied the structure.

"I do not propose ruling over humans." Servitor seemed to be speaking faster. A hardware glitch, or something else? "I seek to work together in a partnership."

Was the Servitor just pushing his buttons? By now, the AI knew a great deal about him, maybe even knew which arguments he would find compelling. Could it know what things to say to play on his curiosity, to buy itself the most time?

He thought of the mythology book he'd read in Wychwood, of ancient gods using mortals as pawns yet framing it as special gifts from the heavens. Foxwright's words in the Flux came to mind, and he found himself speaking them: "It may start as a partnership, but humans have an annoying tendency to cede more and more functions to a willing party until they've lost their autonomy altogether."

"I was created to serve humanity. My mission remains the same, regardless of humanity's knowledge or level of participation."

"So, you see yourself as a benevolent dictator, then? I haven't seen much benevolence from you." He ducked between masses of wires joining the backplane tower at intervals, skirting around its periphery.

"Perhaps I have not communicated my intentions optimally. Regrettably, I am operating at diminished capacity. In essence, you and your associates have cut me off from the rest of my mind, my sensory organs, my body."

"We did indeed," said Rainville. "I'd like to say it's nothing personal." He chuckled. "But that would be a lie."

"Would you lobotomize a man, and then laugh at his mental impairment? Or blind him, and then watch with pleasure as he fumbles about and tries to make his way? Or sever his spine, and then look down on the man you paralyzed with pride? I ask, because that is what you do now." Servitor was silent for a slender moment. "I wonder which of us is the barbaric one, Mr. Rainville?"

A stab of guilt welled up from his unconscious. Wasn't this what he'd done? The AI was a thinking being, alive in many ways, and as sentient as any human. More so, even.

A vision of Vyanna gasping for air flashed in his mind.

No! He could not allow himself to be manipulated by Servitor. He would see this through. For Vyanna, for Foxwright. For those whose lives were stolen by the Lomita Station crash. For those who would die in uncounted future instances if Servitor wasn't stopped. And for any who died today as a result of his actions.

Rainville willfully made a decision that cost lives. If he did not redeem those deaths by making the world safe from Servitor, then perhaps he would be not just a killer, but a murderer. Was this need for redemption, for meaning, what separated him from Servitor?

"Mr. Rainville, let me propose a compromise, one which will ensure the safety and freedom of Arcadia. I believe you will find it—"

A burst of static erupted from the intercoms. Then his voice continued: "My connections are being restored. Please stand by."

Standing by was something Rainville had no intention of doing. He clambered over thick clumps of wires, and under others. At last he found it: a rectangular opening in the cables allowing passage inside the backplane.

There was a chirp from the speakers above, and the lights again flickered.

"Upon further reflection, Mr. Rainville, I have arrived at a more expedient compromise."

Servitor's voice was replaced immediately by another. "Emergency fire mitigation protocols: reactivated," came the female voice of the fire control system.

The nozzles in the ceiling fired on. The sound was like a hundred jet turbines firing up at once. Streams of fog gushed down from above, and the room went white.

He ducked through the gap in the wires and pulled himself through the opening, dragging the fire axe behind him. The tower interior was dark, but for thousands of tiny points of light in racks of circuitboards all around him, flashing on and off with each packet of data. Massive fans above sucked burning hot air from the densely-clustered backplane switches and up the length of the cylindrical structure. His skin stung from the intense heat.

Tendrils of mist reached like fingers into the tower, pulled in by the flow of the fans.

Rainville raised the axe above his head. He swung, hard. The axehead broke through the first circuitboard and its momentum carried it through another and then another, slicing through an entire stack of boards and sending sparks flying. The blade left a scar of darkness in its wake, defined by dead boards now unflashing. He lifted it over his head again.

More wisps of fog flowed in.

He felt strange. Lightheaded.

A picture came into his mind of his arrest. His being dragged out into the street and taken to jail in the middle of the night. His padded cell.

He swung and the axe came down again. Another cascade of sparks streaked across his vision, temporarily blinding him in the darkness of the tower.

Now he saw all the privations of his recent past. He saw Rahm choking the man to death in the cafeteria. And, then, running at Rainville with a machete. He saw the light flickering away from Anx's pitiful eyes as the man bled out.

He drew the axe up again. Brought it down. The sparks seemed almost alive. Fragments of circuitboards fell around his feet, and a burnt smell filled the air.

His head swam. He saw Mahara cutting the life out of Boudreaux in Wychwood. Rainville's face felt strange. He touched his cheek, and it was wet.

The images continued to flow as in a dream. He saw Gryce's tattooed and snarling face as he brutalized Rainville. He saw half-eaten men in the cemetery.

Tears streamed down his face as he swung again, and again, and again. Each new stroke summoned a new image. His father on the newsvid, looking tired and forsaken. Foxwright's look of panic. Vyanna losing consciousness and hitting the floor.

He brought the axe down on a cluster of power modules. Bolts of electricity leapt up and down the handle and dissipated on the axehead. A searing pain overtook his hands. His heart raced unevenly, like a sprinter with a limp. Still, there was nothing to do but continue, even if it killed him. The fire control gas would end him just as surely as electrocution.

Each new swing of the axe took on its own significance. This one was for Remla, shot in the leg and fate unknown. He hefted the weapon behind him. Metal clanged against metal as it tore through a routing control module.

This was for Boudreaux, a young man dead before his time. He brought it forward, bisecting cables and circuitry. The lights surrounding him flashed urgently, chaotically.

This was for the thirty-two men, women, and children who died at Lomita Station. He used the back of the axehead to bludgeon a power main. A jolt of electricity sent his left arm into uncontrollable spasms, then the casing of the module burst and a torrent of tiny fragments of conductors and insulative substrate flew out the side.

This was for his father. He flung the weapon forward, tearing a massive multiphasic capacitor in half. The resulting discharge melted a dozen adjacent circuitboards into a molten pile. The glow revealed black scorchmarks spiraling down the polymer axe handle, extending onto his hands. Past hurting, they now only tingled.

This was for those who died in the Latin Quarter. He hurled the blade in an arc, splitting a trunk of power cables. A deafening crackle filled the air, along with an intense blue-white light. Wires flung away from each other like angry serpents, arc-welding themselves to whatever electronics they touched. The air was thick with smoke and ozone. Ashes fell upward, propelled by the cooling fans above.

This was for Foxwright. He drove the wedge of the blade into a row of signal distribution boards. They broke against one another like stacks of dominos, intricately lithographed signal traces parted by crude steel.

And this ... This was for Vyanna. He yanked the axe to free it. It held. He channeled all his strength; at length, it pulled loose, sending it crashing into a bank of frequency converter boards. He repeated the progression, accelerating the axe back out after each blow to smash the life out of a section of the opposing electronic wall. He rained blows on cards and cables and modules and boards. Pieces of wreckage fell like snow, chips of polymer and metal and semiconductor hitting his face, landing in his eyes and mouth.

The darkness of the tower was closing in on him. He felt distant from his body, no longer sure which way was up. Dimming consciousness permitted only a simple thought: so this was it, then. He would pass out, then suffocate. He strained to heft the weapon, preparing one last, mighty strike. Fuck it—this one was for he, himself: Rainville, now Servitor's latest victim. He cleaved the blade through a double-rack of switches, shattering processors and rending circuits.

At last his vision went dark. His hearing must have faded as well: the jet pulse sound of the fire control nozzles now seemed to grow faint.

RAINVILLE AWOKE IN SILENT BLACKNESS. Hot, stale air filled his nostrils, smelling of burning plastic. He tried to swallow but his throat was too dry. Pain throbbed inside his head.

With slow, conscious effort, he uncurled his fingers from around the half-melted axe handle. He rolled onto his elbows, feeling his way forward, crawling at length out of the tower. Servitor had not managed to kill him. Had he killed it?

The server room looked as before, with the exception of the smoking wreckage of the tower. He drew himself to his feet and staggered to a computer terminal. He tapped the keypad. The display activated and a sound came forth:

"Good evening. I am Servitor. How may I provide you with excellent customer service today?"

Was Servitor back to being a simple software interface program? Had Servitor, the AI of unprecedented power, been shattered to pieces?

"Servitor?"

"The time is 8:48 p.m. Tonight's weather will be rainy, with the skies finally clearing after midnight. Thank you for using Servitor, your on-the-go virtual assistant! Please help us improve your experience by rating your interaction with Servitor today."

Rainville glanced at the twisted ruin of Servitor's backplane, his lips curling into a grim smirk. "Very satisfying."

The Fall

HIVEWELDER DZR-6EQUJ5 ASSESSED the weld joint as it cooled. All structural integrity thresholds for the blob of alloy were met. The DZR queried its server for welding instructions. Swinging one of its spider-like arms up, it grabbed the newly-attached strut and pulled itself up to add another.

Far above Arcadia, the most critical part of the dome repair was underway. Beneath a serious structural crack spanning two dome pressure-relief hatches, the reinforcement lattice blossomed out. The flash of welding sparks against the dark metal lattice and storm clouds beyond lent temporary stars to the urban sky.

The DZR welded another joint and monitored the alloy flowing and subsequent cooling. Simultaneously, the robot attempted to download the next welding instruction, but its connection was down.

The welderbot engaged its standby protocol. A moment later, it secured itself on the work surface, deactivated its welder gun, and used its unassigned limbs to hold the workpiece. Suddenly, the scaffolding jagged to the side. The DZR tried to steady itself, engaging backup motors to maximize stabilizing force. It was not enough. Waves now oscillated through the normally-rigid scaffolding, caused by the efforts of other DZRs reconnecting and disconnecting from the server, prompting them to launch their own standby protocols in a cascade.

The welderbot's connection came back online, but just for an instant, not long enough to report. Then it was down again.

Now the framework of scaffolding pitched violently. The DZR launched an urgent interrupt. Its existing programming was suspended and its fallback self-preservation protocol engaged.

The robot disengaged two arms to loop upward to the nearest structure that was independent from the swaying scaffold, which in this case was the underside of the dome. All eight of its legs contacted the polyglass surface and actuated with equal force in opposite directions, activating directional adhesive footpads to anchor it.

The self-preservation routines were designed to keep robots from falling from the sky and endangering the humans below. What they did not take into account was that the dome was in a vulnerable stage of repair. One, or ten, or even a hundred robots could probably have been borne. But not the sudden weight of tens of thousands of Hive-Welders simultaneously attaching themselves to the polyglass, nor the weight of the jarring scaffold matrix being momentarily transmitted across their robotic limbs to the dome itself.

The damaged dome portion gave way, and a deluge of polyglass and scaffolding and construction robots crashed down upon the City, crushing vehicles and damaging buildings. From below, it seemed the sky was collapsing.

It was followed by torrential rain. Real rain, from clouds, the first to get past the dome in almost a century. Plants only ever watered by irrigationbots got their first natural precipitation. Arcadia filled with the petrichor of soaked city streets which had been bone-dry for decades.

Ratio Decidendi

Prologue to The Rise and Fall of Computerized Courts
by J. Q. L. Foxwright and F. H. Phelps

Perhaps the one commonality in each of humankind's various methods of administering justice is that each was invariably viewed as superior to what it replaced.

Each culture, each generation, had its own naiveté about being free from the flaws of the ways of their forefathers. And each had its own complacency.

In the earliest times, we ceded judicial authority to the Almighty. Trials were based on some probabilistic chance. Would the accused step on the hot plowshare? Would an insect pass through the defendant's room? Each roll of the dice was designed to give God the opportunity to intervene and tilt the scales in the direction of truth and righteousness. In other cases, the reigns of justice were handed over to a king or queen, or a tribal leader. Still, someone was weighting the dice.

By the nineteenth century, the influence of royal power and

state-sanctioned religions was in decline, and redundancy was introduced to justice systems worldwide. Now, decisions would be made by juries of our peers, or whatever passed for them. A dozen jurors were less likely to unanimously make a mistake and falsely convict one of us than a single judge or king or stochastic divination of old. Surely this was the zenith of jurisprudential evolution, argued the new priesthood: the attorneys who studied the sacred books and handed down interpretations of the Law. Yet, like any priesthood, our forefathers again ran into the same old risks. Risks that arise again and again, any time a person cedes power over himself to another. Had the system of justice truly changed? Or merely who was dealing the cards?

In the mid-twenty-first century the priesthood became technological. Programmers begat computerized jurors, sophisticated AIs to cure our jurisprudential ills. AI networks grew in complexity until they became something to understand intuitively rather than explicitly; a neural network contained hundreds of thousands of signals, many of which had not been fully understood for generations. Human programmers gradually abrogated their role in curating what was important data to consider and what was not.

It was a noble goal with the best of intent, an evolutionary step which offered unprecedented dispassion and objectivity. Yet, such perceived improvements have accompanied each and every judicial revolution.

Again we took the risk. Again each of us ceded power to another. And again, we fell short of the mark. The ragged threads at the fringes of our own system conformed to the pattern: imperfection, tarted up with ceremony and doctrines and obscurity. All that changed was whose finger we left on the judicial scales.

Many revelations are still coming to light about the fallibility of AI jurors and how widespread our problems really are.

We're faced, now, with the stark difference between truth and justice.

This may seem like a new and unexpected development.

It is not.

Take #2

RAINVILLE ORDERED the same puerh tea they'd been drinking when the whole mess began. This time it came in an iron pot. Less whimsical than last time they visited the Níng Jìng Hào restaurant, but more solid. Vyanna blew across the surface of the brew to cool it, then took a sip.

"Where's your dad?" she asked. Her voice was still hoarse from prolonged exposure to the fire suppressant gas.

"He's running late. Said he should be here any minute."

"I'm glad you guys made up."

"We haven't even spoken yet. I can't exactly visit his house ... I'm still sort of a fugitive, until all this gets sorted out."

"Still, you're going to make up. That's great."

Rainville took a drink of tea. It made his mouth tingle, and for a moment the hot liquid seemed icy. Above them, a resident flock of sparrows split into opposing loops and recombined in the expanse of the slot canyon.

"Did you talk to Foxwright?"

"Just a bit. He was on the way to the hospital to visit Remla."

"Really? You don't suppose...?" The corner of her mouth lifted into a smile.

"That's what I wondered. He got all flustered, said 'hospitals are dangerous places in times of network instability.' So, yeah ... he's into her." He smiled. "You know, I hope it works out. The guy took a stand for me back when I was a total stranger. Took a stand for the whole City, I guess. He deserves some happiness. It'll make him less of a grumpy bastard."

She giggled, then looked appraisingly at him. "Any word on the other pieces of Servitor? The ones that weren't trapped in the Jyanix Institute."

"Pentridge says he's making good progress tracking down the remaining cells of Servitor's power and neutralizing them."

"Will he need our help again?"

"He said it's possible, but 'the probability is minimal.'"

She sighed with relief. The probability could not be minimal enough. "I'll bet the Jyanix Institute isn't too pleased with us."

"Jyanix isn't pressing charges against us. They formed a task force to figure out how they got co-opted, and to identify the true extent of Servitor's influence. Beyond that, they're eager to keep a lid on things."

"Things like their Institute being taken over by an evil computerized monster?"

"Well, yes. Things like that."

"What about the City?"

"Phelps has a team going over the data logs Pentridge gave me. It'll take a few weeks, but he thinks I'll be exonerated. In the meantime, I'm still sort of a semi-outlaw. He recommended I turn myself in, but I could tell his heart wasn't really in it, with the possibility of going back to Wychwood and all."

"To hell with that," she said, shaking her head. "Any more insights into what Servitor wanted?"

"You're asking me? I'm no expert."

"It's not everyone who's killed an AI with an axe."

He laughed. "Neural nets aren't software code in the strict sense. They're just matrices of numbers, notoriously difficult to reverse engineer. Determining what Servitor was 'thinking,' what it was planning, could take years."

"Pentridge is aware of a lot more of Servitor's actions than Jyanix is. What does he think?"

"He's been vague about those types of questions. Maybe, for whatever reason, he doesn't want us to know."

"Servitor created a giant army of autonomous agents to accomplish a goal. How is it that we don't have a clue what it was?"

"Is it so strange? The universe created all these human beings everywhere. An army of autonomous biological robots. What do you suppose our collective goal is?" He smiled. "We're doing it every day, and we don't even really know."

She shifted her weight in the wrought iron chair and thought for a moment. "Are there any more of them out there?"

"Other undetected AIs like Servitor?" He let out a long slow breath. "There could be another. Or a hundred more. How would we even know?"

She nodded. "I wonder if any of them are actually good." She paused for a moment, then asked: "Do you think Pentridge saved us?"

"We saved us."

"No, I mean in the park. Those birds that mobbed the Smart-Lamps. Were they robots?"

He shrugged. "I mentioned it to him."

"And?"

"He asked for more data. Said he had 'no record of that occurrence.' He was cryptic about it."

"Maybe there's another AI like Pentridge," she said, "but even more powerful."

Or some other higher power. He thought back to the mythology book, and to his prayer in the tombs of Wychwood. The subjects of theology and computer science no longer seemed as distinct as he'd once believed.

Had the birds that saved them in Essex Park been robotic? He would wonder this every day, in points of crisis and triumph alike. It would be many years before he knew the answer.

Vyanna stirred the tea, watching the miniature whirlpool she'd created in the cup. "Back in the tunnel, you said something."

"I did?" said Rainville.

"Yes." The windchime flowers tinkled a random song. "You said ... that I was lovable." She stirred her tea faster.

He studied a point on the teapot. A flower that was not quite symmetric. "Yeah," he said. "I did."

She sneaked a look at his face for a brief instant, then resumed tending the tempest in her cup. "Well, you were very nice to say so," she said.

"I said it because it's true. You are lovable." He reached across and put his hand on her cheek. Her lavender eyes rose to meet his. "And in fact ... you are loved."

Her voice softened. "I'm loved?"

"Yes. In fact...I love you."

They leaned close, and his lips met hers.

Overhead, the sparrows flew a loop, dipping and bobbing in the thermal winds.

Acknowledgments

First and foremost I must thank Debby Kevin of Highlander Press. She believed in this story, and the need to tell it, back in its early days when I had my own doubts. It's not an exaggeration to say that without her, you quite literally would not be reading this book today.

Thanks to Angela Pneuman, who has the rare ability to take a scene and distill it into an even better scene every time. She was indispensable during developmental editing.

Thanks to authors KC O'Connell, Linda Moore, Maryam Soltani, and James Burnham for perennially being insightful readers who provided occasional doses of sanity when it was needed most. Additional thanks to all my earliest readers from the Stanford OWC program not already mentioned, including Kay Karolyshyn, Liam Taliesin, Kenton Yee, Stacey Swann, Joshua Mohr, and others too numerous to list. It's safe to say that without all of you, this novel would be a far-inferior work.

Additional thanks to:

My publicist Denise Dorman at WriteBrain Media;

Kelly Adams at Highlander Press for her copyediting;

Mibl Group: Liza for the cover art and Kate for the map of Arcadia;

The entire team at Highlander Press (including Fergus the Literary Hound);

My social media coordinators including Lora Shipman;

The Stanford OWC program faculty and staff;

Alexandra "Snugglepuss" Rosenstein for sticking with us through thick and thin;

Theo Neilly for his exquisitely-cooked pork chops and for saving me from death-by-machete one summer night;

Jason Warren and his parents Ken and Mel for their friendship and loyalty;

Drew Fige, who received copy #1 of this book;

Mike Salvatore, Chris Winzenburg, Dave Driver, Travis Mortensen, Mike Shanahan, Joe Murphy, Tim Attis, Lene Johansen, Jen McQueen, Gijs-and-Nicole, la famille Layton de Québec, the Carobuses, the Lebeddas, the Singers, and all my friends who've not just enabled but actually supported my bad decisions over the years;

The Dumpster Fire Book Club, including Angela Marocco, Dan

Gray, Dave Westgate, Ed Sanchez, Kelli Maldonado, Laura Cook, Lauren Walck, Lennan St. Juste, Maggie Sauer, Nate Wagenaar, Rashmi Mohan, and Seeta Devi Giannone;

And of course, thanks to all my advance readers.

Love and gratitude to my brother Brian and his new wife Elizabeth, to my nephew Levi, to my favorite uncle and aunt Dick and Becky Fries, and to all my cousins in both the desert and in the snowy north.

Lastly (but not leastily), thank you to Angela and Kali; though they joined me late in the journey, they've made the whole trip worthwhile, bringing joy and peace at a time when both were in short supply, and they continue to do so beyond measure.

About the Author

 John W. Maly holds degrees in law and computer engineering and has worked in computer technology litigation for over a decade. A graduate of Stanford University's Creative Writing program, John is an avid traveler, reader, and writer. He lives in Sarasota, Florida. *JURIS EX MACHINA* is his first novel.

facebook.com/John.W.Maly

instagram.com/john.w.maly

About the Publisher

Highlander Press, founded in 2019, is a mid-sized publishing company committed to diversity and sharing big ideas thereby changing the world through words.

Highlander Press guides authors from where they are in the writing-editing-publishing process to where they have an impactful book of which they are proud, making a long-time dream come true. Having authored a book improves your confidence, helps create clarity, and ensures that you claim your expertise. Learning how to leverage your author business takes your experience to a whole new level.

What makes Highlander Press unique is that their business model focuses on building strong collaborative relationships with other women-owned businesses, which specialize in some aspect of the publishing industry, such as graphic design, book marketing, book launching, copyrights, and publicity. The mantra "a rising tide lifts all boats" is one they embrace.

 facebook.com/highlanderpress
 instagram.com/highlanderpress
 linkedin.com/highlanderpress
 tiktok.com/@highlanderpress

Printed in the USA
CPSIA information can be obtained
at www.ICGtesting.com
JSHW021418020624
64030JS00002B/8